I0527061

Three Families

Three Families

Arthur A. Lee

LEEWARD PUBLISHERS, LLC
Orlando, Florida

Three Families

By

Arthur A. Lee

This is a work of fiction. Names, characters, places and incidents are either the product of the author's imagination or are used fictionally, and resemblance to actual persons living or dead, business establishments, events or locales is entirely coincidental.

Copyright © 2013 by Arthur A. Lee &
LEEWARD PUBLISHERS, LLC.

ISBN: 978-0615848686

www.leewardpublishers.com

In accordance with the U.S. Copyright Act of 1976 all rights reserved. This book, in whole and in part, is the property of the author. No part of this book may be reproduced or transmitted in any form or by any means, graphic, electronic, or mechanical, including but not limited to photocopying, recording, taping, or by any information storage retrieval system, without the permission in writing from the author.

The scanning, uploading, and electric sharing of any part of this book without the permission of the publisher constitutes unlawful piracy and theft of the author's intellectual property. If you would like to use material from the book, prior permission must be obtained by contacting the publisher at:

editor@leewardpublishers.com

Silver Cat Press
An Imprint of Leeward Publishers, LLC

This book is dedicated
to the friends of my youth.
I was the lucky one,
I managed to get out.
So many of the young men and
women I knew didn't.

Other Books by the Author

The Morgan Crew Mystery Series

A Storm In From The Sea

The Las Vegas Murders

A Deadly London Fog

The Four Seasons Murders

The Hawaiian Sunset Murders

The Spy Who Would Not Speak

The West Texas Murders

The Hawaiian Island Murders

www.leewardpublishers.com

Three Families

By

Arthur A. Lee

Contents

Chapters:

PROLOGUE

The three families in this story are:

The Aces – A teenage street gang of 1950's Passaic, New Jersey. They make a living selling protection to the shops and people of their six square block "turf."

The Alberto Falzone Family – A crew of loan sharks, extortionists, hijackers, and thieves, run by Al Falzone. Al is a Caporegime or Capo. He is the Captain of his own crew. He reports to Don Pietro Salvano.

The Pietro Salvano Family – Pietro came to the United States at the turn of the Century and he is the Don, the Capo de tutti Capi, of a crime family that operates in Brooklyn and Northern New Jersey. His son, Peter, is a wealthy Manhattan businessman who tries to separate himself from his father's world.

****

THREE FAMILIES

ONE

Passaic, New Jersey
August 1958
The Moretti Family

The heat of that late August Thursday afternoon was stifling. Outside the temperature had hit the 90s and above every day for the past two weeks. Little air moved through the City, and the humidity thrown off by the Passaic River made sleep at night at least difficult, often impossible in those pre-air conditioned days.

Inside DeSonoto's Pizza the heat from the four big wood burning ovens was even worse. Loud, buzzing fans at open windows in the kitchen sought to expel the heat to the outside, but they did little good. Two big fans inside the restaurant kept the hot air moving for those customers who chose to eat their 'slice and a coke' inside.

The neighborhood, being Italian, kept the ovens burning all day, every day except Sunday, of course. Adamo DeSonoto, sitting on his high stool behind the front counter at the cash register six days a week,

2

owned the shop; his two sons, Michael and Tomas, worked in the heat of the kitchen in the back making the pizzas and cooking them. They were good pizzas, a remembrance of Naples - thin crusts with only a few toppings added to the cheese, basil leaves and spicy tomato sauce, when customers asked.

There were five tables inside, including the big round one where The Aces street gang sat when it wasn't too hot inside. The tables all had red checkered table cloths on them; all old and faded and most with frayed edges. Some were stained because they were changed every other day, regardless of the need to change them. Each table held shakers of peperoncini and parmesan, and there was a small glass vase on each table that held and artificial red rose.

The chairs were a collection of mis-matched wooden and metal chairs Adamo had collected over the ten years he had owned his shop. They were worn and scratched, but no one complained; the pizza was too good to worry about the furnishings.

Framed, faded pictures and photos of Italy hung randomly on the walls, some hanging askew and never straightened. The walls had been papered years ago with murals depicting scenes of Italy, and the paper was now peeling at the seams. But the pizza was good and business was good, even in the heat of August.

The ovens were kept busy all day as people streamed in throughout the day and evening to buy a slice or a whole pizza. And the wonderful smell of the pizza cooking was enough to bring the people in.

Three girls walked into DeSonoto's that day. They were young girls, maybe High School age, maybe a little younger. They wore tan shorts because of the heat, and white blouses, all three dressing alike. They were from Montclair, a long distance from Passaic. It was strange that they should have come all the way to DeSonoto's just to have a slice and a coke. Montclair was an upper middle class community, and Passaic was, at best, a working class city. But DeSonoto's was famous for its Neapolitan style pizzas, and people came from a distance to enjoy a slice.

The three young girls walked to the counter and waited. Adamo was sitting on his stool, at the cash register, reading one of his weeks old newspapers from Italy. They waited for the tall guy behind the counter to turn and take their order. His shirt was wet with sweat and the tail was hanging out over the back of his jeans. His hair was jet black and slicked back with Brillcream as teens were wearing their hair that year. The sleeves of the long sleeve shirt had been rolled up to his biceps, which were thick and attractive to the little girls. From the rear the three girls admired the muscles and elbowed each other, giggling. The waiter heard them and turned. He was a boy, their age, but taller and more muscular than other boys his age. And his eye was black and swollen shut.

"What'll you have, girls?"

One of them answered sounding as mature as she thought mature was; "Three slices," she said. "And make sure they're fresh, ok?"

Another of the three said, "Oh Barbara, don't be so mean. You know they always have fresh pizza here."

"Teresa," Barbara said, "I just want to be sure."

The third girl, Sheila, added, "And three bottles of Coke, please."

The waiter called the order back over his shoulder, and as he was doing that, his eyes caught the dark eyes of the one called Teresa. Their eyes locked on each other's. She was young, he thought, too young, not developed like a woman yet, but she was going to be beautiful very soon. Her hair was dark, like silk, and hung in soft waves to her shoulders, not teased up like the others.

"What's your name?" he asked her and smiled. The other two girls giggled.

She said, "Teresa. What's yours?"

"I'm Tony . . . Maybe I'll see you around here again."

"Maybe," she answered and smiled, not a bit of childish shyness in the smile.

Their pizzas and bottles of Coke were handed through the opening in the wall from the kitchen. Tony carried the plates and Cokes around the front of the counter and to a vacant table, something he had never done before for anyone.

"You girls sit here," he said. "I'll turn a fan on so it'll be a little bit cooler. If you want anything, just yell." He was looking at Teresa as he said this. She smiled.

Outside, on the wide sidewalk, four members of The Aces sat at a dented and rusty metal table, drinking bottles of warm Coca Cola while they waited for their pizza to be brought to them. An awning of faded green, white and red stripes hung low off the building, casting some shade across the glass front of DeSonoto's and onto the table. The awning was torn from back to front on the right side letting the sun's heat penetrate the shade. A small, thin, metal ashtray sat off center on the table; it was overflowing with the cigarette butts crushed out by the four. A cloud of smoke hung low around them as they each chain smoked while waiting.

Eddy Di Bona leaned back in an old wooden chair and stared up at the deep blue and cloudless sky. Sweat beaded on his forehead and dampened his thick, curly, black hair. He was a small boy, thin, and pimply faced. His hair was seldom washed and looked more like a Brillo pad than hair. He wore an old striped T-shirt that would have been too small for any of the other Aces. It hung loose on Eddy. It was stained with three days of sweat under his arms and around the neck of the shirt.

Eddy smoked his Lucky Strike cigarette nervously, quickly taking it back to his lips almost before the smoke had cleared his lungs. His hand shook and he fidgeted in his chair. Eddy had a hard time staying still, whether standing or sitting or doing anything else.

"H . . . H . . . Hey, guys," Eddy stuttered. The Aces had accepted Eddy's stutter and his constant jumpiness. Eddy was sixteen years old and had been a nervous stutterer for all the time the other Aces knew him, since grade school. He took two more quick, deep drags of his cigarette even as it came close to burning his fingers, the ash falling onto his blue jeans, and then continued, "Th . . . Th . . . Th . . . Think this h . . . h . . . heat ever gonna' end? May . . . May . . . Maybe we should go sw . . . sw . . . swimin', huh?"

Joey Castellani flicked his Camel cigarette butt into the litter crowded gutter and spit onto the sidewalk. Eddy was a member of The Aces street gang from the day it was formed, three years ago, when Eddy and Joey and Andy Pecora and Jay Schoemer and Norman Rocque and Richie Pelto decided that fighting as a gang was better than fighting alone. But Eddy's nervousness and trouble talking never stopped bothering Joey.

Joey knew he had a temper. Little things that others laughed at would cause Joey to lash out with his fists or break something. Eddy's stuttering bothered Joey, but after all the years of listening to it, he had learned to hold his temper in. His foot was tapping on the sidewalk nervously; he looked up and down the street trying to control the rising heat of temper inside of him.

Norman crushed out his Lucky Strike cigarette and drank the last of his Coke from the bottle. He said, "Yeah, that ain't a bad idea. I got a date tonight with Carla Esposito. Maybe I'll take her up to Barber's Pond and we can go skinny dippin'."

Richie Pelto had been reading one of his books while sitting at the table with his friends. Richie didn't smoke, and he read anything he could get his hands on. Of all the six teens in the Aces, Richie was the only one with a library card. The others had stopped laughing at that fact. They had gotten used to Richie's addiction to reading and his ability to get A's in school without even trying, because Richie was a fighter. He never gave up, even when he was bleeding and hurt, he would keep fighting. Even when two or three tough guys from some other gang where hitting him, he wouldn't give up. Surrender just wasn't in Richie Pelto.

He closed the book and laid it on the table. He grabbed his bottle of Coke and said, before drinking from it, "Yeah, Norm. Good luck there. Carla, if she was a guy she'd be one'a Father Patrick's altar boys. You ain't gonna get nothin' from her. She gonna' be a nun or a saint someday." The others laughed; Norman just grinned.

Norm was known as a "lover;" he was a good looking teenager whose father was second generation French in the U.S. and whose mother was a good looking dark Italian with big breasts that she let bounce freely as she walked sensuously around the neighborhood. Norm inherited his Italian good looks from his mother and his penchant for chasing girls from his father, who did the same when he was a teenager. He smiled wickedly and told Richie, "You wanna' bet? A buck says I get in her pants tonight."

"You got it," Richie said laughing. The others were finding all this amusing because they knew Norman's reputation. The girls fell hard for his good looks, slicked back black hair, and cool talk. He was wearing a white T-shirt that day, as he always did, tucked into his jeans as he always did to emphasize his slim waist and broad shoulders. His pack of Lucky's was rolled up in his right sleeve as it always was. The rolled up sleeve was intentional so that the tattoo of a heart on his bicep could be seen. The girls liked that.

The door to DeSonoto's Pizza opened, and Tony Moretti walked out carrying the big pizza. He laid the hot pizza on the table and took a step back. Tony was 14 years old but he was tall, as tall as the all the teens of The Aces. And he carried the weight The Aces knew would make him strong and a good fighter.

Tony ate well at DeSonoto's and at Avrum's Deli two doors away. Avrum's was a Jewish Deli that served good meats and salads and kosher foods to the few Jewish people in the neighborhood. Both Adamo DeSonoto and Mr. Abe, as Avrum was known, felt sorry for Tony Moretti because they knew that at home Tony took more beatings from his drunken father than meals. They fed him well without expecting payment. Without their charity Tony wouldn't be as solidly built as he was, his weight wouldn't be what it was, and he wouldn't be the fighter he was.

That day, when he had brought the pizza to the Aces, his right eye was black and swollen shut from the punch he had taken the night before at home. He stood silently, looking from face to face. He wore a wrinkled light cotton plaid shirt, sweat stained, and blue jeans that were torn at the left knee. The tail of his shirt hung out in the back. Sweat ran down his face in rivulets due to the heat from the ovens inside. Richie Pelto was the first to speak, "You waitin' for a tip or somethin', kid?"

Tony said nothing. He was standing in the sun, the shade of the awning a foot away from him. Eddy Di Bona sat forward and asked, "Wh . . . Wh . . . What the h . . . h. . . hell you want kid?"

Tony finally spoke up, in a soft, quaking voice, "I wanna' be in your gang."

The four looked at each other, all wanting to laugh but nobody dared laugh. They knew Tony Moretti from the neighborhood. At 14 years of age he had already acquired a reputation. He didn't wait for others to start a fight; Tony always hit first for any reason he thought good enough. The slightest word that Tony took as an insult resulted in his lashing out. People in the neighborhood said about him, "He always starts fights, and he always finishes them, too."

Norman said, "Ain't you a little young, kid?"

"When you guys got together," Tony said as he took a step closer to them and stood in the shade of the awning, "you were my age. You didn't fight no better than me back then, and you don't fight no better than me now."

"That what you want?" Norman asked. "You wanna' fight? Seems you doin' OK at that right now . . . All by yourself. Seems you don't need us."

"I want the money," Tony said. He looked longingly at the single empty, battered metal chair at the table. No one told him to sit so he stood.

The four looked at each other again. Richie Pelto leaned back in his chair with a knowing grin on his face and asked, "What money you talkin' about kid? You expectin' me t'pay you to be a member?"

"I'm talkin' about the protection you guys sell. I'm tired of workin' my ass off and havin' my old man take everything I earn for his damn cheap jugs of wine. I want money like you guys got. That's what I want."

That brought laughter to the four teens, but it was an uneasy laughter. Each knew that Tony could win a fight with any one of them, maybe not all four at one time, but that mattered little, so they showed him a little respect.

Norman spoke up once again when the others seemed unwilling to do so. "OK, so we collect money from the neighborhood to keep the blacks and spics away. There ain't been no robberies or broken windows in over a year. The old ladies can walk to the store and back home without someone stealin' their bread and pasta. Kids can play in the streets. Now tell me why we need to share that money with you."

"I been lookin'," Tony said. He hesitated at first but then decided to take the risk of pulling the empty chair away from the table. He sat in the shade and waited for the four Aces to tell him to stand. They didn't; he relaxed.

"Like I said, I been lookin'. You guys got four square blocks of this part of Passaic. Two years ago you had six blocks. The white's been moving out little by little and the blacks and spics been movin' in. In a couple more years you won't have even five stores to protect, and you won't get much money from them."

"That's bullshit!" Joey Castellani spat out. His famous temper – or perhaps his infamous temper – was rising inside of him like the heat of that summer's afternoon. "This here's our turf! Ain't nobody gonna' take that away from us!"

"I hope you're right," Tony said. "But I don't think so."

Richie Pelto sat forward. He was the calm one,

the one who reasoned everything, the one who always thought ahead and tried to think rationally. He asked, "So, if you're right . . . And just maybe you are . . . What the hell you gonna' do for us? How's takin' you into the club gonna stop what's gonna' happen?"

"I got ideas," Tony answered and grinned a sly grin.

"Like what?"

"No, Richie," Tony said. "They're my ideas. I gotta' wear an Ace's jacket and be part of the club. Then I'll tell you my ideas."

But before any of the four could say anything, the two other members of The Aces club turned the corner and walked to the table. Andy Pecora was the oldest of The Aces. He was 18 at the time and a drop out from school at the age of 16.

Andy liked knives. He carried a black switchblade knife with a six inch blade of shiny, razor sharp steel in his back jeans pocket. He was quick with the blade, sometimes too quick for some of the other Aces. And he liked guns almost as much as he liked knives. Andy had two guns - a .38 snub nosed police special he had taken from a Clifton, New Jersey Police Detective one night, and a sawed off, double barreled shotgun. Both were kept in the 1949 Ford he drove. Andy, at the age of 18, had already killed three people.

With him that afternoon was Jay Schoemer. Jay was a blond haired, fair skinned boy of German descent. How do you describe a 16 year old boy with the strength Jay carried with him? Jay was big, with thick arms and a barrel chest that a man ten years older than Jay would work hard to attain. Jay did spend a lot of time at Manny's Gym, avoiding the boxing ring and using selected free weights to build his strength.

Jay had a trick he used often when The Aces faced off against another gang. He carried a baseball bat to the rumble, and before the first punch was thrown, he would hold the Louisville Slugger out at arm's length and snap it in two as if it were a thin twig from a dead tree. That simple act, simple for Jay anyway, threw fear into whomever The Aces were facing. A few rumbles were called off when the gang walked away after seeing Jay's trick.

The two were close friends, closer than either was with the other Aces. They stopped at the shaded table and saw Tony Moretti sitting with the other Aces. Andy Pecora touched the heavy switchblade knife in his back pocket and growled, "What the fuck he doin' sittin' with us?"

Richie answered, "Tony here wants to be a member of our club. He says he knows how we can protect our turf."

"I know how we can *expand* our turf," Tony said quickly, putting strong emphasis on 'expand.' He looked up at Andy and forced himself not to swallow hard. He couldn't show fear of any kind; that he was sure of. Andy, he was sure, would slice his stomach open if he said the wrong thing.

"Wh . . . Wh . . . Wh . . . What you mean *our* t . . . t . . . turf?" Eddy Di Bona managed to say.

"Shut up, Eddy," Andy said without taking his eyes off of Tony. He asked Tony, "Where'd you get the shiner? I thought you was tough? Your old man drunk again?"

"Hey, leave him alone," Norman said. "You know his old man beats the crap outta' him and his mother on a regular basis. He's not the only kid in the neighborhood got that goin' for him."

"Yeah, well if this little kid's so tough why don't he fight back?" Andy asked, still staring at Tony.

No one said anything. They all looked at young Tony Moretti and waited for an answer they were all curious about. Tony shyly looked down and twisted his fingers together nervously. He looked down at his torn high-top black and white sneakers. He said softly, "He's my old man . . . My father. What the hell do you expect me to do?"

Norman looked from one teen to another, and when no one was willing to answer he sat forward, leaned his elbows on the table, and said, "Look, Tony. Suppose we let you in the club? Suppose we got work t'do one night? Suppose your old man is beatin' the crap outta' you and you can't make it to a rumble or a job with the rest of us? What happens then?"

Tony just shrugged his shoulders and started to get up from the chair. It wasn't going to work; he seemed sure of that. He was too young. Maybe he should have waited for The Aces to invite him into the gang. But would they ever do that? How many years would he have to wait? And would The Aces even exist a couple of years from now?

They seemed not to realize or understand what was happening all around them. The old Italian neighborhood was dying. The Italians who settled there a generation ago were dying off, and the next generation was slowly moving away, out to the suburbs. Tony could see this and he knew how to handle it. The neighborhood, he understood, didn't have to be Italian to give The Aces an income. All they had to do was do what Tony knew they should do.

Jay Schoemer, who had said nothing so far, and was standing next to Tony, reached down and touched Tony on his shoulder to stop him from standing. Jay lived in the same small, dank apartment house that Tony lived in, in the apartment directly above Tony's. He knew of the near nightly violence, the screaming, the crying. He knew that Tony's father, Lorenzo, was a cruel drunkard who seldom worked.

Lorenzo had been in the Fascist Italian army and was a known coward back then. He surrendered to the British early in the North African war when his comrades were still fighting and dying. He spent the years to the end of the war safely in a POW camp, obtaining a trusted job in the camp's kitchen where he could eat more than the other prisoners were given. He spoke some English, enough to become a translator for the British. In September 1943, when Italy surrendered to the Allies, Lorenzo was sent to Naples from the camp in Egypt to work as a translator when surrendering Italian troops were interrogated.

There he met Graziella, a desperate young woman whose mother and father and two brothers had all been killed in the war. The seventeen year old Graziella had sold herself one night to an American soldier for two cans of Spam. She became pregnant. Lorenzo didn't care if she had a child; all he wanted was easy sex. All Graziella wanted was some security, to not be hungry anymore. They married, and in January 1944 Graziella gave birth to a boy she named Anthony after her father. Lorenzo's name was on the birth record as the boy's father.

When World War II ended Lorenzo had emigrated from Naples with his wife, Graziella and her child. They got on the first boat he could afford passage on, for what he had no doubt was the easy money of the United States. After all, weren't all Americans rich?

The easy money escaped Lorenzo. One job was too hard; the next paid too little; the one after that demanded work beyond what he thought was fair. He found solace hiding away inside bottle after bottle of cheap red wine and raping his wife when he was drunk.

Jay knew all this, and maybe it was because he felt sorry for Tony, maybe he was willing to take a chance on the 14 year old. Whatever it was that caused him to speak up, he said, "Tell you what kid. You want in the club, go beat the crap outta' your father. On the other hand, if you want us to do that . . . We will, but then you ain't gonna be a part of The Aces. That's the deal. Take it or leave it."

The others all nodded their agreement. They all thought it was a good idea. Tony had to prove himself; Tony had to be independent like the six other members of The Aces. None of their parents told them what to do, and none of them cared if they stayed out all night, fighting and maybe stealing when necessary. None had hit their sons since the last time each was spanked when just a child.

Tony got up from the table as the six Aces tore the now warm pizza apart and devoured it. Tony didn't go back inside DeSonoto's Pizza to tell Adamo DeSonoto he was quitting his job. He didn't need the job anymore.

The door to DeSonoto's opened and the three school girls walked out. They walked away, but the one called Teresa turned as she walked, smiled and waved at Tony. He smiled at her and waived. She wanted one more look at the boy, one more look so she could remember him. 'Someday' she thought, 'someday.'

****

Tony went home and stood at the bottom of the four concrete steps that led up to the peeling, red-brown paint on the front door of the brick building where his parents lived. What would happen when he hit his father? What would change? He knew what he wanted his future to be . . . He had it all planned out in his head. He had spent a year thinking it all out. He had his future in his brain and in his dreams. Would this bring that future to him?

He took the steps slowly, one at a time. His hand touched the cold brass door knob, and he found it difficult to turn. He did, finally, and he pushed the door open. The heat in the entry was still and oppressive, hotter than the August afternoon outside. He started up the wooden steps that were barely holding the tattered carpet runner together. The stairs squeaked; he had heard the squeaks so many times over the years, but somehow they were louder that day. He was at the front door of the second floor, one bedroom apartment he had grown up in. Inside he could hear his mother's radio playing. It sounded like The Platters singing "Twilight Time," but he couldn't be sure.

He pushed open the door and walked inside. His mother was in the small kitchen cooking pasta and fat, spicy sausages. 'They must have found some money somewhere,' he thought. Meat for dinner was a seldom enjoyed treat.

Lorenzo was sprawled out on the couch in the apartment's living room. Tony would sleep there each night, smelling his father's unwashed body and spilled wine all night. Tony walked slowly to the couch and his sleeping father. His father opened his eyes and saw Tony standing there, looking down at him. "What's 'matter wit' you?" Lorenzo slurred. He was drunk; an almost empty jug of cheap wine sat on the dirty bare wood floor next to him. Tony didn't say anything and he didn't move. Lorenzo struggled to push himself up to a seated position. "I said, what's 'matter wit' you?"

Tony swallowed hard and said in a weak voice, "You're drunk again."

"What'd you say you little som'bitch?"

"I said you're drunk again."

Lorenzo stood and almost fell backwards as he pushed himself to his feet. He pulled his leather belt from his waist. He wrapped an end around his fist, leaving the metal buckle hanging free.

"I'm gonna' teach ya' some 'spect for you father you little som'bitch."

He swung the belt over his head and started for Tony. Tony lashed out as fast as he could, hitting his father squarely at the side of his mouth. It felt good - he had wondered how it would feel. He had been beaten so many times by his father, and he had often wondered if his father felt good beating his son. There was pleasure in it, Tony felt. He couldn't feel the punch and the expected pain in his fist as it connected with hard bone. And he wanted more of that pleasure.

Lorenzo bent backwards with the punch. He stumbled and fell to the floor. Tony reached down and grabbed the man by his shirt collar, pulling him up and ripping the collar. He hit Lorenzo again and again with his fast swinging and well aimed right fist. He was laughing as he hit the man, a crazy laugh but one that rose from satisfaction after so many years of torture. He didn't feel his fist hitting Lorenzo, it was almost a dream, but he knew he was finally free of the man.

Blood ran from his father's mouth and nose. Tony kept hitting until his own knuckles were bleeding and swollen. Lorenzo slumped back onto the floor. Tony stood over his father and kicked him hard in the ribs. He kicked again, and again. Lorenzo was unconscious and couldn't feel what was happening to him.

Graziella, Tony's mother, had been standing in the kitchen, watching, holding a ragged dish towel. She made no effort to stop Tony. She had suffered so many years at Lorenzo's hands that it felt good to watch him be hurt.

Tony stopped and stepped away from his father. Graziella went to him and hugged him from behind. She whispered in his ear, "Thank you."

Lorenzo was admitted to the hospital forty-five minutes later with broken ribs, a cracked jaw, a broken nose, a dislocated right shoulder, a split and bleeding lip, and several lost teeth. His kidney was bruised, and he wound up blinded in his left eye.

The ambulance would be expensive, but Tony didn't care. In a matter of a month or two he would be rolling in cash. The police knew what had been going on inside the home; they patted Tony on the back and whispered that he was a good kid. Father Patrick came to the home and slapped Tony across his face, hard, and told him God demanded he respect his father and mother. Tony punched Father Patrick in his mouth, knocking the priest onto the floor and unconscious with one punch.

Tony's mother, Graziella, sat on the torn vinyl seat of one of the two kitchen chairs at the table with the cracked vinyl top. She twisted the rosary beads through her fingers and prayed while watching her husband lay in a pool of blood on their dusty wood floor. She sat and watched silently as the man was wheeled away to the ambulance below. She sat and watched as the two policemen congratulated her 14 year old son. She sat in silence and closed her eyes as Tony hit Father Patrick. She prayed, not for forgiveness for her son, but thanking God that her son had put an end to the beatings and violence and drunken rapes she had suffered for so many years. Never again would Lorenzo beat Tony or rape Graziella. His drinking would continue until it killed him years later.

TWO

Montclair, New Jersey
August 1958
The Falzone Family

At the end of a tree lined cul-d-sac, in an upper-middle class neighborhood in Montclair, New Jersey, a new split level ranch home of some 3600 square feet stood proudly amongst its smaller neighboring homes. The house was built on two of the lots being sold by the developer so that neighbors weren't too close and so that the house could be the biggest on the street.

The neighbors were business men, doctors, lawyers, and their families. Children played in the street; dogs chased sticks and the pink rubber balls every boy had to have, tossed for the dogs' amusement. Squirrels and birds frolicked in the big trees. The big split level ranch home at the end of this cul-d-sac was owned by Alberto Falzone. He lived a quiet life there with his wife, Maria and their daughter, Teresa, and their young son, Little Al as he was called.

Their house was furnished in the latest fashion of that time - Danish Modern throughout. It was expensive furniture, much of it imported directly from

Europe. Maria had a natural skill for decorating, as long as she could spend large amounts of money buying the right things. There was color everywhere; cushions of bright reds and blues and greens were casually thrown very deliberately across a light brown corner couch. A lamp of rainbow colors hung from a brass chain. The carpet was red, something Al objected to, but Maria had brushed his objection aside. Everyone entering the house was amazed at the luxury and modern style.

Maria was a beautiful and happy housewife. She had a dressing room next to her bedroom where three dozen dresses hung. She had eighteen pairs of shoes and a four drawer jewelry case to hold all her gold and pearls and gems. She did have costume jewelry, but she had seen several fashion magazines' advertisements, in which housewives were wearing full skirted dresses, tall hi-heeled shoes, and strings of pearls as they vacuumed the house and cooked dinners. So Maria did the same.

Teresa was about to enter High School at the prestigious St. Ignatius Academy, a very expensive and very private school for good Catholic boys and girls. Little Al was just 7 years old and always on the go. Getting the boy to sit still was nearly impossible, until the evening when the family sat and watched T.V. together, watching Sea Hunt, The Donna Reed Show and The Kraft Music Hall.

Alberto Falzone, father and husband, was a Mafia Caporegime who ran Mafia operations in Northeast New Jersey. His neighbors either didn't know that or didn't talk openly of that fact. Al, as his neighbors knew him, coached Little League baseball, seldom missed a Sunday Mass, donated money to charities and the Church, tossed a football in the street for the children, and invited neighbors to his home for parties and cookouts. Those who knew of his Mafia connections dared not talk about it, except in the privacy of their own homes. Al was a Made Man, a ranking member of the Salvano crime family.

Al's office, which his neighbors knew nothing about, was a tavern in Newark named L'oro Luna – The Gold Moon. It was a neighborhood bar, a place with neon lit signs inside the windows and a few tables and chairs out front on the broad sidewalk. But the neighbors of this bar didn't frequent it.

Outside, Al Falzone's crew stood sentry over the neighborhood. They smoked cigarettes and cigars, greeted passersby with friendly words and smiles, they helped old ladies carry bags of groceries across the street, and they made sure that the working class neighborhood of two and three story apartments was crime free.

They would go inside when the heat was too much for them. They would drink beer and rough red wine. And they would cook massive pots of spaghetti with fat meatballs and sausage. They would play cards and watch the TV when the static and fuzzy picture captured by the rabbit ears antenna allowed.

Al Falzone and his crew made their illegal income from loan sharking, extortion, selling protection to local businesses, gambling, and hijacking.

That day Al Falzone arrived at L'oro Luna in time to see a fire engine speed past. Its lights were flashing and its sirens were screaming, on its way to a fire somewhere. He parked his Cadillac at the curb in front of the bar, next to the red fire hydrant. He parked in the same place every day. The police ignored the blocked hydrant.

He stepped onto the curb and turned to watch the fire engine. Benny Rizo, Ted Bianci, Frankie DeLuca, and Mike Colombo stood with him watched, and when the fire engine had passed and the noise had subsided they greeted Al with the hugs and kiss on the cheek that recognized each as friends and members of Al's crew.

Frankie DeLuca looked down the street at the fire engine racing away and said, "That's friggin' loud, ain't it?"

Benny Rizo said, "Hey, f'get about it. They gotta' be loud, ain't they?"

Ted Bianci opened the door of L'oro Luna and Al led his crew inside. He sat at the table he always sat at as the men stood facing him. Al looked from man to man and asked, "Where's Louie?"

"Hey," Mike Colombo said. "You know Louie. Probably stopped for some sfogliatella or sum'thin'. That guy's gonna' explode if he don't stop eatin'."

Benny Rizo said, as he was known to say about everything and anything, "Hey, f'get about it."

Al and the others laughed as Al patted the table top, as he always did, telling his crew to turn over their collections from the past few days. One by one the four men laid fat envelopes on the table, stepping forward and then quickly stepping back. Al smiled; he was happy about the thickness of the four envelopes.

Al's crew ran Northeast New Jersey - Passaic County, Bergen County, Morris County, Essex, Hudson, and Union Counties. The money flowed in; Al counted it out, envelope by envelope. He was happy. Each of the four men was happy. Each of the men gave Al 50% of their weekly income. The 50% each kept for himself gave them a good living and a good income. Al kept half of what they paid up to him and paid half up to Pietro Salvano, the Don of the Salvano crime family.

"So where the hell's Louie?" Al said as he packed the cash into the safe behind the bar. But before anyone could answer, Louie Lombardi walked in. His 300 pound bulk belied his quickness and meanness when he had to beat respect into someone.

Louie walked to the bar behind which Al was standing. "Hey, boss. I'm sorry. I got tied up."

"Yeah," Al said with a laugh. "That powdered sugar on your lips must have come in handy tying you up."

The four others laughed and Louie laughed. He handed a fat envelope to Al. It was bigger than normal. "Where'd you get that at?" Al asked hefting the weight of it in his hand.

"That Abe guy down at Avrum's Deli in Passaic, he thought the vig was too much. So I told him t'pay the vig or the whole five grand he owes. That som'bitch he goes back to that big ice box of his and brings back the whole friggin' five grand plus this week's vig."

That brought hard laughter from Al and his crew. Al asked, "Why'd he want the loan if he keeps that kind of cash in his back room?"

Louie lit a cigarette, blew the smoke towards the ceiling and said, "Hey, you know them Jews."

Benny Rizo said, "Hey, f'get about it," and he laughed.

Al Falzone spent the afternoon at L'oro Luna. It was cool inside since he had the window mounted air conditioner put in. On hot afternoons like that day, he and his crew stayed inside. They played pool and poker and tried to get the baseball game on the TV, arguing about how to get rid of the fuzzy black and white picture. It was half past four when Al decided to go home.

Mike Colombo stepped outside onto the sidewalk. He stood with his back to the closed door and looked up and down the street. No one was there who might be a threat to their boss. He walked to Al's car and looked for anything unusual. The doors of the car remained locked and the car hadn't been moved. He took a key from his pants pocket and unlocked and opened the door. He bent and felt under the seats. Nothing unusual was there, like a paper bag of explosives.

He walked to the front of the car, and reaching under the front of the hood, he pulled the hood release. Pulling up the hood, he looked down at the engine. It was clean, no bomb of any kind waiting to go off when the engine was started. Mike closed the hood and kneeled down to see if anything had been added under Al's car. He stood and called out, "It's OK boss!"

The rest of the crew stepped outside and hovered on the corner as Al got in his car and drove away. He stopped at Belacoza's Bakery and bought a dozen of the cannoli his wife, Maria, loved. They had been married 15 years ago. He thought as he drove away from the bakery, that their anniversary was coming up in just two weeks. He had to find something nice for her.

There were children playing in the street in the late afternoon as Al turned into his neighborhood. He stopped the car and rolled down his window. The children came running up to him. The boys all asked about the baseball game on Saturday, and the girls told him of new dolls and dresses, the children all happily talking at once.

"Hey! Hey!" Al laughed. "Calm down everybody! Tell you what, after the game this Saturday everybody comes to my house for ice cream and soda. Girls, too. And you girls gotta' come to the game. We gotta' have lots of people cheering for us."

The children all screamed in delight and ran in all directions, the boys chasing the girls just as the girls wanted the boys to do. Al carefully pulled into the driveway of his home, avoiding the two bicycles of his son and daughter. They had left them, once again, laying flat on the concrete when they ran into the house for their afternoon cookies and chocolate milk. Before going into the house, Al picked up both bicycles and moved them to the safety of the open garage.

Inside, the two children ran to greet their father. Little Al jumped into his father's arms; Teresa, his daughter, hugged him and pulled him down to her so she could kiss him on his cheek. "Oh, Daddy! Isn't it exciting!"

"OK, OK. What's so exciting?"

"Mommy said she'll take me to the hair dresser and then clothes shopping on Saturday!"

Little Al tried to get his father's attention. "Daddy, Daddy! Guess what I did today!"

Al, although Little Al was in his arms, ignored his son as usual in favor of Teresa. He said to her, "That's wonderful, darling. You're growing up so fast. You're going to be as beautiful as your mother."

Little Al slipped from his father's arms and walked away to his bedroom where he could sulk alone. Being alone was easier for Little Al than being ignored and yelled at by his father and mother.

Maria was standing at the sink in the kitchen, wiping her hands on a dish towel. She was smiling. She was wearing a crinoline under her bright blue dress and a white and pink apron. Around her neck she wore the new string of pearls Al had given her last month. She wore her new hi-heeled shoes even though they pinched her toes; they were too pretty not to wear. She wiped her wet hands on the dish towel and waited for Al to come to her and kiss her hello. He did that every day to the children's delight and laughter.

To Maria, she had a good family; bright children who would grow up well, and a loving husband who was devoted to her and the children. She had a beautiful home and she had friends. And there was a driving force in her life that kept her going. Other people had working careers and the drive to succeed and move up in their careers with the help of good wives, who could be taken to business dinners and be the perfect hostess at business parties. Maria had her husband, and Maria's career and drive was to see him move up inside the Mafia, beyond his Caporegime position, to become the Don of his own family with all the money and respect that came with that high position.

Dinner that night was fried chicken, pasta a'la marinara, and green beans. It was Teresa's turn to say the blessing before they ate. She asked for God's blessing on the food and her family, but in her mind, unspoken, was the thought that God might bring Tony, "That boy from the pizza place," back to her someday.

Little Al wouldn't eat the green beans as usual, but devoured the chicken and pasta. The children had big slices of chocolate cake for dessert while Al and Maria enjoyed espresso and cannelloni as they watched their children eat.

After dinner Al dried the dishes as Maria washed, while the children took their baths and put on their pajamas. An hour of TV, Leave it to Beaver and then Zorro and the children were sent to bed, tucked in by both their mother and father. Little Al was quickly tucked into bed and kissed on his forehead. No words were spoken; the lights were turned off leaving the room in complete darkness. Little Al tossed to his side, facing the wall, and cried again.

Little Al's bedroom was a boy's bedroom, as Maria thought a boy's bedroom should be. The walls were painted dark blue even though Little Al had said he didn't like blue. There was a small desk with a lamp on it and a hard wooden chair pulled to it, even though Little Al had wanted a bigger desk, one where he could line up his little plastic toy soldiers and play war. Pictures of baseball players and football players hung on the walls, even though Little Al said he wanted pictures of race cars. Maria had the painters stencil stars and planets on the ceiling that would glow in the dark, even though Little Al said they frightened him in the night.

Little Al tried out for the Little League teams his father coached because he wanted his father to be proud of him and like him. But he never was able to make it on any of the teams. He just wasn't good at sports. Al always reminded his son of his failure in sports and everything else Little Al couldn't do. "You're just not trying enough, Little Al," his father would tell him every time he failed to make the team.

In Teresa's bedroom, Maria and Al sat on the edge of her bed and talked with her. Her room was a girl's fantasy, all white and pink and lace. Maria and Teresa had worked together decorating the room, and every time Teresa wanted something changed or something new, she and her mother would get it, always working together on the project.

"Daddy," Teresa pleaded as he pulled the cover up to her chin. "I'm 14 years old now. I'm all grown up. Why can't I stay up later?"

Al was about to give in, as he always did when his daughter wanted something, but Maria interceded. "Fourteen is not all grown up young lady," she said and kissed Teresa on her forehead.

Teresa lay back on her feather pillow and said,

"Well . . . Someday I'm going to meet a boy . . . Then I'll stay up as late as I want." She was thinking of the boy who had gotten the pizza and took it to a table for her. He was cute, she thought. He smiled at her. He liked her. And she would never forget his name. Tony, that's right. That's what he said. She would remember that.

Al and Maria laughed and left the girl's bedroom and returned to the kitchen where Maria poured two glasses of Strega. They sat together at the kitchen table. Al pulled a fat wad of hundred dollar bills from his pocket. He pulled the thick rubber band that held the wad of bills together off the roll, and counted out eight of the bills, laying them on the table between him and his wife.

"I'm taking Teresa to have her hair done and get some clothes on Saturday, remember. And she needs the uniforms for school, too. They're expensive. I need more money for that," Maria said and smiled knowing she could ask for anything and get it.

Al took three more hundred dollar bills and laid them on the others. "Anything else?" he asked.

"I'm not happy with the High School Teresa's going to," she said as she folded the hundred dollar bills and put them in the pocket of her apron.

"What's wrong with it? Hell, it's a damn expensive private Catholic school ain't it?"

"Please, Al. Watch your language. Your boss doesn't talk like that."

"Like hell he doesn't," Al laughed. "He drinks like a God damn fish and smokes like a friggin' chimney. And that friggin' son of his is just as bad." He picked up Maria's pack of Pall Mall cigarettes, took one out and lit it.

"Al," Maria insisted. She spoke slowly, as if she

were speaking to Little Al, trying to make her husband understand. "You don't want to stay where you are forever, do you? You want to move up, don't you? Don't you want to be a real boss? Think of all that money, Al. Think of the really great schools Teresa can go to if we had the money. Think about it, Al."

"Move up?" Al asked. "Move up? How many times have we talked about this? How many times do I have to explain it to you? Moving up means being one of Salvano's soldiers. That's the next step for me. Do you really wanna' live in Brooklyn? You think being one of Salvano's soldiers is moving up? Hell, Maria, don't you remember? Don't you remember where we came from? Think back twenty years and all the hard times we had. You think carrying a gun and using my fists like I used to have to do is moving up?"

"No! That's not what I mean. Why can't you be the boss of your own family? Why does Pietro have to be your boss? He's an old man and he doesn't do anything. And that kid of his, why does Peter have to sit up there in that damn penthouse in Manhattan? Why can't that be you?"

"And if we move into Peter's condo, where does he go? Where does Pietro go if I take over the family?" Al waited for Maria to say something but all she did was stare into her husband's eyes. She would never say it out loud, but it was time, she thought, that they broach the subject. Al asked, "Are you telling me it wouldn't be stupid to take Pietro Salvano out? Are you crazy? Killing a Don is a death sentence, you know that."

"Well, why not break off and start your own family? You've got the soldiers . . . You've got the territory."

"And you think Pietro will just shake my hand and wish me good luck? Maybe he'll give me a gold

watch as thanks for all the years I've been with him. If
I tell him that . . . They'll carry my body out of the
room and toss me in the Hudson River."

****

School wouldn't start for another week. Teresa
wasn't looking forward to the strict authoritarian rule of
St. Ignatius Academy any more than she liked the
Catholic grammar school she had just graduated from.
She had heard all the stories of the Dominican Nuns
and Jesuit Priests and how they thought hitting and
spanking were the only way to drum lessons into
students.

Saturday came, and she had been thinking all
week of the boy. She would go to Passaic and see
him again. She dressed in light blue shorts, the shorts
that fit her tightly, because he might like that. She
wore a white cotton blouse and wished that her
breasts were bigger.

She left the house without telling her mother
where she was going. Down the street and to the
corner where the bus stopped. She rode it into
Passaic and walked two blocks to DeSonoto's Pizza.
It was almost ten o'clock but DeSonoto's would not
open until eleven. She waited, sitting at one of the
tables on the sidewalk, she waited for Adamo and his
sons to arrive and open the doors. When they did, she
followed them inside.

"The ovens will take some time to heat up, little
girl," Adamo said. "Sit down, and I'll bring you a bottle
of Coke."

"Thank you," she said and sat at the same table
she had sat at with her two friends. She looked
around nervously.

Adamo brought her the soda. She asked, "Does your waiter come to work soon?"

"Waiter?" Adamo asked. "What waiter?"

"You know . . . I think his name is Tony."

"Oh, Tony! He don't work here no more, little girl. Sorry."

Teresa stood and walked out without drinking her Coca Cola. On the bus back to Montclair she cried. But she was also certain that she would see Tony again. Nothing would stop her, she told herself. She would see him again.

THREE

Manhattan, New York City
August 1958
The Salvano Family

The Dodgers have left Brooklyn. That was the subject at lunch that summer day. Five men sat together at a round table in the middle of Bennett's Steak House slicing through the twenty-four ounce, blood rare Porterhouse steaks Bennett's was famous for. The platters that held the steaks found room for the thick, rich and creamy potato casserole and creamed spinach.

Large mugs of Rheingold beer were exchanged for full mugs when they had been drained. Glasses of whiskey were filled to the brim to go with the beer and steaks. Clouds of cigar smoke hung above, surrounding the thick wooden beams overhead, as the businessmen who frequented Bennett's enjoyed expensive Cuban cigars after their meals.

Bennett's was a restaurant for men only. Every waiter was male and had been at Bennett's for most of their adult lives. The cooks and kitchen staff were all male. The three bartenders were male. It would be seven more years before women were allowed to dine at Bennett's. The male patrons that day concentrated on talk of sports and politics, red meat, beer, fine whiskey, cigars, women, and the business of making money.

"I mean, it's as simple as that," Jack Fulton said while holding a fork overloaded with barely cooked beef, waiting to move it to his mouth. "The team can make more money in California than it can in Brooklyn."

"But what about the fans?" Mike Crawford asked. "I mean, Brooklyn? There's generations of fans there."

"So why can't they fill the stadium anymore?" Randy Maxwell asked. "And the stadium is old after all. They'd have to build a new one sooner or later, and you think the City is gonna' pay for it like L. A. is? That's where all the money is, out west."

"So what does your father think about all this, Pete?" Larry Pendleton asked.

Peter Salvano stopped with his fork halfway to his mouth and looked up from his plate. Larry Pendleton was Peter's attorney and a good friend. They had gone to college together and followed different roads in grad school, Larry to law school and Peter to a business MBA. Their eyes met and immediately Larry knew he had made a mistake. He tried to cover his tracks by saying, "I mean, doesn't he still live out in Brooklyn? That's all."

"Larry . . . You know I haven't spoken with my father in years . . . And you damn well know why."

"I'm sorry, Pete. I just thought . . ."

"Don't think so quickly, Larry. Look, he's my father but we live in different worlds."

Peter Salvano owned Tri-State Investments, a company that owned a large construction company, a trucking company, and a string of restaurants throughout New York and New Jersey. Peter was a very successful business man, a graduate of Harvard, a caring employer who took good care of those who worked for him. He was a church going father of four, a man who made large and very public donations to charities, and a good friend to have when a friend was in trouble. He lived in a grand, two story penthouse apartment overlooking Central Park.

Peter's father was Pietro Salvano, a Mafia Don who had lived in Brooklyn since arriving in the United States in 1893 at the age of twenty, and whose crime family ran some of Brooklyn and all of New Jersey.

Peter lived a life separate from his Mafia father. All his friends and close business associates knew of the family relationship but none talked about it openly. The lunch continued, and the table was cleared of the dishes and glasses. The five men sat for another thirty-five minutes enjoying good cigars, then got up and returned to their work after their two hour lunch, three beers and three martinis.

The heat outside was oppressive so Peter waived down a taxi to take him back to his Madison Avenue office. He had contracts to review and Thursdays were his end of the work week. He would work late that night, finishing up what needed to be finished and then, about eight in the evening, he would either walk home to his Park Avenue apartment or find a taxi to take him to his family. He had bought the apartment two years ago, paying cash for it. A half million dollars was the asking price and a half million was what he had paid.

The next morning, as with every Friday morning, he would wake early and cook thick waffles and bacon for his children before they left for school. It was a treat the children loved and looked forward to. They ran and giggled as they bathed and brushed their teeth and dressed to see who could be first at the table. After they left for school, Peter and his wife, Carol, would return to their bedroom and their bed. Fridays were the only day they had to themselves and they took full advantage of the day.

After lunch together Peter would leave their home overlooking Central Park and take the elevator down to the underground garage. He would drive out of Manhattan to Brooklyn and his father's home. He was very careful making this trip, doubling back often, stopping for coffee at a lonesome diner, and looking in the car's rear view mirror to be sure he wasn't being followed.

The house in Brooklyn was two stories tall, brownstone and newly roofed in the latest asphalt shingles. The window frames were painted bright green, and the wooden porch that ran from end to end of the front of the house was painted a dark red. In the front yard stood a tall flag pole that proudly held a big American flag.

Peter drove into the driveway of his father's home and pulled the car into the back yard, away from sight of anyone on the street. He opened the unlocked back door and walked inside. Bruno Massetti stood as Peter entered the house. Bruno was Pietro's lifelong bodyguard. He dropped the newspaper he was reading and stood silently.

"How is he today?" Peter asked.

"About the same, you know."

"Is my mother with him?"

"Yes," Bruno answered. "She's been up all night. I'm worried about her."

Peter nodded knowingly. "Has the doctor been here this week?"

"He was here yesterday. You want I should have him come back today so's you can talk to him?"

"No," Peter answered. "I'll go upstairs for awhile. When the Capos arrive, have them wait in my father's office."

Peter walked slowly up the wide staircase to his father's bedroom. The door was open; the room was dark because the heavy brocade drapes had been pulled closed. The room smelled of stale air and age. Pietro lay in the middle of the big bed he had shared with his wife for almost fifty years.

Pietro was failing. Dementia, the doctors said. Rapid aging, other doctors said. Whatever it was, Pietro was bedridden and everyone was a stranger. Pietro no longer recognized his wife or his only child. He did not speak; he ate only occasionally and was wasting away. His once powerful body was colorless skin over bones; his once thick black hair was thin and white. His eyes were vacant and simply stared off at some nothingness far away.

It was difficult keeping Pietro's condition secret. The doctors and nurses were paid well, but Peter knew that the threat of death did more to keep the secret. The newspapers, if they ever found out, would surround the house, taking pictures of everyone who came and went. Peter would wait until the old Don died to make a public announcement. Otherwise the headlines would be full of Don Pietro until his death. The neighbors suspected he was ill, but respect and fear kept them quiet. The Caporegimes were the only others to know the truth. Omerta, the code of silence that meant death for the man breaking that code, kept the secret inside them.

Peter stepped inside the bedroom. The room had been furnished years before when Pietro and his wife first moved into it. Dark wood furniture and heavy brocade upholstered chairs filled the room. A mirrored vanity stood against a wall; it was crowded with cut glass bottles of perfumes and other things collected by

Natalia, Pietro's wife, over many years. They sat on top of a crocheted table scarf, yellowed with age. A tall dresser stood nearby, dusty now because keeping the house spotless was less important than seeing Pietro slowly die. There was a smell of nearby death in the room.

Peter's mother, Natalia, stood from the chair she had spent the night in, the one next to her husband's bed. "How's he doing, Mama?" Peter asked.

"Not so well," Natalia whispered. Her eyes were deep within dark rings; her hair had turned grey over the past year. She often wondered if she had any tears left.

"Bruno says you were up all night again."

"I can't sleep, Peter," she said, again in a whisper.

"I don't think he can hear you, Mama," Peter said. He took her in his arms and realized how delicate she had become. He kissed her on both cheeks and hugged her again. "Why don't you go downstairs and make some tea for us, Mama? And maybe some cookies or something. I'll stay with Papa."

Natalia smiled weakly and walked ever so slowly out of the room. Peter watched and thought that she might be carrying a huge weight on her shoulders as she walked. He hated to think it, but if his Papa would just die maybe his Mama wouldn't. He forced the thought away and sat in the chair his mother had been in.

He took his father's hand in his and patted the back of the hand. It was like holding the hand of a skeleton. "Papa," Peter said. "I'm here . . . It's Peter . . . Can you hear me?"

There was no movement or indication that Pietro

heard. His mouth hung open and saliva dripped from his colorless lips. Peter reached out and carefully closed his father's mouth and wiped it dry with a tissue from the box on the nightstand. Pietro was in a near catatonic state and Peter knew his father would never return.

"Everything is going well, Papa," he said softly. "No problems. Everyone's upset about the Dodgers moving west." He stopped and a smile crept across his face. "Remember when we used to go out to Flatbush? . . . To Ebbets Field? . . . Those were fun days, Papa . . . I wonder if Mama ever found out you let me cut school to see the ballgame?"

Bruno stood in the doorway. "Excuse me, boss," he said quietly. "The Capos are here. I got them in the office like you said."

"Find the nurse," Peter said. "I'll be down in a minute." Peter had to do his father's business because his father could no longer do it. He had to receive the money, listen to the Capos, pass judgments, settle disputes, issue orders, and when absolutely necessary, order a murder. Because Peter was now the Don of the Salvano Family.

FOUR

Montclair, New Jersey
September 1958

Teresa was in her room the day before the new school year was to start. Her two friends, Barbara and Sheila, were with her. The room was a mess of clothes spread over the bed, the two chairs, the dresser, and all over the floor. There were dresses, slacks, blouses, shoes, jeans, sweaters, scarf's, and even three new bras that Teresa was proud to finally have. No more wearing those silly, childish camisoles, she would say proudly. And there were three sets of the school uniform she would wear. Blue and white plaid skirts and white blouses that Teresa hated.

"You're so lucky, Teresa," Sheila said as she went from dress to dress, holding them up to her and looking at herself in the tall mirror next to the closet. "I wish I had this many new clothes."

Barbara was trying on a pair of Teresa's new tennis shoes. They were too small for her but she wedged her feet in anyway. "I wish I had that boy we saw at the pizza place the other day," she said. "Wasn't he dreamy?" Barbara sighed.

"I guess so," Teresa said. But she knew he was good looking. His dark eyes and his muscled arms were what she wanted in a boyfriend, someone to be proud of. And of course he had to be tall and strong, like the boy she couldn't take her eyes off of the other day. And she knew he had looked at her too, liking what he saw.

"You guess so? I saw you look at him," Barbara said. "And he looked at you, too. I saw it. Love at first sight!" she laughed. "Just like in the movies!"

"I'm glad we weren't caught down there," Sheila said. "My dad would have a fit if he knew I was down in Passaic."

Barbara tossed the tennis shoes across the room and picked up a pink cashmere sweater from the bed. "That's where the best pizza is," she said. "I told you that. Wasn't it scrumptious? There's nothing like it around here."

Sheila held up a pale blue dress with a high white lace collar in front of her. "And that boy was scrumptious, too. Who do you think he is?"

Teresa was sitting at the vanity mirror combing her hair. She liked her hair to hang long and soft when so many of the girls wore their hair teased high on their heads. She stared at herself and wished her mother and father would relent and let her wear makeup. "I don't know who he is," she lied in a dreamy voice. "But I wish he would go to our school."

Teresa's two friends looked at each other and giggled, and Barbara said, "I'll bet you wish he'd do something else, too."

"You're so lucky, Teresa," Sheila said again. She was jealous of everything Teresa had. She wanted to say Teresa was lucky just because her father was a crook and had tons of money, but her parents warned her against saying anything like that.

"I wish I was lucky enough not to have to go to

St. Ignatius tomorrow," Teresa said.

Sheila was holding another dress with a very full skirt up in front of her. She said, "Why? It's a dreamy school. They have the cutest boys on the football team. Remember Robert Johnson? He played last year. He's dreamy. He's going to Notre Dame this year. They want him to play football there. Isn't that dreamy?"

"Yes . . . But I'd rather go to Montclair High. There aren't any Nuns and Priests there. And we wouldn't have to wear those goofy uniforms." Teresa said.

Barbara added, "You'd rather go to Passaic High so you can see that boy at the pizza place." And they all laughed, even Teresa because she knew that was the truth. She hadn't told the girls she had gone back to Passaic all alone, to DeSonoto's, and was disappointed to learn Tony didn't work there anymore. But she kept hoping . . . And saying prayers every night before bed . . . That she would see him again.

Teresa slowly ran the comb through her hair and thought, 'I'm going to meet that boy again. Someday, I'm going to meet that boy again.' But she didn't say it. Keeping the secret felt good, it made her feel somehow older, knowing that she had a secret about a boy. And as she thought about Tony, there was a strange warmness inside of her that she had never felt before. She would keep the secret and she would go on dreaming of Tony, until she could see him again. And she knew inside of her that she would.

They went on playing with the clothes Teresa's mother had bought for her. Maria and Teresa had spent the last week shopping. They went all over New Jersey and then into New York. Store after store, without missing even the most expensive places, and everything that Teresa said she liked her mother bought for her.   Package after package was brought into the house every afternoon.

They ate lunch every day in a different expensive restaurant.   Both mother and daughter were dressed up every day. They wore their best dresses, hats, and white gloves, in spite of the late summer heat. Teresa, just entering High School, felt like a grown woman.

And each afternoon Little Al would wait at the door for them to come home from their shopping trip. Little Al, at seven years old, was left alone each day. Maria would make a sandwich for him and pour a glass of milk.   He stood at her side as she put them in the refrigerator, on the bottom shelf so he could reach them.

"Now you be good Little Al," Maria would say. She always called her son Little Al.   He hated the name because it made him feel small in size.   "Why Little, mama?   Am I never gonna' be big?" he would ask.

"Sure you will, Little Al," his mother would say. "Someday."

The boy always felt like his mother was saying that without really knowing what he had said, how he felt.   She wasn't really listening to him.   Why was he left alone when his sister was treated so special?   He didn't understand, but he hoped it wasn't because there was something wrong with him.   He often felt that maybe he was not normal, that maybe he was stupid, not like the other children.   Why else would he be abandoned day after day?   Why else would his father be so ashamed of him?

Teresa called Little Al, Alley.   He didn't like the name but he didn't complain either.   It was better than Little Al.   And Teresa was, at least, kinder to him. When she wasn't busy with something else, she might actually smile at him; sometimes she might even talk to him for a minute or two. He waited for those times and lounged in how good they made him feel.

FIVE

Passaic, New Jersey
December 1958

That Saturday, Tony Moretti sat at the table inside DeSonoto's Pizza with The Aces. They sat at the only round table in DeSonoto's. It was cold and snowy outside; neighborhood people crowded inside for a slice and a Coke. But none dared to sit close enough to The Aces to hear what was being said.

"OK, Tony," Joey Castellani said. "So we're movin' out. So we got another street and a few more bucks comin' in. We had t'fight the damn Los Reyes twice. Now I hear they want to join up with the damn Mau Maus up in New York. Them damn Mau Mau bastards been wantin' to move into Jersey for a couple years now. What's next? Them damn Pachuco bastards formin' up again?"

Tony bit into a slice of pizza and drank from the bottle of Coke before answering. The Aces waited. Tony had made promises to them; promises of more money and more turf. He had them walk into a Latin and Black neighborhood and demand payment from the shopkeepers there. They objected and went to the Latin Los Reyes gang. The Aces met them one night in the playground of Public School Number 5. The fight was a draw in reality, but the Los Reyes gang was put in fear. They had come expecting a fist fight; The Aces came with knives, chains, baseball bats and Andy's sawed off shotgun. No, he hadn't fired it, but he hit with it, and the Los Reyes' teens were scared that he might fire it and kill one or two of them.

Tony spoke in a convincing way when explaining what they needed to do to expand their turf and The Aces listened. But Joey had a quick temper. He was known as an angry young man who more often than not let his temper take control of him. He wanted more than just a few more stores paying protection; he wanted it all and he wanted it immediately.

Tony, intentionally making The Aces wait for him to say something, finally spoke, "Me and Andy are going to take care of that." Andy Pecora was a full member of The Aces. Andy liked guns. Andy liked knives. And Andy liked to use them. Tony knew that at 18 years of age Andy had already killed three people. Andy smiled knowingly; the other Aces looked from one to another, all sharing the same thought: Someone was going to die.

Tony knew that in order for him to wear the colors of The Aces, to have a full share of the cash, he had to succeed in what he had promised. Tony had promised that The Aces would retake the turf they once owned, which was six square blocks of what was once an Italian neighborhood. The Italians were being squeezed out by the Puerto Ricans and Blacks. That day, as The Aces sat and listened to Tony, they controlled five square blocks including the stores recently taken from the Los Reyes gang. Tony wanted more. He wanted the money expansion would bring to him.

He stood, and as he started to walk away he tapped Andy Pecora on his shoulder. Andy smiled, stood and followed the fourteen year old Tony Moretti out of DeSonoto's Pizza. What little was left of the late afternoon sun was blocked by the thick clouds that were dropping heavy, wet snow. Tony pulled his torn corduroy jacket up around his neck. It did little to keep him warm but it was all he had. Andy wore his Aces jacket, a shiny satin material that was lightly padded. But Andy was not aware of the bitter cold. He knew he would have the chance to kill soon. Tony wanted one of those jackets. He would have one soon if his plan worked.

Andy followed a step or two behind young Tony. Andy was four years older than Tony, yet he followed, understanding that Tony had ideas, he had plans. They turned a corner and then another. They walked for five blocks and then Tony quickly turned into a thin alleyway. It was dark inside the alley, bitterly cold with an icy wind cutting through the narrow walkway. It was lined with trash cans and spilled garbage that was being blown around by the winter wind. A big rat jumped from an open trash can and ran away from the two. Tony stopped at a door. He looked left, then right and left again, then opened the door and stepped inside. Andy followed.

They stepped carefully up a dark wooden staircase. The building was vacant from the second floor up to the fourth, top floor. On the street floor, at the front of the building, was a new business, a small grocery and news stand, run by Manuel Rodriguez and his wife. The street was slowly converting to Spanish speakers.

On the fourth floor Tony led Andy to a window that looked down onto the street. The glass was cracked and yellow with grime. Cobwebs covered a couple of corners. The floor was thick with dust and dirt and garbage and cockroaches. The window was hard to see out of until Tony wiped his hand across the dirt. They looked down at the street that was almost crowded with the Puerto Ricans they didn't know or like. He lifted the window open; slowly, as the wood was warped and squeaked loudly, it was raised. "Look down there," he said, and Andy stepped close to the window.

"Yeah, so what?" he asked.

"Down there, directly across the street. That's where Paco lives." Paco was the head of Los Reyes. He was 21 years old and a professional criminal. Paco stole whatever he could; he sold heroin; he carried an eight inch long knife that he liked to use, and he used it very well. "He's got his girlfriend there with him," Tony said. "She's pregnant. His little brother lives there, and two others of the Los Reyes live there. Paco's bodyguards."

"OK," Andy said. He knew what was coming but he had to hear it from Tony.

"I want them dead," Tony said as he stared out the window. He said it almost casually, softly, almost as if he was asking for a glass of water. There was no passion or fear in the words he spoke.

"That's great," Andy said. "You askin' me to kill five people? Just how do I do that?"

"From here," Tony explained. "From this window."

Andy Pecora looked at the boy, questioning what he was hearing. He asked, "Do you know what you're talking about? First, how the hell do I do that? Throw friggin' pebbles at them? And if they all get killed, then what? Those damn spics'll come at us from all over."

Tony walked away, to a dark corner of the room, and picked up a pile of rags. From the pile he pulled an M1 Garand rifle with a scope attached to it. He left it wrapped in a grimy cloth so that his finger prints would not appear on it. He carried it back and held it in front of Andy. "This is how," he said. "And when it's done, everybody will be too scared to do anything. Don't you see? Nothin' like this has ever been done before. It's a step up. They'll run before they face up to anyone who would do this."

"You're sure about that?" Andy asked.

"I'm sure," he said simply. Tony wasn't as sure as he made it sound. He had a natural instinct for psychology, however. He seemed to know how to handle people, how to bend them to his will with words and actions. In honesty, he was hoping that the Los Reyes would run in fear; he wasn't sure they would. But he had to try.

Andy took the rifle still wrapped in a rag and felt the weight of it. "Where the hell'd you get this thing?" he asked smiling, feeling good about holding the murderous weapon.

"Never mind," Tony answered. Tony had broken into the home of an Army veteran, a drunk and warehouse laborer. The man had the rifle and several pistols in his house. He had bought them illegally and could not report the theft to the police. The man had been seriously wounded in the South Pacific during the war. He was known as the "neighborhood crazy guy." Tony had seen the pistols and knew that he could get one anytime he needed one.

"Look," Tony explained. "Paco and his people go out almost every night to some damn Mexican bar place across town. Wait here every night around nine. When all five of them leave at the same time . . . Kill them all and then get the hell outta' here. Don't take the gun with you . . . Leave it here. Make sure you wear some kind of gloves so's you don't leave prints on it."

Andy smiled the smile of a kid who had secretly

gotten into the cookie jar. He was going to like this. He played with the rifle, sliding the bolt back and forth and hefting the rifle to his shoulder. From inside the pile of rags on the floor Tony took out two eight round clips of bullets. He showed Andy how to load the rifle and how to focus the scope. "Leave the gun wrapped in these rags until you're going to use it. Leave it here every night you don't get them. And don't get greedy. Wait until you have the opportunity to get all of them at once."

Tony, at the age of only fourteen, was as tall as Andy. He patted the older boy on the shoulder and left Andy alone in the room. He knew Andy would do it; he knew Paco would be dead soon; he hoped that fear at such an outrageous massacre would spread through the Latin gangs. They would retreat, and it would be a long time before they found the courage to come back. Tony would have the time to expand the streets that The Aces owned, and he would have the money he wanted from joining the gang. And Tony also knew that he would soon be wearing the colors of The Aces.

SIX

Montclair, New Jersey
December 1958

Christmas was the most important time of the year for the Falzone family, especially for Maria. The Falzone home hosted three extravagant parties each December - one for their neighbors, one for Al's crew and their families, and one for the politicians and police on Al's payroll. After the Thanksgiving dishes were washed and put away, Maria began managing her husband and children as they decorated their Christmas tree, the inside of their home, and especially the outside where everyone could see their lavish wealth. And, in the front yard, there was a life size display of Mary, Joseph, and the baby Jesus in a manger, lit by flood lights every night.

The days were long and the work seemed to never end. But when they were done the rambling split level home was lit, inside and out. It was brighter and more festive than anything that Maria would see during the season. She made sure of that.

That evening was the neighborhood party, and the house, as big as it was, was crowded and loud with dozens of children running around. The adults were enjoying a well stocked bar that never ran dry.

The food was catered by Costello's, a famous and popular restaurant in Montclair. The conversation went in every direction, except for the neighbors carefully avoiding talk of the Mafia.

Maria was dressed in a bright red cocktail dress. She wore the five carat diamond ring Al had given her on their anniversary and jeweled Christmas tree earrings.

Teresa was wearing the new dress she and Maria had spent days shopping for. It was blue, sequined, and cut low enough for her to show off her teenage cleavage. Maria had let her wear her string of pearls. And for the first time Teresa wore adult makeup, applied lovingly by her mother.

She stood with several neighborhood girls and boys, enjoying the punch Maria had made and wishing some alcohol could be in it. One of the boys, a pimply faced kid with bright red hair, edged his way next to Teresa, and when he was finally standing close to her, he whispered in her ear, "Wanna go see a movie with me?"

Teresa looked at him, refusing to smile, and said, "No, leave me alone."

Al wore a grey tweed jacket and black pants that Maria had taken from his closet for him. She wanted him to wear a white shirt and tie, but Al insisted he wanted to wear a red polo shirt, open at the collar.

Little Al was dressed in grey slacks and a white shirt, open at the collar. He stood motionless most of the night, leaning against the wall near the entrance to the kitchen. No one noticed the boy.

The men were still complaining about the Dodgers moving west; the ladies exchanged recipes and stories of their days of Christmas shopping and the bargains they had found. Al walked from group to group, talking, smiling, laughing, and being the perfect host as he always was. He heard a snippet of conversation behind him that drew his attention.

"What the hell's happening to our world?" Jessie Palmer complained. He was drinking Crown Royal straight over ice and he had finished several already. The others with him tried to quiet him. "I mean, five people gunned down in cold blood! What the hell!"

Jessie's wife, Betty, tried to shush him but he was too drunk to understand. Al turned and asked, "Did I hear correctly? Five people were killed? When? Where?"

Bob Parker stepped in front of Jessie and said, "I'm sorry, Al. Jessie didn't mean anything." Talk of crime of any sort was avoided for fear of offending Alberto Falzone. The fact that he was a criminal was widely known, but never talked about in the neighborhood. Al did too much for the neighborhood; he was too good a neighbor for anyone to take the risk of offending him.

"No, it's OK. I hadn't heard. Maria has kept me so busy the last couple of weeks I haven't had time to read a newspaper. What happened?"

Bob looked from person to person then took the risk of telling the story. "Five Puerto Rican kids . . . They say gang members . . . They were all shot."

"When? . . . Where?" Al asked. If these murders happened in his territory, he would have to find out why and who murdered them. The police would do their job, but justice would be rendered by Alberto Falzone. His neighborhoods had to remain safe if the money was to continue to flow in. Unsafe neighborhoods would cause people to leave, and they would take their money with them.

Bob felt more comfortable talking about it. After all, if Al had anything to do with the killings he wouldn't be asking about them. He would be sending signals that the subject was one that should not be talked about.

"Out in Passaic," Bob said. "Day before yesterday. It was some guy named Paco Ramirez. His girlfriend and his brother and two others were with him. They were all shot. The papers called it a massacre." Bob stopped there. He dared not ask the big question: Do you know who did it?

Al said nothing; he frowned, turned and walked away leaving the group of people looking at each other, wondering. Al went to his den, a place where no one was allowed except Kathleen, the lady who came to his house three times a week to clean. Maria had furnished the den as she thought a man would like. It was nautical . . . Everywhere. Ship's wheels, expensive brass lamps, and pictures of sailing ships decorated the room, while dark wood paneling richly covered all four walls. Al didn't really like it; he had no interest in boats, but he never told Maria that.

He closed the door behind him and sat behind his desk. He picked up the phone. He dialed the L'oro Luna Tavern. Benny Rizo answered.

"Hey, boss. How's the party goin'?"

"What happened out in Pasaic?" Al asked. Passaic was part of Al's territory. He had to know everything that happened everywhere in his territory. It was his responsibility to keep the police happy. Murders that might send some suspicion his way he had to know about. And a slaughter, a mass murder, would be in the headlines for days to come. The police would have to respond.

"What'ya mean? Nothin' happened."

"Five kids were murdered," Al said, angry and feeling his temper rise. "Didn't you friggin' hear about that? Don't you read the friggin' newspapers?"

"Yeah," Benny answered. "Sure I heard. Just some spics. Probably somethin' 'bout the drugs them damn kids sell."

"Find out what happened," Al ordered. "Whatever cops we got on the payroll up in Passaic, get everything they know. Tell them we want everything . . . And tell them we're gonna' take care of this. Tell the cops to go chase some speeding cars. And we have some people on the newspaper there. Tell them to ditch the story."

"Sure boss. But why? I mean, they was just a bunch of street kids."

"Just do what I tell you to do, Benny. Get everyone on this. I want an answer fast. This is important."

Al slammed the phone down, took a couple of deep breaths to calm himself, filled a glass with the bourbon he liked from the bar that held the crystal ship's decanters, and returned to his party with a smile.

SEVEN

Brooklyn, New York
December 1958

Peter Salvano sat behind his father's desk in the den of the Brooklyn house where he had grown up. The house was dark in that mid-afternoon. There was no Christmas tree; there were no lights, no decorations, no presents for the children. A large picture of Pietro sat on a brass easel in the living room, draped in a black scarf. Don Pietro Salvano had passed away two days before.

The living room was crowded with neighbors, friends, and the many men who were in Don Salvano's crime family. The small room was furnished in the couches and chairs and tables from years before, unchanged since Pietro and his wife moved into the house. Peter had grown up in that house; he had played in the street in front of the house, but he had never really been happy there. Happiness came when he went off to Harvard where he stayed for four years and then three more to attain his MBA. Too many memories of those days growing up amongst the thugs and soldiers who worked for his father came back to Peter that day. As much as he would honor his parents, he did not honor their world.

The next day, at the cemetery, many more people would show their respect. There would be police and politicians; there would be the other Dons from the Five Families and many from other parts of the Country. Dozens of huge flower arrangements would adorn the gravesite.

The men were all dressed in black, the women in black veils with tightly tangled rosary beads in their fingers. The four children of Peter and his wife Carol sat quietly and stiffly, crowded onto a small couch in a corner of the living room. They were dressed somberly and secretly wished they would soon go home to their Christmas presents in Manhattan. Other children scampered about but the four grandchildren of Pietro could not.

Peter thought it was safe to be there and to bring his family. How could even the FBI object to him being at his father's funeral?

Pietro's wife, Natalia, moved from person to person, listening to each mourner tearfully express the depths of their loss. Don Pietro's loss meant more questions than sorrow to these people, unspoken questions but questions in any case. Who would take his place? Would the money continue to flow? What would change once one of the last of the old world Italians was gone?

The door to the den opened and silence fell throughout the house. Peter stopped in the doorway and looked around the crowded room. Soon, after everyone had had their fill of food and wine, they would return to St. Dominic's Church for the second mass of the day in memory of Don Pietro. And then to the cemetery the next morning. There wasn't time for more thought. Peter had to make his decision now.

He caught his mother's attention and waved her into the den. Inside he closed the door and pulled a tall leather chair a few inches toward her. She sat and waited for what she knew was coming. Peter paced back and forth, looking at the dark furniture in the room and the big hand carved desk that his Dad had reigned from.

"Mama," he began as he sat in his father's chair behind the desk. "You know I didn't want this. Will you come live with Carol and me?"

"No, Young Pietro," she said, calling him by the name she called him when she wanted to express her love for him. "This is my home. I will stay here."

"Who can I give the family to?" he asked.

Natalia smiled softly and kindly. She wiped a tear from the corner of her dark eyes with the small lace handkerchief that had been overused already. It was the question she knew was coming. "You should do what your father wanted."

"What did he want?"

"He spoke his last will and testament in front of me and Father Mario," she said, still smiling at the man who would always be her little boy. "He wanted you to take care of the family."

"But the others . . ." he began.

"The others will understand," she said. Natalia struggled to stand; she had not slept for more than a few hours each night in the last week, waiting at her husband's bedside until the light finally left his eyes. Peter watched her leave. She left the den's door open and walked out to the crowd, as he sat behind his father's desk. One by one, Don Pietro's Capos walked into the den. Bruno Massetti, the now deceased Don's bodyguard, led the way. Michael Funno, Charles 'Chi Chi' Torrel, and Manny Esposito followed. They stood in front of the desk while Peter waited. He looked behind the four men and through the open door.

"Where's Al?" he asked because Al Falzone was not there. Peter had been in the living room all that day, but hadn't given any thought to who was there and who wasn't.

Mike Funno answered, "Al will be here," he said. He and Al were friends. His territory was along the Jersey shore, south of Al's territory. They had grown up together and remained friends after both dropped out of High School.

Al should have been there. It was his Don who had died. To not be at the wake was a terrible insult. Mike knew that Al's wife was hosting a Christmas party that night. But he wouldn't mention that to Peter. "I'm sure he'll be here, Peter. I'm sure something came up . . . Business probably. He'll be here."

Peter said, "Close the door, please." He stood and paced back and forth behind the desk, his hands behind his back. Without stopping and without looking at the men, he said, "My father wanted me to take over." He paused and continued pacing nervously. "Do any of you object to that?"

No one answered. It was a strange question, maybe a challenge, maybe a test of loyalty. To object, if Peter had already decided he would follow his father and head the family, would mean certain death. To keep quiet was the smarter move, regardless of what each man thought. So no one answered.

Peter stopped his pacing, turned and looked from face to face, man to man. Michael Funno could pass for a banker or mid-level businessman anywhere. He dressed in good quality off the rack suits; he was thin with only a slight paunch that came with middle age; his glasses were rimmed in thick black plastic.

Chi Chi Torrel liked his gold jewelry and he wore a lot of it. Heavy chains draped around his thick neck, and a heavy gold wristwatch were the most noticeable, but he liked his gold so much that he wore as much of it as he could. Chi Chi was the shortest of the four men. He was heavy, but that did not stop him from dancing with his many girlfriends and his wife, when she was the only woman around.

Manny Esposito's weight showed his love of food. He was sweating as he always did.

And Bruno Massetti was the Bruno Peter remembered from his childhood. Bruno never seemed to age. He was Don Pietro's bodyguard for what seemed forever, yet even after all those years the strength in the man's arms, barrel chest, and thick neck gave warning to anyone coming near him or the Don. His life as Don Pietro's bodyguard had filled his days and years. There was no time to marry; he was alone.

Peter sat once again, behind his father's desk, elbows on the chair arms and fingers intertwined at his chin. He said, "OK, I will follow my father as head of this family. Nothing will change . . . For the time being anyway. Bruno, my mother wants to stay here in her home. You will move in and stay here and protect her. This is going to be an important job because I want this neighborhood kept safe. I want to know if the police take an interest in this neighborhood. I want the local police on our payroll if they aren't already. This house is where we will meet. It is your job to make sure that this is a safe place to meet.

"No one will come to Manhattan," Peter continued. "No one will use the phone to contact me. Michael, your son Theo just graduated from NYU. He has a job waiting for him in my company . . ."

Michael smiled, happy that his son would not follow in his footsteps. "Thank you, Don Peter," he said.

"Theo will deliver messages to me in person.

Nothing will be put in writing, and you will not contact him by phone at my office on family business. Meet him for lunch or somewhere and relay everything by mouth."

The smile left Michael's face. Theo was going to be drawn in whether he liked it or not.

Peter, now Don Peter, paused to let the discomfort amongst the four men continue for a moment or two, and then said, "That's all. Thank you all for showing your respect to my father."

As the men started to turn, Don Peter at first thought that each would kiss his hand as the old gangsters from the 30's did. But they lived in a modern world, not the world of prohibition and the old Mustache Pete's and the Black Hand. Ceremony had taken a back seat to business. He said, "Michael, tell your friend Al Falzone that I expect to see him here tonight and tomorrow at the cemetery."

It was a command, Don Peter's first threat. To disobey would be impossible.

Peter left the den and his wife walked up to him. "What was all that about?" she asked.

"I had to keep my mother safe and let them know I wasn't going to replace my father. Carol, you know I'm ashamed of all this. I want no part of it. All I want is to get us all back home and away from this."

"How will your mother be safe?" Carol asked. "Isn't she coming to live with us?"

"No, she wants to stay here. I asked one of the men to move in here and see to it she's taken care of. That's all I can do. I just don't want to be dragged into all this."

Carol understood and touched his arm approvingly. The newspapers ran the story of Pietro's death for a week, every day. It was common belief that Bruno Massetti, having moved into Pietro's house, was the new Don of the Salvano Family.

EIGHT

Passaic, New Jersey
December, 1958

This meeting of The Aces was too important to be held at the round table inside DeSonoto's. They sat in private, in the storage room at the rear of DeSonoto's. There were no tables and only one chair. Jay Schoemer sat in the wooden chair, while the others stood and leaned against stacks of boxes and wooden shelves. Big cans of tomato sauce and boxes of cheese lined the shelves. Tony Moretti stood with his back to the closed door. The room wasn't big, with the six Aces and Tony inside there was little room left.

It was a week since Andy Pecora had killed Paco and his friends. He had done what Tony had told him to do. He had waited until all five were outside and together; he had worn gloves; he had left the rifle in the vacant room for the police to find. The room had been on a street once owned by Paco and his gang. Nothing pointed to The Aces as having committed the crime. The police, for lack of any other evidence, declared that some other rival Latino gang had done the murders, some other gang who were dealing in drugs.

And Tony was right. The Los Reyes were

frightened and without a leader. They felt surrounded by potential enemies; they didn't know which way to turn or who to attack. Fear crept through the eleven remaining members of the Los Reyes and one by one they started to drift away, to join other gangs in other neighborhoods. And street by street The Aces took over. Their income from protection and extortion doubled.

Tony was proudly wearing the jacket The Aces had given him. The white and gold satin jacket, with the sown on patch of four aces on the back, felt good. He was proud, and he had money in his pocket for the first time in his life. His fifteenth birthday was in four weeks and he felt like a man.

Joey Castellani was speaking. "There's this one store on Twelfth Street. The guy says he don't need no protection. Says he pays somethin' called The City Merchant Protection Group. What the hell's that?"

Richie Pelto laughed and said, "That's the damn Mafia, you jerk."

The six looked at Tony. He had become, in a short amount of time, the one the others turned to for answers to questions and for advice on what to do. The Aces had never had a formal leader before. Tony had stepped into the role of having the answers. Perhaps he wasn't the leader, but the others had come to rely on him for the right answers.

Tony smiled and said, "The Mafia, huh? Well, I think they should have theirs and we should have ours."

The six others looked from one to another, questioning what Tony meant by what he had said. Richie Pelto, perhaps smarter than the others, asked, "Tony, I think I know what you mean. But I think you better explain it, just in case."

"What kind of store is it?" Tony asked Joey.

"The guy sells newspapers . . . magazines . . . cigarettes.   That   kind'a   stuff."   Joey   Castellani answered. "Why?"

Tony thought about that and then asked, "How many of you ever been in there?"

Again the six looked from one to another. No one answered, but their silence was the answer Tony was looking for.

He said, "That neighborhood ain't nothin' but blacks and Puerto Ricans.   They might smoke cigarettes but how many of them can read?" he said derisively. "I think maybe the guy that runs that place is doin' some other kind of business."

Richie Pelto said, "And I think you know what kind of business he's doing."

"Yeah, I think I know," Tony said, grinning. "He's running a numbers drop for the mob. That kind'a thing is a growing business. What's the guy's name runs the place? I think I should talk to him."

Joey Castellani said, "Sammy Washington. He's this black guy. What the hell good's it gonna' do t'talk to him? I think we should go over there and wreck the place." Joey's famous temper was rising again. Tony had to control him and the best way to do that, Tony knew, was by flattering him.

He said, "If he doesn't come around when I talk t'him . . . You an' me are gonna' wreck the place . . . Turn it into a friggin' warehouse. I need you if I'm gonna do that. There ain't nobody better than you at that kind'a thing."

That seemed to satisfy Joey. He smiled and relaxed back in the chair. What Tony didn't say was that wrecking a Mafia front would be a deadly thing to do for all of them. He pulled the door open and walked out of the storeroom and into the restaurant. It was snowing outside, and the wind was blowing as they left DeSonoto's. Tony pulled his brand new Aces jacket tightly around him. It did little to keep the cold away from him, but he wasn't about to wear anything but it, regardless of the weather.

He found the store Joey was having trouble with. Inside was warm but there weren't any customers. It smelled bad, of old, damp paper. And there was dust and dirt everywhere. It was dark inside, the one room lit by only two small light bulbs hanging from the ceiling. As Tony stepped inside he felt a crunching under his foot. He looked down and a big cockroach lay flattened on the dirty floor. 'Damn place is a pig sty,' Tony thought.

Sammy Washington stood from the stool he was sitting on. He put his hands on the battered wood table that held an old cash register and a pile of dusty magazines.

He glared at Tony and said, "I told you guys to stay away from here. I got me protection enough, you unner'stand? Now get the hell out!"

Tony walked slowly to the man and stood on the other side of the table. He stuck his hands inside the pockets of his Aces jacket. He smiled a friendly smile and said, "Mr. Washington. I know who runs this place. Believe me I don't want to step on their toes. But there are gangs . . . Like The Aces . . . Out there fighting over this street. You know that as well as I do. Every other business on the street has hired The Aces to keep these other gangs away. These other gangs will steal from you, strong arm you, and demand everything you have. They'll piss on your door and shit on your floor. Now, the people you work for aren't going to risk taking on a bunch of kids. Can you imagine the headlines when they do? I can see it now, 'Mafia thugs kill children.' You don't want that . . . I don't want that. The Aces can keep these other gangs away from you. And all we want is ten dollars a week from you. That's what every other business on the block is paying. And they're getting what they're paying for. Hasn't there been peace around here in the last couple of weeks?"

"So if there's this here peace you're talkin' 'bout, why should I pay you anything?"

"Because I can let these other gangs know that I don't give a fuck what happens to you. I can let them know they can have you. I can let them know that The Aces will sit outside and watch them tear your place apart."

Sammy Washington said nothing for a moment or two. He stared at Tony, looked him up and down, and saw a teenager who didn't sound like the other gang kids. He asked, "You with The Aces? You don't sound like it. Who are you?"

"I'm Tony Moretti. When I talk business, I talk business. When I need to talk to some other people, I talk the way they expect me to talk. I want to do business with you. You're a business man and I respect that. I'm not going to insult you by sounding like some street thug. You're a grown man and you deserve my respect."

Sammy Washington nodded and opened his cash register, pulled a ten dollar bill from it and handed it to Tony. "I hope you kids know what the hell you're doin'," he said.

"I know what I'm doing," Tony said. "Joey Castellani will be around every Wednesday. You pay him, is that OK?"

"Joey's that big kid? The one who's always pissed off?" Sammy asked. "I don't like him. He tosses threats around. Gonna' get the boy in trouble some day."

"Joey won't give you any trouble," Tony said as he pocketed the money. "Just give him the ten dollars and he'll go away. He won't say anything to you. Come see me if he gives you trouble." Tony reached out his hand. Sammy hesitated and then took it. They shook hands; Tony smiled, Sammy didn't.

NINE

Passaic, New Jersey
February, 1959

The Aces sat at the big round table inside DeSonoto's Pizza Parlor. It was bitterly cold outside; the temperature that late afternoon was barely above freezing. The ovens helped to warm the place, but because of the cold outside, customers were few that day.

Adamo DeSonoto sat on his stool behind the counter reading one of the Italian newspapers that was a week and a half old. He didn't mind The Aces being there. They always paid for their pizza and Cokes, and they never caused trouble. They were polite to the customers and one of them would always jump up to open the door for any lady entering or leaving the store. Except, that is, for Joey Castellani. He was quiet most of the time, but all of the time had an angry scowl on his face. Adamo didn't like Joey, but he never risked telling anyone that. He saw Joey as a trouble maker, an angry young man with a terrible and quick temper. 'That boy is crazy,' Adamo often thought.

Jay Schoemer reached for the last slice of the pizza before anyone else could get it. He devoured half of it in one bite. Tony laughed a little and leaned back in his chair. Tony ate well and stayed fit, but he could never bring himself to overdo eating as the others did. Even Eddy Di Bono gorged himself when there was food in front of him, but he never seemed to gain the weight the others did.

Tony Moretti was fifteen years old now. He was the youngest of The Aces but through unspoken consent he was now the head of the gang. He had been right when he had told them he knew how to expand their turf. The others respected that and looked to Tony for ideas and answers.

The money was rolling in, several hundreds of dollars a week, divided equally between the seven teens. Their turf was theirs; seldom did other gangs dare invade. Peace reigned, and kids played in the streets, and old ladies could walk to the market safely. In the heat of the coming summer, doors and windows could be left open because no one dared steal from anyone in the blocks owned by The Aces. The ten dollars a week each business owner and landlord paid turned out to be a good investment and no one complained about the payments.

The glass door of DeSonoto's opened and a man stepped inside. He was too well dressed to be from the neighborhood. His camel hair overcoat was unbuttoned revealing an expensive grey suit, certainly not off the rack, over a grey striped silk shirt and bright red tie. The man stood with his back to the closed door and looked at The Aces, from teen to teen. His gaze stopped with Tony. He smiled as he said, "Tony Moretti. I would like to talk to you."

"And who the hell are you?" Tony asked. He knew, of course, who the man was. He had seen him many times walking down the streets of Passaic with his crew.

"I'm Al Falzone," he said. "Is there somewhere where we can talk? In private?"

Tony stood as slow as he could, making a show of it. He smiled proudly and arrogantly as he walked to the back of the restaurant and to the storage room The Aces used whenever they needed to talk without people hearing. Al followed.

Inside Al closed the door, leaving the two alone. Tony was as big as Al, and Al knew Tony's reputation as a fighter. In two month's time Al's crew had found out everything there was to know about the boy. He also had a good hunch that it was Tony Moretti who had ordered the killing of Paco Ramirez and the others. There was no evidence, of course, but there was no other reason why the Los Reyes had retreated and The Aces moved into their turf. If someone other than The Aces had done the killing, that person or persons would certainly have taken over the streets The Aces now owned.

"So, Mr. Falzone," Tony said. "What can I do for you?"

"You know who I am?" Al asked.

"Certainly," Tony said. "I know everything about my turf. So what can I do for you?"

"Actually, it's what I can do for you, Tony." Al said. "I've been hearing good things about you."

Tony recognized the use of a compliment. Empty flattery often brought results. Tony often used the same technique. He wasn't about to fall for the trick, however. Al Falzone was a dangerous man, Tony knew that. But he also knew that if Mr. Falzone wanted him dead or hurt, he would be dead or hurt already. So he thought it best to get right to the point, to show Mr. Falzone he wasn't scared. He asked, "And do you have a problem with us protecting the neighborhood?"

"Not at all," Al said. He smiled but Tony thought it might be a forced smile. Al pulled the lone chair in the room to him and sat. He lit a cigarette and offered one to Tony who refused. Tony disliked the smell of cigarettes, the smoke and the after smell on people who smoked. It reminded him of the smell of cigarettes and sweat on Lorenzo. At the table with The Aces he had managed to convince the others not to smoke when he was with them. It was a huge concession on their parts, but it was but a small payment in return for the money that came to them. But he said nothing when Al lit a cigarette.

"So you don't have a problem with the money we've been making. What do you want?"

"Your business is not a problem to me," Al said again. "In fact, I appreciate your initiative. The ten bucks you get is small potatoes and it does a lot to keep the peace here. I like that. When you guys keep the peace, I don't have to." Al paused long enough to make Tony wonder what the hell this was all about. He wanted to shout out *'SO WHAT THE HELL DO YOU WANT THEN?'* But he waited, patiently, saying nothing. He leaned back on some shelves that were full of cans of tomatoes and bags of flour, leaning his elbow against the shelves, and he smiled.

Al crushed out his cigarette on the floor and looked up at Tony. The smile hadn't left his face. Tony was trying to look casual and calm, but Al had enough experience with people to know that below the exterior calm, Tony was worried. He finally asked, "How would you like to work for me?"

"You want me to work for you? You've got to be kidding!"

"I'm not kidding," Al said and the smile fell suddenly from his face. "I've got work for you to do. You gonna' do it? Or does that cash you kids been taking in dry up?"

So that was it. Tony had built a reputation as a fighter and as a smart young teenager, only fifteen years old, but a kid who was to be feared. And now the local boss wanted that reputation to bring more cash to him. He had grown up in that neighborhood and had seen other young men, teenagers at best, drawn into a life of organized crime. It was where the Families got their recruits, their new, young soldiers to replace the dead soldiers and the soldiers who would spend years in jail.

Tony knew that if he refused, he would pay a terrible price and The Aces would lose everything they had gained. All the fights and the murders will have been for nothing. Yet, if he said 'yes', and he wasn't as smart as he thought he was, the rest of his life would be in the service of one Mafia boss or another. And what would be asked of him, if he could not succeed in his plan?   Certainly there would be violence, but he knew how to use violence.   Would there be more? Would he be asked to commit murder?

He was at that point in his plan where he always knew he would have to make a choice. He was at a fork in the road and he had to decide which road to take. He could continue with his plan for his future or he could go back to work at DeSonoto's.

"What kind of work did you have in mind?" he asked.

"You know who I am and the kind of business I do. I need someone who can fight. Someone like you," Al said. He lit another cigarette and offered one to Tony who said no again.

"You think I'm going to get into the ring and fight for money?"

Al laughed.   "You know that's not what I'm talking about."

Tony pushed himself away from the shelves and paced back and forth, as far as the small room would allow. He wanted to make it obvious that he was thinking, at least that's what he wanted Al Falzone to believe. Tony had already made his decision but he had to make Al believe he hadn't. Al could not know that the meeting was part of Tony's plan for his future. He had known, sooner or later, Al Falzone would come to see him.

Tony stopped and looked down at the man sitting and smoking. He said, "You've got Benny Rizo, Ted Bianci, Mike Colombo, Frankie DeLuca, and Louie Lombardi. Why me?"

"You know a lot," Al said.

"I'm not dumb," Tony answered. "I know everything that happens around here. It's as much my neighborhood as it is yours. So why me?"

"Like I said, I want someone who can fight."

"Fight who?"

"That's my business," Al answered.

Tony grinned and said, "Let me guess. You plan on expanding your territory. Don Pietro is dead and leadership in the Salvano Family is shaky. You want to take advantage of the situation to move out, to move into someone else's territory, to take over. I'm guessing that would be Chi Chi Torrel's territory and I'm guessing Chi Chi won't like that. I'm guessing that if you send one of your own crew to do the dirty work, Chi Chi is going to find out too soon and he might send some of his own men up here. You want someone to take the heat, to do the dirty work and steer Chi Chi away from you for awhile. But what happens when Don Peter finds out?

Al didn't answer. He crushed the cigarette out under his heal and lit another. He smiled up at Tony.

"Oh, I get it. You want Don Peter to want Chi Chi out and you in. You're figuring that if I hit Chi Chi's money sources he won't be able to pay up to the Don and he'll eventually be on the short end of the stick with Don Peter. Don Peter will put a contract on Chi Chi, and you'll take over his territory." Tony paused and grinned slyly. "I hope you know what you're doing."

"You're a smart kid," Al said. "How'd you get so smart?"

Tony didn't answer. He didn't want Al Falzone to know that in that part of Passaic he was respected more than he was feared. He was feared, yes. But people knew he kept his word, and the neighborhood was safer with him than without him. So they told him everything. Instead of answering he asked, "What's in it for me?"

"How much money do you have in your pocket, Tony?"

"About a hundred," he said and that was a lot of money in those days, especially for a fifteen year old boy.

But it didn't impress Al. "Small potatoes," he said again. "How's ten times that sound?"

Tony nodded and smiled. He knew he had to keep Al going if he were to get what he wanted. "What about The Aces?"

"We'll find work for them. But they can't know what we're doing. That has to be between you and me and no one else. You'll be the boss of everything I give you and you can use your friends but you can't tell them why. Can you do that?"

Tony paced again in the small storage room. He wanted Al to feel anxious and maybe a little nervous. The minute and a half that went by seemed much longer. He wanted Al Falzone to feel some heat, to realize that he wasn't dealing with a child. Tony stopped pacing and said, "Let me guess. You came here on your own. You didn't talk to anyone about meeting here with me. You couldn't risk someone running off and squealing to Chi Chi or the new Don. So no one knows you're here. Suppose I were to call Andy Pecora in here and tell him to cut your throat from ear to ear? Hell, no one would know. We could bury your body somewhere later on tonight. No one would ever know."

"Do you know who the hell you're talking to kid?" Al demanded.

"Sure, Mr. Falzone. I just wanted you to know that you're not dealing with some punk who's afraid of you. Sure, you can have me killed, but I can have you killed too. So if we're going to do business let's keep it as business. No threats . . . Just business."

Al said nothing as Tony started pacing back and forth again. He stopped pacing suddenly, turned to look down at Al sitting on the chair and said, "I want a thousand a month for me and another thousand to split among The Aces. If we hit one of Chi Chi's places we keep whatever we take. And I don't want trouble with our turf. If the Mau Maus come down from New York or the Los Reyes come back up . . . I want guns. And if you want someone dead we'll discuss a price depending on who. That'll be extra."

Al stood and held out his hand. "You've got a deal."

TEN

Brooklyn, New York
June 1959

Peter Salvano left his Manhattan office at twenty past noon that day. He was as cautious as he always was. He had heard that J. Edgar Hoover and the FBI were intent on breaking up what they called 'organized crime.' He had started to take extra precautions earlier in the year. Rather than drive his own car to Brooklyn to meet with his Capos, he switched cars twice. He drove his car from the parking garage in the basement of his building to a parking garage three blocks away. He parked his car there and walked down two floors where a nondescript grey Chevy was waiting. He drove that car into Queens and parked in the lot of an A&P grocery store. Inside the store he bought a pack of cigarettes and left the lot in a third car, a brown Ford.

He drove taking turns and u-turns, making the route to Brooklyn as difficult as possible. He kept close watch on the car's rearview mirror. If anyone was following him that day, they had to have some kind of invisible car, he thought and laughed.

He circled the block where his mother's house was three times before pulling into the driveway and parking behind the house, out of view from the street. Bruno Massetti opened the back door, the screen door squeaking loudly on rusting hinges. He held it open for his Don. "They're all waiting for you," he said as Peter stepped into the house.

"Put some oil on those hinges," Peter said as he entered the house. The four Capos were in what was now Peter's office, once his father's den, waiting for Peter and Bruno to join them. Chairs had been put in the office for them and Natalia, Peter's mother, had filled a small table with coffee and cookies, as she did every time the family's leaders met. The four waited patiently.

Bruno closed and locked the back door; Peter turned to face him and said in a whisper, "Come into the kitchen with me, Bruno."

He followed his Don knowing the questions that were going to be asked. Bruno felt good that he had such an important place in the Salvano family. He was being well paid to ensure the necessary security his Don demanded, and doing that was easier than breaking legs to collect money after all those years.

Natalia was sitting at the kitchen table. There was a delicate china cup of tea on the table. She stopped her crocheting and looked up at her son. The pride she felt in him grew every day. He was dressed in expensive clothes; his shoes were always highly polished. He held a respected position in the world of business, and he had followed in his father's footsteps at the same time. Her one regret was that she could never see her grandchildren. Her son insisted that his two lives remain separated and never be exposed to each other. Natalia didn't fully understand this, but in her world she did whatever the head of the family demanded. Women had a place in that world; they raised children and cooked meals and were good, faithful wives. She expected nothing else out of life.

He asked her over and over again to move to Manhattan and live with his family, but she refused. Brooklyn was her home, and she was afraid that if she left, her memories of her husband would fade away.

Peter went to his mother, kissed her on the cheek and asked softly, "Mama, I have to speak with Bruno. May we please have the kitchen?"

Natalia struggled to stand; age was overcoming her more rapidly than it should have since her husband had passed away. Her fingers, knotted with arthritis, lifted the cup and saucer. She smiled as she walked away, leaving her crocheting on the table.

When they were alone Peter asked Bruno, "Bring me up to date on Chi Chi's territory."

Over the past three months the income from Chi Chi Torrel had dropped by almost a half. The old Don would have killed Chi Chi and put someone else in as head of his crew. But Peter had other ideas. Peter didn't like Chi Chi to begin with. He was too flashy in dress and lifestyle. He wore too much gold. He talked too much and told too many people about 'the business.' And he had too many women, not hiding them from his wife.

Chi Chi drew too much attention to himself, and Peter wanted his organization to hide in the shadows. Chi Chi had to go, but Peter didn't want a simple and quick murder on his hands. Simple murders were messy and hard to recover from. The days when a body was left in the middle of the street were over with. Oh, that still happened in New York and Chicago every now and then. But Peter was of a new generation, it was business to him, and violence cut into the profit picture.

The other Capos had to respect Peter more than they feared him. That was not what his father had wanted, but it was what Peter wanted. He wanted his organization to run like a business, making huge profits that would be invested in legal businesses that would make more profits. But Chi Chi had to go. He was a risk; he was of the old world and sooner or later the FBI would have enough from Chi Chi's own mouth to bring the entire organization crashing down.

Bruno started to report on Chi Chi's operations, "Four of his books have been hit in the last three months. Guys dressed in blue jeans and black sweat shirts. They were wearing these here Halloween masks. Stupid kid's masks. Smiling clowns they was. The same masks on all of'em. Same masks each time so I figure it was the same guys."

Chi Chi Torrel's business was based in and around Trenton. It stretched east to Asbury Park and north to Perth Amboy. His business was illegal gambling and loan sharking. He had a dozen dirty, dusty little backroom 'books' where bets were taken on horse racing, football, baseball, basketball, anything that anyone wanted to bet on. The police, particularly the State Police, were always after him because in his books fights were common and stabbings even more common.

It was what Chi Chi preferred, but he also had good income from loan sharking. People who borrowed money from Chi Chi would be charged interest at five points – five percent – per week. There was no paper work involved. You paid or one of Chi Chi's soldiers would make the collection.

Peter leaned back in the kitchen chair his mother had sat in. He lit a cigarette and blew the smoke slowly towards the ceiling. At home, in his Manhattan apartment, Carol, his wife, would not allow him to smoke. He didn't smoke in his office in Manhattan so that he would not go home smelling of cigarettes. But in his mother's home in Brooklyn, he took the risk and chain smoked.

"What else?" he asked Bruno.

"His collections are down," Bruno said, almost whispering. "Says people ain't payin' like they should."

"So what do you think, Bruno?"

Bruno shifted from one foot to the other nervously. His eyes were down; he could not look at his boss.

"Let me tell you what you think, Bruno," Peter said as he crushed out the cigarette in a delicate china saucer and lit another. "Chi Chi's income is down because his books are being hit. He's got a couple of women on the side. They cost a lot of money. He's skimming from his collections to make up some of the losses from his book. He's paying his women before he pays me . . . Am I right?"

Bruno said nothing, but after a moment he nodded his agreement. Chi Chi was a longtime friend of Bruno's, not close friends but friends anyway. Bruno knew what was going to happen.

"What has Chi Chi done to stop these people from hitting his books?" Peter asked.

"I don't know . . . I ain't spoke t'him about it, boss."

"Find out," Peter ordered. "Keep it quiet, don't tell anyone. Don't raise his suspicions, but ask anyway."

"OK, boss," Bruno said.

Peter stood, crushed out the half smoked cigarette and led Bruno to the old Don's den where the Capos waited with the money they would give him.

ELEVEN

Passaic, New Jersey
June 1959

Five of The Aces sat in their new clubhouse, a vacant storefront near the railroad tracks that they had bought with their new found fortune. Only Tony and Andy Pecora were not there. The teens didn't really care where all the money was coming from or why they were robbing bookie joints. They didn't know they were Chi Chi Torrel's places and that the orders had come from Al Falzone. They were just happy to see Tony bring the money in as he said he would. Tony kept all the money they stole from Chi Chi and all of it was divided equally amongst The Aces. He never offered any to Al, and Al didn't ask for any; that was their deal. Al didn't need the money; what he wanted was to put Chi Chi in trouble with Don Peter.

They knew, of course, that he and Andy were out doing things they knew nothing about, and none of them really wanted to know. If Andy Pecora was involved they knew it had to be something it was best not to be involved in. Everyone knew that Andy was a little crazy. But the money was good, better than good, and they were happy. In fact, Andy was driving Tony down to Newark in his 1949 Ford, now painted

Candy Apple Red, to see Al and get instructions on a new place to hit. They would then go to wherever it was they would storm into and make sure there was an easy escape.

It wasn't so bad robbing the bookie joints. They didn't have to hurt anyone, and no one would ever know who was doing it. Tony had supplied each of them with a short barreled Winchester pump shotgun given to him by Al. It wasn't too strange that Andy never went with them on one of these robberies. They just figured that Andy, with his penchant for killing, might get trigger happy. No one wanted that. And Joey Castellani was always the driver, waiting in the stolen car for the others to do the robbery. Tony knew that Joey's temper might not be good for a violence free robbery.

They had converted the empty storefront near the railroad tracks to the kind of place they had always talked about but never imagined they would ever have. In the middle of the room stood a brand new poker table with a green felt top and black rim, surrounded by seven black leather club chairs. A big, oak pool table filled the area between the table and the back of the room. A dozen pool sticks rested in a rack on the back wall. A shiny, white Westinghouse refrigerator at the side of the room was stocked with bottles of beer for the guys and soft drinks for the girls who liked to be near The Aces. The girls had ideas of one of The Aces falling in love with them.

A colorfully lighted juke box had been delivered that afternoon and stood near the refrigerator. It was playing all the top ten hits, as loud as The Aces could get the volume to go. The girls were dancing as seductively as they knew how, and the boys watched, liking what they saw.

There were three girls there that day. They were dressed in the latest teenage fashions. One wore a cashmere sweater that fit tight over her tissue stuffed bra, and blue jeans rolled up six or eight inches above her ankles. Another wore a calf length skirt, grey in color with a pink Poodle stitched onto it. It flared out and twirled as she danced. She wore a white blouse with a high collar, and she had left the top three buttons unbuttoned to expose her white bra. The third wore bright pink pedal pushers and a boat-neck sweater, striped in white and navy blue. They wore saddle shoes over white cotton socks, and they swayed and danced the afternoon away, letting their ponytails swing back and forth.

The walls of the new clubhouse were covered with Playboy centerfolds, posters of cars, and old photographs of boxers and wrestlers. Over time The Aces would add souvenirs of sporting events - most they would steal, but some they would buy at the ball games they spent some of their money on.

The double glass doors of the storefront opened, and Tony walked in followed by Andy Pecora. They stopped in the doorway as Tony looked around the room. With a flip of his arm over his shoulder, Andy closed the doors behind them. Tony walked across the room to the juke box, reached down behind it and unplugged it. The music stopped.

"You girls have to leave, please," Tony said.

Norman Rocque grinned and said, "Hey, we was just getting' the party goin'. Grab yourself a girl, Tony." Norman was the lover of the group. He was handsome, and the girls liked him as much as he liked the girls.

Tony repeated, "You girls have to leave, please."

Andy opened the door and stood aside. The girls walked outside, slowly, pouting and frowning as best as they could at Tony. When they were outside Andy shut the door and stood with his back to it. Andy had quickly become what he liked to think of as Tony's bodyguard.   He liked the work Tony gave him. Fighting was OK, but using his guns and knives gave him the greatest pleasure. Andy was at Tony's side everywhere Tony went, waiting for the next opportunity to kill someone.

Tony pulled a chair to the poker table; the others joined him there leaving Andy alone at the door. There was work to do that night. They all knew that. Tony broke the news to them when all were seated and waiting.

"There's a car that's going to have ten thousand dollars in it tonight. We're going to stop that car and take the money.   All of us this time.   And this is important. The guys with the cash might want to shoot to keep it."

No explanation was asked for because The Aces knew they wouldn't get one. Tony, they had come to understand, knew what he was doing. Any job they would do would have been well studied and planned out by Tony and Andy. No one bothered to ask how Tony knew about this car. It really didn't matter.

****

A black Buick pulled away from the lot behind Mario's Italian Restaurant in the outskirts of Philadelphia. In the trunk of the car was a black bag filled with cash. Inside the car, two of Chi Chi Torrel's men, Tommy Rosario and Stevie Conti, sat in the front seat, silently chain smoking Camel cigarettes from the single pack they shared. They stayed off the main highways. Neighborhoods were less likely to have State Police patrolling them, and in the late hours of the day, the cops were probably too busy drinking coffee somewhere, trying to stay awake.

So they took surface streets, neighborhoods, heading for Chi Chi's home on Staten Island. Chi Chi had bought what he thought was a palace. It wasn't a palace, but he had mortgaged the property for two times it's worth. He didn't care, because before the first payment was due, he had two of his men corner the bank manager. The mortgage was filed in the back of the bottom drawer of ten year old papers where no one would find it.

The money in the trunk was eventually going to go to Chi Chi's boss, Peter Salvano, in an attempt to ease the tension between the two. Chi Chi had been losing a lot of money in the past few months. Someone, and Chi Chi thought he knew who, was systematically hitting his businesses. Peter certainly wasn't like his father, the old Don, but he was Chi Chi's boss, and because of that he had to show Peter the respect due a Don.

Chi Chi had kept cash at his home, tens of thousands of dollars, but he had gone through most of that paying up to Peter, even though it was less than Peter expected. His wife was demanding money from him, and he had two girlfriends he had to pay for. He was rapidly going broke.

He had stolen heroin from a Harlem drug dealer and shipped it to Philadelphia and sold it for ten thousand dollars. It was enough to satisfy Peter, at least for a few weeks. In that time Chi Chi would be able to get evidence to prove Alberto Falzone was responsible for Chi Chi's problems.

The car and the money would arrive at his house at nine that evening. Chi Chi's wife, Monica, had tried to cook the food that her husband liked, manicotti and broccoli rabe, but as usual the manicotti was overcooked and the broccoli rabe was too salty. Monica had been a stripper in a cheap nightclub in The Bronx. Chi Chi found her there and quickly married her. She was blond and sexy, and she knew her way around a bed. But Chi Chi's lust for her soon turned to loathing.

Chi Chi tried to eat the food, but he couldn't. He settled for a bottle of rough Sicilian wine and some Sicilian Provola cheese, and waited for the money to arrive.

Nine o'clock passed . . . Ten o'clock passed . . . At ten to eleven Chi Chi started making phone calls. None of his men had seen Tommy or Stevie. They, the car, and all the money had simply disappeared off the face of the earth.

****

What Chi Chi didn't know was that while Tommy Rosario and Stevie Conti were maneuvering through the back road farmlands of Western New Jersey, they came upon an auto accident. One car was on its side, the other blocked the thin two lane road, keeping Tommy and Stevie from passing. There was a man lying face down in the road and another, sitting on the back bumper of the blocking car, who seemed to be wiping blood from his face.

Tommy, behind the wheel, stopped the Buick. "Get out and see if we can get by," he said to Stevie. Stevie walked slowly towards the wreck, and as he did, the barrel of a shotgun was placed against Tommy's head, through the open window. The man with the shotgun, Jay Schoemer, was dressed in a black sweatshirt and blue jeans. And he wore a Halloween mask, a smiling clown.

As Stevie reached the wrecks, the man on the ground rolled over. Norman Rocque also had a black sweatshirt and blue jeans on, and he, too, wore a similar Halloween mask. He pointed a shotgun up at Stevie. The man sitting on the bumper of the car dropped the cloth he had been wiping his mask covered face with. He was dressed as the other two. He walked past Stevie. He opened the passenger side door of the Buick, leaned in and said, "Keys." Jay nudged the shotgun against Tommy's shoulder and Tommy tossed the car keys to Tony Moretti.

Tony opened the trunk and took the black bag holding the money from it. Jay opened the door for Tommy and he was pulled out of the car. Two more of The Aces, both dressed as the others, roughly threw him to the ground. The two Aces who had Stevie pushed him to the ground. Andy Pecora, dressed as the others, walked from the shadows. He pulled a revolver from his belt, but Tony stopped him. "They have to live," he said.

"Why?"

Tony looked at Andy and held the stare for a moment, long enough for a chill to run up Andy's spine. Tony said in almost a whisper, "Because I said so."

They tied Tommy and Stevie, leaving them in the dirt of the unpaved road. They left the two cars they had stolen and drove away in the Buick Tommie and Stevie had driven, laughing wildly at their good luck. All but Richie Pelto who sat quietly in the corner of the back seat. He was staring out the window, not seeing the passing farm land. When the others had laughed and joked all they could, Richie asked, "Whose money is it, Tony?"

Tony sat in the front, Andy was driving, and Norman Rocque sat between them. Tony turned and looked at Richie. He said, "It's our money, Richie. You know that. We split everything equally."

"That's not what I meant," Richie said. "I mean,

whose money was it? Who did we take it from?"

Tony turned back to look out the front window. He took a minute and then said, "You don't need to know. Trust me. You don't want to know."

The next morning Tommie and Stevie showed up at Chi Chi's front door. They had walked and hitch hiked all the way. They were scared, but they didn't know what else to do. They couldn't run; they couldn't hide. If Chi Chi thought they had stolen the money, he wouldn't rest until they were dead.

When they explained that it was the gang in Halloween masks again, Chi Chi slammed his fist into the wall of his living room. He broke two knuckles, but he also left a hole in the wall.

Who could have known? He had tried to keep the secret among just a few people. He thought, 'That damn Falzone had to find out somehow.'

Al did find out because Chi Chi had talked in a bar about making a lot of money in a drug deal with Philly. The bar was a place Chi Chi liked to go to because it was a business place for hookers. The owner of the bar owed Al Falzone a lot of money. When Chi Chi had bragged to a hooker about how he would get all that money safely out of Philly, the hooker told the owner, who in turn told Al. Al told Tony, and Chi Chi lost $10,000.

TWELVE

Brooklyn, New York
July 1959

Bruno Massetti's position of trust in the Salvano Family had grown to the point at which he felt comfortable sitting in a chair very close to the old Don's desk, at its side, facing the Capos when they met. The big desk still separated Bruno from Peter, but at least he could sit. Standing was demeaning after all the years as the old Don's trusted body guard. He did not yet feel comfortable enough to smoke even as Peter chained smoked. That would come soon enough.

Bruno had not changed anything in the den. The old furniture, dark woods and heavy brocades bought by Natalia thirty years ago, were still there, unmoved. The old Don had a ficus tree in a big Oriental vase sitting in a corner. Peter didn't know, but the plant had died some months before. Bruno had spent several days driving from landscaper to landscaper trying to find one that would pass for the dead plant. He found one, and so far Peter did not question it.

Bruno was doing a good job taking care of the neighborhood where Peter's mother lived in the house Peter had grown up in, the house where Peter met with his Capos. The neighborhood was safe; no crime dare be committed. Bruno was police, judge and jury for any indiscretion that might be committed in the neighborhood, and no one wanted to be the subject of Bruno's justice.

Peter's mother, Natalia, was aging quickly. Her hair, once only flecked with grey against its deep black, was now completely white. Her skin was free of color, and the weight she had lost exposed itself in the lifeless skin that sagged on her face and arms. Bruno was reporting his concerns for Mrs. Salvano; he was truly worried, perhaps more for his own fate should she die. What would become of him then?

"Yes," Peter said as he lit his third cigarette. "I've noticed. Ever since my father's death she seems to have lost the light that used to be inside her. Maybe we should bring in a nurse. What do you think?"

Bruno nodded and said, "The neighborhood ladies, they bring food for Mrs. Salvano. The young ones, they've been cleaning the house and washing the clothes. Some boys have been taking care of the yard. But I think maybe your mother, she needs more than that. She sits all day with her bible and rosary. She hardly ever speaks. I think maybe a nurse to care for her would be a good idea."

"OK, Bruno. Make the arrangements. Find someone good. Don't worry about the cost. And see to it that Doctor Mathews comes in to see her once a week."

"OK, boss," Bruno said. He wished he could light a cigarette but he dared not. Not yet anyway.

"Tell me about Chi Chi," Peter moved on to what might be a more important subject.

"I don't know boss. Somethin's not right there. He says he's bein' hit over and over again. But I was thinkin', if he's bein' hit, why ain't he doin' somethin'? He's losin' a lot of money yet he ain't increasin' his security. If it was me, I'd put a bunch of guys with guns inside his books and outside, too. But he ain't doin' nothin'."

"And why do you think he's not doing anything to stop what is happening?" Peter asked. He was blowing the cigarette smoke up, towards the ceiling, but enough of it filled the room to make Bruno's hands shake. What would happen if he just lit one, he thought?

"Boss, Chi Chi and me, we been around a long time. We was young kids when we started working for your father. We was just fifteen years old." Bruno paused and he lowered his eyes. The frown creasing his forehead and the sadness in his eyes told Peter what he wanted to know. If Bruno defended Chi Chi, then Bruno was placing his friendship above his loyalty to his Don. If he told Peter his honest thoughts, then Peter would know Bruno's loyalty to Peter was firm.

Bruno looked up and said, his voice exposing his sadness, "Chi Chi's got a life outside the family and outside his own family . . . His wife and kids, I mean. He's got a couple whores on the side; pays their rent and buys their clothes. He spends big bucks at nightclubs up in New York. He buys a lot of clothes and gold stuff. None of us know how the hell he can afford it."

"How *does* he afford it?" Peter asked. "How do you think he affords it all? What do the others think?"

Bruno hesitated, Peter saw it. Peter knew it must be hard for Bruno to tell secrets about a man whom he had been close to much longer than he had been close to Peter. But Bruno, although reluctantly, was loyal to the Salvano Family, loyal above everything else. He had taken an oath of loyalty when he was initiated as a 'Made Man'. That loyalty would be taken to the grave by Bruno.

"It looks like Chi Chi maybe has become too close to some of our New York friends," Bruno said. His voice revealed the tears that Bruno was holding back. "He's been spending a lot of time up at high class nightclubs, like I said. Some of the other Families go there all the time."

"So you think he's paying up to some other Family and covering it up by claiming these thefts?"

"It seems likely," Bruno said. "And maybe he's losing less to the guys who are stickin' up his books. Maybe he's spending money on his whores in New York and covering it up claiming the stick ups get more money than they do."

"OK, send the Capos in," Peter ordered.

"Chi Chi ain't here," Bruno said.

Peter nodded and repeated, "Send the Capos in."

Bruno left the room and returned with Michael Funno, Manny Esposito, and Al Falzone. They gathered around the big desk that separated them from their boss and stood nervously. Bruno had been in the den with Don Peter for a long time. Something was up; some trouble was obviously in the air.

Peter looked from man to man; enjoying the pregnant silence and enjoying seeing them feel some discomfort. He was at first reluctant to follow his father as Don, but in time he had come to like the power, not to mention all the money.

Power was becoming very important to Peter. He felt good when these men of respect stood in front of him, afraid to sit without being told to do so. He was beginning to understand why his father put so much effort into being a Don. But he knew that he had to ease their minds, that each had to know the respect he demanded of them was returned by Peter to them. So he took an unusual tack by saying, "Please, everyone sit down."

That was the first time any of them had ever sat in the presence of their Don. Peter's father, Don Pietro, would have never allowed it. Old world respect laced with fear was very important to the old Don. Peter had different ideas. He wanted loyalty, but he also wanted respect based not on fear but on his leadership. That is how he ran his legal business in that other world he lived in, that is how he wanted to run his father's business.

There were a leather couch and a leather armchair in the room, besides the two chairs in front of the Don's desk. The four men looked around and, obviously ill at ease, sat, leaving the two chairs in front of the desk vacant.

Peter lit yet another cigarette and said, "I'm moving Bruno up." The shock of the words hit Bruno hard. He wasn't expecting that, but he was happy, proud, and he knew that his honesty with his boss had paid off. Peter went on, "Bruno will now be what you call an Underboss. From now on my orders will come to you through Bruno. You will pay up to him as usual. Your problems will come to Bruno. And you will obey all his orders and commands. Is that acceptable with each of you?"

Each of the three men agreed quickly. The four stood, and Manny and Michael and Al each embraced Bruno in the old world style. They sat again, all smiling regardless of their personal feelings. Why Bruno? Why not one of the others?

Peter said, "I will not be coming here as often as I have. From now on I will visit my mother but not when you are here. I am changing my phone numbers, and only Bruno will know what the new numbers are. I'm not going to use your son Theo, Michael. He'll keep his job, but he won't be a middle man to send messages back and forth. If there is any contact between us, it will be for emergencies only. You will never mention my name to anyone. I am still your Don. Don't ever forget that. Do I have your agreement on this?"

Each man agreed quickly, but each knew there was trouble coming. The old Don would never have gone into hiding, into the shadows. The old Don would have fought against incursions by the police or by some other family. If the new, young Don was going to go into hiding, it was to protect himself, leaving each of them to take whatever hit was coming.

Peter stood, slowly and dramatically, and went to a small table in the corner of the room. The table held three crystal decanters and several glasses that had been untouched since his father's death. He took one decanter and opened it. He filled five glasses with grappa as the four men stood. He handed each man a glass and together they drank the strong liquor down in a salute to the Salvano Family.

Peter returned to his chair behind the big desk, and each man pulled thick envelopes of cash from their jackets. As they began to lay the envelopes on the desk Peter waived them away and pointed to Bruno. Bruno took the envelopes dramatically and laid them on the desk.

With a silent nod from his boss, Bruno said to the Capos, with no end of pride in his voice, "Thank you, and you may leave now." The men walked out of the den in a stiff procession. Bruno closed the door leaving Peter and him alone once again.

"Thank you, Don Peter," Bruno said in his gravelly voice now tinged with emotion. "It's a great honor, and I will do everything to carry out your wishes. Tell me what to do, and it will be done."

Peter opened a drawer of the desk and took from it a small brown book. He handed it to Bruno and said, "This contains all the police and politicians on our payroll. Continue the payments to them. I will give you instructions on how to handle the money. Keep it here until I tell you what to do with it."

"Yes, Don Peter."

"One other thing," Peter began. "I want Chi Chi taken out. Put Al Falzone on it. And Al will take over his crew and businesses. There will be no disputes over this, understand?"

"Yes, Don Peter."

THIRTEEN

The Bronx, New York
July 1959

Andy Pecora sat next to Tony Moretti in the front seat of the 1954 Chevy Bel-Air they had stolen. It had New York plates on it, and it was a dull tan in color, nothing that would stand out as noticeable or unusual. Tony was behind the steering wheel. It felt strange to him as Andy always did the driving. It was ten minutes to four in the morning and not as hot as it had been earlier in the day. They had the windows rolled down, but there was no air moving through the thick night. Both Tony and Andy wore black sweatshirts and blue jeans. They were warm, but they had to wear these so they couldn't be identified. Halloween masks, smiling clowns, lay on the seat next to them.

The car was parked at the curb across the street and a block away from the three story brownstone where Chi Chi Torrel was visiting one of his whores. He had rented the top floor apartment for Margie Winston. Margie was a prostitute until she met Chi Chi. He took her off the street and out of the bars, and gave her a lifestyle she had not known before. She was given clothes, a car, food, jewelry, and all the cash she could spend. Her life was so much different than the years before Chi Chi had picked her up for an hour of sex.

Margie was a runaway from an isolated Iowa farm. She started working the streets as a teenager when she couldn't find a job in New York City. She soon had Mickey Adams, a Harlem drug dealer, as a pimp. She had to turn over all her earnings to Mickey, who gave her a rat hole of a single room in Harlem to live in. Food was in short supply, and clothes were just enough to keep her from working naked. Chi Chi picked her up one night, and the next day Mickey Adams was found dead in an alley behind the bar he kept as his office. Margie was moved into the Bronx apartment.

Tony reached under the seat and pulled a Smith & Wesson Model 15. It was a .38 caliber revolver with a four inch barrel. It was the kind of pistol many police departments issued at that time. He had wrapped the pistol in a red bandana, and as Andy watched, he carefully unwrapped it. Andy smiled, pleased at what he saw. He reached for it but Tony pulled it away. "The gloves, Andy," he said. Andy pulled his thin leather gloves on and then took the pistol, weighing it satisfactorily in his hands.

"Nice piece," he said, fondling it like it was a woman in his hands.

"Remember," Tony said. "Two shots in the head, and drop the gun."

"Hey, this here's a nice piece," Andy said. "Why can't I keep it?"

"Do you really want the cops to find you with the gun that killed Chi Chi Torrel? How about one or two of his crew learning you killed him? Andy, that gun was reported stolen by a New Jersey State cop. He happens to be a dirty cop. He's been on the take for years. They'll come down on him and not us. Now, drop the gun, OK?"

At twenty minutes past four that morning, Chi Chi stepped out on the sidewalk in front of the Brownstone. He looked left, right, and then left again. He turned right and started for his car. There was just enough time to drive to Queens and screw Dorothy once or twice before going home for breakfast.

Dorothy was a waitress in a coffee shop who liked the money Chi Chi gave her. She despised Chi Chi. She didn't enjoy their time in bed. He was too rough, and he smelled of cheap cologne. But she liked the money.

Andy was out of the Chevy pulling the Halloween mask on as he walked. He crossed the street quickly and quietly. On the other side of the street he kept to the shadows. He walked quickly to Chi Chi from behind. When Andy was a few feet behind Chi Chi, Tony started the car and drove quickly to get to Andy as two shots rang out like thunder in the still night air. Andy dropped the pistol and jumped into the car as the two sped away.

There were no witnesses; people were asleep, and the few who awoke at the sound thought it was thunder and rolled over and went back to sleep. A milkman found Chi Chi as the sun was rising. His murder quickly became a closed file because the police assumed it was just another Mafia murder. The detective who had been in charge wrote by hand in the file before it was closed, "Just another Wop thug,"

****

Tony found a bench in Newark's Branch Brook Park under a tree. The shade felt good in the heat of the afternoon. It was a few days from August, and the heat of the summer was destined to continue. He wore a brand new white T-shirt that hung loose outside his blue jeans. It wasn't the heat that kept the T-shirt hanging loose; it was the Colt 1911 .45 caliber pistol that he had tucked under his belt at the small of his back. He didn't know why Al wanted to talk to him, but he wasn't going to take any chances.

He might be getting a lot of money from Al for very little work, but he didn't trust Al, 'Not as far as I can spit into the wind,' he liked to tell Andy. Al had never asked for any of the money The Aces stole from Chi Chi Torrel, and Tony never offered to give him any. That was the deal they had made, but how long could that continue? Tony had the lingering idea that one day Al would ask for everything they had stolen.

In spite of the afternoon heat, some birds jumped from branch to branch overhead. They sang and chirped; Tony liked that. A squirrel ran down the trunk of the tree and scampered across the dirt in front of Tony. It stopped, sat up on its back legs, and looked at Tony. Tony smiled, and the squirrel ran away. 'That's cute,' he thought.

Al Falzone came from behind Tony and sat beside him quickly, making Tony flinch. "Don't be scared, kid," Al said. "It's only me." Al was dressed in light grey slacks and a loud Hawaiian shirt left to hang outside his pants.

Tony said nothing. Al had wanted to meet Tony in a warehouse down in Trenton. Tony didn't like that. Trenton may be part of Al's new territory now that he had taken over from Chi Chi, but it wasn't Tony's turf. He and The Aces had grown rich doing jobs for Al. But that didn't mean Tony trusted Al Falzone. He knew who Al was and the kind of business Al did. Tony had a fear that now that Al had Chi Chi's territory and money, maybe he didn't need Tony anymore. Maybe he needed to get rid of Tony. Maybe Tony knew too much. Did he think Tony might talk? Maybe, he thought, he had grown from an asset into a liability.

"You look nervous, kid," Al said.   "Something wrong?"

"No. Of course not. It's just damn hot."

"So why are you carrying that gun under your shirt?" Al asked, his voice a mere whispered threat.

Tony looked across the brown, dry grass. Andy Pecora was where he was supposed to be, not too far away, with his hand on the butt of his gun. Tony stood and looked around, taking a full turn. There were a couple of women in skirts and thin, sleeveless blouses, each pushing a baby carriage; four kids were tossing a baseball between them; an old man was walking an old dog, both moving as slow as their age demanded. Tony knew what all of Al's crew looked like, and he didn't see any of them. He sat and looked sideways at Al. "Why did you want me in Trenton?"

"Hey, Tony!" Al said. "You think I'm going to kill you? Why would you think something like that? After all you've done for me? I'm insulted. If I wanted you dead, do you think I'd be here right now sitting next to you and talking to you?"

That seemed like sense, Tony thought. It was something he would have done had the positions been reversed. He asked, "So why Trenton?"

"Because that's part of my territory now. I'm trying to get it all working right and straightened out."

"And what does that have to do with me?" Tony asked.

"Look, kid. I've been good to you, haven't I? Haven't you made a lot of money? All I want to do is move you up."

"Move me up?" Tony asked.   "What's that mean?"

"I want you in my crew . . . Up here . . . While I straighten things out down south."

"You've got your own crew," Tony said. "Why do you need me? I'm a fifteen year old kid. Why me?"

Al shifted on the bench, turning to face Tony. This wasn't going as he had planned. He had wanted Tony to be happy and proud to become one of his soldiers quickly, to jump at the chance. But Tony was suspicious. That suspicion told Al that Tony was maybe smarter than Al had thought.

He had given Tony a free hand to plan all the thefts from Chi Chi and even the murder of Chi Chi. Tony had done everything perfectly; no evidence left behind and no shadow of suspicion fell on anyone. Tony was smart, and if Al could handle him correctly, that could work to Al's advantage. His intelligence could put more money in Al's pocket.

"Tony," Al began. "I was your age when I started. I was raised not too far from where your folks live. I was part of a crew. I did heists and tough collections when I was fifteen. I did other stuff that I don't talk about. I moved up. I'm in charge of a crew now. I'm giving you the same chance."

"And if I say no?"

"Then you go back to Passaic and The Aces. You go back to your ten bucks a week extortion. And you'll never hear from me again. You've got a choice, Tony. Move up . . . Or move down."

"What would I be doing?" Tony asked.

"I'm taking Benny Rizo and Frankie De Luca with me," Al said. Al had five men in his crew. Along with Benny and Frankie there were Ted Bianci, Mike Colombo, and Louie Lombardi. Tony didn't know them personally, but he knew about them. Al was taking his two best soldiers with him. "I need you to make their collections, to provide security at the books and poker games. You'll have fifty thousand dollars to loan out. You'll get my cut from the crew and get it to me. You'll keep twenty percent of the vig you collect and five percent of what the crew takes in and send to me. Is that enough?"

"And The Aces?" Tony asked.

"No changes there. They'll still get their thousand a month, and you can use them however you want. But they'll stay a street gang. Only you will move up." Al waited for Tony to say something, but before he could, Al looked across the grass at Andy Pecora, standing ready under a tree. "And keep a chain on your friend over there. He's useful, but he needs to be controlled."

"I'm not sure I like that," Tony said. "If the other gangs learn I'm not there all the time, they'll try to take over The Aces turf."

"Tony, think about it for a minute. Do you think the gangs . . . the Los Reyes, all the others, and even the Mau Maus up in New York . . . Why they haven't tried to move into Passaic? Do you think there's been some peace all this time just because your pretty face has been hanging out there?"

"What are you saying?"

"I take care of the people who work for me," Al said. "None of the other gangs are going to try to push The Aces aside as long as you work for me. What I'm asking you to join is a bigger gang than The Aces or any of the other street gangs. I have a family behind me. I have power. I have money. You can be a part of that. If you say no . . . Well, then I can't protect The Aces anymore. That's the deal. Do you want in or not?"

Tony acted like he was thinking about the offer. He frowned and rubbed his chin. In fact he had already made up his mind. He had made a lot of money with The Aces and doing dirty work for Al, but he knew everything he had earned was small change compared to what he could make as part of a crew. And from that crew, he knew he could move up. That's where the money was. His plan for his own future was rooted in being in a crew. He would do what the crew does . . . For awhile. Then he would move on with his own plans.

Tony held out his hand, Al took it, and they shook hands, binding the two to their agreement. Andy saw this and thought that something big just happened, but what? His hand had drifted to the gun held tightly at his waist without Andy realizing it. He would have to wait to find out what was happening. He never gave a thought to the possibility that Tony would drop him. Wherever Tony was going, Andy was going, also. He knew that. Tony would have more work for him, and that was a good thing.

FOURTEEN

Passaic, New Jersey
June 1960

The Aces sat quietly in their storefront clubhouse. The jukebox wasn't playing; the girls weren't there; one of the three light bulbs hanging from the ceiling was burnt out. Only Andy and Tony weren't there, but that had become normal. The two seldom came to the old storefront anymore. Oh, the one thousand dollars arrived every month, and the shopkeepers in the neighborhood still paid their ten dollars a week. But there wasn't any work, nothing for them to do. Joey Castellani wanted to go out and "bust into a couple places and steal stuff." But that was Joey, a hot gun ready to go off.

Richie Pelto was reading one of his books. Richie was always reading something. He alone of all The Aces had not dropped out of school. In fact, he had graduated High School that month. The Aces all attended the graduation, and they all had a good time making jokes about the gown and mortar board hat Richie wore. But he was proud and took the joking well. He never talked down to his friends; he never mocked their lack of education. They were, in his opinion, a product of their environment. They were doing the best they could, considering where they came from.

Richie's parents were different from the parents of the other Aces. His father held a steady job, although it was a low paying job. He was not a heavy drinker, and he had never struck Richie in anger. His mother did the best she could, keeping their apartment clean and cooking good meals for Richie and his sister.

They didn't like the idea of Richie being a member of The Aces, but they also knew that he had been beaten up enough as a child. How many times had his brown bag lunch of a bologna sandwich and an apple been taken away by bullies? How many times had he come home from school with a black eye or split lip? They had come to accept the fact that The Aces was the only thing that could keep their son safe until they could save enough money to move from Passaic.

They were proud that he stayed in school and did so well there. They spent many evenings talking with Richie, offering advice but never demanding anything from him. They helped with his homework and encouraged his reading, never criticizing what he read. They were good parents, and Richie thanked them for it. They gave Richie a vision of what a good life could be.

Richie had seemed restless the last two weeks. He had something on his mind, something serious. The others saw it but they said nothing. He was different then they were. He was thoughtful, reasoning, and calm when the others weren't. He was quiet when they were loud. But they thought of Richie as a brother, a person to be trusted. If he was worried about something, if he had a problem, it was their worry, it was their problem.

That was the day that Tony would bring the envelope with their one thousand dollars in it. And where the hell was that coming from? They all had their own ideas, but they all agreed it was not legal money. To them, there was no legal way to get that much money on a regular basis. That didn't make any difference to them. It was cash, and they all made good use of the cash.

Suddenly the front door opened and startled the five teens. Andy Pecora held the glass door open for Tony, standing aside so Tony could walk in. The Aces hardly recognized either of them. They weren't wearing their club jackets and blue jeans; they were dressed in dark suits. Tony was wearing a starched white shirt and a blue tie under a muted dark blue pin stripe suit. And he had found a barber. "Cut it like Sinatra," he told the barber. Gone was the long, greased back hair that had been so familiar.

Andy wore a charcoal grey suit and tan silk shirt open at the collar. Their shoes were shined to a brilliance. Andy wore a big diamond pinkie ring on his right hand. Andy's hair, like Tony's, was no longer greased back, long and unkempt. It was cut short and neatly combed back, like any adult businessman any of them had seen.

Tony had been going to the gym and working out with weights on a regular basis. He was bulking up, building up good muscle. The suit he wore had been altered to fit his slim waist and broad shoulders.

None of The Aces had ever seen anyone dressed as well, not in their neighborhood anyway. Their world was the six square blocks of Passaic they controlled. None had ever set foot more than a few blocks outside their turf. Suits in that part of New Jersey were limited to cheap, second hand, ill fitting suits, if any suits could be seen at all. These two men, because they looked like men and not teenagers, looked like they came from some other world unknown to The Aces.

Tony was happy to see his friends; he smiled and greeted them, "Hey, guys! How're you doin'?"

No one answered; no one knew what to say. Tony felt the icy chill from The Aces. 'Oh well,' he thought. Times change, and he had work to do. He needed to get done what needed to be done and get back to Newark where he could make more money, the money he needed to bring his dreams to reality. Tony pulled the envelope of cash from his jacket and dropped it dramatically on the poker table. It fell open and the cash spilled out. No one touched it.

Tony pulled a chair from the table and sat. Andy stood behind him, grinning but looking ominous. Andy had put on a lot of weight, not all muscle. Once he was tall, not skinny but not fat either. In the last several months he had put on weight from his seemingly never satisfied appetite for food of any kind. And there was an all too obvious bulge in his suit under his left shoulder. Andy had acquired a shoulder holster for his big .45.

Eddy Di Bona was the first to speak as he stuttered, "H . . . H . . . Hey, Tony. You . . . You . . . You lookin' g . . . g . . . g . . . good."

Andy started to say something, to make fun of Eddy's stutter, but with a very slight movement of Tony's hand, raised just inches off the table, Andy stopped and said nothing. The Aces took notice of this and would remember it. Tony had grown up quickly. He was no longer just a kid who could set up robberies that brought money into the club. He was now a man with some power. They were still unsure of where that power came from, but that power was guaranteed by Andy Pecora's gun.

"Thanks, Eddy," Tony said. "I kind'a like wearing

suits, ya'know?" Tony spoke at the level of the people he was speaking to once again. He had dropped out of school after the eighth grade but he had a natural instinct for psychology. He knew that he had to be careful not to 'talk down' to people and never to talk below people either. Doing either would make the person he was talking to feel ill at ease. When he talked with The Aces, he spoke at their level; when he spoke with Al Falzone, he spoke at his level.

Richie Pelto was the exception. Richie was smart, Richie was educated, at least he was better educated than the other Aces. When Tony spoke privately with Richie, he needed to come across as smarter than Richie; he needed to be at a level higher than Richie Pelto to make Richie respect and fear him.

They spent a few minutes talking of meaningless things, baseball and the new records on the jukebox. It didn't take long for the subjects to drift off to nothing. Everything that could be talked about was spoken. Too many things could not be talked about. The silence told Tony it was time to go. He had moved on. He may be able to tell The Aces what to do, he may be able to give them money, but he was no longer one of The Aces. As Tony pushed his chair away from the table, Richie asked, "Tony, can I speak with you for a minute?"

"Sure. What's up?"

"It's personal, Tony. Can we go outside for a minute?"

Joey, Norman, Jay, and Eddy looked at Richie. So there *was* something bothering Richie. They all knew it was something serious; something was bothering him that he could not talk to them about. There never were any secrets among them before. They didn't like what they heard when Richie asked to speak with Tony in private. Things were changing, and changing too quickly for The Aces.

Tony stood, and Richie followed him outside. At the door Tony whispered something to Andy. Andy closed the front door with him still inside. He turned his back to the door, crossed his arms across his chest, and smiled across the room at The Aces. "So how all you guys doin'?" he asked.

Outside, Richie paced nervously on the sidewalk. It was hot outside; he took his Aces jacket off but didn't stop pacing back and forth, shifting from one foot to another.

"OK, Richie," Tony said. "Tell me what the problem is."

Richie stopped his pacing. He turned to face Tony and looked down at the sidewalk, at the old black and white high top sneakers he was wearing and the polished wingtips Tony had on. He said, "I want out, Tony."

"You want out of what, Richie? I don't understand." Tony felt he knew what Richie was getting at. Richie was nervous, scared. It was serious, and the only thing that could be that serious would be a desire to leave The Aces.

"I want out of The Aces," he said nervously, his voice shaking, confirming what Tony guessed.

"You want out of The Aces," Tony said. It was not a question but there seemed to be a threat behind the words. "Why?"

Richie looked up and into Tony's eyes. Richie was two years older than Tony yet there was a sense that Richie was talking to a mature man with some authority and power over Richie's life.

He had taken the first step and there was no retreat now. He had to go on; he had to explain. He couldn't just go back to The Aces because he had lost the trust and brotherhood of the gang's leader. Nothing would ever be the same after confessing that he wanted to leave The Aces.

"I want to go to college, Tony. I want to go out to California and go to college. I got an acceptance letter from UCLA. I have to go, Tony. It's something I've wanted my whole life. I just have to go."

"That's an excellent aspiration, Richie," Tony said, speaking in a tone he imagined a caring father or counselor or priest might sound like. "I admire you for wanting to take on that kind of hard work. I can only imagine what people in college must go through. Oh, I imagine there's some fun, too. But the study must be very difficult. And the cost. I've heard how expensive a good college can be. How will you do that? Your parents aren't going to be able to help you."

"You've brought in a lot of money, Tony. I've saved most of it . . . You know me. I'm not big on parties and girls."

"Yes," Tony said as he looked deeply into Richie's blue eyes. "Are you homosexual?" He had always wondered why Richie wasn't as free spending as the other Aces. He had never seen Richie throw away money on girls and good times like the other Aces did.

Richie tried to laugh that off. "Of course not," he said. "You know I've had my share of girls. Hell, I'm going steady with Mary Ann right now. I just had this plan to go to college for a couple of years. I've been putting money aside."

So Richie had a plan. Tony knew what was inside of Richie; he had a plan, too. His plan might be different than Richie's but Tony knew what it felt like, inside, to want something better. "That's good, Richie. Smart."

"I've got enough money to last the first year.

After that, I'll get a job or something." He paused and grinned mischievously. "I can always steal some stuff. I learned how to do that really well."

"You know, Richie, there are big things ahead for The Aces."

Richie swallowed hard and took a chance at telling the truth. He said, "I don't want those big things, Tony. When I was a kid I liked to fight, I liked the excitement, I liked it when people stepped aside for us when we walked down the street. I liked it when I wasn't beaten up and stuff stolen from me. But . . . I think maybe I'm growing up. I don't want those things anymore."

"You know if you leave, the money will stop. Can you handle that?"

"I know it'll be tough. Like I said, I've got enough cash for a while. I'll get a job somewhere. I guess I'll do any kind of work . . . Washing dishes maybe, I really don't care. But I feel like I have to go get this college thing. It's something I have to do. It's burning inside of me, Tony. Please let me do it."

Tony thought about this. He could, of course, tell Richie 'No,' but then he could not trust Richie anymore. There would come a time when Richie would defect to someone, someone who was at war with Tony and the Salvano Family. He could have Andy kill Richie; Andy didn't mind who he killed; he just liked killing. But Richie was a friend; he respected Richie. They had been together a long time and had come a long way. Tony could accept neither of those options. Maybe there would come a time to take Richie out, but not then.

Tony took Richie's jacket from him. It was all the ceremony there would be. Richie understood this. He was out of The Aces. He smiled and let out a deep breath. Tony said, "You better leave quickly. Just pack and get out of town. When people find out you're not in The Aces any longer, they'll come after you. There are a lot of guys out there who would love to kick your ass all over town. The guys won't want to protect you."

"Thank you, Tony. I owe you one. I won't forget. You'll see. I'll be in your debt forever. I'll go tell the fellas . . ."

"No," Tony interrupted him, grabbing him by his arm to stop him. "I'll tell them. They might not understand."

Tony held out his hand and they shook hands, one friend to another. Richie turned and walked away. His steps started out slow, hesitatingly slow, then quickened, and finally he was running. Tony watched him until he disappeared around a corner. He thought, 'I hope he makes it.'

Tony returned to The Ace's. The four of them were still seated but wondering what the hell was going on. He had Richie's jacket in hand. He laid it across the table, and they all looked at it, not knowing what to make of it. Tony sat again, Andy stood behind him again, and Tony said, "Richie has quit. He's leaving town."

Jay Schoemer pounded his fist on the poker table and jumped up, knocking the chair across the room. "What d'fuck! What'ya mean, he quit? You can't quit the damn Aces!"

Tony didn't flinch as the others did. Andy reached inside his jacket but Tony stopped him again with a raised hand. Jay was standing and not very happy. Jay was big, strong, muscular, and he loved to fight. None of The Aces had ever seen anyone as strong as Jay. But Tony didn't move. He slowly crossed his legs and folded his hands on his lap. "Sit down, Jay," he whispered menacingly. When Jay didn't sit he repeated, "I said sit down, Jay," only this time there was command in his voice.

Jay hesitated; he stood straight and looked from Tony to Andy Pecora. Andy grinned at him. Things had changed; times had changed. Tony was more than a kid who could plan robberies. He was a boss, a dangerous man now. Fighting would do no good. And besides, Andy Pecora looked like he was willing to kill Jay to protect Tony. Jay pulled the chair he had knocked over off the floor, and he sat.

Tony cleared his throat and said slowly, "I told Richie he could leave. Does anyone want to discuss that decision with me?"

He looked from young man to young man. Norman wouldn't give him any trouble. He cared about his girls, his women. Little else mattered to Norman. Eddy would do what he was told. He was a good man to have around when a fight broke out, but he was limited by his fears. Jay could be controlled. He was strong but he was slow witted and needed someone to tell him what to do. Joey Castellani could be a problem. Joey had that famous short temper of his. He would be hard to control and there would come a time . . . Soon Tony thought . . . To have Andy take care of Joey.

When no one challenged Tony he said, "That's the way it is. He knows what he's done. He knows we won't be there for him or help him in any way. He's on his own, and he's willing to take the consequences. He can handle the ramifications."

Eddy asked, "W ... W ...W ...What's ramficasuns?"

The others laughed, Tony didn't. He said, "Don't worry Eddy. Everything's going to be alright."

Jay, calmer now, asked, "There's only four of us now. What we gonna do when someone comes after us?"

"Only four?" Tony asked. "What about Andy and me? I count six."

Norman said, "Are you still with us, Tony? Where's your Ace's jacket? It wouldn't look too good over that Brooks Brothers suit of yours."

Tony sat forward and leaned his elbows on the table. He said, "I'm still with you; I always will be. As for someone coming after you and your turf . . . That won't happen. I guarantee it. Trust me. It's all taken care of."

The four heard the words: 'you and your turf', not 'us and our turf.' The words did not go unnoticed and were never to be forgotten.

****

Tony and Andy were driving back to Newark. Tony had bought a brand new Cadillac, white in color 'so everybody will know it's me coming,' with a red leather interior. He had walked into the dealership, Andy two steps behind him, and laid a thick stack of hundred dollar bills on the salesman's desk. "I want the white one that's out in front," he said. "How much?"

The salesman was surprised and didn't know what to say. Was this guy a kid in man's clothing or a very young looking man? He asked to see Tony's driver's license, and of course he didn't have one. He said, pointing over his shoulder, "My friend will put the car in his name."

Andy was nineteen at the time and old enough to have a driver's license and have a car registered in his name. So Tony went over all the paper work, agreed on a price, paid in cash, and Andy signed on the dotted line.

Andy was driving as he always did; Tony sat in the front passenger seat as he always did. Andy liked the new car, lots of class. He knew it wasn't his car, but that made little difference to him. It made him feel important to sit behind the wheel. He sold his old 49 Ford and liked to be seen in the brand new Cadillac.

Feeling important was very important to Andy. He had a small opinion of himself, but he never let anyone know that. He considered himself dumber than others, not quick of wit, not good at understanding jokes and conversation. He was slow at just about everything except his willingness to hurt other people. He envied those who were smarter than he was, but he didn't envy them when he killed them. He liked that; it gave him a good feeling that he somehow was better than they were, that he was good enough to kill anyone who was smarter than he was.

Tony was slumped down in the seat. He was tired. He had too much responsibility. Letting Richie Pelto go was a big step. It was a hurdle he had to take, to let someone out of The Aces where membership meant a lifetime, and not have the others rebel. He was successful, he had won that one. How many more could he win?

Not that he disliked being a leader. It had been easy enough to take over The Aces. They couldn't see the future as he could. They were limited in what they could envision for the future. He had known that with the right moves The Aces could bring in the money he needed and be the start of a career. The Aces, with him at their head, would attract the attention he wanted, and in fact that is just what happened, as he had planned.

He had wanted to be in that group of men he had

seen making their collections and driving their
Cadillac's. He wanted to be one of those men known
as 'Men of Respect.' He had wanted to be able to
stand on the corner and have people walk around him.
And it had, so far, worked out for him. He was now a
part of Alberto Falzone's crew and the respect . . . And
money . . . He desired came to him. But that was only
the first 'easy' step in his plan. The future would be
harder and more dangerous.

He had to admit to himself that the easy days of
hanging out with The Aces, fighting other gangs with
The Aces, being a kid with The Aces, were days he did
miss. Life was easy 'back then' he thought and
laughed at the thought. It was only two years ago
after all.

That life he had chosen was, to him, his only
option. It was move forward with his plan or work for
peanuts the rest of his life, never be anything, live in a
second floor walk-up slum, and die a poor man.

Life had progressed, and now his plan was to
slowly take over Al's Newark crew. No one knew that
plan, not even Andy. Step by step he was climbing
over Mike Colombo and Louie Lombardo. That was
easy to do. Neither were very smart and neither were
leaders in the making.

Ted Bianci, on the other hand, was quick and
smart. He had stayed in school and even had two
years of City College behind him. He had a family he
was faithful to and had aspirations of moving up in the
Mafia. But Ted also saw what Tony had to offer, a
mind that could plan ahead and weigh options. That
ability, Ted thought, he could use, and Tony let him do
it. One day, Tony knew, he would step over Ted
Bianci, also.

"Hey Andy," he said. "Remember those egg
creams at Pops Candy Store?" Pops Candy Store was

a Passaic drive-in restaurant that served hamburgers, French fries and milk shakes to the local teens and sometimes their parents, if their parents dared embarrass their children by entering Pops.

"Yeah, they was real good. But did you know egg creams ain't got no eggs in them? I heard that somewhere."

Tony knew that, of course. But he also knew that Andy needed reassurance. He never corrected Andy except when business was at hand. He said, "Yeah? Is that right?" It made Andy feel good to be able to know something he believed Tony didn't know. "How about we go there now and get us a couple of them egg creams?" Tony suggested.

"Yeah, that's great," Andy said and suddenly spun the car around in a u-turn in the middle of the street's traffic. Tires squealed and horns blared, but Andy didn't care, and Tony let him have some fun. When the car was headed in the right direction, Andy asked, "You think we maybe aren't dressed like we should for Pop's?" Their suits would be something not generally seen there. They would stand out, but Tony had a feeling that would be a good thing. Respect was important. People needed to know who they were.

"No," Tony said. "We're OK." He explained, "It's important for people to not see us as a couple of kids."

Pop's was across the Passaic City line from Clifton. It was crowded most days and every weekend night with High School kids. And recent grads from both Passaic High School and Clifton High School would gather there. Often times, especially at football season, the two groups of teens would fall into fights over whose school was the best.

That afternoon Andy parked the brand new white Cadillac at the curb in front of a red fire hydrant. Any police car passing by would recognize the white

Cadillac and drive by without stopping. And if one felt he needed to write a ticket, Tony would just tear it up anyway.

Pop's was a polished aluminum building with round corners and a black shingle roof. It had red neon running around the front and both sides of the building and two big glass doors in the front. On either side were parking lots that would be filled with the cars teens lucky enough to have cars would park there to show off to the girls and make other guys envious.

The front sidewalk of Pop's that afternoon had a couple of groups of teens standing around. They stepped aside and let Andy open one of the doors and hold it open for Tony. Tony walked in grandly, stopped and looked around attracting the attention he wanted. Everyone inside looked up from their hamburgers and Coca Colas. Except for the juke box blaring out the Everly Brothers singing 'Bye Bye Love,' silence suddenly filled the room. There was a booth near the rear of Pops. Andy led the way there, and they sat on opposite sides of the table, Andy with his back to the door because Tony wanted to look at the people there. Andy didn't think that was a good idea; he wanted to see trouble entering Pop's and he couldn't with his back turned away from the front door. But Tony insisted. Little by little, people started to talk again.

A waitress with an order pad and pencil in hand uncomfortably approached their booth. Tony was happy, he was smiling. It felt good to be back where he had spent so much time what seemed like a lifetime ago. He looked up at the woman. "Hi," he said. "We've been thinking about one of those egg creams. It's been a long time since we've had one. How about a couple of them?"

"Yes, Mr. Moretti," she said. She knew who he

was. Most people knew who he was. Most people knew how he made his money.

Andy said, "Nah. How about a cheeseburger and fries? And one of them thick chocolate milkshakes."

"You eat too much, Andy," Tony said.

"Nah, I just like good food is all. All that pasta stuff they cook up at the L'oro Luna is good. My old lady, she don't cook that good, and she learned back in Sicily. I love all that Italian stuff, but I can't eat it all the time. I need some other stuff . . . Like the burgers they got here."

Tony laughed; he was in a good mood. He slid out of the booth and put some quarters into the jukebox. He pushed the buttons for Sea Of Love, Stagger Lee, and Dream Lover. There were a few records left to choose from the coins he put in the slot. He looked at a young girl sitting nearby, winked and waived at her to pick some more music. She ran to the machine, giggled and started pushing buttons.

Back at the booth the waitress brought their food. Andy dived into his, while Tony savored the frothy egg cream of milk, chocolate, and soda water, made as good as he remembered. He looked around the room, enjoying being there and remembering when he used to be there unnoticed.

A booth on the other side of the restaurant was occupied by four girls. They were all staring at him, smiling and hoping Tony would take notice. Three of them giggled and acted silly, the fourth just stared at him. She was pretty. Her hair was dark, like silk, and hung softly to her shoulders, not teased up like the others. The little makeup she wore was not like the ill-done and thick make up the others had pasted on their faces. Tony liked what he saw and their eyes locked on each other's. She was smiling. He had seen her somewhere before. He tried to remember.

Then it came to him. It was that hot afternoon in DeSonoto's. It must have been two years ago, he thought. Three little girls who wanted pizza. He had found her cute then, and now she was more so. She was pretty, he thought. It hadn't been that long but she seemed older, more grown up. She wasn't some little kid anymore. She was a woman, and he liked what he saw.

She was wearing a simple light blue sweater with a small gold cross on a thin chain that hung around her neck and rested on the sweater. She wore tight fitting Capri pants that did justice to her curves. And she said a silent prayer of thanks to God for letting her find Tony once again. For two years she had prayed nightly, silently, that God would bring them together.

Andy saw what was happening and asked, "You OK, Tony?"

"Yes," he answered still looking at the girl. "I think I have a date for Saturday night."

At the table the dark haired girl spoke to the others. They turned and looked at Tony, giggled and then the three got up and walked away, leaving the girl alone. Tony grinned knowingly and left Andy to join the girl.

"Hi," he said. "Mind if I join you?"

"Sure," she said. "Sit down."

Tony slid into the seat opposite her and said, "I'm Tony . . . What's your name?"

"I'm Teresa," she said. "I know who you are."

"That's nice. Who am I?"

"You're Tony Moretti. I was in DeSonoto's a long time ago. You were behind the counter. You looked different back then. Your hair . . . And you had a black eye. I like your clothes by the way, better than what you were wearing that day. And your hair is a lot better now. I like it. Do you remember me?"

"Yeah, I remember. You're Teresa. You were cute back then . . . You're beautiful now."

She blushed and said, "Thank you, but I know that's not true."

"Oh yes it is. If you knew me you'd know I never lie."

"I'm glad you remembered me," she said. It had been her hope that when they met once again he would remember her. She had dreamed of him for all those months, dreamed of him kissing her and holding her, and she had dreamed of making love with him, feeling his muscles and wrapping her arms around him. Now, she prayed, those dreams might come true.

"Yes. You're hard to forget. I mean, you were a just a kid back then. But you're not a kid anymore. How do you know me?"

Teresa smiled and said, "Of course I know who you are. Everybody knows you."

"Does that bother you?" he asked.

"No . . . Not really. I guess I kind of admire you."

"Why is that?" he asked. Tony could see that Teresa liked what she saw. She liked sitting with him. She liked being near him.

"I mean, you're fifteen . . . sixteen right? Yet you have a Cadillac and a driver. And your shirt doesn't hang out of your pants anymore like it did at DeSonoto's. You dress like a man, not a kid."

"Thanks, and he's my friend," Tony said. "Not my driver."

"I know who he is," Teresa answered. "He's Andy Pecora. People are scared of you but maybe they're scared because of Andy, I don't know. But people are scared of you. Look around. People stay out of your way. I'll bet if you got up and walked out without paying for your drink, no one would complain."

"Is that fear or respect?" Tony asked.

"Maybe both," she said. "But I kind of think if people respect you, it's because you have a reputation at a young age. Not many kids have done what you've done."

"And you like that?" Tony asked.

"Not really, maybe in some ways," Teresa answered. "I don't like people to get hurt. But I like that you are brave enough to do what you do. You live dangerously, and that's exciting. Kind of like the roller coaster out at Coney Island. Scary, but fun."

Tony nodded as he looked around the room. He hadn't noticed, but no one in the restaurant was talking. Everyone was looking at them. She had her back to the people watching. "Are you uncomfortable that everyone is watching us?" he asked her. "Because they are. I can stop that if you want."

"No . . . I guess I sort of like it. I guess it makes me feel . . . special."

"I think I'd like to take you to a movie Saturday night," he said. "How about it? You pick the movie."

"My father won't let me date," she said. "He says I'm too young. Sorry. My mother would say it was OK, though."

"I'll talk to them," Tony said. "I'll come to your house. I'll introduce myself. I'll bring you flowers. I'll show them I'm a gentleman and they have nothing to fear."

Teresa put her hand to her mouth and laughed. "You have no idea what you're saying."

"I don't get it. Why shouldn't I come to your house and meet your parents?"

"That just wouldn't be a good idea," she said. She started to get up but stopped when Tony touched her hand. There was an electric shock they both felt. Neither one pulled their hand away. It was special, they both knew it. There was a connection there. Something neither had ever experienced before. He said, "You like to live dangerously? Meet me here at six on Saturday."

Teresa smiled and walked away, back to her friends. She was happy, but she was also frightened. Her prayers had come true, but what should she do now, she wondered? Tony left the booth and went back to where Andy was waiting. Andy didn't look happy. "What's the matter?" Tony asked as he slid into the booth.

"Do you know who that is?"

"Yeah, her name's Teresa. She looks like a nice kid. We're going out next Saturday."

"Do you know who her old man is?"

Tony said nothing. Andy leaned close, across the table, and said, "Al Falzone . . . Your boss."

Tony was taken aback. He looked around the restaurant, but she was gone. She had known how impossible it would have been for Tony to come knocking on her door. She probably knew that Tony worked for her father, most people knew that. She would never be allowed to go out with him. Her father had destined her for college and a college man with a good career as her husband.

But Teresa did meet Tony the following Saturday. Tony waited for her, knowing she would be there.   Andy sat nearby, waiting just in case Al Falzone should have learned of their date.

Teresa walked into Pop's with two of her girlfriends. They saw Tony, and the two walked to the counter and sat while Teresa walked to Tony. They sat next to each other at the rear of Pop's. Little by little she edged closer to him until they touched.

They talked and laughed and shared a strawberry milkshake with two straws. They left Pop's and went to see a movie, 'The Magnificent Seven', that Teresa had heard was good. Andy drove as they sat in the back seat of the Cadillac. In the theater, Tony and Teresa sat in the last row, holding hands, while Andy sat across the aisle. Half way through the movie, Tony put his arm around Teresa's shoulders. She leaned towards him and they kissed for the first time.

After the movie ended, Teresa said, "I'd better go home now. It was fun, Tony. I had a good time."

"I did, too. I'll take you home, OK?"

"No," she said. "That's not a good idea. I'll take the bus."

"Teresa, I know who your father is. Let me take you home and talk to him. I promise it will be OK."

"No, please. No trouble, Tony, OK? Let's not ruin this. Let's see where it's going, OK?"

"Ok," Tony said. "But you have to meet me at Pop's next Saturday. Make it around noon, and we'll spend the day together."

She said she would, feeling good that he wanted to be with her again. She stood on her toes and kissed him lightly and quickly.

So Andy and Tony took Teresa to the bus stop and waited while she sat next to a window and waived as the bus drove away.

They met the Saturday after that as Tony had wanted . . . And the next Saturday. It was soon almost impossible for them to wait for the next Saturday to arrive. The week between their meetings was terrible for both of them. Time slowed down and all both could think of was the day they could be in each other's arms. It was as if love hadn't come quickly to them, love seemed to have been there all along.

And Andy was always nearby. Not too close, but close enough to protect Tony on that day when Al Falzone would find out his daughter and Tony Moretti were in love.

FIFTEEN

Passaic, New Jersey
August 1960

Tony had settled into the crew's business at L'oro Luna. Newark was a new city to him, and he felt he had to take his time and learn what was there, what he could use to move his plan forward. Mike Colombo and Louie Lombardi didn't like having the kid there at first, they didn't like the idea of him collecting from them, but as the weeks went by they came to understand that Tony was smart and had good ideas. His ideas brought more money to their pockets. Ted Bianci was cautious and waited to see what Tony could do for him.

The drive down to Newark was taking too much time, and Tony needed to get away from his parent's home in Passaic. Lorenzo had stayed drunk almost continuously since Tony had put him in the hospital, but Lorenzo never again hit Tony or Tony's mother. It had been over two years, and Lorenzo hadn't left the house except to buy another jug of cheap red wine. Work for Lorenzo was a thing of the past. And speaking to Tony or even looking at him was a thing of the past, also.

Tony's mother, Graziella, found work cleaning houses in nearby wealthier communities, and sometimes she would waitress in diners and small restaurants. Tony tried to give her money, but she had refused to take it. She was grateful that the beatings and rapes had ended, but she knew where Tony's money was coming from. She couldn't bring herself to dirty her hands with money from crime. She silently went on with her hard life, leaving Tony to the life he had chosen.

So, Tony soon decided that he had to move out of his parent's home. He found a small apartment in a working class neighborhood of Newark, a better place, he thought, than the neighborhood he had come from. He had found a chair he liked in a second hand store, an overstuffed arm chair covered in a rose pattern similar to the one in his parents' apartment. It was soft and comfortable, and he could relax back in it after a long day of the work he had chosen.

It, a radio, and a small black and white TV were the only furnishings in the apartment's living room. There was no rug on the wood floor, and only a single bare light bulb hung from the ceiling. The bedroom had a mattress on the bare floor and a short lamp on the floor next to it. The small kitchen had a two burner stove and a coffee pot resting atop it. An old refrigerator held milk until it soured and beer, Tony's only alcoholic indulgence. In the corner stood a small metal table and two chairs. Two mugs for the coffee sat on the table, one for him and one for Andy, finishing the kitchen.

It would have been a barely adequate place for anyone else, but it satisfied Tony. It was his first real home where he could relax and know that no violence would occur, and he liked that. He liked the independence, and he liked the quiet solitude, when he could sit in his chair and listen to music on the radio or watch a ballgame on the TV.

It was a hot Saturday that day; the August heat reaching nearly 100 degrees at noon. Tony and Teresa sat close to each other in the cool of Pop's. He leaned against the wall without windows and Teresa leaned against him. His arm was wrapped around her shoulders. They had two egg creams and a big plate of French fries in front of them, neither of them taking much notice of the food.

The air conditioner was working overtime to keep it cool inside. They talked about maybe seeing a movie, maybe a meal somewhere. Teresa was fighting the urge to tell Tony she just wanted to be alone with him . . . Somewhere . . . Anywhere. She needed his strong arms around her and his lips on hers.

She whispered, shyness in her voice, "Is there someplace we can go, Tony?"

"I guess that's what we're trying to figure out," he answered. "Suppose we go get you a swim suit and we go swimming somewhere?"

"I don't mean that," she said. "I want to be alone with you. I don't want people watching us. I . . . I . . ." She tried to say the words but she couldn't.

"Teresa," Tony started. He turned her face up towards him. There was the slightest glimmer of a tear in her eye. "Tell me what you want. You know I'll get you anything. I'll do anything for you."

She turned her eyes away from him and forced the words out, softly and nervously. "Do your parents ever go out? I mean are you ever alone at home?"

"I don't live there anymore," he said.

She turned back to him quickly, sat up straight, her mouth open in surprise, and she said, "You don't live there anymore? Where do you live?"

"I have my own place," he said. "Down in Newark. I work down there now. You know that."

"I want to see it, Tony. Take me there now," she said excitedly. She slid out of the booth and waived across the room for Andy to come with them. Andy dropped a ten dollar bill on the table and he and Tony ran to keep up with her as she left Pop's running for Tony's Cadillac.

She jumped into the back seat leaving the door open for Tony. At the curb Andy asked, "What the hell's happening?"

"I'm not sure," Tony answered. "I think we're going to my place. We better get her there fast."

And fast is what Andy gave them. They swerved around cars and trucks, ran red lights, and broke speed laws. Teresa kept telling Andy to drive faster. Tony tried to tell him to slow down before they all got killed, but Teresa would have none of it. So Andy drove as fast as he could and came to a sliding stop in front of the plain brown wooden building that Tony called his home.

Teresa jumped from the car and ran up the five scuffed wooden steps to the front door. She stopped and turned, looking down at Tony and Andy who were standing on the weed lined sidewalk. She asked, "Is this whole place yours?"

Tony said, "No, I've only got a small apartment."

"So show me!" Teresa said excitedly. "Don't just stand there! Get up here and show me!"

Tony shrugged his shoulders and walked up the steps. He unlocked the front door, and Teresa pushed her way past him. There was a slim hallway and stairs on the right going up. "Which is yours?" she demanded.

He walked past the staircase, down the hallway

to a door on the left, unlocked it and held it open for Teresa. She stepped inside and looked around quickly. She said, "Well, it's not much now . . . But it has potential. We can fix it up really nice."

She walked through the small apartment, the living room and kitchen, and into the bedroom. She ducked her head into the bathroom and returned to the living room where Andy and Tony waited, not really understanding what was happening.

But Teresa was radiant; she was smiling and almost giddy. She said, "Oh, how I wish my mother could be here. She's very good at this you know."

"At what?" Tony asked.

"We're going to fix this place up. It's going to be really nice when we get done."

She turned around and took in the living room once again. She said, almost speaking to herself, "I think paint . . . Not wallpaper. The room's too small. Light colors I think . . . Yes, cream maybe . . . Light yellows would be good. And of course we'll have to get carpet for the floor . . . Wall to wall, I think."

She turned back to look at Tony and said, "That chair has to go, of course . . ."

He interrupted her and said, "But I like that chair."

"Well . . . OK, I guess. It's not really a guy's chair . . . But if you like it, I guess you have to have one thing of your own. Let's get started, OK? Let's go buy some paint and then we need to find a furniture store. Is there one nearby?"

As Teresa walked out the front door and down the stairs to Tony's Cadillac, Andy said, "Hey, Tony. I think you got one of them interior decorator people."

The two laughed and followed Teresa to the car.

****

The next Saturday was as hot as the week before. The best that could be hoped for was that August was almost over and September might bring the first taste of autumn. Tony sat in the front seat, Andy behind the wheel, as they waited for the bus that would bring Teresa to them. She had said she would be early that day, "We have a lot of work to do," she had told them.

When the bus arrived at the stop, she jumped from it and ran to the Cadillac. Tony opened the car's door and stepped into the early morning heat and humidity. The Cadillac had air conditioning, but it did little except keep the heat barely lower than outside the car. Teresa ran to him, threw herself at him, and they kissed with a passion Tony had not known before. "God! It was a long week," she said. "I missed you so much."

They sat in the rear seat, Tony holding her close to him, as Andy took them to Newark. Half way there she said, "Andy, I need a coffee. I skipped breakfast this morning. And I need a bathroom. Can we stop somewhere?"

"Sure thing, babe," he said. They found a diner and a table inside. When Teresa retuned from the restroom, a coffee and a big cinnamon roll were waiting for her.

"Thanks," she said. "But I can't eat that thing. Coffee is enough."

Andy didn't wait. He grabbed for the sticky roll and dug into it. When he was done he said, "I gotta' go wash my hands. Be right back." When he stood he turned slowly, doing a 360 degree turn, looking around the diner at everyone there and into the parking lot.

Teresa thought that strange, and after he walked away she asked, "Why did he do that?"

Tony answered, "He's my bodyguard. He makes sure there's no one around who could hurt me."

She looked at him with a wondering frown on her forehead. Then she asked, "That's nice, I guess. But does he always have to be with us? Can't you and I ever be alone?"

Tony thought about that for a moment and then said, "Teresa, in life there are things we want and things we need. I want you . . . But I need Andy. If you ask me to, I will choose you over Andy every time. But then one day my life might be cut short. With Andy around, that may never happen. We'll have our chance, trust me. I'll make everything work out for us."

Andy returned, grinning as he always did. And they continued on to Newark. Andy parked at the curb and waited behind the wheel, letting the engine run, as Tony and Teresa got out. He rolled down the window and said, "Look, you guys are gonna' do paintin' and stuff. I ain't the kind'a guy that likes that stuff, so I'm gonna' go up to the L'oro Luna and check on business. I'll be back in time to take you home, babe. Is that OK?"

Teresa smiled happily and leaned down into the car. She kissed Andy on the cheek and whispered, "Thank you, Andy." She walked up the steps to the apartment.

What Teresa didn't know was that Tony had asked Andy to do just that before Teresa's bus arrived in Passaic. Andy was at first not happy with the idea. His job was to protect Tony and kill when Tony wanted him to kill. But Tony asked, he didn't insist, and Andy finally got the idea that Tony wanted to be alone with his girl.

While they were waiting for the bus, he opened the glove box and took out the .38 police special he had taken from the Clifton Detective all those years ago. He handed it to Tony who tucked it inside his belt, under his suit jacket. "Use it if you have to, Tony," he said. Then Andy reached again inside the glove box and took out a pack of three condoms. "You don't haft'a use these," he said. "But now's not a good time to become a father." He winked and smiled slyly.

Inside the apartment, in the middle of the living room floor, were seven gallon cans of paint, drop cloths, brushes, rollers, and everything else the salesman could think of selling them the Saturday before. "This is going to be fun," she said.

Tony left her there and went to his bedroom to change clothes. From the back of his closet he pulled out a pair of blue jeans left from his days with The Aces, and he slipped on a white T-shirt. He hid the pistol under the mattress on the floor and put the condoms next to it.

Back in the living room he found that Teresa had spread drop cloths across the wood floor and had separated the cans of paint. She said, "Good, you've changed clothes. I think this nice beigey cream will go in here. It will make the room look bigger. Look, I can't get paint on my clothes. Do you have something I can wear? Maybe cover up what I'm wearing?"

"Back in the bedroom," Tony said. "Take what you need but not one of my suits."

She laughed as she walked past him, patting him on the cheek. "Don't worry, dear. I won't ruin your clothes."

In a few minutes she came back to the living room wearing one of Tony's white dress shirts. And other than her bra and panties, that's all she was wearing. The shirt was much too big for her, of course. It hung down to her knees over her bare legs. She had rolled up the sleeves to her elbows and left the shirt's top three buttons unbuttoned. She stood in the doorway, barefoot and smiling.

"Wow!" was Tony's reaction upon seeing her.

"OK," she said. "Enough of that. Let's get to work. We have to make this place a home."

Teresa had, of course, worked with her mother on decorating their house in Montclair. She knew how to paint and was patient with Tony who had never held a paint brush in his hands before.

At one o'clock that day they had finished painting the small living room, and Tony was happy with the result. Teresa really did know what she was doing, he thought. But it was hot, almost as hot inside as it was outside. The two windows at the front of the apartment were open. The single window in the bedroom was open but no movement of air came in, only more heat from the hot August afternoon.

"We need an air conditioner in here, Tony," she said, wiping sweat from her forehead. "Do you think the landlord will let you put one in the window?"

Tony laughed and said, "I kind of think maybe the landlord will let me do whatever I want to do."

"Oh, yeah. I forgot." And Teresa laughed, too.

Tony sat in his chair and peeled off his wet T-shirt. He leaned back and said, "Man, I could use a cold beer right now."

Teresa stared at his bare chest, longingly wanting to touch the muscles, and said, "I've never had a beer. Can I try one?"

"Sure . . . If you get one for me, too."

"Yes, my lord and master," she said, exaggerating a bow. She went to the kitchen and took two bottles of beer from the refrigerator. She found a church-key bottle opener hanging on a string from the knob of a cabinet door. When she came back to Tony, she sat on his lap and handed a bottle to him. He drank the cold beer quickly. She sipped at hers and said, "Eeeuwww! You like this stuff?"

They gazed at each other; no words were spoken. Teresa reached out and touched Tony's bare chest. She liked the feel of the muscle; it stirred a passion inside of her. She leaned down and kissed Tony. She put her bottle on the floor next to the chair and took his away, placing it next to hers. She touched his bare chest again and ran her hands across the muscles of his shoulders and arms. She took his hand in hers and raised it, putting it on her breast. The feel of his hand as it caressed her breast sent a shiver through her, and she closed her eyes to enjoy the sensation.

She whispered, her eyes closed, "I've never done this before." She was afraid she might not please him, that her innocence might not be what he wanted.

He pulled her down to him and kissed her. He said as softly as she had spoken, "I've never done this before, either."

She opened her eyes, sat up, and looked at him. "You've never done this? I can't believe that. There must be hundreds of girls chasing after you."

"I've been too busy," he said. "I've had to work too hard. Long hours and a lot of thinking time. I haven't had time for girlfriends . . . Until you that is. And I don't like whores. I keep wondering . . . Was I waiting for you? Was there something in the deep recesses of my mind that told me you would be with me?"

She smiled and said, "I like that." She stood and

took Tony's hand, pulling him from the chair. She led him to the bedroom and told him to sit on the bed. Tony had made sure the white cotton sheets were fresh and clean, and he had bought a new light weight cotton blanket. Standing in front of him, she slowly unbuttoned her paint stained shirt and let it drop to the floor. Reaching behind her, she unfastened her bra, and it joined the shirt. She slid out of her panties and moved into Tony's arms. They fell back onto the bed, holding each other. They made love for the first time, slowly, each wanting it to last forever.

****

At half past nine that evening Andy knocked on the apartment door. Teresa opened the door for him and hugged the big man as tightly as she could. She said, "Thank you, Andy."

They drove slowly back to Passaic, not in any rush to get there. This time the three of them sat in the front of the car, Teresa between the two men. They turned up the volume on the radio and tried to sing along with the songs being played. The three of them laughed, and Teresa said a silent prayer of thanks to God for letting her find Tony and fall in love with him.

The last bus leaving Passaic for Montclair had left five minutes before they got there. "Oh, great!" Teresa said. "Now what do I do?"

"Let me take you home," Tony said. "It's time I meet your parents."

"No, not now," she said. "Someday, but not now. Take me to the bus stop at my home. I'll be OK."

So Andy drove to Montclair and stopped at the corner of her street, at the bus stop. Tony opened the door and got out. Teresa said as she got out, "Early again next week, Andy. We've got to finish that damn painting."

He laughed and waited as she kissed Tony and then ran up the street to her home.

SIXTEEN

Montclair High School
October 1960

Teresa wasn't listening to Father James, a Jesuit Priest, speak to the class about the glories of heaven and the sufferings of hell. It seems, as Father James explained, that if a good Catholic were to spend a life praying on their knees and having kids, luxury in heaven was guaranteed. On the other hand, sins, particularly masturbation and sex outside of a Catholic marriage and for any purpose other than having children, were a one way ticket to hell.

The clock on the wall said it was eight minutes to two. Eight more long minutes and the bell would ring. She would have to run to get to the gym and not be late again. The girl's Phys. Ed. Instructor, Mrs. Rogers, who Teresa was absolutely sure was a dyke, would write her a late slip again and two more meant detention.

It was Friday, and all she could think of was waking early the next morning and running for the bus to Passaic. Andy, who still lived in Passaic, would be waiting, and they would drive to Newark and Tony. She and Andy would laugh and talk and listen to music on the radio while he drove as fast as he could without taking the risk of a cop stopping them. She looked at the clock again. Her foot was tapping anxiously on the floor under her desk as she stared at the slow moving hands of the clock.

The room was old, as was the entire school. It had been built twenty years before, and in spite of the money it cost to send a student there, nothing had been done to update the classrooms. Wood, darkened with age, lined the walls. Pictures of Christ and the Saints were thumb tacked to the wood. The one thing added to each classroom, in deference to the cracked blackboards in each, were new 'green' boards. Something modern in the old school.

"Teresa . . . Teresa . . ." Father James repeated. She didn't hear him; her mind was on Tony. She was longing to feel his arms around her and to feel his lips against hers. "Teresa Falzone!" he said very loudly, and the class laughed when Teresa jumped.

"Yes, Father. I'm sorry, Father. I was just thinking of Jesus and how good he is to us."

Father James nodded and said, "Yes, I'll bet you were."

Tim Robinson, sitting across the room, said, "You wanna' make a bet, Father? Teresa can help you with that."

The joke didn't go over well. Silence fell on the classroom, and Father James stared at Tim. Everyone knew who Teresa's father was, and no one dared talk about it openly in front of Teresa. Tim was tall, handsome, blond and a football hero at St. Ignatius Academy High School. He was popular with the girls and he knew it, playing it to the fullest. He knew the girls would line up to be one of his girlfriends.

The bell rang, and the class erupted with students gathering up their books and running for the door. Sister Mary Mathew called out, "Walk, boys and girls! Walk, please!" Teresa was quick jumping from her chair. Before she could reach the door, Father James called her name, "Teresa. Please wait. I want to talk to you."

"I'll be late, Father," she said smiling sweetly.

"Sister Mary Mathew will give you a late slip," he said. "Please wait."

Sister Mary Mathew nodded and went to her desk to get the note that would keep Teresa from trouble with Mrs. Rogers. When the students had all vacated the room, Father James shut the classroom door and returned to Teresa.

"I want to talk to you, Teresa," he began. "I'm very worried about you, my daughter."

"You don't have anything to worry about, Father. I'm fine. I'm not sick or anything."

"It's not that I think you are not well, Teresa. I think your soul is in jeopardy."

Teresa knew exactly what Father James was saying. She had heard it all before, from practically every Nun in school. But she put on an actor's face of not understanding. "I have no idea what you're talking about Father. Don't you see me at Church every Sunday?"

"You know what I'm talking about, my daughter."

"Father . . . I mean no disrespect . . . Please forgive me . . . But I'm uncomfortable with you calling me your daughter. It implies something that I'm very uncomfortable with."

"Teresa!" Sister Mary Mathew exclaimed.

Father James knew what Teresa was doing. She was smart, at the top of the grade list at St. Ignatius High. He smiled and said, "Please don't change the subject, Teresa. I want to talk with you about your

Saturdays."

"I'm sure I don't know what you're talking about, Father James," she said innocently.

"Please, Teresa. Your Saturdays are going to send your soul to hell."

There was no use playing games, Teresa decided. He knew. Sister Mary Mathew knew. She put her armful of books on Sister Mary Mathew's desk and looked up at the middle aged Priest. "Father . . . I don't believe God put us here to be unhappy. I don't believe He meant us to live a life of pain and suffering. I believe there is good in love, and I believe that's what God believes also. I don't believe we have to give up happiness to get into Heaven. I believe that if we live a good life and love as God wants us to love . . . . Heaven will be there for us."

Neither Father James nor Sister Mary Mathew knew what to say. Both were shocked. How could a good Catholic girl believe that? How could she believe that happiness and not pain, sacrifice, and suffering would get her into Heaven? It must be just a childish fantasy, something she had seen in some movie somewhere. Something she probably read in a book that had been banned by the Church.

Father James said, "I don't believe that you think that's the truth. The Church teaches . . ."

"Father," Teresa interrupted. "I mean no disrespect. I love the Church, and I love God. But I simply can't believe that God put us on this earth to suffer. Love is what God wants in every aspect of our life. God wants us to love our neighbors, the poor, people who are angry with us. Why doesn't he want us to love one person, also? To truly love one man for our whole life? And Father, I believe God has shown me that love is good. He has answered my prayers. I've prayed every night for God to bring the man I love to me. He has answered those prayers, so it has to be right."

"Teresa," Father James said sadly. "I'm going to have to speak with your parents about this. What you are doing is wrong."

Teresa laughed, raising her hand to cover her mouth. "Oh, great!" she said. "I'd love to see that! Can I be there the day after you talk to my parents?"

"What does that mean, Teresa?"

"What that means is, if you know who my boyfriend is . . . You'll know what he'll do to you if you hurt me. I'd suggest you move to a new parish, very far away, if you go to my parents."

The threat was made, received and understood by Father James, and not taken lightly. Teresa picked up her books, still laughing, and left the classroom. The hallway was empty; the bell had rung signaling that classes had started, and she didn't have the late slip that was promised. 'Oh well,' she thought. She walked slowly towards the gymnasium. 'If I'm going to be late, it might as well be really late.'

Tim Robinson stepped from the doorway he had been hiding in. He stopped Teresa, standing in front of her, too close as far as Teresa was concerned.

"Hey, beautiful," he said. "Got a minute?"

"No."   She tried to step around Tim but he wouldn't let her. He grabbed her arm and held her tightly.

"Tell you what," he said. "Let me take you to the game tomorrow.   After the game we'll go get something to eat. Then we can go up to Barber's pond and park for awhile. I've got my father's car. We can have a good time."

"Thanks but no thanks," Teresa said.   "I've

already got a date. Now please, I have to get to gym class."

"Yeah, I know all about your date. Why some hood? Why not me?"

"Because he's a man and you're not. And he's not a hood."

"Yeah he is . . . Everybody knows that. I'd like to meet him alone somewhere. Without all his hood friends. I'd kick the crap out of him."

Teresa looked up at Tim, into his blue eyes, and paused for a moment. Then she said, "Maybe I can arrange that."

She pushed past him and ran to the gymnasium.

The next Monday, Teresa was sitting in Sister Mary Margaret's classroom as the other students filed in. Tim walked in, his left eye black and blue, and swollen shut, his lower lip split and stitched closed. He walked past Teresa but did not look at her.

SEVENTEEN

Brooklyn, New York
October 1960

Bruno sat outside Natalia Salvano's bedroom. Doctor McGuire was in there, and Abby Williams, the nurse Bruno had hired, was in there. Natalia had started screaming during the night, calling out profanities in Italian and struggling with Abby. Natalia was barely more than colorless skin over bones. She was so fragile that the nurse was afraid she would injure the woman trying to keep her quiet. Bruno phoned Doctor McGuire at half past two in the morning, and he was at the house a half hour later. A quick injection calmed the old lady, and she slept quickly. Bruno phoned his boss and insisted the Doctor stay until Peter arrived.

Peter drove to Brooklyn, without worrying about someone following him. His mother was very ill, what could be more innocent than visiting her? Peter had become used to the police and the FBI questioning him. His father had been a powerful Mafia Don. It was easy for them to suspect that Peter had followed in his father's footsteps. But there was no evidence of that, and so their suspicions never rose above unsubstantiated suspicions. His lifestyle in Manhattan was all the FBI could find out about him. Phone taps of the new numbers he had installed in his office and home revealed nothing. Peter and Bruno had worked out a simple code, words that seemed innocuous enough but often had dire meanings.

That day Peter parked at the curb in front of his mother's house, innocently visiting his ailing mother. Dr. McGuire's black Buick was there, Bruno's blue Ford was in the driveway, and the street was crowded with neighbors gathered together in inquisitive groups, all wondering and worrying about Natalia. They whispered amongst themselves, everyone having their own idea of what was happening. But everyone knew that Natalia Salvano was dying. The only question was, when would she die?

Peter jumped from his car and ran up the steps to the front door. Bruno was standing at the open door. Peter asked as he quickly stepped past him, "How is she?"

"Not good, boss. I kept the Doctor here."

Peter took the stairs two at a time up to his mother's bedroom. The door to the room was open; Abby Williams was sitting on the edge of Natalia's bed, holding the woman's skeleton-like hand. Dr. McGuire was sitting in a chair. He stood when Peter walked into the room. The Doctor was dressed as if he had just jumped out of bed and thrown on some clothes, which in fact he had when Bruno phoned. His grey slacks were wrinkled; his white shirt had been worn the day before. He did not wear a tie or jacket. He had an overnight stubble of grey/black beard. His thick glasses hung low on his long nose. He looked tired. The nurse stood and stepped away to let Peter stand close to his mother.

He looked down at the woman and hardly recognized her. There was no color to her; her hair was fully white and hung in thin strands; her eyes were closed and her breathing was not natural. Gasps of breath were separated with no breathing at all for long moments. It was forced and seemed like attempts at her body to fight off death.

Peter asked the doctor without looking at him, "Shouldn't she be in a hospital?"

"I'm sorry, Mr. Salvano. Moving her now would just end it more quickly. She's dying, Mr. Salvano. She hasn't much time left. There's nothing can be done about it."

Peter sat at his mother's bedside throughout the rest of the night and into the morning. The sun lit the room and Natalia's breathing became more forced and irregular.   The intervals between breaths became longer and longer, and more struggled. And finally they stopped. Dr. McGuire stepped closer and felt for a pulse at her wrist and neck. He shook his head, Bruno touched his boss' shoulder, and Peter knew his mother was gone.

As if by some old world Sicilian magic, the old ladies of the neighborhood, standing outside under Natalia's window, began crying and wailing. He didn't know how they knew, but they knew. It was of the old world of which he was not a part.

Peter's eyes filled with tears.   He bent and kissed his mother on her cold lips and left the room with Bruno following close behind.

As they walked slowly down the stairs Peter said, "Please call Romano. Tell them I'll be there to make arrangements for the funeral and burial."

"I done that already, boss. I wanted them to be ready. You want I should drive you there?"

"Thank you, Bruno. Yes, I think you better drive. Call some of the men. Get them here fast. I want security."

"Yes boss."

"I don't want the press getting near the house. No one is to talk to the press. Only a simple obituary and I'll write that. Keep the neighbors outside. I don't want anyone inside the house."

"Yes boss."

****

When Don Pietro died, the hearse carrying him from the church to the cemetery was followed by fourteen limousines and a procession of twenty-three cars. There was a forest of flowers at the gravesite. Made Men from as far away as California stood and watched Don Pietro's coffin be slowly lowered into the earth. He was of a world of crime that was dying off quickly, one of the last of the Old Dons. He had come from nothing and had risen to power in pools of blood. So different from what Peter wanted for himself.

At Romano's Funeral Home, few people came to show their respect and condolences at Peter's loss of his mother. Al Falzone was there, Michael Funno and Manny Esposito were there, but only for a short time. They paid their respects and left. But that was expected because they were the Salvano Family Capos, and Peter wanted no public relationship with them. They were showing respect to the wife of their Don, that's all. They walked past Peter as if they didn't know him.

Their wives made an appearance but didn't stay long either. Peter's wife and children were there. He had to keep his two lives separated, but Natalia was the grandmother of his children after all. Who could object to that?

Bruno Massetti was there of course, standing at the rear of the funeral parlor where Natalia lay at rest, without thought of rest or food for himself. His loyalty knew no end. And the neighborhood men and women came to mourn the loss of Natalia. The old ladies, from the old Country, dressed in black and hooded in black veils, cried and prayed their rosaries.

Sitting at the back of the small chapel where Natalia's coffin rested was a young man Peter didn't know. He was dressed in a well tailored black suit, white shirt and black tie. Sitting next to him was another young man, slightly older and much heavier. They sat there for hours, through the night. Peter whispered in Bruno's ear, "Who are they?"

"I don't know," Bruno said. "I'll find out."

Bruno went quietly from man to man and returned to sit next to his boss. "One of Al Falzone's people . . . And his bodyguard."

"That kid has a bodyguard?" Peter asked. "Tell him I want to speak with him," Peter whispered. "Tell him to wait outside."

Bruno did as he was told, and Tony rose, telling Andy to wait there. He went out into the sunlight, the warmth feeling good after the somber cold of the night in the funeral home. A few minutes later Peter joined him. As he walked to him Peter looked the young man up and down. An expensive suit that had been altered because of the muscle built up on his arms, shoulders and chest, and shoes that if not custom made were at least expensive. His hair was short and combed neatly. Peter thought to himself, 'Whoever this guy is, he's got a future.'

"I'm told you're with Al Falzone," Peter said.

"Yes, Don Peter," Tony answered proudly.

"In public you should never call me 'Don',

understand? I thank you for being here and showing your respect, but you and your friend must leave now."

"My deepest condolences on your mother's death, Mr. Salvano. I've heard stories of what a great woman she was."

"Thank you again," Peter said. "But you must leave."

"With respect, Mr. Salvano . . . Why?"

Peter's stare cut deep into Tony's eyes. There was anger there; Tony could see it, and he wondered if he had gone too far. But as quickly as it came, it went, and Peter said, "Because I said so." How many times had Tony said the same thing to The Aces and to Andy? It was the mark of a leader to demand unquestioned loyalty.

Peter turned and walked back into Romano's Funeral Home and to his mother's casket. Within minutes Andy stepped outside after Bruno told him to go to Tony. They drove away, but Tony could not put aside the desire to be at the cemetery the next day.

At the cemetery a small crowd of neighbors and friends stood by, as Natalia's parish priest prayed in the Latin that only the old ladies understood. Tony and Andy stood at the curb, under the red, brown and yellow leaves of an old oak tree, a distance away, watching.

Single roses were laid on the coffin by those attending, and slowly it was lowered into the earth. The people filtered away. But Peter walked in a different direction. There, standing in the shadows of tall oak trees nearby, unseen by Tony, were Al Falzone and his wife and two children.

Teresa had seen Tony when no one else did. She wanted to run to him and throw her arms around him and kiss him. She wanted to be with him, be with him somewhere where their lives would not interfere with their love. But that was not possible; she knew that. 'Time will bring us together,' she thought.

Peter shook Al's hand and brushed a kiss lightly across Maria Falzone's cheek. He rumpled young Al's shock of dark hair and touched Teresa's cheek fondly. Tony bristled at that. He wanted Teresa, and he didn't want anyone else touching her. But Andy put his big hand on Tony's shoulder, as if knowing what Tony was thinking.

"I'm not going to do anything," Tony said. "Let's get outta' here."

EIGHTEEN

Newark, New Jersey
October, 1960

Al Falzone had been living in Trenton since he was given Chi Chi Torrel's territory. At first he came home to his family in Montclair every weekend. Then he would skip a weekend because of "business". Soon he was coming home once a month. Often it was less than that.

He had an apartment there, of course. And he had a girlfriend living there with him. She was young, she was beautiful, she had been a street walking prostitute before Al found her, and she was a dark skinned Mexican. If his Don found out she was Mexican and dark skinned, Al hoped he might not care. It was one thing to have a whore on the side, to take the whore out bar hopping on a Saturday night, to buy her furs and jewelry, to give her cash. But to have a dark skinned whore living with a Made Man and have that Made Man not be home with his wife and family, was not acceptable.

If the other Capos found out, he might lose some respect. If his crew found out, they would keep their opinions to themselves and laugh behind his back. If his wife found out there would be trouble. Maria was a

151

strong willed Italian woman who demanded the fidelity of her husband . . . At least the outward appearance of fidelity. If Al had a girlfriend, it should be a secret and quiet affair, a Saturday night affair once a month perhaps. In her life she had seen almost every man do that.

Al's girlfriend was great in bed, at least Al thought so. That's what he wanted her there for. At home, sex with Maria had become routine and quick. It didn't seem as if she enjoyed having her husband on top of her, grunting like a pig until it was over for him and he rolled over to sleep. Rosalita, Al's whore, wasn't like that. She took a very active role in their sex life. And she did things Maria refused to do. No matter how many times Al ask for a blow job, Rosalita fell to her knees and seemed to like it almost as much as Al did.

At home, with Maria, Al was too often subjected to Maria's whining, as Al thought of it, about his not moving up in the organization. She was pushing too hard, he thought. Night after night and every time they were alone she would start on him to move up and start his own family. The money, she kept saying, was the important thing. She wanted more money.

In Trenton, he didn't have to listen to that . . . Or to anything else for that matter. Rosalita spoke broken English with a heavy accent. When she did talk, which wasn't often, Al simply ignored her. It was good, he felt, to be able to get a good blow job whenever he wanted and not have to listen to a woman complain.

And so over time Al missed more and more weekends in Montclair. And he missed more and more time in Newark with his crew there.

His absence at L'oro Luna in Newark was being felt by his crew. He hadn't been seen there in months.

He had left Ted Bianci, Mike Columbo, and Louie Lombardi on their own, an experience they were not used to. Making decisions was new to them.

In Trenton, Chi Chi's crew had been shepherded out to work the streets and do robberies and hijackings. They couldn't be trusted. Al hoped they would go to other crews, abandon him. He didn't need them, he felt, and he didn't want them around. He wanted his own people in Trenton, people he could trust. He was there and kept a close eye on them.

In the past Al had approved or disapproved of everything that the Newark crew did. They now were left to decide when someone was to be hurt and when latitude was to be given, to decide who got a loan and what the vig was to be. It took time for them to discuss everything, hoping to do what would not get them in trouble.

And then there was Tony Moretti. The three men looked at him and saw a boy with muscles in an expensive suit. But when he spoke, they heard a man who was smarter than the three soldiers put together. He at first made subtle suggestions that they listened to only half the time. Little by little those suggestions were listened to intently because Tony, it seemed, was never wrong.

The people who worked at the booking parlors owned by Al became used to phoning Tony at L'oro Luna when problems occurred. He told them when to lay off big bets on other bookies and when to refuse a bet altogether.

A great deal of the income Al's crew realized was from loan sharking. Tony began to make the decisions on who got a loan and what the vig would be, and he picked which man would make the hard collections when a person couldn't or wouldn't pay. He decided what would be done to late payers, how much they would be hurt, or if they were to be hurt at all.

Tony had pulled himself away from the loan sharking and hijacking part of the business. He let the others do that if they wanted. He would make decisions, but that was their business, not his. Tony was more interested in the gambling end of Al's Newark territory. That was where the money he wanted was. He would keep his percentage of their take, as he and Al had agreed, but he let the others do that kind of work.

There was a long standing weekly poker game in the back room of L'oro Luna. Just about anybody with a few dollars could sit in. Tony changed that. He initiated a once a week game open only to invited players with fat wallets. It was a closed game, high stakes, and for only people who could afford to lose. It started slow, but word got around, and within a month the players were doctors, lawyers, business owners, and the police who were on the books. The police always won, a few hundred, never more, but they walked away happy. They were happy enough to keep the games from being raided.

The games always made a profit, and Tony kept half of that profit, sending the other half to Trenton to keep Al happy. Tony collected the money from the Capos to send to Al. He kept 10% of what he collected, although they had agreed he would have 5%. And he kept 25% of the vig he collected himself, even though they had agreed on 20%. And Al didn't complain. Al liked that the income he was getting was increasing, and it let him have more time with his whore and more money for her.

Tony's apartment in Newark had been transformed by Teresa from a dull and drab bachelor's place into a bright and comfortable home for the two of them to spend their Saturdays. She had picked out the few pieces of furniture that were there, a comfortable light brown upholstered couch with colorful pillows, two glass topped wooden end tables and matching lamps for each, and a wicker chair with thick cushions that Tony didn't like but Teresa insisted on getting. He had to compromise, since she agreed to let him keep his flowery stuffed armchair. Expensive, beige, wall to wall carpet covered the floor of the small living room. The single bulb ceiling light that hung from an old wire had been replaced with a simple chandelier that lit the room with soft, pleasing light.

All the paint on the walls had been chosen by Teresa, and Tony had to admit that he liked the end result. She had found framed pictures, prints of famous paintings she assured him, and chose where to hang them. She had hung drapes and curtains. She kept a few vases of fresh flowers there, changing them every Saturday. And she had brought in a few green plants. "They're nice, and they're supposed to keep the air fresh," she said when Tony laughed at them.

Tony had air conditioners put in the living room window and the lone bedroom window. They cooled the apartment and made it comfortable for the two of them when they spent the day making love.

They had fun furnishing and painting the apartment together but they were having more fun in the big bed Teresa had picked out. It was the biggest bed Teresa could find, very soft, and she made sure the springs didn't squeak. At her insistence, Tony bought a white canopy for the bed. "I'm going to feel really dumb sleeping under that thing," he had said. She answered quietly so no one else in the store could hear, "Not while I'm there." Night stands and a matching five drawer bureau filled the room. And carpet to match the living room covered the floor.

Teresa took three of the drawers of the new bureau for her clothes and filled more than half the closet with more clothes that Tony bought for her. Anything that she looked at and liked, he bought, often surprising her when she got to the apartment on Saturday mornings.

In the tiny kitchen, Teresa had the old two burner stove removed and hauled away. She had a four burner stove with an oven squeezed into a space by removing one of the old cabinets. She and Tony painted the cabinets and had new doors brought in. And a small light wood table and two chairs finished the room.

It took five Saturdays to transform the old, dull apartment into a pleasant, bright, and comfortable home for the two of them. When it was all done they sat on the couch, listening to music on the radio, holding each other, and feeling good about how their 'home' looked. "You did a good job, Teresa," Tony told her. She liked that. She kissed him.

Their Saturdays together continued uninterrupted. Rather than wait for the afternoon, they began meeting early in the morning so they could have more time together. Andy would drive to Newark before sunrise and get Tony. They would go back to Passaic early in the morning. Sometimes they would take Teresa to breakfast; sometimes they would go to a movie. But more often than not Teresa and Tony would wind up in bed at their apartment in Newark. Andy would drive and they would sit in the back seat as they took Teresa home, each night a little later than the Saturday before.

That day Teresa's silky black hair fell across Tony's chest as they lay together under the soft blanket. She liked the feel of her breasts pressing against him. Tony was running his fingers through her hair and dreaming of the day they could be together all the time. Late Saturday night was a terrible time. It meant they had to be apart again.

Tony loved her, he knew that. He hadn't told her that yet, but he loved her. He had to figure out a way that they could be together without hiding and sneaking around. Kids did that; maybe they were only sixteen years old but they weren't kids. What they shared was more than that.

He put his hand to her face and turned her to him. They kissed deeply and she moved on top of him. Teresa couldn't get enough of him. She loved him. She needed him. But she feared her father at the same time. Something had to be done. Somehow, she had to have him all the time.

It was evening and they had spent the day making love. Teresa had to get home. As they were dressing she said, "We have to do something about this."

"About what? Am I doing something wrong in bed?"

"You idiot!" she laughed and threw one of her shoes at him. "I can't stand being with you only once a week. All my friends at school know; the Nuns know."

"Why don't they tell your parents, then?"

"Because they're all afraid."

"Of what?" Tony asked, although he knew the answer.

"Of you . . . Of my father. God, I wish things were different! Why couldn't I fall in love with someone from the Chess Club . . . Or one of those creepy Alter Boys at Church? Why did I have to fall in love with someone so much like my father who has to work for my father?"

"You love me?" Tony asked.

"Of course you idiot! Would I be standing here

naked in front of you if I didn't love you?"

"Well, that's good, because I love you, too," he said. He hesitated at first but then took three quick steps to her and wrapped his arms around her. She was soft, young, beautiful . . . And dangerous. "So, I think we should go tell your parents," he whispered into her ear.

"I wish we could . . . Oh how I wish we could," she sighed, kissed his lips lightly and whispered, "Not now . . . Soon, but not now."

****

It was a cold Monday morning when Tony walked into L'oro Luna. Winter had set in early and foretold of bad weather to come. Ted Bianci was there, reading a horse racing form. Mike Colombo was behind the bar making coffee. Louie Lombardi wasn't there yet, and neither was Andy Pecora who everyone knew was Tony's bodyguard. Tony expected Andy soon. Andy had been with a woman the night before, in a motel out on the highway. Tony took a taxi to the L'oro Luna, letting Andy sleep in.

He felt comfortable at L'oro Luna. He was in charge; he felt he needed Andy outside but not there. That day Al Falzone was there, standing with his back to the bar, leaning both elbows on it. Tony was surprised to see him there, away from Trenton. It had been more than three months since he had come to Newark. Tony and the others wondered why. 'Maybe Andy should be here,' Tony thought.

"Hey, Tony!" Al said loudly. "Glad you could make it! The boys were just telling me how good everything was going! You're making quite a reputation for yourself!"

Tony pulled a chair away from the table Ted Bianci was sitting at. He sat, smiled and said, "Yeah, things are going great. Good money coming in and no real problems. I had to have a couple of guys roughed up a little, but no real problems."

"So I heard. So I heard," Al said. "Anything else happening that I should know about? Anything at all?"

Tony assumed that Al had learned about Teresa and him. It was bound to happen. Someone would tell Al, someone maybe looking for revenge. Someone who was jealous or envious of Tony's rise to power.

"You're lookin' good, Tony," Al said. "You been workin' out, haven't you? You got strong arms and shoulders there, kid." He pushed away from the bar and strode around the room slowly. Ted Bianci put the racing form down on the table. He knew something was going to happen. Mike Colombo had walked to the table and sat down after putting the coffee pot on the flame. "How many suits you got, Tony?" Al asked.

"I don't know. Maybe six or eight. I don't count'em."

"And that fancy white Caddy you drive around. That's a real beauty."

"Yeah, but I don't drive it. Andy Pecora does that," Tony said, mentioning Andy's name on purpose. Andy was feared by everyone, even Al Falzone. No one wanted to be on his bad side.

"Oh yes, Andy. He's a real asset. Glad you brought him on."

Al circled the table Ted and Mike and Tony were sitting at, and then he circled it again. "I hear you've been giving orders up here while I'm down in Trenton," he said.

"I don't give orders, Al. I maybe make a suggestion or two, that's all."

"So tell me, do you ever suggest that an order I give not be obeyed?"

"That's crazy, Al," Tony said. "What order?"

Al circled the table once again and then said, "You tell him, Mike."

"Hey, Al," Mike Colombo started. "I told you what happened. What's a'matter? You don't believe me or sump'tin?"

"Tell Tony," Al demanded.

"OK, you tell me to take out a guy. A guy what's been causin' trouble for you. So Tony here says maybe he can talk to the guy and straighten things out, ya'know? That's all."

"Well Tony?" Al asked.

"That's bullshit, Al. You know its bullshit. When have I ever gone against anything you've ever said?"

"You know, Tony?" Al started. He pulled a knife from inside his suit coat, reached around Mike Colombo and put the blade at the man's throat. "I think you're right." He slashed across Mike's throat sending blood streaming across the table. Tony jumped up and away; Mike Colombo fell forward across the table where he bled out.

"What the hell, Al!" Tony shouted. "What the hell!"

"Mike's been holding out on me for a long time. Not a lot of money . . . So I really didn't care. What the hell, everybody's got their little expenses they gotta' take care of. But when I told him to take out a guy, he let the guy pay him a thousand bucks instead. Mike blamed it on you. I got the truth from the guy. He's dead now anyway."

Between Al and Ted and Tony, they dragged Mike's body into a back storage room. They wrapped the body in some old burlap bags and spent a couple of hours cleaning up the bloody mess as best they could. Ted was sent down the street to the A&P to get a couple gallons of bleach. No one would dare question the blood stains anyway.

As Al left the L'oro Luna bar he said to Tony, "I think my daughter's doing something she shouldn't be doing. You have people up there . . . Near Montclair. See if you can find out what she's doing, OK?"

Later that night Tony would watch as Andy and Ted and Louie Lombardi cut up Mike's body. Tony would have none of it, refusing to help. He would do a lot of things, bad things, in order to get what he wanted, but butchering a man was beyond what he would do. He watched. The pieces of Mike's body would be wrapped and would be buried in several different places before the sun came up.

NINETEEN

Newark, New Jersey
November 1960

Tony waited in L'oro Luna that cold Friday morning. He was reading a newspaper while Andy was making a fresh pot of coffee. They were alone because the crew was out making their collections. The phone call in the middle of last night had caused his temper to rise, and he didn't like to lose his temper. Self control let him think clearly and make good decisions. So he had calmed down and waited. The phone call was the end of what had happened weeks before.

Tony had been making a lot of money in the past year from the high stakes gambling. The poker games were now twice a week, and he was opening betting rooms where anyone could bet on any sports action they wanted.

He had a lot of cash stashed in his small apartment, in paper bags and old pillow cases stashed under his bed and in the back of his closet, where it wasn't doing any good. He needed to invest that cash if his long term plan was ever to come true. He couldn't just put it in a bank because the bank would have to report it. And nothing else he could think of was free of required government reports and record keeping. Tony wasn't filing Income Tax Returns, and he didn't want to start doing so. He had no way to explain all his income.

Then he happened to meet Connie Baker at the bar of a restaurant one evening a few weeks ago. That meeting was the start of it. Tony and Andy were sitting in a booth in the restaurant enjoying thick steaks that night. Connie was at the bar with a man she clearly didn't enjoy being with. He was fat, bald, and old, and he was leering lustfully at the woman who was his employee. The man was drunk and loud.

Connie was thirty years old, divorced, tall, slim and good looking. Her blond hair was cut short and combed back professionally but still sensually. Connie was a Real Estate Agent, working out of Brewster Realty in Newark. Her boss, sitting uncomfortably close to her at the bar, was Milo Brewster.

While Milo was drinking too much and trying to talk Connie into going to a cheap motel with him, she was looking in the mirror behind the bar at Tony. He looked so young, but he was wearing an expensive suit, and he had a diamond tie pin holding his red silk tie down. The suit and his shoes, she knew from experience sizing her clients up, were custom made. He looked big and strong, and he had to be, she thought, older than he looked. Men with 'baby faces' turned her on.

Tony looked across the room as he ate and saw her staring at him in the mirror. He turned away quickly and asked Andy, "That blond at the bar, is she some kind of cop?"

Andy looked and said, "I ain't seen her anywhere. Maybe a Fed, though. Why?"

"She's been staring at me."

"Well, she's cute enough," Andy said. "Might be

worth while seein' what an older dame is like in bed."

Tony didn't answer. There was only one woman for him, and she wasn't with him that night.

Connie stood from the barstool; Milo grabbed her arm. She tried to shake herself free of him, but she couldn't. They were making a loud scene. Tony saw what was happening and the bartender wasn't doing anything. He told Andy, "Go do something about that, will you?"

Andy stood and walked menacingly towards Connie and Milo. People sitting at the tables saw what was happening and stopped talking and eating. Milo saw Andy, too. He let go of Connie's arm and stood up, unsteady on his feet.

Milo was a foot shorter than Andy and had a bulging waist line. Being drunk was the only thing that kept him from running out of the restaurant.

"What the hell you want, kid?" he slurred.

"I want you to leave this lady alone, please," Andy said.

"And what if I don't?"

Andy bent down and whispered in Milo's ear so only he could hear, "If you don't leave her alone . . . I'm going to take you out back and cut your balls off."

Andy stood back up and grinned. Milo stumbled backwards and then left the restaurant as quickly as he could. Andy turned to Connie and said, "My boss says he can escort you home if you need to be away from that fat pig."

"Your boss?" she questioned. "Who is he?" she said looking across the room at Tony still in the booth but watching what was happening.

"He's Tony Moretti," Andy said. "So you want us to take you home or what?"

"Thank you," she said to Andy but still smiling at Tony. "Can I finish my drink at your table?"

"Yeah, I guess so."

Connie followed Andy to the booth. Tony stood as she approached. Andy said, "She wants to finish her drink here, boss. Is that OK?"

"Sure . . . If you'd like."

Tony waived to a waiter and asked that a chair be brought to the table for the lady. Connie asked, "Can't I sit with you in the booth?"

Tony slid into the booth and said, "No. I can offer you protection . . . Nothing more. Sit if you want and when we're done with our meal we'll see if your fat friend is waiting for you outside."

She sat in the chair and placed her martini on the table. Tony and Andy went on eating, ignoring her.

A few minutes went by, uncomfortable minutes for Connie, and she asked, "What's going on here? Who are you anyway?"

Tony moved his hand slightly, waving towards Connie. Andy saw it and said, "I told you, lady. He's Tony Moretti."

"And who is Tony Moretti?"

Neither Tony nor Andy said anything. Connie had had enough. She finished her drink quickly and stood. She pulled a business card from her purse and laid it on the table. She turned and walked out.

After they had finished their meal, Tony grabbed the card off the table and put it in his jacket pocket. He had to be careful. She might have been a cop, and the whole thing could have been a setup.

In the car, as Andy drove back to Tony's

apartment, Tony looked at the card. "What is she?" Andy asked.

"It says she's a Real Estate Agent."

"That right? She's good lookin' though."

Real Estate? Maybe that's what he was looking for? The next day he phoned her and asked to meet her and talk about real estate investments.

She remembered him, of course, and she wasn't happy at her treatment the night before. "Why are you phoning here?" she demanded angrily.

"I've got some money I want to invest. I don't know anything about real estate but I thought it might be the place to put some cash."

'Cash'. That one word piqued her interest. Getting right to the point she asked, "How much cash?"

"A hundred twenty thousand," Tony said. "I can come up with more if I have to."

The number astounded her. It was a fortune in those days, if it was all cash. "How old are you?" she asked.

"What difference does that make? Money is money. What can I invest in?"

OK, so his age maybe didn't make a difference to her so long as the money was really there. Maybe he was some rich kid, a rich man's son, a kid who had inherited a lot of money? So she decided to move ahead. "Do you want a house to live in?"

"No, I don't want to be tied down right now."

"Then income properties, rentals. I've got a few good buys there. When can we get together?"

"Give me an address of something I should buy. I'll meet you there in about an hour."

She gave him an address in an area of town that Tony knew a little about. He had started a numbers operation there. It was a part of Newark where laborers lived, where blacks and Latinos were prevalent.

Connie was waiting in her Jaguar XK150. It was completely out of place in that neighborhood. Andy pulled Tony's white Cadillac to the curb, parking behind her. They and she all got out of their cars at the same time and stood on the sidewalk.

The building was, at best, a slum. "This is what you want me to buy?" Tony asked.

"You don't want to live in it . . . All you want is to collect rents, correct? This is a good investment. One hundred twenty thousand will get it. You'll get around eight hundred a month in rents . . . Unless you want to jack the rents up. A year from now you can sell it for a hundred fifty thousand."

Andy thought that sounded like a good deal. Good money with no work to get it. Tony thought it might be a good deal, too.

"I've got one problem," Tony said.

"Mr. Moretti," Connie said. "I've asked around the office. I know who you are. I'm guessing you can't openly spend the money you have. There's a way around that."

"Tell me."

"It's called a straw buyer. There are a lot of people who have to keep their money quiet . . . Away from the tax man. You pay someone to buy the property for you. It's that person's name on the deed. You pay that person a fee and you get the rents and the cash when you sell."

"Is that legal" Tony asked.

"No . . . Does that make a difference?"

"No. Set it up and get back to me."

"How do I get in touch with you?" she asked as Tony walked away.

He said without stopping, "If you want to make the deal, you find that out."

Connie did get the number for L'oro Luna and ten days later Tony gave her a small suitcase that he had bought the day before. Inside was $120,000 in cash. "I want the name and address of this straw buyer guy," he said.

"You'll meet him when you pay him the five hundred dollars he gets."

"Fine," Tony said and started to walk away.

"Wait a minute, Tony," Connie called after him. "May I call you Tony?"

"What is it?"

"I thought we might celebrate. Can I buy you dinner tonight? Maybe some champagne?"

"Thank you but no."

She walked up to Tony and stood very close. She ran her fingers up and down his jacket's lapel and smiled seductively. "I can cook a great steak, Tony. That's not all I can do. How about you come to my place for dinner . . . And dessert?"

"Thank you," Tony said. "That's very tempting . . . But I'm spoken for."

"I don't want to marry you, Tony. I just want to go to bed with you."

Tony just turned and walked away.

****

A month after buying the building, Tony was asleep in his apartment. That's when the phone call came in. It was Andy Pecora.

"Trouble. Your apartment building is on fire."

"Do I need to be there?" he asked, still groggy.

"It ain't good. I got a call from one of our cops. People died in the damn fire. Looks like it might be arson or somethin'. It ain't good."

"Don't go there," Tony said. "Find out what's happening by phone. And get that damn Connie woman on the phone. I want to talk to her in the morning. Find some place quiet, out of the way. I don't want anyone to see us together."

At nine the next morning Andy and Tony waited in the parking lot at Caldown Park. It was a school day and it was very cold. No one would be there that morning. Connie drove up in her Jaguar and parked next to them. She was smiling broadly and she was very happy.

They stood in the cold and Tony asked, "OK, what happened?"

"It's beautiful, Tony," she said. "You're going to love it."

"Love what?" he asked. "Andy, how many people died in that fire?"

"Husband and wife and their two year old kid," Andy said.

Tony looked at her and asked, "Did you start that fire?"

"Of course not, Tony." She said. The smile had disappeared from her face. She shivered, maybe from the cold, maybe because she was getting scared.

"Did you hire someone to start that fire?"

"Tony, that slum was insured for twice what you paid for it. There won't be any evidence. It's perfect. We'll split the profit. That's $60,000 to you, Tony."

"You killed three people for $60,000?" Tony asked.

"Tony, I'm sorry about them. That wasn't supposed to happen. If the fire department had gotten there sooner . . . It's their fault."

"Tell you what I'm going to do, Connie." Tony said. "Tomorrow you're going to bring me my $120,000 . . . In cash. Then I'm going to see to it that the investigators find evidence of arson so you don't get a penny of insurance."

"Tony . . . But Tony . . ."

"Andy, tell her what you're going to do if she doesn't bring the money to me tomorrow."

"I'm gonna' have some fun with her first. Then I'm gonna' kill her."

Tony and Andy drove away. The next day was that cold Friday and Tony and Andy were waiting in L'oro Luna. A messenger brought a brown paper wrapped package to Tony. It had $120,000 in hundred dollar bills inside. Tony never saw Connie Baker again. She and the man she hired to burn the building down were prosecuted and sent to jail.

TWENTY

Brooklyn, New York
November 1960

Bruno Massetti sat behind the Old Don's desk. He had taken that position ever since the new Don separated himself from the Family. He was, after all, the Underboss. Michael Funno and Manny Esposito sat on the other side of the desk and listened intently. Don Peter had given instructions to Bruno, and Bruno would pass those orders on and see to it they were carried out. This was the routine they had come to accept as normal.

The old ways were different. The old Don was involved and made decisions himself. Now orders were given by code but decisions were made without the new Don. Times were changing, but the Capos were not of the new world Don Peter chose to live in. They didn't like the changes.

After the Death of Natalia, Bruno had his widowed sister move into the house with her family. She had four daughters, the youngest nineteen years old. The daughters were all unmarried and without prospects because they were not pretty, and they liked to eat too much. But Bruno cared for them and provided a good home for them. They did not cause trouble in the house, they helped their mother cook and clean, and they stayed out of the way when the Capos were there.

The neighborhood had welcomed Bruno when he moved into the house after the old Don's death, knowing that the neighborhood would be a safe place for their children to play and grow up. They welcomed his sister and nieces as well. The house was alive again, and Bruno was happy.

In the den Bruno looked from one Capo to another, enjoying his position of power. He said, "The Don wants proof that Al had Roger Tifton killed."

"Who is this Tifton guy?" Michael asked.

"He did some business with Don Peter . . . That's all you need to know."

"This order came from Don Peter?" Michael Funno asked.

That question wasn't taken well by Bruno. It was an insult. Would he tell them something the Don had not told him? Bruno's stare sent a cold chill up Michael's spine.

"I'm sorry," Michael said. "Of course the order came from Don Peter. I was stupid to ask. I'm sorry."

Manny Esposito merely shook his head and looked down at the floor. He knew that Michael was Al's friend. They had come up together as young soldiers. But friendship only went so far. Loyalty to their Don was more important than friendship.

Bruno spoke without answering Michael, "Send some people down to Newark. Speak only with this kid, Tony Moretti, no one else. Tell him to find out who killed Tifton and why. Tell him his Don has ordered this, and he is not to talk to anyone about this."

****

Newark, New Jersey

That Saturday the knock came on the door at half past two in the afternoon. There was a second knock. And then a demanding pounding on the door. Tony stumbled out of bed and across the small living room. He opened the door a crack, leaving the chain in place. In his right hand, held behind his back, was the small .38 revolver that Andy had given him to keep at his bedside, "Just in case," Andy had said.

"Whatta'ya want?" he slurred, his voice full of sleep.

"I got a message from your Don," the man said in a deep growl of a voice.

"What?" Tony asked, rubbing sleep from his eyes.

"I said I got a message from your Don. Let me in."

Tony closed the door enough to slip the chain loose. He stepped back as he opened the door, tightening his grip on the pistol. Tony was dressed in white boxer shorts, bare chested, his hair was rumpled, and he needed a shave.

The man stepped into the apartment and looked around, then at Tony. He thought, 'This is a kid? He's got muscles like I wish I had. This kid is dangerous.' "Why you ain't dressed . . . This time a'day?" he asked.

"I was sleeping," Tony said. "I was up late last night . . . Poker game. Who the hell are you anyway?"

"Your Don wants you to do a job for him," the

man said. "Are you gonna' do it?"

"I'm not a Made Man," Tony said. "You must know that if you came from Don Peter Salvano. If you didn't, and this is some kind of scam . . . You may never leave this place alive."

"Tony, it would be best if you put that gun you're holdin' down and hear what your Don has to say."

Tony moved hesitatingly to the couch and sat. He laid the .38 on the end table under the table's lamp where he could get it quickly if needed. "OK," he said. "Now talk to me."

"I'm gonna' ask you once more. You gonna' do what your Don asks?"

"Yeah . . . Sure . . . Of course."

The man looked around the room. It was a small room, simple, but nice and comfortable. 'A woman's hand here,' he thought. He found a glass ashtray on a corner table near a thatch woven chair. The ashtray was clean, like new, never been used, he thought. He sat in the wicker chair, noticing how uncomfortable it was as it squeaked under his weight, and lit a cigarette. Tony didn't object this time, although he seldom let people smoke near him. He needed to be sure of what was happening, and pissing this guy off wouldn't help him get to the truth. So he let him smoke.

He began, "There was a guy who got killed. Guy called Roger Tifton. Down in Trenton. Your Don wants to know who killed him and why."

"Why not ask the cops? They should know."

"Your Don wants you to do it. You shouldn't be askin' questions. Do I tell your Don you'll do what he asks or not?"

Tony hesitated, thinking of his options, but if this

man was really from Don Salvano he had no choice. He would agree and then find out what was going on. Let the man talk, find out what he could, and then ask questions. Be sure the man was who he said he was . . . Except Tony didn't know the man's name.

"Of course I'll do what the Don asks," he said, trying to sound sincere. "Who're you?"

The man ignored Tony's question and said, "You do this and report directly to Bruno Massetti. He will contact you. No one is to know what you're doin', unner'stand? You talk to no one. Got it?"

"Yeah," Tony said. "I got it." This guy knew the name Bruno Massetti. That was good. 'Maybe this wasn't some con game after all,' he thought.

The man stood, crushed out his cigarette, looked around the room once again and said, "Nice place. You keep it clean. How old are you kid?"

"Sixteen," Tony answered.

"You got yourself a reputation, kid. Good for you." With that the man walked out and Tony never saw him again.

When the front door closed, the door to the bedroom opened and Teresa walked out. She was dressed in her bra and panties, her hair still rumpled from having been in bed with Tony.

"What was that all about?" she asked.

Tony was still sitting on the couch with the pistol lying on the table next to him. "I'm not sure," he said.

"I listened," Teresa said. "I heard through the door. Something's wrong, Tony."

"Yeah, something isn't right."

Teresa sat next to him on the couch, close to him; she wrapped her arms around him and kissed him. "If you work for my father why does Mr. Salvano contact you without going through my Dad? It doesn't work like that, does it?"

"I don't think it's supposed to work like that. At least I've never heard of it working like that. I'm too new to all this. What do you think I should do?"

Teresa's voice was full of fear as she said, "I don't think you have a choice, do you? Do what they say and be quiet about it. Be careful. I'd hate to lose you now."

"What about your father?" he asked. "Are you going to tell him?"

"Are you crazy," she said and laughed. "How do I explain that one of Mr. Salvano's people came here when you and I were in bed together? Do you think he'd like that?"

Tony nodded and said, "Hey, look. I've got two more rubbers. Let's go back to bed for awhile."

****

Detective Lieutenant Max Sieberg of the NYPD had been on the Salvano Family payroll for five years. Tony considered contacting one of the cops in Newark or in Passaic or someplace closer to home, but that might not be a safe way to find out what he needed to find out. They would be too close to Al Falzone's crew and they might talk to one of them. He had been warned to keep this quiet, to not let anyone else know. 'Best to go out of town,' he thought.

Sieberg was at his desk, trying to find something he hadn't seen before in the thick file of a three year old murder case. His desk was crowded with papers and files and an overflowing ashtray filled with two days worth of cigarette butts. He leaned back in the hard wooden swivel chair and tried to think. The chair squeaked. His mind was on six o'clock when he could head for Sam's bar and his nightly pint bottle of cheap rye whiskey. The ringing of the phone brought him back to that Monday morning.

He picked up the phone and said, "Yeah, Detective Sieberg. Whatta'ya want?"

"My family wanted me to call."

Sieberg knew what the words meant. He was being asked to do something to earn the hundred dollars a week paid to him by the Salvano Family. It wasn't a lot of money but it was all his. His two ex-wives didn't know about it.

"Yeah, OK. What?" he said.

"I'd like to buy you a cup of coffee . . . And maybe a donut or two," Tony joked. 'Cops always eat too many donuts,' he had thought. "There's this little place down in Jersey on Route 4 near Teaneck. Place called The Rose Diner. Be there tomorrow at nine AM."

Before Sieberg could say anything, the line went dead. He slammed the phone down hard. Papers flew off his desk and fell to the floor. He didn't care, 'Let'm stay there,' he thought. He wanted to say 'screw you' to these guinea wops, but he would do as he was told. That hundred dollars a week kept him drunk every night.

The next morning, he arrived at The Rose Diner at half past eight. He wanted to be early to make sure it wasn't a set up. Maybe the Internal Affairs cops were on to him? Maybe not. But he had to be sure. He parked his unmarked car with the New York plates a block away and walked to the diner. He walked slowly, deliberately, looking and watching for anything out of the ordinary. Utility workers, someone changing a flat tire, guys in parked cars, anybody like that could be a cop waiting to throw cuffs on him.

The diner's parking lot had a few cars in it, all older models and none with guys sitting in them. The Highway was fairly busy; there were no cars or trucks parked on the shoulders for cops to sit in and watch. The diner had a dozen people, men and women, eating breakfast. None looked like cops, but you never know.

Inside he sat at the far end of the place, facing the door. He drank a cup of coffee and then another. Coffee would clear his head, he hoped. As with almost every night, he had gotten drunk the night before. His head hurt and he wished he had taken a handful of aspirin before leaving his one room flat that he jokingly called 'home'.

He sat by the front window and watched. A big white Cadillac pulled into the parking lot, circled slowly around to the back of the diner and then appeared back in front. It parked, and a man got out of the passenger side.

He was a young man, well dressed, good polished shoes, well groomed short hair. He was big, tall with broad shoulders. 'Tough guy,' Sieberg thought. His suit was too expensive to belong to a cop, and he was sure I.A. didn't own any big white Cadillac's. Maybe it was the feds? They had all the money.

The driver stayed in the car. That was strange, but better there then inside, where the two of them could throw cuffs on him and drag him away.

Tony stopped in the doorway and looked around. He had never seen Det. Sieberg but he recognized him immediately. His rumpled hair, cheap wrinkled suit, and stained shirt open at the collar told Tony who he was.

Sieberg stayed in the booth, facing the door,

watching Tony intently. Tony walked slowly to him and sat opposite him. He said, "Glad you could show up."

A waitress came to the table with her pad in hand. "What'll you have?" she asked.

Tony smiled up at her and said, "Nothing . . . But they'll be a big tip in it for you if you leave us alone."

She glared down at him and gruffly walked away.

"Who are you?" Sieberg asked.

"Just a messenger . . . From my family, ya' know? We got work for ya'." Tony, as usual, spoke at the level of the person he was speaking to. He found it put the person more at ease.

"How old are you?" Sieberg asked.

Tony ignored his question and said, "There was a murder down in Trenton. Guy named Roger Tifton. We wanna' know why and who did it."

"So go there and find out, kid. Ask the cops there. They'll probably open their file for you. You look up to it."

Tony stared deeply into Sieberg's brown eyes. They were bloodshot, and his lids drooped over them. His hair was greasy and unkempt. Cigarette ash had been spilled on his jacket's lapel. Dandruff was flaked on the coat's collar. Tony thought, 'This guy's a real bum.' He pulled his cash from his pocket, a rolled up wad of hundred dollar bills wrapped by a thick rubber band. He pulled two one hundred dollar bills away and laid them on the table. "Your fuckin' bonus, asshole. Now do what I tell ya' t'do."

Sieberg looked at the bills but didn't touch them. Here was a kid, a big, well dressed kid, but a kid all along, trying to buy favors. Was it a set up? Before he touched the money he had to be sure.

"You wired up kid?" he asked.

Tony leaned back and said, "Take a look out the window. See the car I arrived in? See the guy behind the wheel? If you touch me . . . That guy'll blow your fuckin' brains out. Now, I ain't no cop. You gonna' do what my family wants you t'do or not? You get paid every week to do what you're told, so do it."

Sieberg picked up the two bills. Tony took another two from his roll and laid them where the others had been. "That's to keep your fuckin' mouth shut. You do this quietly and don't tell nobody, unner'stand? You got one week. I'll be right here this time next week. You better be here, or you won't see the end of the day."

Tony slid out of the booth and walked out of the diner.

TWENTY-ONE

Montclair, New Jersey
November 1960

Al Falzone hadn't been home in three weeks, and Maria had become resigned to the fact that he might not be home that week either. He had a woman down there, she was sure of that. But the money kept coming in, and there was more of it then there had been. So, she brushed aside the fact that her husband was a cheating son of a bitch. At least he had moved up a little; his territory had expanded. His income . . . And of course her spending money . . . Had expanded.

In the back of her mind, unspoken, but she knew the thought was there, she didn't miss Al at all. When he was there, it was a different Al than she had married. Since taking over Trenton, he had changed. He wasn't a husband and father like he had been. On those days when he was home, it had been all family. He had been a good neighbor and Little League baseball coach.

On those few weekends he was home after moving to Trenton all he wanted to do was sit in front of the TV and finish a bottle of whiskey. Then, in bed, smelling of booze and unwashed body, he would push himself on top of her. She never said 'No'. It was an unlikeable task she had to put up with for the money Al brought to her. And she was getting tired of trying to talk him into moving up, starting his own family. 'To hell with Salvano,' she would say to herself as Al grunted on top of her. 'Why can't he just say that to Salvano and move up?'

It was Sunday morning, a cold and blustery day foretelling of a long, cold winter. There was snow on the ground from the day before. It had snowed hard; the cold had been bitter. The wind had blown like a summer storm. Yet, when Teresa came home past midnight from wherever she had been, she was not wet or cold. There was a glow on her teenager's face that Maria had been seeing lately. And she thought she knew what was bringing the color to her daughter's face. Teresa was happy, more so than usual.

She was in their big kitchen flipping the pancakes and turning the sausage. Once, months ago, Al would have made the breakfast when he been home. He always did on Sunday mornings. It had become a tradition that Maria missed, but the children didn't seem to care. It wasn't baseball season, so the neighborhood children hadn't missed him yet. Maria wondered if the children missed their father.

Church would be skipped that morning; it was just too damn cold outside. She had started missing Sunday Mass more and more often lately.

Al's wanderings were heavy on her mind. He would come home some day, she hoped, without some disease from one of his women. Too many of the wives of people in Al's line of work wound up with diseases from the philandering of their husbands. It was all part of the life, and it kept the doctors busy.

Her son, Little Al as everyone still called him to

his continuing dismay, sat at the table devouring the pancakes that he had lathered in syrup and butter. He ripped off big hunks of pancakes and fat sausage with his fork and stuffed his mouth with the sweet breakfast.

He was getting too fat, Maria thought. It was time to do something about that before it was too late. He was nine years old and the heaviest boy in his class. It was time to limit his food, but sweet things and pastas were the only things he seemed to eat a lot of. Vegetables were something he would never eat.

Little Al held his plate out for more pancakes. Maria said, "There aren't any ready yet. Go up and wake up your sister."

"But I'm still hungry," he complained.

"You've had enough. Now go upstairs like I said."

Little Al pushed his chair away from the table roughly, angrily. It hit the wall and left a mark there, on the newly painted kitchen. "Damn it, Little Al!" Maria yelled. He ran out of the kitchen.

Ten minutes later, Teresa came into the kitchen. Maria had finished the two hotcakes and one sausage she had cooked for herself. She was smoking a cigarette while she finished her coffee. Teresa stood in the doorway; she was dressed in flannel pajamas, her feet were bare, her hair rumpled, her eyes still full of sleep. Maria turned and looked at her daughter. She said, "You should put something on your feet. It's cold."

Teresa nodded but said nothing.

"You want something to eat, Teresa?"

"No . . . Thank you," she answered. "Maybe some coffee."

She sat at the table and leaned her elbows on the vinyl. Maria asked, "So you want me to get your coffee? What's this look like, a restaurant or something?"

Teresa got up in a huff and poured a cup of burnt coffee from the electric percolator near the sink. She returned to the table and sat as far from her mother as the table would allow. She sipped at the coffee and tried to waive her mother's cigarette smoke away. "Do you really have to smoke, Mama? It's really disgusting." Teresa thought of her time with Tony. He didn't smoke and wouldn't allow anyone near them, even Andy, to smoke.

She laughed at the thought. It seemed like everything reminded her of Tony anymore. Music on the radio reminded her of hearing it when she was with Tony. The sun setting reminded her of those late days with Tony. Rainfall reminded her of rainy days with Tony. The simple noise of a car passing on the road outside, and she would think of those hours in the back seat of the Cadillac with Tony holding her tightly.

Maria continued to smoke and drink her coffee. It was unusual for Maria to be so short with her daughter. Never before had she refused to get up and get Teresa anything Teresa wanted. She doted on Teresa, spoiling her with clothes and money. In an effort to please Teresa, she crushed out her cigarette in the saucer holding her coffee cup.

But that morning Teresa could feel something else in the air. Her mother seemed angry somehow. Maybe she was just concerned, maybe just upset that her husband, Teresa's father, was not at home once again. But something was wrong.

Maria let a few minutes go by, trying to ease the tension brought on by her angry words. She smiled and asked again, "Are you sure you don't want some pancakes, baby? I can do some if you want."

"No," Teresa said. "Thank you though. Maybe later after I wake up."

Maria drank some more coffee. She thought about lighting another cigarette, but that would annoy her daughter, she thought. Best to keep things friendly. She let another minute go by saying nothing and then she asked, "Teresa, do you have a boyfriend? Anybody who you're interested in?"

"Mama! What a question!" She paused and thought for a minute. Something was wrong. Her mother was acting strange. Does her mother know? Did somebody tell on her and Tony? A lot of kids at school knew, of course. Did one of them make a mistake and talk too much? She said, trying to change the conversation, "I go to a Catholic School with a bunch of jerks. Who could I be interested in? Aren't we going to Church this morning?"

"It's too cold," Maria said. She smiled and looked lovingly at her daughter. "You seem different, Teresa," she said. "You're growing up too fast. I want my little girl back."

"Well, Mama, I guess I have to grow up. I'm not a child anymore."

Maria picked up the pack of Pall Malls from the table. Teresa glared at her. Maria dropped the pack onto the table. Little Al walked into the kitchen and asked, "Can I have some more pancakes?"

Without looking at her son, Maria said, "No, you've had enough. Go upstairs and watch TV."

"Shit! Damn it!" Little Al yelled and stomped out of the room.

Maria longed for another cigarette but put the temptation behind her. There were things she had to find out. Teresa tried to stay awake over her coffee.

She had stayed later than usual at Tony's apartment the night before. It was almost one AM when she snuck into the house. She thought her mother would be asleep, but Maria had heard her. She had heard the car drive up, and she had heard the engine running for at least a minute or two before the car drove away and Teresa opened the front door. That night it was cold, and it was snowing. Tony insisted she not walk from the bus stop as she usually did. He and Andy took her right to her house.

Maria said nothing as she heard her daughter come home but spent the rest of the night tossing and turning, planning on what to say in the morning. She fiddled nervously with the pack of cigarettes and asked, "So who is he?"

"Who is who, Mama?"

"The boy you're sleeping with," she said flatly.

"Sleeping with! What the hell, Mama!" Teresa sat up and looked straight at her mother, looking as surprised as she could. Acting and lying had become one of her skills. She had to become good at it since falling in love with Tony. It had to remain a secret. But soon, she hoped, soon it could all be out in the open. Tony had promised that. He had promised that he had a plan and he was well on his way, he assured her. Soon, he told her; soon they could tell the world about their love. But right then, as she sat at the kitchen table with her mother, it had to be a secret. She was fully awake now and frightened.

Her mother said, "I can remember the first boy I had sex with. I can remember how I felt . . . And how I looked when I looked at myself in the mirror. You have that same look, Teresa. It's OK," she smiled and reached out to take Teresa's hand in hers. "Don't worry. I'm not mad. I just want to know if he's good for you or not."

"Mama! Please! I'm a virgin!" she lied with as straight a face as she could manage. "You want me to go to the doctor so he can tell you that?"

"Teresa," Maria said and tried to smile as a loving mother would. She gently squeezed her daughter's hand in hers. "It's OK, baby. You're not in trouble . . . Not with me anyway. Now your father . . . He might not feel the same way. You know how men are. They want their women to be vestal virgins their whole lives. But I'm not going to tell your father. Don't worry."

Teresa was scared. She couldn't tell her mother. What if she didn't approve of Tony and told her father? Certainly she wouldn't be allowed to see him again. And if the worse happened, Tony could be hurt.

She tried to change the subject. "Mother, Vestal Virgins weren't virgins. They were concubines for the Emperors and the rich men of Rome. They used sex to gain power. Do you really think I'm like that?"

"Honey, please. There's nothing wrong with having sex, so long as it's with the right man. All I want to know is who you're sleeping with. Let me meet him and his parents. We can do this out in the open if we handle it correctly. I'm sure you've made the right choice. I'm sure we will all be proud of him."

"You're embarrassing me, mother!"

Maria lit a cigarette and leaned back in the chair. She folded her arms in front of her and thought. It probably wasn't worth arguing with Teresa. It might only drive her away. Staying close, buying her things, that was the way to handle it. Keep her close and get her to trust her mother. That was the way. Be her friend, not just her mother. She blew the cigarette smoke towards the ceiling.

"I hope you're using protection, Teresa. I can

get you condoms if you don't have any already. And they have those new birth control pills now. I read about them the other day. You take one a day and you can't get pregnant. We can see your Doctor about getting those if you want."

"Mother! Please!" Teresa jumped up and ran from the room. She had to get to a phone quickly. She couldn't use the one phone that was in the house, her mother would hear. She had to get out and phone Tony. She ran up the stairs and into her room.

She showered and dressed as fast as she could. Downstairs she grabbed her coat and ran outside. She had a school friend, Mary Margaret Murphy, three doors away whose parents converted their basement into what they called a 'rumpus room', a finished basement with a bar and a TV, something new that a lot of parents were doing. It had a telephone down there that the girls often used to talk 'privately'.

Teresa ran through the wet snow to her friend's house. Mary Margaret had to be home. 'Please let her be home,' she said out loud as she slipped and slid down the street. She ran to the back door of Mary Margaret's home and knocked. She knocked three times and then realized that Mary Margaret had gone to Church with her family.

She was desperate and afraid. There had to be a way into Mary Margaret's house. She began checking windows trying to find one that wasn't locked. She was about to break a window when she found a small cellar window that had been left unlatched. Opening it, she slid down into the basement. She slipped across the linoleum covered floor in her wet boots to the bar where the phone was. She dialed Tony's number. He answered on the second ring.

"Tony," she whispered. "She knows. My mother knows."

"Knows what?" he asked. His voice was filled with sleep. He rubbed his eyes and tried to focus. She had wakened him from a sound sleep. "Is that you Teresa?"

"Yes! It's me! My mother knows about us!"

"Did she say my name?"

"Well, no . . . But she knows I'm having sex."

"Did you tell her you were?"

"No, of course not. I'm not crazy. What should we do?"

"Nothing," Tony said. "Just keep denying it. Look, you've got a Christmas dance at your school next month, right?"

"Yes, so what?"

"I'm going to take you to that dance. I'm going to pick you up at your house and take you to that dance. Your parents are going to be happy, and they're going to like me. They'll be happy that you and I are together."

Teresa felt like a weight had been taken from her shoulders. She felt a lightness fill her where panic had been. Joy took over from fear. Tony really loved her, she knew that now. He was willing to risk everything to be with her . . . Out in the open . . . No more secrets . . . No more lies. He would face her father with the truth and take the consequences. But how would he do that? What would he do? What would he say?

"Oh Tony," she said. "How are you going to do that? What about my father?"

"Let me worry about that," he said. "I've got it all figured out. Trust me, and let me get back to sleep now, OK?"

"I love you, Tony."

"I love you, babe. Now hang up, will you?"

TWENTY-TWO

The Rose Diner
November 1960

Tony and Andy Pecora arrived at The Rose Diner at eight o'clock the morning they were to meet Det. Sieberg. He was told to be there at nine. They wanted breakfast before dealing with the cop. Tony figured Det. Sieberg might spoil his appetite; he was that disgusting to be around.

They sat in the same booth at the far end of the diner where they had talked with Det. Sieberg a week before, Tony next to the window and Andy on the outside, in case he had to move fast and start shooting. They sat, watching the door, as Sieberg had done. Andy carried his .45, and he had given Tony a small 9MM pistol he kept in the glove box of the Cadillac. "Gotta' be ready," he said. "Just in case. I don't trust that guy." The .38 Police Special had found a permanent home in the drawer of the nightstand next to Tony's bed.

Andy had a tall stack of pancakes, sausage and scrambled eggs. Tony had eggs and hash browns, and two slices of wheat toast. Andy finished his meal and ordered more pancakes. "You're gonna be a fat son of a bitch someday, Andy." Tony said.

"Yeah, but I like it," he laughed.

Tony was laughing until he saw Det. Sieberg walk into the diner at precisely 9 AM. That changed his good mood. Sieberg was smoking the stub end of a bent cigar. He needed a shave, and he needed to run a comb through his hair. But he was there as Tony had told him. He stood at the table Tony and Andy were seated at. Along with the rest of his disheveled appearance, he smelled really bad.

"Who's this guy?" Sieberg asked pointing at Andy.

"He's the guy gonna' put a bullet in your friggin' head if you haven't done what I told you to do," Tony said, speaking at Sieberg's level. "Now sit down and tell me what you got."

Sieberg sat across the booth from Tony and Andy. He started to relight his cigar with a scratched and dinged up Zippo lighter, but Tony stopped him. "Don't smoke that dog shit in here," he said. "There are real human beings tryin' to eat here."

"Why can't you guys ever be nice? Why you always gotta' sound like sons'a bitches?"

"Shut up, and put out the damn cigar," Tony said.

The Detective crushed out the cigar on the table top and looked as nasty and mean as he could manage. It was all the offense he could muster at the time.

He smelled bad, of stale booze and cigarettes, because he had been up all night drinking once again. His eyes were cloudy, and the lids hung low over them. He coughed a couple of times and hacked to clear his throat. He wiped his nose clean with the sleeve of his wrinkled sports jacket. His shirt was filthy with spilled food and booze from the night before. The collar was hanging open, and what was probably supposed to be a tie hung tattered and torn around his neck.

Tony shook his head; he couldn't stand to be near this man but he had to. "OK," he said. "Tell me what you found out."

"Roger Tifton. Real Estate guy. Buys and sells apartments, houses, land, that kind of stuff. He has a rep as a real estate con artist. Rips people off on phony schemes. Been doing it for years. Starts development companies and gets people to pour money into them. They fail all the time, and the investors lose their money. The Feds been looking at him for a couple of years, but he has this bunch of really good lawyers and accountants. The books are always clean, and there's always excuses for every failure. The stuff he puts his own money into never fails. They had nothing on him when he got killed. Had his throat sliced . . . Nearly cut his damn head off. The Trenton City Cops don't know nothin' yet. They got the murder case. The FBI dropped their investigation of his fraud stuff and closed their case."

Andy laughed and said, "That don't surprise me. Cops don't know nothin' ever."

Tony laughed, But Det. Sieberg didn't. He didn't like being talked to the way these cheap Mafia hoods spoke to him. They had no respect for him. He had almost twenty years as an NYPD cop and detective. That counted for something, or it should have. They thought all they had to do was give him a hundred bucks a week, and he'd kiss their asses. He needed the money; two ex-wives had drained him clean. He would take money from anybody for anything, just to stay alive and drunk. They didn't understand how it was. 'One day,' he kept telling himself, 'one day they'd learn a lesson from him. Just wait.'

Tony asked, "So who killed him?"

"You ain't gonna' like this," Sieberg said.

"Tell me."

"Word on the street is this Tifton guy liked parties, women, and social crap. He liked to put a load of cocaine up his nose all the time. He met one of yours . . . A Capo . . . guy named Al Falzone at some party somewhere. Do you guys know him?"

Tony and Andy said nothing and the expressions on their faces didn't change.

"Anyway," Sieberg continued. "Tifton found out Falzone is screwing some Mexican bitch. A real looker, I understand, but dark skinned and a real whore. Tifton found out this Falzone guy was shacked up with her, leaving his wife someplace else. Word is Falzone killed this guy when Tifton told him he knew about the bitch. Tifton wanted money to keep his mouth shut. Apparently he was doing business with some other of you guys, and Falzone didn't want that guy to know about the bitch. I guess you guinea sons of bitches don't think much of inter-racial fuckin'. Anyway, that's what's on the street."

"That's it?" Tony asked. "Nothin' else?"

"That's all," Sieberg said. "Just rumors, but there ain't no evidence to be had. If there was, the Newark police would have found it."

"Who was Tifton doing business with?"

"Don't know," Sieberg said. He was eyeing Andy's hotcakes, but the sight of them started turning his booze filled stomach. "I'm told it was one of you guys, that's all."

"OK," Tony said. He peeled another hundred dollar bill from his roll and laid it on the table in front of Det. Sieberg. "That's for keeping your friggin mouth shut, unner'stand?"

Sieberg stood and grabbed the bill. He didn't try to hide his look of contempt. He wanted to spit in their faces, but he knew that would be stupid. Better to just turn and walk away. Tony whispered to Andy as Sieberg walked out of the diner, "Go after him. Take care of him. I don't trust him. He'll blab to somebody."

"How about you?" Andy asked.

"I'll take a cab home. Meet me there. We have work to do."

****

Andy pulled the Cadillac to the curb in front of Tony's apartment building. Tony had been watching for him. He came down the front porch stairs and slid into the car.

"Everything OK?" he asked Andy.

"Yeah, that guy ain't gonna talk to nobody."

"I need someone we can trust, Andy. Do you think The Aces can still be trusted?"

"Don't see why not," Andy said as he started the engine. "They still getting' their money, ain't they?"

Their thousand dollars a month had stopped some time ago, but Tony couldn't admit that. He had not been delivering it himself anyway. One of the young soldiers had been told to drive up to Passaic and give them the cash. Then a month went by and then another month. Soon no one was making the trip.

"Let's go there."

It had been a year since Tony and Andy had

been to The Aces' storefront clubhouse. The neighborhood hadn't changed much. A few stores that used to be there were closed and shuttered. A few new stores had appeared, most of them for the Latin community. Some of the old ladies of the neighborhood had died, and younger women were walking from store to store now, buying what they needed for dinner. A few new kids were in the streets and on the sidewalks. Black kids and Latino kids. The neighborhood was changing.

Andy slowed the car and pulled to the curb in front of The Aces' clubhouse. It was dark inside. They couldn't see anyone through the dirty windows. One window had a crack running from top to bottom. There was trash lying in the doorway.

"Maybe it's too early for 'em." Andy said. It was just half past eleven in the morning.

Tony said, "Yeah, you could be right. Let's go inside and wait for them."

The front door was unlocked. They stepped over the trash in the doorway and went in. Inside was dusty and dank. It had the smell of age and urine. Trash and dirt covered the floor. The jukebox was gone, and the poker table had been replaced with an old metal kitchen table with a torn linoleum top and one bent leg that set the table off level.

"What the hell?" Andy said. "What happened?"

Tony walked around the room slowly; it was like a dream. Memories of how he had moved into The Aces gang, fought with them, arranged a murder for them, and filled everyone's pockets with cash spun in his head. He had come a long way in so short a time. What could have happened?

The noisy hinges of the front door took Tony from his reverie. "What the hell you doin' here?" the boy said. He was a small boy, perhaps nine or ten years old. He was black, something that Tony and Andy had not seen in the neighborhood before.

"Who are you?" Tony asked.

"Who am I? Who the hell are you? This here's my place," the boy said in a swaggering voice.

"Your place? Where are The Aces?"

"The Aces? What the hell is The Aces?" he laughed.

Tony took a couple steps closer to the boy. He was dressed in dirty clothes, a striped T-shirt that was torn at one shoulder, and brown corduroy pants with holes torn at both knees. It was freezing cold outside, but this boy didn't have a coat.

"This is your place?" Tony asked. "Do you live here?"

"Nah, my Mom, she got a place. I just come here when I haft'a."

"There used to be a club here. Teenage kids. They wore these gold satin jackets."

The boy laughed and said, "You mean them white guinea fuckers. They gone man."

"Gone?" Tony looked at Andy who shrugged his shoulders. "Gone where?"

"Hell, I don't know. They just gone. I done heard one of'em got his ass killed and the others they just faded away."

One of The Aces was dead. But why? How? Did the other gangs decide to take over? What about Al Falzone's promise to keep the gangs from coming into their turf? What the boy had said struck both Tony and Andy hard. They had to find out what had happened.

Tony handed the boy a twenty dollar bill. The

boy's eyes lit up as he took the bill and held it lovingly, gently. 'Probably more money than the kid had ever seen,' he thought. He waived for Andy to follow him. In the car neither one of them spoke. Neither knew what to say. Finally Tony said, "Let's go to DeSonoto's."

DeSonoto's Pizza Parlor hadn't changed at all. Old man Adamo DeSonoto was still there, sitting on his tall stool, behind the counter, shouting orders to his two sons who were tossing rounds of pizza dough in the air and working the ovens. He hadn't changed much. He had always been old and wrinkled with thick grey hair. His leathery face was that of someone who had seen hard times. But he had always been a good man, kind to the neighborhood children and always willing to give away free pizza to hungry kids without money.

It was warm inside, as it always was. The wood burning ovens were kept fiery hot from early morning to late at night. The tables were the same. The old photos on the walls were the same. The wall paper was still peeling at the seams. The big round table where The Aces had once held court was still there. Andy opened the door for Tony. As he walked in, Adamo recognized him immediately, despite Tony's changed appearance.

"Tony Moretti! What the hell! How long's it been?"

"A long time, Adamo," he said. "How about one of those great pizzas? Everything on it, like always."

"Sure, Tony!" he said and called over his shoulder to his sons.

Tony and Andy sat at a table, not the big table they had once sat at. That would have felt strange, almost sacrilegious. Adamo joined them, bringing three cold bottles of Coca Cola with him. "So how you been, Tony? And you, Andy Pecora. You look like you been eatin' OK."

"Hey, I can't pass up any of that great pasta and cannelloni. How you been, Mr. DeSonoto?

"Ehhh, things change, ya'know? But business is still good. New people in the neighborhood, though. I sure wish you guys was still protectin' us. We got some tough punks movin' in. They want strange stuff on their pizza. You know . . . Pineapple an' peppers and stuff. An' sometimes they walk out without payin' nothin'."

Tony lowered his voice because he believed he knew the answer to his question, "What happened to The Aces?"

Adamo's face went sad. He looked down and his voice spoke in sorrow. "When you and Andy stopped comin' by, and when Richie moved away, things sort of fell apart. Poor Eddy, he got killed, ya' know."

"Eddy? Eddy's dead? How?" Tony was shocked. He had never thought about any of The Aces actually dying, especially Eddy. Without speaking it, he had assumed it was Joey Castellani who had died. Joey and his hot temper, Tony thought, probably pissed somebody off.

"Nobody knows why," Adamo said. "He got found one morning back at your old clubhouse . . . That store front, ya' know. He had hung himself, poor kid. Hung by the neck. Police say it was suicide. I guess it was. He was never a happy kid. I think all he had was The Aces."

"Shit, that's bad," Andy said. Andy had never liked Eddy Di Bona. Eddy's stuttering bothered Andy. That and Eddy was always too skinny and nervous for Andy. But he never wanted to see Eddy dead.

"Christ!" Tony said. "Because I wasn't around?"

"It wasn't your fault, Tony," Adamo said kindly. "Don't think like that. We was all proud of you for bein' successful and all that. It wasn't you. Eddy, he was just like that. Growing up was too hard for him. He had no place to go, ya'know? He couldn't move on."

"When?" Tony asked.

"Couple a'months ago. Poor kid. I always felt sorry for him."

"What about Joey and Jay and Norman? Where are they?"

"Jay got a job down at the YMCA. He's runnin' the gym down there. He seems OK with it. Got himself a girl, too. She's not too pretty, but she's real nice, an' they seem to like each other. He says they gonna get married."

"What about Norman?"

"He's in a bad way, Tony. He started drinkin' a lot. Works odd jobs when he can. He comes in here when he's real hungry. I take care of him."

"How about Joey?"

"I ain't seen him in . . . Must be almost a year. I guess he just ain't around no more."

"Where can I find Jay and Norman?"

Adamo reached for a paper napkin and scribbled an address on it. He handed it to Tony. "That's where Jay is. That's where he an' his girl live. I don't know where Norman sleeps. Maybe Jay'll know." He took the napkin back and wrote another address on it. "That's the YMCA where Jay works."

The pizza was brought out, but neither Tony nor Andy could eat it. It was all like a nightmare to both of them. Their friends, the guys they had been friends with, fought with, were brothers with, were all gone their separate ways. One was dead, one was in college out in California, one was a drunk, and one had just disappeared. It was all too terrible and unbelievable, and too hard to fathom. They stood, and Tony dropped a twenty dollar bill on the table.

"Good bye, Mr. DeSonoto," Tony said. It was the first time Tony had ever called Adamo 'Mister'. He looked around and remembered those days when he used to work there after school. And when he quit school in the eighth grade, Adamo had given him all the hours Tony could work.

'Poor kid,' Adamo used to think. 'Wonder what's gonna become of him?' Well, Adamo had seen Tony wearing his expensive suit and expensive shoes and riding in an expensive car, his hair groomed rather than slicked back and greasy. How was he getting his money? What kind of work was he doing? He had heard all the stories, of course. The Falzone crew . . . The Mafia . . . Organized crime. He thought as Tony and Andy walked out, 'Wonder if he would have been better off staying here?'

In the car Andy suggested, "It's probably too late to find Jay at home. How 'bout we go to the Y and see if he's there?"

At the YMCA, Tony and Andy ignored the man at the desk telling them they had to be members and yelling at them as they walked past him into the gymnasium. Jay was carrying a mop and bucket out of the shower room. He saw them immediately and dropped the bucket splashing dirty soapy water onto the floor.

"Jesus Christ!" he shouted. "Look who came back from the dead! Where you guys been?"

Jay hadn't lost any of his muscle, in fact he was

bigger and stronger looking then Tony remembered. Tony assumed working at the Y gave Jay time to use the weights and machines free of charge. He was dressed in kaki cotton pants that needed a washing and ironing, and a grey T-shirt that needed the same. He had an old pair of black and white hi-top tennis shoes on and no socks. He needed a shave. His hair had been cut very short in the new flat top style, a change from his curly, slicked back hair.

Andy took a step back, finding it hard to look at his friend. He felt like running. He and Jay had been closer than they had been with any of the others. But that was all over now. The Aces were dead and gone. Andy felt ashamed; he wasn't sure if he felt ashamed of Jay or himself. He had walked away from The Aces so that he could use a gun and have money. Maybe that was a mistake? Maybe if he had stayed? . . . But who could tell for sure?

Tony was able to hide his feelings. He smiled broadly and almost ran to shake Jay's hand. "Son of a bitch!" he laughed. "It's been awhile. How are you doing, Jay?"

"Hey, I'm OK, Tony. I got me a girl, and we got our own place to live. I'm doin' OK."

"Do you have time to talk? Can you take a break or something?"

"Sure," Jay said. "That old fart up front don't run the place. I do pretty much what I want around here. Come on back. There's a break room and some coffee. Andy!" he called out. "Come on! Don't be afraid!"

The break room was only slightly larger than a closet, but there was a table and four chairs, and there was a coffee pot with stale but hot coffee and a stack of paper cups. Jay poured three cups and set them down on the table. He drank his, but Tony and Andy didn't.   They had learned to like better coffee than that.

"So how's it going, Jay?" Tony asked.   "You like working here?"

"Nah," he said still smiling.   "But it's a job, and I'm savin' up some money.   Me and Nancy . . . That's my girl . . . We're gonna' open our own gym someday."

"But you like workin' a regular job?" Andy asked.

Jay laughed again and said, "When that thousand a month stopped comin' in . . . No hard feelings there, Tony . . . And there was only the three of us left, the old gangs and some new ones started movin' in.   It all kind'a fell apart, especially after Eddy hanged himself.   But you guys are lookin' great. Those suits you're wearing must'a cost a hell of a lot of money.   Doin' good, huh?"

"Why did Eddy kill himself?" Tony asked.

"I don't know.   I don't think nobody knows.   I think he just got tired of it all, ya' know?"

"How about Norman?" Tony asked.   "I'd like to see him.   Do you know where he is?"

"Ol' Norm?   He's in a bad way.   He been drinkin' a lot.   I think he had a hard time growin' up.   Him and me, we ain't teenagers no more, ya' know.   Them days is all gone now.   I'm not sure where he's livin' at. Sometimes he comes here, and I let him sleep it off in one of the rooms upstairs."

"Look, Jay," Tony said.   "I've got a little job I need done . . . Down in Trenton.   You could make a few bucks.   How about it?"

"Nah.   I mean, thanks for thinkin' of me, Tony. But I don't do that stuff no more.   Thanks anyway.   I got a future now . . . With Nancy I mean.   I don't wanna' screw that up."   He smiled uneasily, not sure if he had done the right thing. He didn't want to make Tony angry, and he certainly didn't want Andy losing his temper.

"That's OK, Jay. I understand. Can you use some money? You can pay me back whenever."

"Nah, that's OK. I'm alright . . . Money-wise anyway." He laughed at that. "But thanks."

"How about Joey? Have you seen him around anywhere?"

"Nah," Jay said and sipped at the coffee. "Joey ain't been around. He was real pissed off when The Aces broke up. You know Joey, always hot headed that kid. Don't know what he's doin' now. I ain't seen him in almost a year now."

Tony stood, and Andy followed him to his feet. Tony said, "If you see Norman, tell him I said 'hi'."

They each shook Jay's hand and left the Y. In the car as they drove away from Passaic, Andy said, "I guess we gotta' go to Trenton ourselves, huh?"

"Looks that way, Andy. I guess The Aces are done. I don't know who else we can get. There's nobody else I can trust."

"Why do you think they all just broke up? I mean, I heard what Jay said. But why do you think?"

"Things change Andy. People grow up. You can't stay a kid forever. The Aces were kid stuff, like it or not. Guys who grow out of their teen years can't stay in a kid's street gang. They change. They can take one of two forks in the road. You and me, we took one . . . They took another. I guess that's what happened."

They drove for fifteen minutes without speaking. Then Tony said, "We've got some work to do Andy. It's dangerous. It could mean we'll get killed. You can stay out of this one if you want."

"Nah, boss. I'm in for anything you want." Andy said. It was the first time Andy had ever called Tony 'boss' to his face. Tony liked that; it made him feel good and confident that Andy would have his back. It was said with respect; Andy meant it. He knew that Tony was moving up, and he wanted to go with him. He had no future without Tony, he knew that. He would wind up like Jay or Norman or worse yet, like Eddy Di Bona. No, from that day on Tony was Andy's boss. He reached over and patted Andy's shoulder.

"We have to figure out a way to handle this Roger Tifton mess. I think that slob cop was right. I think Al killed Tifton, and we have to prove it and go to Peter Salvano. If Al finds out, he'll come after us. We're going to have to spend some time thinking about this one. Do you mind sleeping on my couch for a few days?"

"Hey, boss, anything you want. But I gotta' go back to my Mom's house and get some clothes." Andy had never moved out of his mother's Passaic apartment. The drive between there and Newark where Tony's apartment was had become routine for him.

"Sure," Tony said. "Turn around and we'll stop there."

"Sure thing," Andy said. He spun the Cadillac around, grinned and looked at Tony. "You wanna' tell that little girl of yours you ain't gonna see her on Saturday?"

Tony smiled and said, "Nah, we're going to be done with this by Friday night I hope . . . Or we may not see Saturday. If we spend too much time on this, Al is sure to find out."

They stopped in front of Andy's mother's apartment house. It was very close to where Tony's parents lived. The same kind of old brick, four story building with garbage cans on the front walk and litter on the stairs leading up to the front door. Andy jumped from the car, and Tony waited, listening to The Silhouettes singing 'Get a job' on the radio. That's really funny, he thought.

Andy came down the stairs with a beat up old suitcase. He threw it in the back seat and got behind the wheel. He was angry at something.

"What's wrong?" Tony asked.

"Ahh, my old lady's always getting' on me."

"Why don't you move out? You've got enough cash. Get your own place."

"She cooks too good, and she cleans the place. Where am I gonna' get that in my own place?"

"Where do you take girls?" Tony asked laughing. "Does your mom cook breakfast for the girls you spend the night with?"

"You kiddin'? I go to some hotel or somethin'. She'd beat the crap outta' me if I was t'do somethin' like that."

Tony laughed, forgetting for the moment what he had to do in the next few days.

****

While Tony was pulling sheets and a blanket out of the closet for Andy, his telephone rang. "Tony, this is Bruno Massetti," he said, his voice gravelly and deep. "I been tryin' to get you for a couple days. Ain't you never home?"

Tony had never met nor spoken with Bruno before. His normal suspicion of everyone was not diminished. "Excuse me," he said. "But how do I know who you are?"

"You don't," Bruno said. "You're doin' a job for your Don, right?"

Tony didn't answer.

"You been talkin' to anyone about that job?" Bruno asked.

Again Tony remained silent.

"If you ain't been talkin' then how would I know about the job you got?"

"What job?" Tony asked.

"You're suppose t'find out who killed Roger Tifton."

Tony weighed what he knew. A man he didn't know told him Don Salvano wanted him to investigate a murder. Det. Sieberg was dead, so he couldn't talk. Only he and Andy knew about the job. If the man on the phone knew, then either he was Bruno Massetti or someone was setting Tony up for a fall. Maybe Al had learned something. If it was one of Al's men, he was in trouble. The stranger who gave him the job a week ago; who was he? There were too many things he didn't know.

He would go along with whatever was happening until he figured out who these people were. He had an idea of how he could use this mystery to his own benefit, regardless of who had set him on this task. Somewhere along the line, he would know, and he would take it Peter Salvano.

"OK," Tony said. "So you're Bruno Massetti. I know the name . . . But I've never met you. So tell me what you want."

"That's good, kid . . ."

Tony interrupted and said, "Please don't call me kid. I'm Mr. Moretti if you're a cop and Tony if you're Bruno Massetti."

"OK, Tony. That's good. So what you got for me?"

"I've got some questions I'm going to get answers to, nothing more."

"What questions?" Bruno asked.

"With all due respect, I'd rather keep that to myself. I don't like to spread rumors, and I don't like talking over the phone to someone I don't know. When I have answers I'll contact you. Like the guy at my door said. Until then I'll keep what I have to myself."

"You killed a cop," Bruno said. "Was that necessary?"

"I have no idea what you're talking about. And if I had killed anybody, would I be talking about it on the phone with a stranger?"

"That's good, kid . . . I mean Tony. Smart. When will I hear from you?"

"When and if I get answers," Tony said. "But I've got a question for you. Where does Chi Chi's crew hang out?"

"Chi Chi ain't around no more."

"I know that," Tony said with an exasperated sigh. "Don't tell me things I know already. Where can I find the crew Al Falzone is now running down in Trenton?"

"There's a second floor pool hall. On South Madison in Trenton. It's not a real good area of town. Be careful."

"Yeah, right. Gosh, I guess I will be careful . . . Whoever you are." Tony didn't hesitate to hang up the phone. He swallowed hard, hoping he was doing the right thing. He wanted to show some strength, show that he was a man and not some teenager trying to act like a man. He was a man in his own mind, and smarter than everyone he had met in the Salvano Family so far. All he needed was a chance, an opportunity that would move him up. 'This might be it,' he thought. 'This might be it.'

"Andy, I guess we're not going to stay here after all. Do you know how to get to Trenton?"

"Sure, boss. I got a map in the car. Why Trenton?"

"Because that's where the answers are going to be. If Al really did kill this Tifton guy, someone there is going to know. We need to know for certain before we take it upstairs. Suspicions and rumors aren't enough."

Tony packed a bag with the clothes he'd need, and he and Andy drove away from Newark. As they drove, Tony asked, "How many guns do you have with you, Andy?"

"I got my .45 . . . And a shotgun in the trunk. You got that 9MM?"

"Yes, it's in my suitcase."

"You think that's gonna' be enough, boss?"

"Andy, I don't want to go to war. I've got an idea how to handle this that might work out well for us. We could move up. Do you want to move up, Andy?"

"Boss, you been good to me so far. I got money an' clothes. Hell, I'd be back there in Passaic wanderin' the damn streets if it weren't for you. You wanna' move up . . . Then I wanna move up with ya'. That OK with you?"

"That's fine with me, Andy."

Tony wished there was some way for him to talk to Teresa, but that was not possible. Soon, if he did everything right, he would be able to see her and talk with her whenever he wanted to. He would be able to go to her home, have dinner with her and her family, and be normal like they should be. Their love would be out in the open, the secret left behind them forever.

It was Wednesday. He needed to be done with everything in time to see her on Saturday.

TWENTY-THREE

Trenton, New Jersey
November 1960

They found a Holiday Inn near the downtown area and got two rooms next to each other. They found a small restaurant away from the hotel to have dinner. Andy ate too much again; Tony had a hard time finishing his sandwich. It had no taste, and he didn't even know what was in it. He had too much on his mind, too many things to weigh, to be thinking of food. He was walking on that proverbial thin ice, and if he wasn't careful, he was going to fall through that ice and drown.

Back at the hotel, Andy checked and cleaned Tony's 9MM pistol. "Don't trust nobody down here," he told Tony. "Don't open the door to nobody, and don't go anywhere. I'm gonna' be right next door if you need me."

Tony had a hard time finding sleep that night. Visions of Teresa filled his mind. Half asleep and half awake, he dreamed of holding her close to him. He could almost feel her lips on his. Her hair was falling in soft waves across his chest, as she lay next to him.

He needed her so badly; he needed her with him all the time. The days between their Saturdays were like years, eternities. He had never imagined that he would feel that way. The way he felt, it had to be real, he told himself. Such longing to be with someone, to hold her in his arms, to make love to her, to feel her kissing him and caressing him, that had to be more than just a crush. It had to be real love.

In those waking hours, he tried as hard as he could to keep going over and over in his mind what he would do and say the next day with Al and his men. He and Andy would be outnumbered, of course. Al still owned the loyalty of his crew in Trenton. Up in Newark that might have been changed. Tony's ideas, having been put into action, were bringing in more money for the Newark crew. But in Trenton, he was a stranger.

Andy could handle being out gunned, but could Tony? He wasn't sure. He had to handle it correctly, and if he did, everything would be alright. If not . . . Well, he would be dead. The worse part of death to Tony was the loss of Teresa. Sleep finally was found before the sun came up. The phone at his bedside table was ringing. It was Andy.

****

Thursday Morning

"Hey, Tony," he said. "You gonna' sleep all day?"

"What time is it?"

"Past ten. You gonna get this done or not?"

"Yeah, I'll meet you downstairs in the restaurant."

"I had breakfast already," Andy said. "But you should have sump'tin. It's gonna be a tough day, ya' know?"

"OK. Give me fifteen minutes. I'll meet you in the lobby. Get me some coffee, will you?"

Andy had a large paper cup of hot coffee waiting for Tony. In the car, before they left the hotel lot, Tony said, "Al took Benny Rizo and Frankie De Luca with him when he took over Newark. Those are the guys we don't trust. They'll hold some loyalty to Al. Whoever is left from Chi Chi's crew might still be holding some resentment over his death and one of them being passed over as Capo. Don't let anyone know that we took Chi Chi out, no matter what happens. And watch Al in particular. He's old school, and he sees himself as superior to everyone. He might do anything. Like when he cut Mike Colombo's throat. He's unpredictable and maybe a little crazy."

"Yeah, boss. But a lot of people say the same thing about me."

"Just hold your temper and follow my lead."

"Hey! I ain't got no temper," Andy laughed at his joke.

"Yeah, right. Hold onto it anyway. If anything bad happens take out Benny and Frankie but leave Al alive. You got all that? Al has to live, or we don't have any evidence of who killed Tifton. If we do this right, we'll be OK."

"Yeah boss." They stopped at a Shell gas station and bought a street map of Trenton. They got lost once but eventually found South Madison Street and the second floor pool hall. The neighborhood was run down, dirty, with garbage lining the street's gutters. Overturned garbage cans had lain in the street and on the sidewalks for days, maybe even weeks. A mangy yellow dog was digging through one, looking for something to eat.

Most of the stores on the street were deserted, vacant, with broken windows and graffiti everywhere. There was no street traffic at all. Paper and trash blew down the lonely pavement. On the sidewalk, outside the pool hall, a drunk was asleep next to three garbage cans that were overflowing with rotten trash. "What a friggin' place," Andy said. "Can you believe it? Al's guys hang out here? There's gotta' be somethin' wrong here, boss."

Tony thought that this might be the set up he had feared. Maybe he had been lured to this place where he was to be killed? Maybe this wasn't where the Trenton crew spent their time? If they walked in, maybe there were guns waiting for them?

If Al had found out about Teresa and him, Al would be angry enough to have Tony killed. Tony was just a soldier, a throw away when a sacrifice was necessary. But Tony couldn't run either. If this job was really from his Don, he had to follow through on it. Time would tell, and if he was lucky . . . And careful . . . He would walk away alive. But that didn't stop him from being scared.

"You got that gun?" Andy asked.

"Yeah," Tony answered feeling for the weight of the small pistol that was tucked under his belt at his side. "I assume you have your own?"

Andy reached under his suit jacket and pulled out his Colt .45. He pulled the slide back and jacked a round into the chamber. "I got my knife, too. Should I get the shotgun from the trunk?"

"No, leave it. We shouldn't go in looking for trouble. Just be ready, OK?"

Tony waited, hesitated, his hand on the door latch of the Cadillac. He had to open the door and get out. It had to be done, he told himself. But pulling the handle and opening the door would mean there was no turning back.

"We gonna do this, boss?" Andy asked. He seemed anxious to get at it. Maybe he was hoping it was a trap.

Tony nodded, took a deep breath, opened the door, and got out of the Cadillac. The street was deserted, and a cold, bitter wind blew. Andy stepped up onto the sidewalk, holding his .45 at his side. Tony took the 9MM from his belt. Andy walked ahead of Tony to the door that would open onto the stairs up to what they had been told was the pool hall that the Trenton crew worked out of.

It was as cold inside as it was outside. The stairs were dark, and they squeaked loudly as the two walked up. At the top was a heavy wooden door. It was open a crack, and light shone through from inside. Andy used his foot to slowly open the door, as he leaned against the wall. Tony backed himself against the wall, standing behind Andy. From inside a man said, "Come on in, Tony. You don't need no guns here."

Inside it was dark and smelled of dampness and age. One light, hanging from the tall ceiling, was all the light there was in the big room. It hung over three men who were sitting at a long table that was surrounded by the pool tables that filled the room. Tony recognized Frankie De Luca. The other two he had never seen before. He assumed they were part of Chi Chi's former crew.

Andy looked at Tony who nodded. Andy holstered his .45. Tony handed his pistol to Andy and he put that in his jacket pocket. They stepped carefully into the room. Andy led the way, peering into the shadows and dark corners.

"Come on in!" Frankie said again. "Sit down. We got some coffee if you want some . . . And some donuts. You hungry?"

Tony walked to the men, as Andy waited with his back to the wall next to the door. Tony pulled a metal chair away from the table and sat. Andy took in the room, planning what he would do if shooting started. There was another door at the opposite end of the room. It was closed. That would be where it would come from, he thought. Tony was facing the door; the three others had their backs to it. That was good, he said to himself. 'I got clear shots at everybody and Tony can see what's comin'.'

"Is Al here?" Tony asked.

"No. I phoned him. He'll be here soon."

"You knew I was coming here?" Tony asked.

"Nah," Frankie said and laughed. "That big white Caddy of yours. We seen it comin' from a couple blocks away. It's like you're sendin' a friggin' telegram ahead of you. But it's a good lookin' car all the same."

"You saw it . . . From blocks away?"

"Yeah. We got lookouts up on roofs. This neighborhood is a tough place to be. We keep some guys up high to keep watch so's we know what's come'n our way."

"Why are you guys here?" Tony asked. "I mean, this neighborhood is shit. Can't you find some better place?"

"The cops been comin' down hard on us since Chi Chi got wiped out. This place gives us a chance to see 'em coming."

"Local or State cops?"

"State," Frankie said. "We still got most of the

locals on the books. But the State cops are hard to get to. They're workin' close to the FBI."

Tony nodded. "So who killed Chi Chi?" he asked, waiting to see if they knew he and Andy had killed him. "I mean, if you know, why not just give him to the cops and get them off your back?"

"If we knew, which we don't, we'd give it to the cops," Frankie said. "And if it was a friend of ours, we wouldn't turn him over to anybody but the Don."

Tony knew the meaning of 'a friend of ours'. It was code for anyone from the rank of 'associate' or a guy who liked to hang out around crews, and above. Tony and Andy were classified as 'a friend of ours'. Tony had been promoted to soldier; Andy would always be Tony's bodyguard but never more than an 'associate'.

Frankie hadn't looked accusingly at Andy when he told Tony they didn't know. That was good. It would have been a message that Tony was looking for. Frankie could lie, but Tony was watching his face and eyes. If Frankie was lying, Tony felt he would know it, or Frankie would be the best poker player in the world.

Tony looked at the two men sitting with Frankie. "Who are these two?" he asked.

"Oh, yeah," Frankie said. "You never met any of Chi Chi's crew did you? This here is Mickey Donzella. And this is Charlie Russo." He stared at Tony and said to the two sitting with him, "And this here is the famous Tony Moretti. Would you believe he's sixteen years old? And he's coming up fast . . . Real fast."

The door behind Tony was slammed open. Andy reached for his gun but stopped when Al Falzone stood in the doorway. "Well, well," he said. "If it ain't Tony Moretti! I haven't seen you in a long time. What brings you down here?"

Tony stood. Showing the proper respect was important. Al wasn't yet guilty of killing Tifton, of violating his oath to his Don. People would be looking for that, and Al would be expecting it. Without respect, Tony's appearance would mean trouble.

"I need to talk with you, Al. In private."

"About what?"

"In private," Tony repeated.

Al didn't like what he was hearing. Tony worked for him, not the other way around. He looked at the three men sitting at the table, unmoved so far. They were waiting to see how this played out. They had heard all about Tony Moretti and Andy Pecora. They wielded a lot of power and were held in respect by a lot of people. Maybe they were there to take over? If so, they had to be careful and keep their mouths shut. That way, no matter who wound up in charge, they would be OK.

Al looked first at Tony, this kid who was giving him orders, and then at Andy Pecora, standing at the door and smiling like a wise-ass son of a bitch.

"OK," Al said. "In the back room." He turned, and Tony followed Al to the door Andy had seen. Andy rushed forward to get in front of the two of them. He wanted to be the one to open the door and be the first inside for whatever was there.

Andy pushed his way between the two and got to the door first. Tony stepped aside, and Andy pushed the door open. It was dark inside, but enough light from the pool hall filtered in to let Andy see whatever was in there. He first looked inside and then stepped into the dark room. No one was there.

When Al and Tony were in the room, Andy pulled the door shut leaving them alone. Andy stood with his back against the closed door and smiled across the room and at the three men sitting there.

"So how's it hangin', fellas?" he said.

Inside the small room was pitch black. There were no windows to let light in. Al flipped a switch on the wall, and four lights sprung to life. The room held a poker table, a small refrigerator, a sink, an upholstered couch that had seen better days, and cabinets that ran along the back wall. A fan hung from the ceiling, but it was turned off in deference to the cold. Tony sat at the poker table and said, "Please sit, Al. I have a message from your Don."

"My Don?"

"Yes, *your* Don . . . And mine. I think we all do what he wants, right?"

Al waited for a moment, just to make it clear he didn't like to be ordered around by a kid, and then he sat.

"So what?" he asked. "And I don't like this," he added.

"As a matter of fact, I don't like it either. But when Don Salvano orders, we do what he says. Isn't that right? Isn't that what I've learned over the last year? Did I learn right or not?"

"Yeah, you learned," Al said snidely. "It looks like you maybe learned too good."

"I doubt that. I'm still your student, Al." Flattery seemed to always work with these men, Tony had learned. They had inflated opinions of themselves, and Tony played on that. "I watch you, and I learn from you. What better teacher could I possibly have, Al?"

"OK, what are you supposed to tell me? Quit screwin' around."

Tony shifted in the chair, sitting as upright as he

could, and said, "A man, Roger Tifton, was murdered. Don Salvano wants to know who killed him and why."

"How the fuck am I supposed to know?"

"I think you do know," Tony said. He crossed his legs, ran his fingers down the sharp crease in his pants, leaned back in the chair, and stared deeply into Al's eyes. There was nervousness in those dark eyes. They were jumping around; he couldn't hold his eyes on Tony's. And that telltale bead of sweat appeared; it told Tony that he had been told the truth. Det. Sieberg had been right in what he had found out.

"You fuckin' little kid," Al said. "I ought'a get the guys out there to cut your fuckin' heart out."

Tony laughed and lowered his eyes; he shook his head. He brushed some unseen flecks of dust from his pants leg and said, "You know Andy Pecora? Do you think he can kill those three guys before any of them can stand? And after he does that, he'll kill you, too. How would you like Andy to kill you? Would you prefer a bullet in your friggin' head . . . Or maybe something slower, more painful? All I have to do is tell him to do whatever he feels like doing. He'd thank me for letting him kill some more. He's a little crazy . . . But he's loyal to me."

Al said nothing because he knew it was true. He knew Andy's reputation, and he was afraid of Andy Pecora. Every sane person who knew Andy was afraid of him. Al would have to be stupid not to be afraid.

Tony said in a calm, low voice that carried a heavy threat with it, "So anyway, now that that's out of the way, tell me about Roger Tifton."

Al's forehead had broken out in a flood of sweat, dripping across his eyebrows into his eyes. He wiped his forehead with the back of his hand. Tony saw that, and he knew he had him. It was the next step in his plan for the future. He had known that sooner or later he would be able to do something important for Peter Salvano. Now was that time, and Peter would be grateful and would move Tony up.

Tony said, "OK, I'll tell you, if you don't want to tell me. You're shacked up down here with some whore. I mean, that's OK with me. I don't care. Everybody to their own thing, you know? But you think the guys up north wouldn't understand. A lot of the guys are old school, and they wouldn't understand you living with a dark skinned Mexican and not your good Italian wife. And you're afraid your wife wouldn't understand either. Divorce, especially a messy and loud divorce, isn't something the Family would appreciate. Too much publicity, and that can never be good.

"You met this Roger Tifton at a party. The guy's into real estate, parties, broads, and cocaine, and he makes a lot of money, too. So you thought you'd be his friend and maybe make some money, working along with him on some of the scams he runs. But Roger found about your Mexican bitch. And you found out that he and Peter Salvano were in business together."

That was just a guess on Tony's part. But why else was all this happening? Why did Peter Salvano want to find out who killed Tifton? Detective Sieberg said Tifton was working with 'one of you guys.' That had to be Peter Salvano. It could be no one else for Peter to be so involved. What would he care if anybody else were working with Tifton?

Tony continued, "Roger came to you and told you he was going to tell his friend, Peter Salvano, about the woman you're living with down here. That couldn't happen. He demanded money from you, and that couldn't happen either. You're Alberto Falzone; nobody blackmails Alberto Falzone. Roger had to be shut up. You couldn't let the people up north know, and you couldn't give up your whore or your money. So you told Mike Colombo to kill him, but Mike took a thousand bucks from the guy and let him live. He was stupid enough to try to frame me. You killed Roger, and then you killed Mike. All that for some cheap Mexican whore."

"She's not a whore," Al said. It was over, he knew that. Don Salvano would not let him live. Tony saw in Al's face that Al knew this, too. But what could he do? He had a gun . . . He could kill Tony but how would he get past Andy Pecora? He would never get out of the room once Tony was dead. No, it was all over. All he could do was call in favors and plead for some kind of forgiveness.

Tony stood and walked to the cabinets. He searched through them one by one until he found several bottles of liquor. He took a bottle of Irish whiskey and a glass from the sink. He poured a full glass and laid it on the table in front of Al. "Drink it, Al," he said. "It isn't as bad as you think."

Al took a long drink of the whiskey, almost emptying the glass. He coughed and choked, and then finished the glass. "Whatta'ya mean, it ain't bad?"

"I mean there's a way out of this. You're my boss, Al. I respect that. We can make a deal."

"What deal? Talk to me." A ray of hope appeared on Al's face. He tried to smile, tried to look like a buddy. It didn't quite work. Tony saw that. He had him, and he had what he was after.

Tony sat again, crossed his legs, cleared his throat just for the affect of doing it, and said, "I phone Brooklyn. I tell Bruno Massetti that Roger Tifton was the victim of a robbery. Some cheap street punks ganged up on him. I can make the police reports show that. They can say his wallet and watch were stolen. I'll get the local cops on our payroll to do that. Bruno tells the Don, and everything is OK."

"And what do you get?" Al asked. He anticipated giving Tony a lot of money, maybe regular payments. But what Tony told him surprised him. And it gave Al a greater depth of respect for . . . And fear of . . . The boy.

Tony said, "This January I'm going to be seventeen. That's two months away. That time will be used to separate my story from anyone thinking we made a deal. We don't want to be too anxious. When my birthday happens, I want you to tell Bruno that you need to spend more time down here in Trenton. Tell him that Chi Chi left a real mess, and it's going to take more time to clean it up. Tell him you suggest that I take over the Newark crew and business."

"You want to be a Capo?" Al asked, astonished at the audacity of this kid.

"I want to be a Capo," Tony answered simply.

"You have to be a Made Man to be a Capo, Tony. You ain't a Made Man."

"You put me up for that. Sponsor me." Tony paused, waiting, watching the expression on Al's red face. "That's the way it is Al. Take it or leave it."

Al weighed his options. He could laugh and say no, but that would send Tony off to Bruno Massetti with the truth, and that would end Al's life. He could lie to Bruno, but Bruno had sent Tony for a purpose. Tony must have some weight with Bruno and the Don. Tony was trusted. He was respected. If he took Tony's offer and then squealed on Tony, the truth about Tifton would have to come out, and he would die. Tony's offer was all there was.

"OK, I'll do it," he told Tony. He started to stand but Tony raised his hand and told him to stay seated.

"That's not all, Al," Tony said. "There's

something else, another part of the deal. You asked me to find out what your daughter was doing. You said she was up to something."

"Yeah, that's right," Al said, interested in something that might be good for him. "She's been hiding something. What's she doing?"

"I've been dating Teresa," Tony said. "Every Saturday we get together."

"WHAT! You! Teresa!" Al shouted. He stood quickly, kicking the chair away. "How the hell . . . How dare you, you son of a bitch!"

Andy, standing with his back to the door, heard all this and smiled.

"Calm down, Al. We're in love. We deeply love each other. She loves me, and I love her."

"You bastard!"

"Part of the deal is that we don't have to keep that secret anymore. I want to see her out in the open whenever I want. I want to date her like real life ordinary people. You know, go to the movies, and have dinner together and things like that. Maybe even come to your house now and then and have dinner with you and your family. There's a dance at her school next month. I'm going to pick her up at home and take her to that dance."

"You can't do that! I won't allow it!" Al stammered.

"Learn to live with it, Al. Remember what will happen if Don Salvano learns you killed his business partner." Tony paused and then said earnestly, "Look, I'm going to take care of her. No harm will ever come to her. She'll always be happy. I guarantee it, trust me. When she finishes college . . . Like you want . . . We're going to get married, and you're going to become a happy Grandfather. Won't that be great?

Her life will be the best. She will have everything. She will never be unhappy. Trust me."

"She knows who you are?" Al asked.

"She knows, and that's why we had to keep our little secret."

"Teresa loves you?" Al asked. He pulled the chair off the floor and sat down again. "She told you that?"

"Yes, she did."

"You been screwing her?" Al asked.

"Have you been screwing the Mexican? Have you let her suck your cock?"

"Sure I have! She's great," he bragged, throwing out his chest and laughing.

"You see Al," Tony said. "That's the difference between you and me. A gentleman doesn't talk about the woman in his life."

TWENTY-FOUR

Trenton, New Jersey
November 1960

Thursday Mid-Day

Al opened the door and walked out of the room ahead of Tony. Tony wasn't about to let Al get at his back. Al looked unhappy, a scowl on his face made that clear, as he left the back room. Tony, as he passed Andy, nodded and smiled, telling Andy it went well, and they were on their way up. Andy laughed and said out loud, "Yes! Holy shit, yes!"

Al heard this, stopped and turned. Andy was smiling broadly. Andy knew then that the choice he had made, to follow a kid four years younger than he, was the right choice. Everything now was possible, he thought. The money, the power, the easy life away from the slums and streets of Passaic, were all there for the taking now.

Al saw in Andy's face that he had no choice at all. He was finished. The best he could hope for was to remain alive. Both Peter Salvano and Andy Pecora would be there, watching him closely, for the rest of his life. He tried to figure out what mistake he had made. But Al was unable to see what he had done.

Living with his whore rather than his wife, killing Roger Tifton, seeing some importance in himself that didn't exist, all escaped him as reasons for the place he found himself in.

Tony walked to a telephone that was on a small table in a corner of the room. He called to Al, "I need Bruno Massetti's phone number, Al."

"You don't know that, kid? I thought you was somethin' special."

"Don't give me any of your crap, Al. What's Bruno's phone number?"

Frankie De Luca, Mickey Donzella, and Charlie Russo, sitting at the table still, all heard this and looked at each other. Something had changed. Never before had anyone ever dared speak to Al Falzone like that, especially some muscle bound kid who was little more than an associate, hanging out on the corner. And they saw Al shrink back at Tony's words. He spoke Bruno's phone number. Never again would Al demand the respect from his crew that had been due him.

Tony dialed the number, Bruno answered.

"Are you Bruno Massetti?" Tony asked.

"Yeah . . . is this you, Tony?"

Tony didn't answer. 'Best to keep names to myself' he thought.

"Did you send someone out to find out who killed Roger Tifton?"

"Yeah, that's smart kid. You should be careful who're you talkin' to."

"OK, the answer is that Tifton was hit by some punks who got him on the street. Probably two or three of them. They went after his wallet and wrist watch."

"You're sure about that, kid?"

"Don't call me kid."

"Ok, Tony. Sorry 'bout that. You sure about who killed Tifton?"

"I'm sure."

Bruno was silent for a moment or two, thinking, and then he said, "OK, I wanna' know who they are. Go find out."

"How the hell am I supposed to do that? I don't know anything about Trenton."

"You tell Al that I said he's supposed to help you. You want I should tell him that?"

Tony considered and then said, "No, I'll take care of that."

"That's good, kid . . . Sorry, I mean Tony. Find 'em quick. You ain't got much time."

Bruno hung up and Tony heard the line go dead. Now what? He had made the cover-up to protect Al Falzone but now he had to prove the lie. He looked at the three men sitting at the table, listening. He looked at them, he frowned, and said, "You three . . . Go make your collections . . . Get some lunch . . . I don't care what you do, just get the hell out of here."

Without looking for approval from Al, the three stood and quickly walked out, down the stairs, and away. Tony picked up the phone and dialed another number. It was to a police Captain in Newark who was on the Family's books. He told the Captain that he needed the police reports in Trenton to reflect that Tifton had his wallet and watch stolen. "I need that done immediately, and I don't care how you do it. Get it done today, and there's a thousand dollars in it for you. It's that important."

Tony walked to the table and waived at Andy to

sit with him. He said, "Al, sit down. We have some shit to bury. And you're going to help dig the hole."

Tony told them what Bruno had demanded. "So, we need to find some people to take the hit. We're going to need some people who are in the business of street assault and robbery. Al, you've been here long enough. Who can we use?"

"How the hell should I know?" Al said angrily. "You think I have friends like that?"

"Al, we have a choice here. I lied to Bruno Massetti, and that lie will go up to Peter Salvano. Understand that if they find out I lied, it will mean you and I both die. Not just me. You want to go on living? You're in this up to your damn neck. Now help me out here. I need a couple of people to hang this on."

Al lowered his head. He was thinking, but he was also trying to hold his temper. It was not an accident that his men were sent away and Andy Pecora was sitting next to him. 'Jesus! This kid is dangerous!' he thought. 'When is he gonna' make a mistake?' For the time being, until he had his opportunity, he would have to work with Tony.

He looked up and said, "There might be a couple of black guys. They deal in heroin, and they do other stuff. They've been busted more than once for assault."

"OK, how do I find them?"

"Hell, I don't know. I don't do business with them."

"How do you know about them, then?" Tony demanded. He could feel his temper rising, and he had to control it. Al was angry, that was obvious, and he should be. But Tony had a job to do that would, if he could do it, keep him alive and would mean he could look forward to a long life with Teresa at his side and in his arms. That was the only important thing to him. So he took a deep breath, calmed himself, and said, "Please Al. We need to work on this together. It's to both our benefits."

Al said nothing. If he didn't help Tony, maybe Tony would fail and be in trouble. But if he failed, would Peter Salvano find out that Al did kill Tifton?

Andy got tired of Al's hesitation. He leaned forward, his elbows on the table and said, "Look, Al. You either do what my boss wants, or you and me are gonna' go into that back room . . . Just the two of us."

Al heard Andy say 'my boss.' This kid was moving up faster than Al had ever seen anyone move up before. And he, like everyone else he knew, was afraid of Andy Pecora. He quickly said, "They hang out a couple of blocks from here. Night is the best time to find them all together. During the day, there's usually only one of them on the corner selling their dope."

Tony looked at Andy, and Andy nodded, knowing what he would have to do. "How many of them are there?" Andy asked.

"Three . . . Two of them are brothers; the other one is just a friend."

Tony leaned back in the chair and thought of what he had to do. Al pulled a cigarette from a pack he had in his shirt pocket. Tony looked at him and said, "Please don't smoke right now, Al. I've got some things to consider, and I don't need to breathe that shit."

Al put the cigarette back in the pack and looked really unhappy about it. They sat without speaking for a few minutes, while Tony thought and planned. He stood and started pacing around the room. It had to be done, of course, but how? It couldn't look too easy; Bruno would be suspicious if it were all too easy.

These things took time, and if this didn't take some time, it wouldn't work. If he were to hang Tifton's murder on these three men, Bruno would certainly tell him to kill them. 'Revenge is what these people are all about,' he told himself. If it were to be done, it had to be done cleanly, with nothing to show Tony was part of it. He really didn't care if Al hung for murder . . . Except how that would affect Teresa. It had to be done carefully, slowly.

But time was important. Saturday and Teresa were just a day away. His heart yearned for her. But then he realized that the days of secrecy were over. Al finally knew, and that meant the problem that had been the wall standing between their love of each other had been done away with. He had to make the finding of Tifton's killers look good.

That would take time, and time meant missing Saturday with Teresa. He would phone her. He could do that now; Al wasn't in the way. He would phone her and explain. 'Business,' he would tell her, and he would say he would see her . . . At her home . . . In a few days. That is what he would do. She would be happy, and that was the most important thing.

He returned to Al and Andy, he sat and said, "OK, we have to make this look good. That's going to take some time. Al, I want you to go home . . . Not to Montclair . . . To your place here. Stay there until I tell you that you can leave. Don't go out . . . Don't go anywhere. If you need food or cigarettes, anything, tell me, and someone will get it for you.

"Andy, we're going to stay here for a couple of days. I want you to pick up Al at his place tonight, after dark. Al is going to show you where these guys do business. Don't do anything tonight; just find out where you can find them when I say it's OK.

"Don't use the Cadillac . . . It's too easy to see it

coming. Use Al's car or steal one that won't stand out too much. I'm going to wait until Saturday and then phone Bruno and tell him I found the guys. Bruno will have to report to Peter Salvano and get instructions. Those instructions will mean taking out the three guys. Andy, check out the area and see what's the best way to do that."

He paused for a second and then grinned. "You remember Paco and his friends back in Passaic? Maybe that's the best way. Anyway, check it out. Now, nobody but the three of us can know anything about this. Al, if you blab this to anyone . . . I'm going to have Andy kill you and the person you talked to, understand? That includes the woman you're living with."

Al understood, only too well. The kid had taken over, and nothing yet would change that. Andy grinned like a kid offered candy. Al didn't.

Tony went to the phone again. He picked up the receiver and asked Al, "What's your home phone number?"

"Why?"

Tony sighed deeply and repeated, "What's your home phone number?"

Al gave it to him, and he started to dial before it occurred to him that Teresa would be in school at that time of day. He was just too anxious. He hung up without dialing and said out loud, "Later."

He told Al to go back to his apartment and reminded him to stay there. When he had left, Tony said, "I need something to eat, Andy. And I need to get some sleep. Let's head back to the hotel."

****

They found a clean enough looking diner to get some food, which Tony only half tasted. His mind was on Teresa. At the hotel he told Andy, "Look, I'm exhausted. I need some sleep. Tonight you go get Al and see what can be done. Wake me, if he's been lying to us. Otherwise make a plan, but don't do anything yet. I'll see you in the morning."

Tony looked at his watch in the room. It was three in the afternoon. He set the room's alarm to wake him at seven that evening when he would phone Teresa. He stripped off his clothes, took a quick shower and fell into bed, asleep almost immediately.

He dreamed of Teresa, holding her, touching her, enjoying the sweet smell of her. Then the dream turned into a nightmare. Someone, a dark monster of some kind, came between them, and Teresa ran away. He tried to kill the monster but he couldn't. It seemed the monster had to go on living no matter what Tony did. He called for help, but Andy wasn't there. Tony was alone in the blackness of the nightmare. Calling after Teresa, pleading for her to come back, did no good. She just kept running away.

Tony woke up in a sweat, out of breath. He sat up in bed and looked around trying to remember where he was. The bedside clock told him it was a quarter past six. He rubbed the sleep from his eyes and reached for the phone. Teresa would be home.

A boy's voice answered the phone. Tony said, "May I speak with Teresa, please."

"She's not home," the boy answered.

"Is this her brother?" Tony asked, trying to sound friendly.

"I'm not supposed to talk to strangers."

"I'm not exactly a stranger," Tony said. "Look, please tell Teresa Tony called, and I'll call back later,

OK?"

"I'm not supposed to talk to strangers," the boy repeated.

"OK, that's right of course. How about your mother? Let me speak to her, please."

"She's not home . . . But I'm not supposed to say that."

"Where is she?"

"Out," was Little Al's answer.

"So who is there with you?"

"Nobody . . . But I'm not supposed to say that, too."

Little Al hung up. Tony laughed and decided he would simply call back later. With all the things Teresa's mother bought her, they were probably out buying more things. He fell back on to the bed and was soon asleep again. When the alarm rang, he hit it to turn it off and wandered back into his dreams.

****

Friday Morning

The phone woke Tony. He grabbed for it and said, "Yes! Teresa?"

"No," Andy said. "It's only me."

"What time is it?"

"Past nine," Andy told him. "You been asleep a long time, boss. You OK or what?"

"Yeah, I'm OK. Come to my room. I'm going to

jump in the shower . . . I'll leave the door unlocked for you."

"I'll be right there, boss."

Andy was sitting in the room's only chair. He had turned on the TV and was switching through the few channels that the hotel provided. He turned it off when Tony walked out of the bathroom, with a towel wrapped around his waist.

Tony sat on the edge of the bed and asked, "So what did you find out?"

"It was like Al said it would be. The three of'em were on the street corner in the damn cold. They was selling shit to people walkin' by and drivin' by. Like it was nothin'. They took in a hell of a lot of cash, boss. Is that somethin' we maybe should get into?"

"No, I don't think so. Gambling is too easy to do and the cops love to win a little. They leave us alone so long as they can walk away a winner. I think we'll stick with that. How about taking these guys out?"

"Tough, boss. All the buildings nearby are full of people. Crappy places though. Real slums. I wouldn't wanna' live there. No place to set up, ya'know? But I got an idea." Andy was smiling and waited for Tony to ask what his idea was. Tony wanted to make Andy feel good; it wasn't often he came up with a good idea.

"That's great. What's your idea?"

"Me an' Al drive up to them like we was gonna' buy some shit from them. Al drives and I sit next to him. When they come to the car, I roll down the window and BAM! I get'em all."

"That's a good idea, Andy. Risky but a good idea."

"How's it risky, boss?"

"People could see you and identify you if the police pick you up. How about this? We have to make this look real. So we wait another day . . . To make it look like we're working on it. Then I phone Bruno and tell him we got the guys, that we took one of them and he confessed. You know, we say we beat it out of him. Bruno will check with Peter, and then he'll tell us to take them out. We put Chi Chi's guys on it, like you said. If we need to, we can take them out, too. You and me and Al will come out clean, and Peter Salvano will be happy."

"That's smart, boss. I like it. One question though. If we wait another day and then some more for Bruno to get an OK, you're gonna' to miss your Saturday with your girl."

"That's all taken care of, Andy. Al has given me his blessing to see Teresa. He's resigned himself to the fact that one day he's going to be my father-in-law."

"You're kidding, right?"

"No, that's all part of the deal to save his rotten ass."

TWENTY-FIVE

Montclair, New Jersey
November 1960

Friday Evening

Teresa had finally gotten detention from her Phys. Ed. Instructor, Mrs. Rogers. It didn't make any difference. It was Friday, not Saturday, and it gave her a chance to do her homework. She wouldn't have to worry about it on Sunday. From 3 PM to 6 PM, she would sit there under the watchful eye of Sister Mary Catherine. The Nun sat at the desk in the front of the room, silently mouthing the prayers as her fingers moved the rosary through its circle of faith.

Bobby Jean Trinsett sat behind Teresa. She bent forward and tapped Teresa on her shoulder. She whispered, "Hey Teresa. Does Tony have a brother? How about setting me up?"

Teresa looked at the Nun; she had her eyes down in fervent prayer. Teresa turned slightly and whispered, "Watch your mouth Bobby Jean."

Bobby Jean just laughed. Teresa thought that she might be able to get away with turning around and smacking Bobby Jean. But why risk another detention? Words can't hurt, she assured herself. And Saturday was almost there.

Teresa's mother, Maria, had gotten the telephone call from the school telling her about Teresa's detention.

"Why are you picking on Teresa? She's a good girl," she said to Sister Mary Thomas, the principal of St. Ignatius High School.

"She's a very good girl, Mrs. Falzone. Her grades are some of the best we have. But she's consistently late for her classes. She dreams a lot and doesn't pay attention."

"She's a teenage girl, Sister. Don't you remember? Weren't you ever a teenage girl?"

Sister Mary Thomas had no answer for that. Yes, she was a teenager once, but never a teenager like Teresa. The only thing she could say, without talking about the subject everyone was frightened of, was, "She'll be released from detention at 6 PM. You may come to get her then."

Maria dressed and did her makeup and hair. She would go to the school and get her daughter and the two of them would go out for a mother and daughter dinner. Someplace nice, Maria thought.

She stopped in Teresa's room and picked a new dress and shoes from her closet. 'Teresa can change in the girl's room at school,' she told herself.

At the door Little Al ran to her. "Mama! Mama! Where are you going?"

She had forgotten about Little Al. She took him to the kitchen and made a peanut butter and jelly sandwich for him. She poured a glass of milk and put it and the sandwich in the refrigerator.

"Don't go again, Mama! Don't go again! I'm

scared when you leave me all alone!"

"That's silly Little Al. Just keep the doors locked, and don't talk to anyone. I won't be long, and I'll tuck you in bed when I get back."

Ten minutes after Maria left, the phone rang. Little Al remembered his mother's warning not to talk to anyone. He stood by the phone and watched it as it rang. He counted the rings, six, seven, eight, nine, ten and then it stopped. He walked away to eat his sandwich.

Little Al was lying on the floor in front of the television. He had found a bag of potato chips and was eating them. The phone rang again but he didn't get up to go to it. 'Twelve rings this time' he said to himself, proud that he had kept count correctly.

It was nine o'clock, and Maria and Teresa weren't home yet. Little Al was scared. The house was dark. How was he going to get to his bedroom? He cried himself to sleep on the floor. He didn't hear the phone ringing the third time.

****

Trenton, New Jersey

Tony hung up the phone. No answer still. Maria must have taken Teresa and her brother out somewhere on Friday night. Andy knocked on the door. "Hey, boss. You awake?"

Tony went to the door and opened it. He waived Andy in. "What's up? You want to go get some dinner?"

"Nah, I ate already. I thought you'd be on the phone with your girl. You wanna' go get something?"

"Yeah, I guess I should. And why don't we drive by those three drug dealers. I want to see the layout for myself."

"Sure thing, boss."

In the car, Andy started for the slums and the three men they would sacrifice to save Al Falzone. Andy said, "I saw this here steak house when me an' Al was going out there. Wanna' stop there?"

"No, something lighter . . . Unless you want a steak."

"Nah, I had one already, back at the place at the hotel. By the way, I been thinkin'. Your girl, she's Al's kid, right? Is that why you're protecting him?"

"That's one of the reasons, Andy. I guess it is. I don't want to do anything that would hurt Teresa, you know? But Al's going to do other things for us. As I said, we're moving up. Al is going to sponsor us. There are big things ahead for us, Andy . . . If you want to stick with me, that is."

"Hell, boss. I guess you're stuck with me. I ain't goin' nowhere," he laughed.

They found a little Mom and Pop place where Tony had a ham and cheese sandwich and Andy had two cheeseburgers and fries. Andy found the street where the three men were huddled on their corner. Loud music was playing from speakers in an open window on the second floor of the building behind them. They drove past without slowing down, the big white Cadillac drawing a lot of attention.

Without taking the same street again, Andy drove throughout the neighborhood. The place was a mess; junk cars and over turned trash cans were everywhere. Hookers, shivering in the cold night air, walked the streets and called to them as they passed. The white Cadillac was mistaken for some pimp's car.

Few street lights were on, and the dark was frightening.

Tony said, "Even the worst parts of Passaic aren't this bad."

They drove out of the neighborhood and past Al Falzone's apartment. "That's it, boss. Second floor front. The lights are on, so he must be there."

"Where's his car?"

"There's a lot out back."

Andy drove into the lot, and there was Al's Buick.

"Let's go back to that pig sty Al's guys hang out at. I want to see if anybody's there and what they're talking about."

When they got there, they found the street door closed but unlocked. They walked up the dark stairs and found the heavy door to the pool room closed but unlocked, too. They walked into the dank room the crew worked out of. It was dark inside, and no one was there.

"Damn," Andy said. "They leave the friggin' doors open? I can't believe it."

"There are changes coming, Andy. I want to see what's in the back room."

They searched through all the cabinets and looked for anything that might be concealed. In one of the bottom cabinets, Andy found a false floor and inside, a cloth bound book. It was a list of everyone who had been loaned money, the vig they paid, and a history of payments to politicians and police.

"Christ, boss! Is Al crazy? If I can find this the cops can."

Tony took the book with him and replaced the

false cabinet bottom. "Don't tell Al about this," he said.

It was midnight by the time they got back to the Holiday Inn. It was too late to phone Teresa. He would try in the morning. He was missing her already but there was nothing could be done about that. He had to be patient; Teresa would understand, and she would be happy that they didn't have to keep their secret anymore.

He smiled at the thought. It would be nice to be able to go up to her front door and walk inside her house. He had called it her 'house' because his apartment had become their 'home'. And he smiled at the thought that it was just their first home. What would she want after they were married? Surely something with a big yard for the kids.

'Kids! My God,' he thought. What kind of father would he be? Certainly, he was sure, a better father than he had. And then he remembered that he had never played baseball or football or anything. How was he going to teach his sons those things? He had a couple of years; he had to learn.

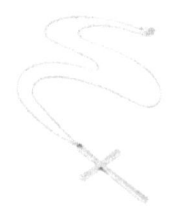

TWENTY-SIX

Montclair, New Jersey
November 1960

Saturday Morning

The alarm clock went off at 6 AM. Teresa jumped and hit it quickly so that it wouldn't wake her mother. She showered, dressed and quickly did her make-up and hair. She dressed warm and took her new winter parka with the thick fur hood. It was bitterly cold outside with fresh snow on the ground. She waited until she was at the front door before putting on her fur lined boots so as to make as little noise as possible when leaving the house.

She ran down the street, slipping once and falling on the slick snowy sidewalk. It was still dark; the sun wouldn't be up for at least another half an hour.

She reached the bus stop just as her bus was arriving. The driver waited for her with the door open. She ran up the steps and dropped her twenty cents into the coin slot.

"Mornin' Miss," the driver said. "Must be Saturday."

"Thanks for waiting for me," Teresa said, smiling sweetly.

"It wouldn't be Saturday without seeing you, Miss."

The bus took Teresa into Passaic and to the stop where she got off every Saturday. Andy would be there, and they would be off to Newark. But Andy wasn't there that morning. She looked up and down the street, and then looked again. She was in the right place. It was Saturday. Where was Andy?

The sun was just breaking through the clouds, but it didn't help to cut the cold of the morning. She needed to decide if she should wait or go home. No, going home wasn't the thing to do. She had to see Tony. She was burning for him, and she had to be with him. But what was wrong? Something was wrong.

'My God!' she thought. 'Did my dad find out?' But the thought was too terrible to think. She paced up and down the block, back and forth, pulling the thick fur hood of the parka around her face to fight off the biting wind. A police car pulled to the curb and stopped. The passenger side window was rolled down, and the cop said, "What are you doing out here?"

At first she thought about giving the cop some kind of wise answer, but that would just make him mad. If she was sarcastic with him he might not believe who she was. So she tried to be sincere and truthful. She said, "I'm waiting for someone. He's late."

"Who are you waiting for?"

OK, she had to continue with the truth. She said, "Andy Pecora."

The two police officers inside the car looked at

each other. The officer at the open window asked, "Do you know who Andy Pecora is?"

"Yes, he's a good friend of mine. Why?"

The driver leaned towards the open window and asked, "You a hooker? You look awful young to be walkin' the streets."

"I am NOT a hooker! My name is Teresa Falzone. Do you know the name?"

The car's window was rolled up and they drove away. DeSonoto's Pizza was four blocks away . . . But it was too early for them to be open. She started walking, she wasn't sure where.

All kinds of horrible thoughts were spinning around in her head. Tony was dead . . . No! That couldn't be. Maybe her father just hurt him, put him in the hospital. But would Andy let that happen? Was Andy dead? She turned a corner, and there was a taxi cab. The driver was inside, drinking a paper cup of coffee; the engine was running to keep the heater working, sending clouds of exhaust into the cold morning air. She ran to it, opened the back door, jumped in and said, "Take me to Newark." She pushed the parka's hood back, off her head.

"You kiddin' lady? That's a long way."

"I don't care. Take me to Newark and make it fast."

"You got the money, honey?" he said leering at her in the mirror, maybe hoping for something besides a cash fare.

Teresa opened her purse and pulled three twenty dollar bills out. She threw them at the driver and yelled, "Get going!"

****

The taxi stopped in front of Tony's apartment building. Teresa looked out the window. There were no lights on. It was past 9 AM. The white Cadillac was not there.

She told the driver, "I've got your name and tag number. I'm going to go up to the door and see if anyone is home. If you leave me here I will do more than report you to the cab company. My name is Teresa Falzone. My father is Alberto Falzone. Tony Moretti lives here. Do you understand?"

"Yeah . . . Sure . . . I ain't goin' nowhere."

Teresa ran up the front steps and rang the bell for Tony's apartment. She rang it again and then a third time. She was fighting back the tears. Something terrible must have happened. Was he lying dead on the floor?

She ran back to the taxi and said, "Montclair . . . And make it fast."

****

Trenton, New Jersey

Tony woke up at half past seven. He splashed some water on his face in the bathroom and went to the phone. He dialed Teresa's number. Maria answered.

"May I speak with Teresa, please?" he said.

"I'm sorry, she's not here. May I take a message?"

"Oh shit!" he said. He'd phoned after she left and Andy would not be there waiting for her. "I'm sorry Mrs. Falzone. Is she on her way to Passaic?"

"Passaic? Why in heaven's name would she go to Passaic?"

"To meet me, Mrs. Falzone."

"And who are you may I ask?"

"I'm Tony Moretti," he said.

"Oh my God! *You're* Teresa's boyfriend? Oh my God! I didn't know!"

"Do you have a problem with that, Mrs. Falzone?"

"Do I have a problem? No! I'm so happy I don't know what to say. Tony Moretti! This isn't a joke, is it?"

"It's no joke, Mrs. Falzone. You might as well know. I'm deeply in love with your daughter."

"Oh my God! I'm so happy, I feel like crying!"

"Look, she's on her way to see me. I'm working . . . Out of town." There was no sense in telling her he was with her husband. "She's going to be upset because I wasn't there."

"Where is she? I'll go get her."

"No. It's best that you wait for her. She'll come home, and she'll be very upset. Tell her I'll be home soon."

"Yes . . . Certainly . . . I'll take care of her. Is there anything else I can do?"

"No, just tell her I'll be there as soon as I can."

****

Montclair, New Jersey

The taxi pulled to the curb in front of the Falzone home. Teresa jumped out and ran to the front door without giving the driver any more money. He didn't ask for any more; he drove away as fast as he could.

She threw open the door and ran into her mother's arms. She was crying hysterically. Maria held her and whispered over and over again, "It's OK baby. It's OK, baby."

"Oh Mama," she cried. "Something terrible has happened to him!"

"No, baby," Maria said, holding her tightly to comfort her. "He phoned, baby. He's OK."

Teresa backed away from her mother. She wiped her eyes with the back of her hand and looked at her mother who was smiling happily. Her face was bright with joy. "Who phoned?" she asked.

"Tony," Maria said. She did nothing to hold back the happiness she felt. She felt like dancing and celebrating. She reached out and put her hands on her daughter's shoulders. Teresa was shaking, stunned, almost ready to faint.

"Tony phoned here? Tony phoned? You know? Are you mad?"

"Mad? Oh baby, it's the most wonderful thing. He said he loves you. I'm so happy. Do you love him, baby?"

Teresa wiped the last of her tears away and she fought to smile. "Oh, Mama. I love him so much. I'm so happy. I never thought I could be this happy. What did he say, Mama?"

"He said he's working out of town. He said he'd be back soon. He said to take good care of you."

"And you're not mad?"

Maria took Teresa's parka, threw it on the couch,

and walked her daughter into the kitchen. She sat Teresa at the table and said, "I'm going to make some tea, and then we can talk."

Teresa sat, using a paper napkin to wipe her face clear of tears. She watched her mother make a pot of tea. Maria thought of herself as an expert at making tea. When she and Al were on their honeymoon trip, they had gone to London. Maria was fascinated with the British penchant for tea. The British were so refined, she thought, that tea must be for refined people. She had been making tea ever since.

Maria filled a kettle with water and placed it on the stove, waiting for it to boil. When steam started from it, she took the kettle and poured a little into a fine china tea pot. She waited and then poured that water down the drain. Into the tea pot went three spoons of black tea leaves and more hot water was added.

Teresa was thinking as she watched. It would be so wonderful now. They could be together all the time now. Then another thought occurred to her. "But he would have phoned to tell me he was going out of town," Teresa said.

"How, baby? It was all a secret until now. No one was supposed to know, right? He broke the secret because he was worried about you."

Teresa thought about that. It sounded true . . . But he had phoned . . . On Saturday. Why not before? If he was going to break the secret why wait until Saturday? Teresa got up and walked to the stairs going to Little Al's room. "Alley," she called from the bottom of the stairs. "Alley, please come down, honey," she called to him.

Little Al came down the stairs, worried that he might be in trouble once again. He stopped a couple of stairs from the bottom, what he thought was a safe distance from Teresa.

"What?" he asked. "I didn't do nothin'."

Teresa reached out and swept him up in her arms, laughing and hugging her brother. She carried him into the kitchen. He was fat, heavy, almost too heavy to carry, but this was too important to think about that. She had to know why Tony had waited until Saturday to phone.

"I didn't do nothin'," Little Al said again, worried that he was in trouble.

"You didn't do *anything* Alley."

"That's what I said."

Teresa laughed and sat her brother in a chair. "Alley," she said. "This is important. In the last couple of days, when Mama and I weren't home, did anyone phone here?"

Little Al looked quickly to his mother. Her back was to him, as she prepared the tea. He looked at his sister. She knelt in front of him but she was smiling. He thought he had to be careful. Don't admit to anything. Lie, of course, but deny everything.

"I'm not supposed to talk to strangers," he said.

"That's right, Alley. But did anyone phone here when I wasn't home?"

Tears started to fill the boy's eyes. He started to cry and said, "You left me alone again, Sister. Why did you leave me alone again?"

"I'm very sorry, Alley," she said. "But did anyone phone here?"

"Am I in trouble again?"

"You're not in trouble at all, Alley. I guess someone did phone, right?"

He nodded and wiped his nose on his sleeve.

"Who phoned, Alley?"

"I don't know . . . I don't remember . . . Some man . . . He wanted to talk to you."

"That's fine, Alley. Thank you. How many times did he phone?"

"I don't know . . . Maybe a couple."

"Thank you, Alley," Teresa said. She leaned towards him, kissed his cheek and rumpled his hair lovingly. "Now go back upstairs."

He ran away and up the stairs to hide in the safety he knew, under his bed in his dark bedroom.

Maria finished the tea and brought the pot and the two china cups on a silver tray to the table.

"What about Papa, Mama?" Teresa asked. "What will he say?"

"I'll take care of that, baby."

"Why are you so happy about this, Mama? I didn't think you would be. You're not mad that I lied to you?"

Maria poured two cups of tea with milk, as she had seen in England. A small silver tea strainer was pulled from a drawer and hot tea was strained into the two delicate china cups. She sat and sipped at the tea and said, "Teresa. Of course I wish you would have come to me and told me. But I understand why," she said and took her daughter's hand in hers. "I know all about the business your father is in. It's the same business Tony is in. I know all about it. Your father has reached as high as he's ever going to go . . . In the business. I think Tony will go further. That's what I always wanted for myself, and that's what I want for you. Do you know what a Capo is?" she asked.

"Yes, Mama. I'm not stupid.   I know what Daddy does."

"There are people who give orders to Capos. They are strong men, powerful men, men who are feared and respected by everyone. They are Dons and Capo di tutti Capi. Capos give some of their income to these men and take orders from them. Peter Salvano is your father's Don. The money Peter gets is in the millions. Peter pays some of that up to one or more of the Five New York Families. I will never see that money and power. I will never be a part of that. I think Tony can give that to you. I think Tony will one day be a Capo di tutti Capi or perhaps even a Don. I want you to have what I will never have."

****

Trenton, New Jersey
Saturday Afternoon

Tony had told Andy he would phone Bruno that night. He couldn't wait any longer to get back up north and see Teresa. Andy agreed, "I think we waited long enough. If he thinks we found'em fast, maybe he'll think we're pretty good."

They found a place that said they were selling pizza, but it wasn't what they were used to, certainly not as good as DeSonoto's. The crust was thick and pasty, the sauce was bland, and the cheese had little taste to it. And the woman taking their order couldn't understand why they didn't want three or four different things added to it. "Maybe there ain't no Italians down here, boss," Andy said.

Back at the hotel Tony went to his room and phoned Teresa. She had been sitting by the phone, waiting for him to call. Her legs were tucked under her, as she nervously filed her nails and worried. She grabbed the phone before the first ring had ended.

"Oh, Tony! I was so scared. I didn't know what to do. Are you OK?"

"I'm fine, honey. I'm OK. I just had to go out of town for awhile . . . On business."

"When will you be back?" she asked.

"Soon. Maybe a day or two. I'll come right to your house, OK?"

"My Mama is really happy about us, Tony. Isn't that great?"

"Well, I have a surprise for you. I told your father, too."

"Oh my God! What did he say?"

Tony laughed and said, "Well, he's not exactly overjoyed, but he knows, and he's accepting the fact that I love you. I think he was hoping you'd marry a doctor or something. I think maybe he's looking forward to being a grandfather though." They both laughed at that.

"Well, I'm going to marry you, and he's going to walk me down the aisle. He's going to have to wait for that to be a grandfather."

They were quiet for a moment. Tony said softly, seriously, "I miss you, Teresa. I want to be with you right now."

"Oh, Tony. I miss you so much. Can we be together all the time now?"

"Well, not all the time. That will come when you've finished college. But we can see each other out in the open now." He debated whether or not he should tell her about his dream. The nightmare of the dark monster coming between them, and her running away from it. No, that wouldn't be a good idea, he thought. It was just a stupid dream after all, not something that anybody would believe in.

They talked for nearly an hour, as if they hadn't seen each other in years. It had been only a week ago that they lay together in their bed. On the phone they talked about their future together, being married, where they would live, what they would name their children. They laughed and then they were serious and quiet, and then they laughed again. They were happy. Their talk was interrupted when Andy knocked on the door and walked into Tony's room.

"Sorry, boss," he said. "But maybe we should get busy . . . Before it gets too late, huh?"

Teresa heard and said, "You have to go?"

"I guess I do. I have to get this work done if I'm ever going to get back to you."

"Where are you?" she asked.

"I'm sorry. It's better you don't know."

"Be careful, Tony. I don't want to lose you."

"You're not going to lose me, honey. I'm afraid you'll have to put up with me forever."

****

Saturday Evening

Andy sat in the room's chair as Tony, sitting on the edge of the bed, took a deep breath and dialed Bruno Massetti's number. Bruno answered on the fourth ring.

"Bruno, this is Tony."

"Good, what did ya' find out?"

"There's three drug pushers down here . . . Black guys. They have a history of assault . . . Robbing guys. They hit Tifton. They took his wallet and wrist watch. They killed him."

"You sure 'bout that?" Bruno asked. There was suspicion in his voice. Did he know? How could he know?

"Sure I'm sure, Bruno. Andy and I collared one and made him talk. He confessed."

"They took his wallet and watch?"

"Like I said," Tony answered, trying to keep the fear from his voice. "I got some cops who can tell you that. If you want, I'll get copies of the police reports and get them to you."

Bruno was silent. Tony made an effort to keep his breathing normal. "Bruno?" he said. "You still there?"

"Yeah, I'm here."

"So what do you want done with them?"

Bruno was quiet again and then he said, "Give me your phone number. I'll get back to you."

"When? I want to get back home," Tony said, giving Bruno the hotel's phone number and his room number.

"Don't be so anxious, kid . . . I mean Tony. You're doing your Don's business. Why you gotta' get back there so quick?"

Tony had to think about that one. He couldn't tell Bruno the truth, that he needed Teresa. He said, "I've got collections . . . I've got work back there."

"Don't worry 'bout your damn collections. This is more important. Just wait there."

Bruno hung up and Tony, looking dejected, told Andy, "I guess we're here for awhile longer."

****

Monday Evening

Saturday went by, then Sunday. Tony phoned Teresa a couple of times each day from Andy's room. He had to keep the line open in his room should Bruno phone. Teresa tried to understand, but she kept asking when he would be back anyway. Monday evening the phone rang. It was Bruno.

Tony answered, and Bruno said, "Take'em out . . . To the ball game." He hung up. Tony knew what that meant. He went to Andy's room. He was in bed with a prostitute.

"Oh, sorry Andy. I'll come back."

"No, it's OK." He got out of bed and started to dress. The woman stayed in bed and pulled the sheets up to her neck. Andy looked at her and said, "OK. You can go now. Your fifty bucks is on the dresser over there."

She got out of bed, standing naked, and asked, "Can I take a shower?"

Andy didn't stop pulling his clothes on. He said, "No. Get out."

She threw her clothes on, grabbed the money, and left. When she had gone and Tony and Andy were alone in the room, Tony said, "We just got the OK. Let's go get Al. I want to get this over with as fast as we can."

"You bet, boss. We gotta' get a couple of Chi Chi's guys, too. You want it done tonight?"

"Yes, tonight."

They drove to Al's apartment. Inside, his whore was lounging on the couch. She was maybe pretty, sexy, but she wasn't beautiful. She was very dark skinned and her eyes were as black as the night. Her hair was a tangled mass sitting high on top of her head. She wore a red silk Asian robe, tied at her waist but open enough to reveal big breasts and skinny legs. 'Oh well,' Tony thought. 'If that's what he likes.'

Al walked out of the bathroom. He was dressed in white boxer underwear and nothing else. His stomach stuck out in a paunch, and the hair on his chest ran down across his ballooned stomach. He was unshaven, and he smelled bad.

"Hey," he said. "You should'a phoned first, ya'know?"

"Get rid of her," Tony said. "We've got work to do."

Al flicked his thumb over his shoulder and the woman got off the couch. She sort of swayed, trying to be seductive, as she slowly walked out of the room, one hand on her hip as she smiled a big toothy smile. When she was gone, Tony said, "Get dressed. It's tonight."

"You mean we . . ."

"Shut your mouth, Al. Do you talk about everything you do?"

Al glared at Tony. He spit on the carpeted floor, away from Andy and Tony, then turned and went back to his bedroom to dress. Ten minutes later he was back, dressed in old jeans and a leather jacket, still unshaven.

"Did you talk to her?" Tony asked.

"Of course not. I'm not new at this."

"You better not have," Tony warned him. "If you did . . . She's dead. You know that, don't you?"

They walked out and to the Cadillac. "Sit up front," Tony told Al. "I don't want you behind me."

"You're a real wise ass, aren't you?"

Tony sighed deeply and explained. "This whole damn mess is yours, Al. If you could have kept your pants on and remembered you're married with a good family, we wouldn't be here tonight. Now, it's not too late. I can always phone Bruno and tell him I made a mistake. I can tell him the truth, and then Andy and I can blow your friggin' brains out. Is that what you want?"

Al didn't answer.

"Then get in the front seat, Al."

They arrived at the dump where Al's Trenton crew worked out of. The front door was still unlocked. Up the dark stairs and into the clammy room they called an office. Al switched on the lights and said, "OK, now what?"

Tony answered, "Now you phone two of Chi Chi's old crew. Anybody will do, but they shouldn't be too smart. Get them over here fast. Andy and I will be in the back room. You tell the two guys to steal a car. Tell them about the three drug pushers. Tell them the corner they hang out on. Tell them to go there tonight, around eleven PM. Tell them to take the three of them out from the car and drive off as fast as they can."

Al thought about that. He wasn't stupid, just nasty. He said, "So the only people who can be ID'd when the cops start asking questions are Chi Chi's two guys. And when they talk . . . It'll be me gave them the OK to do the killing. You two will be safe and warm in that back room. That sounds good . . . For the two of you."

"Al, you're losing it. Think about it for a minute. We're using Chi Chi's guys. They're probably hiding anger about their boss being killed. Do they really like you? Probably not, since they were passed over to take over the crew. Now, tell me what you would do to protect yourself after the drug pushers are murdered by two guys who don't like you anyway?"

Al thought about that and then smiled, "I'd take Chi Chi's guys out."

"Right! Now you've got it, Al. So you tell the two of them to dump the stolen car away from here and come back here right after the job is done. When they get here . . . You put a bullet into each of their heads. When you've done that, Andy will help you get rid of the bodies."

"You think I should kill'em? Why not your buddy? He likes killing people."

"Because this is your fault, Al," Tony said, exasperated with his future father-in-law. "All this is because you wanted to screw your girlfriend. Jesus Christ . . . I just don't get you. You risk giving everything up for a piece of ass. You'd give up your position in the Family; you'd give up your own wife and kids. No, you're going to take care of Chi Chi's men yourself. It's the price you're going to pay for what you've done."

And Al did exactly what his daughter's boyfriend told him to do. He knew he had little choice. Tony had a knife at his throat, and he would keep it there for the rest of Al's life. It would be so easy for Tony to go to Bruno and say he had made a mistake and put Tifton's death on Al. After all, Tony was just a damn kid. Kids make mistakes. He would be forgiven, but Al would die.

TWENTY-SEVEN

Montclair, New Jersey
December 1960

After Al had done what Tony told him to do, after the bodies of Chi Chi's soldiers had been dissected and disposed of, after the guns they used were thrown into a furnace to destroy any evidence of their use, Tony told Al he had to go back to his wife and family for Christmas. Al didn't want to and argued with Tony that his wife didn't want him anymore, and he was happier with his Mexican girlfriend. But Tony had taken charge, and Al knew it. He had to wait, wait for Tony to make the mistake Al hoped he would make. So he agreed to go home, but he would wait a few days. He needed to 'make it right' with his girlfriend. Tony finally agreed.

Day by day, Al was getting ever angrier at Tony. At one point, the day Tony and Andy left to go back to Newark, Andy pulled Al to the side and they spoke alone.

Andy said, "Al, I'm not the smartest person working for Mr. Salvano. I know that. But Tony, he probably is the smartest person Mr. Salvano's got. You need to do what he tells you to do. He can save your ass, Al. I can see you got stuff between the two of you. You'd best let it drop. You ain't gonna win one with Tony."

"And why the hell should I let it all drop?"

"Because if you hurt Tony in any way . . . I'll kill you."

"I'm a Made Man you son of a bitch."

"Yeah," Andy said. "I'm seeing that old stuff going away. You seen Made Men up in New York get wasted with nothin' happenin'. You could be the next Made Man to have his brains blown out."

Al took this advice to heart. He would never like Tony again; he would never admire him; he would carry anger inside of him . . . More so for him taking his daughter away than anything else. But he packed his bags, and he went home for Christmas a week after Tony and Andy left Trenton.

****

Montclair, New Jersey

It was early in December and it was cold and snowy. Tony had returned to Newark as he had decided he would, before Al left Trenton. There was time, Tony assured himself. Al wasn't home yet but he would be with his family for Christmas, Tony would make that happen for Teresa. Teresa would be happy, that's all that mattered. If for no other reason, Tony let Al live so that Teresa would be happy. She would have her family back together again, and it would be a happy Christmas.

It was Tony's first day home from Trenton. He

dropped his suitcase at the apartment in Newark, and Andy drove him to Teresa. He walked up the flagstone path to the front door proudly and very happily. He rang the doorbell and stood, looking around the front yard and the neighborhood. How many people were watching from their front windows?

Teresa had said he should have dinner with her and Maria that night. It would be the first time Tony was inside the Falzone home. In spite of being happy, he felt a little uncomfortable, a little uneasy. It would be the first time he would meet his lover's mother. He had to keep reminding himself that the love he and Teresa shared was no longer a secret.

Teresa ran to the door and threw it open. She was ecstatic, and she was beautiful. She had taken a long time picking out a dress and doing make-up and combing her hair. She had to be perfect that night. She pulled Tony into the house and threw her arms around him, pulling him down to her. She kissed him as hard and passionately as she could.

Maria was standing at the kitchen doorway, smiling and happy, wiping her hands on a dish towel. There was nothing she wanted more than to see her daughter happy and with a powerful man who could provide what her own husband could not. She had never seen Tony before. He was handsome, bigger than she expected, taller and more muscular than a mere teenager. That was good, she thought.

"OK, you two," Maria said. "Come inside. And Teresa, take Tony's coat."

As he slipped out of his long coat he said, "Andy drove me here. Do you think there's enough dinner for one more?"

Maria went to the door, opened it and yelled from the threshold, "Andy Pecora! You come in here right now!" She hoped some neighbors heard her.

What a privilege, in her mind, it was to have both Tony Moretti and Andy Pecora in her house.

That's all Andy was waiting for. He jumped from the Cadillac and ran into the house. "Thanks Mrs. Falzone. It's cold out there."

Maria took his coat and asked, "Were you going to wait out there all night for Tony?"

"Of course," Andy said, as if it were a stupid question. "He's my boss."

Maria smiled and looked at her daughter. She nodded, telling Teresa how important that was. A man with absolute loyalty to Tony.

Dinner that night was antipasti of peppers and Italian meats, baked ziti, broccoli rabe, and a ricotta cheesecake. Tony sat back in the tall dining room chair and said, "I haven't eaten anything that good in a long time, Mrs. Falzone."

Andy had helped himself to a second helping, a big second helping, of the baked ziti, after he had finished the cheesecake. The others found that funny but Andy just said, "This stuff is good."

Maria said, "You know Teresa cooked most of this. I just helped out a little. She's going to be a wonderful wife, you know."

"And I'm looking forward to that," Tony said. "As soon as she finishes college."

"College?" Maria asked. "You want Teresa to go to college?"

"Of course. It's what she wants, it's what her father wants, and it's what I want. I hope it's what you want, too. She's going to have everything she wants, Mrs. Falzone."

"How about you call me Maria?"

"I guess I can do that.   Thanks."   He took Teresa's hand, smiled at her and said to Maria, "In a couple of years I'm going to be calling you Mom."

Little Al was at the table with them.   He said nothing until Tony spoke to him.   "So, Little Al.   What grade are you in?"

"Fourth . . . I guess," he answered shyly.   He wasn't used to people taking notice of him, except for his sister who did show him some love and caring . . . When she wasn't busy with something else.

"Fourth, huh?   That's great.   Are you doing well? How's that math thing?   I always found math tough."

"It's OK . . . I guess," the boy answered.   'What was happening?' he thought.   Someone was talking to him.   He fiddled with his food, pushing it around on his plate nervously.

"You like sports?" Andy asked.   "I used to like baseball a lot."

"Nah," Little Al answered.   "I like drawing," he said brightly and smiled.

Teresa added, "Yes, and he's very good at it, too.   I think he's going to be an artist."   Little Al smiled again and ate a bite of food.

"Tell you what," Tony offered.   "When it's warmer . . . In the spring . . . Andy and I will take you up to New York, and we can go to a couple of museums. They have some really great works of art up there. Old Masters they call them.   I think you'd like it."

Little Al smiled and sat up straight.   Color flooded his face.   He started eating happily, and Teresa squeezed Tony's hand in thanks and love.

After dinner they retreated to the big living room. Andy   found   the   Swedish   Modern   furniture uncomfortable.   He was too big for everything there.

And he wanted a cigarette. He knew he shouldn't smoke near Tony; it was often hard to go without a cigarette when they were in the car for hours, driving between Newark and Trenton and back again. But he did it because that's what Tony wanted.

Maria wheeled in an elaborate cart with a silver tea set and delicate china cups and saucers on it. "I made some tea," she said proudly. Beside the teapot, there was a plate of Italian cookies she had bought at the local bakery. She wouldn't admit she had bought them and not made them herself.

Andy pushed himself out of the unusually shaped chair he had wedged himself into and said, "I think I better go check on the car, boss. I'll be right back."

He went outside, leaving his heavy coat behind. Maria looked questioningly at Tony. Teresa laughed and explained, "He just wants to smoke a cigarette. He'll be back in a minute or two. Tony doesn't like people to smoke around him." It was a hint that her mother shouldn't smoke either.

The evening went well, and when Tony and Andy left, there had been a comfortable relationship built between Tony and Maria. Tony returned many times after that, and Teresa continued going to Tony's apartment in Newark, now spending the entire Saturday night and returning home on Sunday. Maria never complained about that.

During the first weeks of December Tony was at the Falzone home almost every day, helping with the Christmas decorating, pulling boxes out of the attic, stringing lights outside the house, and going Christmas shopping with Teresa. He and Teresa took Little Al out to buy a Christmas tree. One afternoon Tony and Andy took the boy Christmas shopping, and he was in heaven. He was excited; he danced around, he laughed, and he ran from store to store. He ate a huge lunch, competing with Andy's appetite. No one had ever done that for him before. Little Al picked out presents for his mother and his father and four presents he wanted to give to Teresa. Tony paid for them. And he made Tony wait outside a store while Andy took him to buy a present for Tony. He spent that evening at home talking endlessly and happily about his day out.

Al had come home in time for the Christmas celebration to begin. Tony attended each of the three Christmas parties the Falzone's hosted. Teresa clung to him proudly and showed him off, introducing him to everyone. Al wasn't very happy about Tony being there, but he knew he had little choice.

Little Al saw what was happening. Tony would be the center of attention, and Little Al's chance at some attention for himself was quashed.

On the night of Teresa's Christmas dance at her High School, Tony stepped out of his big white Cadillac in front of the Falzone house and walked proudly up the flagstone path. Maria had made sure the path was shoveled free of snow and ice. He wore a brand new black wool overcoat over his brand new tuxedo. The salesman at the store who fitted him for the overcoat and tuxedo tried to sell Tony a pair of patent leather dress shoes. Tony thought they were just a bit 'girly' as he described them. He had taken his new black dress shoes to a local shoe shine stand and had the guy there put a glossy spit shine on them. The guy did such a good job that Tony gave him a hundred dollar bill for his work. He carried a boxed orchid corsage for Teresa and a bouquet of red roses for Maria.

Maria answered the doorbell. She was happy to see Tony; she could barely hold in how happy and proud she was. She stepped aside to let Tony walk in.

"You look beautiful, Tony!" she said as she wrapped her arms around him and hugged him. Tony handed her the roses. She beamed with pride and happiness. "Oh, thank you so much, Tony. Look Al! Look at what Tony brought for me! Aren't they beautiful?"

Al Falzone sat on his couch. He had been home for a week and a half so as not to miss the three Christmas parties. Tony demanded that. He wasn't as happy to see Tony as his wife was. He wanted to be back in Trenton with his Mexican girlfriend. He didn't want to see Tony with Teresa, and he didn't like his daughter being so happy with Tony. But in his mind he knew he had to wait. Sooner or later Tony would make a mistake, at least he hoped he would.

Teresa stood on the landing of the staircase. She was wearing a floor length, simple, soft blue satin dress, fitted at her waist, with thin straps over her shoulders. Her hair was pulled up in a swirled French twist with a butterfly brooch of sparkling diamonds on one side. She took each step very slowly, like a model, to be seen. She finally stood in front of Tony, and they kissed, gently, with love. She was glowing with happiness. Tony picked her up and spun her around off the floor to Teresa's delight. Little Al stood in the doorway to the kitchen, leaning against the wall. The scowl on the boy's face was easy to read. He wanted attention from Tony, but he didn't get it. Tony didn't notice. He was too enthralled with Teresa. She was absolutely beautiful that night.

In the past weeks Tony had come to Teresa's house many times. She had always run down the stairs and thrown herself into his arms. They would kiss and hold each other, to the delight of Maria. That night, although Maria was very happy, Teresa's father wasn't happy. His expression told the story of his contempt for what was happening between his daughter and Tony Moretti.

Maria Falzone once had high hopes that her husband would rise up in the mafia. But those hopes were frittered away over the years, as Al wasted his talents on other women. The girlfriend in Trenton was just the latest. Oh yes, she knew all about the woman living in his apartment down there. Gossip took time to reach her, but it always did. But she said nothing, as she had said nothing each time Al found a new whore.

Her hopes now rested on her beautiful daughter. Just as 'Stage Mothers' lived their failed lives through the children they pushed onto the stage, she was pushing Teresa onto the stage she knew, life with a powerful man of respect. She was ecstatic that Teresa had found a rising star. Teresa would live the life Maria had hoped for. There would be money and respect. That was what was important.

Tony handed the corsage to Teresa. "Oh look, Mama! Isn't it beautiful!" Maria helped her pin the corsage to the bodice of her dress. Maria took an ermine wrap from the arm of a chair and wrapped it around Teresa's shoulders. Her husband had given it and many other things to her in years past, in better years. Teresa pulled it around her and stood before Tony, to be seen and appreciated. He said, "God, you're beautiful."

She hugged him joyfully and then hugged her mother. Al remained seated. He said, "I want her home by 11:30. Got it?"

Tony didn't look at Al. He was too busy gazing at Teresa. He said, "Sorry, Al. I rented a suite at the Plaza. Damn thing overlooks Central Park. A bunch of us are going there to have a Christmas party. But I'll have her home in time for school Monday."

Teresa laughed. Maria laughed. Al didn't.

Teresa took Tony's arm, and they started for the

door. Maria ran ahead and opened the door for them. She hugged her daughter once again and whispered, "Have a good time, dear. I love you so much. I'm so happy for you."

Teresa whispered back, "I love you too, Mama."

Outside it was bitterly cold, but neither Tony nor Teresa felt it. Andy jumped from the Cadillac and opened the back door for them.

"Hi, Andy," Teresa said as she bent to get in the car.

"Hi, Teresa. You look great."

She slid across the back seat and looked at the girl who had turned to look at her. "Hi, Suzy." Teresa said. "Isn't this exciting?"

Susan Townsend was Andy's date for the dance. She was a classmate of Teresa's. Her father had been a Montclair cop who had been shot and killed when Susan was just three years old. Her mother made a good living running numbers for Al Falzone. Andy was four years older than Susan, but she didn't care. After all, she was with Andy Pecora who was with Tony Moretti. She would have the whole of the rest of the school year to brag about that.

She said, "That wrap is something else. Where'd you get it at?"

"It's my mother's," Teresa said. "I've got to be careful of it."

Tony sat next to her, close to her, his arm around her shoulders holding her close to him. He said, "Don't worry. If you spill something on it, I'll buy you a new one."

They parked the big Cadillac in the school parking lot, in front of a sign that read 'Teachers Only'. They walked across the lot; groups of students and teachers standing out in the cold stood aside as they passed. Inside the school gymnasium, the floor was filled with students dancing and talking. As the four walked in, the dancing and talking stopped, and the band stopped playing.

Everyone knew who Tony Moretti was. They knew who Andy Pecora was. Everyone knew that Teresa was Al Falzone's daughter. One of the Nuns approached them. She was smiling kindly when she said, "Welcome to Saint Ignatius Academy High School, Tony. I'm so glad that you've brought Teresa. She's one of our best students you know. I hope you have a good time . . . But please, no trouble, Tony."

"No trouble, Sister," Tony said, smiling broadly. "All we want to do is dance. Teresa said she'd teach me."

And they had a good time. Tony had not had much practice dancing, in fact he had never danced even once before that night, but he let Teresa show him, and they danced and laughed the night away. It didn't take very long for everyone there to accept the fact that the four of them were there, and they all began to dance around them and laugh with them. The music played on, and the kids danced and laughed and ate the food that the girls from Home Economics Class had prepared.

After midnight, they left, and the four drove across the George Washington Bridge into New York, to the Plaza Hotel, and the suite Tony had reserved. Andy and Susan quickly disappeared into one of the bedrooms. Tony took Teresa to the suite's balcony, opening the French doors for her. Outside, on the balcony, they held hands as they looked out over Central Park and the lights of the City.

Tony said, "This is great. It's like the whole world is lit up for us."

Teresa leaned against him and hugged his arm.

"I'm going to give you the world, Teresa," he said.

She smiled up at him and said softly, "I don't want the world, Tony. I just want you."

They were quiet for awhile, enjoying the view of Central Park.

"I had a good time tonight," Teresa said. She shivered a little at the cold. Tony put his arm around her shoulders and held her tight to him.

"I had a good time, too. I wish I was a better dancer."

"Oh Tony, you were great. You were the best dancer there tonight," she said and smiled up at him.

"Actually," he said, "you were the best. You're beautiful. Everything about you is great."

She smiled up at him and stood on her toes to reach his lips with hers. "I love you so much, Tony."

There was a sadness in her voice, Tony heard it and asked, "What's wrong? Did I do something?"

"No, Tony. It's just . . . Well Dad wants me to go to college in the fall."

"That's right. We've talked about that. I want you to go, too. Don't you want to go? I thought you were excited about it?"

"I want to be with you. I don't want to be away from you."

"You'll never be away from me, Teresa."

"But I want to be *with* you."

Tony took her back into the suite and closed the French door. He took her to a big couch that was in front of a fireplace that had been laid with wood and lit. The warmth felt good to both of them. He pulled her close to him and wrapped her in his arms. Tears were filling her eyes. Tony whispered, "Please don't cry. It's all going to work out. I'll see to that."

"Are you sure?" she sobbed. "It was so good tonight. I don't want it to end."

Tony let go of her and knelt in front of her. She covered her eyes with her hands as she cried. Tony touched her hair. It was soft and silky and wonderful to his touch. He gently pulled her head onto his shoulder. He whispered in her ear, "I love you Teresa Falzone, and no matter where you are, you'll be in my heart. Miles can't separate us. I believe God or fate or something has brought us together, and nothing is going to tear us apart. I don't know what I'd ever do without you. I'm not sure I could go on living. I know that sounds like something from some lovesick kid, but I feel that in my heart. You are so special, so unique. Being with you is like being in heaven."

He remembered the nightmare he had suffered down in Trenton all those long nights without her. Was the nightmare coming true? Was the dark monster coming between them? Would she be running towards college and away from him? There were men there, men with money, good looking men. Men who would be doctors and lawyers. Honest men who had nothing to hide.

"But college is such a long time, Tony," she said. "I'll miss you terribly."

"Look, Teresa," he began. He knew he had to be supportive of her and not demand anything of her. If she was destined for college, he would support her in that. "I need you . . . More than anything. But you know the life I've chosen. I'm good at it, I have instincts, but there are things I don't know, things that I need to know. I don't have an education like most people. Hell, I never got past the eighth grade. I want you to learn those things, and then when we're married you'll be able to help me."

"Married? Do you really mean that?" she said. She looked up as Tony knelt before her. Tears streamed down her face ruining her makeup.

"Of course. Haven't we talked about that? How many times have we talked about names for our kids?" Tony laughed and took a handkerchief from his pocket. He wiped the tears and said, "What the hell did you think this is all about? Do you think I was just kidding when we talked about being married? I'm serious . . . I'm not lying . . . We're going to get married and settle down and have a couple dozen kids."

"Whoa big boy." She tried to laugh as she wiped the tears away. Tony felt good about that. "Let's try to make do with two or three, OK?" she said, laughing that wonderful laugh that Tony liked so much.

"So anyway," Tony said. "I've got plans, and if they work out, everything will be OK. You go to college . . . But not too far away. We'll be together a lot, weekends and holidays and summers. I might even take you to Europe one summer, you never know. And then when college is over, we'll have the biggest damn wedding anybody's ever seen."

They kissed, and Teresa let the ermine wrap slide from her shoulders. She reached behind her and unzipped her dress. He picked her up into his arms and carried her to the bedroom. They slept late on Sunday, and Teresa was home in time for a late lunch with her parents that day.

****

Christmas Eve found Tony at midnight mass with

Teresa, Maria, Al and Little Al. Andy went to his mother's house and took her to church on Christmas morning. At the Falzone home, after mass, coffee and small cakes and cookies and sweet wine were served. Tony spent the night at the Falzone home, in the guest bedroom so as not to anger Al too much. Al had made it obvious that he didn't want Tony there at all. Sleeping in Teresa's room would have been too much.

The next morning there were pancakes and sausage and presents and laughter. Al had given his whore a diamond bracelet for Christmas as a pacifier for him not being with her on the Holiday. The bracelet had been stolen from a jewelry store. Al got it cheap. He bought his wife a new Sears and Roebuck vacuum cleaner.

It was the first really good Christmas Tony had ever experienced. In the past, Christmas for Tony was dark and usually spent hiding from his drunken father. It was the best Christmas Teresa ever had. That night when she went to bed, she prayed, "Please God. Let me be with Tony forever. I love him so much."

TWENTY-EIGHT

Newark, New Jersey
March 1961

Tony was seventeen years old. Work in Newark had been going well. He was expanding the gambling operation little by little, but it wasn't what he dreamed of yet. Shortly after arriving in Newark he had started a weekly, very high stakes poker game going in the back room of L'oro Luna, which quickly expanded to twice a week. The house, that was Tony, kept 5% of every pot on the table.

He had opened what he called 'betting parlors', what everyone else called bookie joints, where anyone could make a bet on just about anything they wanted to lose their money on. He had closed the old and dirty bookie joints that Al had going. Tony's new places were clean and modern. And he added something new that no one in the business had ever dreamed of before. He welcomed ladies in to place their own bets.

He had started to take over a numbers operation in the slum areas of the city. That wasn't very difficult to do; Andy and his own soldiers made sure the people running numbers there started working for Tony.

He was leaving the strong arm loan sharking to

the others. He had money out on the street but he had, little by little turned it all over to others in the crew. He didn't want any part of that part of the business. Depending on gambling only, his income had doubled. He and Teresa were together often, but never enough.

The phone call came at three in the morning that Tuesday. Tony had been dreaming of Teresa; a good dream, a sexy dream, not the nightmare he dreaded so much. He jumped when the ringing started. "Damn!" he said. He wished Teresa could be there with him. He rubbed his eyes and swung his feet out of bed onto the floor. On the fifth ring he picked up the phone.

"Who the hell is this, and you better have a damn good reason for waking me up!"

"Your Don wants to see you." It was Bruno Massetti. The voice was easy to recognize. In fact the deep, gravelly voice was hard to forget.

"Now?" Tony said. "Do you know what time it is?"

"Not now," Bruno said. "In the mornin'. Be here at ten, and don't be late. And wear your best suit. The Don expects the best."

"Wait a minute," Tony complained. "Be where? I don't know what you're talking about."

Bruno gave him the address of the Old Don's house in Brooklyn. "Can you find that?" he asked.

"Yeah, I can find it," Tony said. "Now tell me why."

"Don't question what your Don wants. Just be here."

The phone line went dead. Tony dropped the receiver on the floor and lay back on the bed. Why? What the hell could the Don want to talk to him about?

What went wrong? What had he done? Where had he slipped up? What mistake had he made?

Had Peter found out the truth about Roger Tifton? Was the trip out to Brooklyn a one way trip? He picked up the phone from the floor, hung it in its cradle and then picked it up again. He dialed Andy Pecora's number.

"Andy, this is Tony. Sorry to wake you. Something's up. I got a phone call from Bruno Massetti. He said I'm to meet the Don in Brooklyn in a few hours."

"I don't like it, boss. That don't sound right."

"I agree. Be here at seven, OK? I want to be early and see what's happening out there."

"You're actually going?" Andy said.

"What do you think I should do? Pack a bag and move to the mountains or something? Just be here at seven, and bring an extra gun with you."

"OK, boss. I'll be there."

****

Brooklyn, New York

Tony and Andy sat in the car a block away from the Don's house. The big white Caddy stuck out like a sore thumb. Neighborhood people were watching from their windows; children gathered on the sidewalk next to the car and looked in the windows at them.

"I think they might know we're here, boss," Andy laughed.

"Yeah, you're right. Screw this. Let's just go to

the front door and see what they want."

Andy pulled a small semi-auto pistol from the belt at his waist. He pulled the slide back, let it fall forward, and handed it to Tony. Tony took it, looked at it, and put it in his suit jacket pocket. "Look," he said. "I don't know what's going to happen in there. There's a good possibility that they are going to try to take both of us out. You can stay in the car if you want. I'll understand and I won't be angry."

"Hey, boss. That's an insult. I been with you a long time. We made a lot a'money together and had a lot of fun. I ain't gonna' let you walk in there alone. So f'getta' 'bout it."

Tony touched Andy's shoulder. He had understood a long time ago that he had made the right choice with Andy Pecora. Yes, Andy was probably a little psycho, but Andy knew what loyalty was. Andy started the engine, and the car moved slowly up the street. The crowds of people who had been watching remained . . . And watched. He stopped the car in front of the Don's house, and they both got out.

It was an end-of-winter cold morning that day. The sky was dark with black clouds that would bring rain soon. The tall trees of the neighborhood swayed under the cold wind that blew from the north. As they walked up the cracked concrete walk that had weeds and grass filling the cracks, Tony whispered, "No shooting until I say so, OK?"

"OK, boss," was Andy's reply.

Tony rang the doorbell and then knocked on the door. He was nervous, he was scared, his hands were shaking. He thought about Teresa and touched the bulge of the gun in his pocket. He knocked again, and the door opened. An old man stood there. He was short, fat and grey haired. He had a big mustache that needed trimming. It hung long, down the sides of his mouth and over his upper lip. And he needed to shave yesterday's beard. He wore a rumpled blue pin striped suit that had dandruff flaked on the shoulders. An old wrinkled blue tie, stained from last night's pasta gravy, hung lose from his white shirt that was open at the collar.

"You must be Anthony," he said. His voice was raspy and carried a heavy accent. But it didn't have the gravel in it that Bruno's voice had.

"Yes," Tony said. "I don't suppose you're Don Salvano?"

The man laughed in a short burst that ended almost as soon as it started. He stepped back and said, "Come on in." The 'in' was pronounced 'een'. He led Tony and Andy through the house, walking maddeningly slow. It was dark as night in the middle of the day, due to the heavy drapes that covered the windows and the aged dark wood walls. There were several lamps, but none were lit. He opened a door and stepped aside. "Inside," he said and walked away.

Andy asked, "Maybe I should go first, boss."

"No," Tony said simply. He stepped into the room and found two men there waiting for him. Andy was at his heals, his hand inside his jacket grasping his .45 Colt in its shoulder holster.

The man sitting behind the big desk was older and bigger than the other man. That other man sat crossed legged in a tall leather wing back chair at the side of the desk. He smiled and shook his head. The bigger man said, "You must be that Andy Pecora I heard 'bout." The gravelly voice was familiar to Tony. He was Bruno Massetti. Bruno said, "You ain't gonna' need the gun, Andy. Take it easy, and sit over there." He pointed to a chair in a far corner. Andy looked to Tony, who nodded, and Andy went to the chair.

Bruno and the other man saw this nod and smiled at each other knowingly. The stories they had heard about Tony and his loyal bodyguard were true. Bruno stood and said, "Tony Moretti, this is your Don, Peter Salvano."

Tony looked down at the man. He was middle aged, fit, with dark hair and dressed as if he had just come from a golf course. His yellow Polo shirt was cut to tell people he had some muscle under it. He wore tan cotton slacks, and good leather loafers with no socks. It took a second or two, but Tony finally recognized the man he had spoken with at Natalia Salvano's funeral. He was dressed for the summer in the middle of a cold March.

Tony said, discomfort in his voice, "So you said not to call you Don in public. Do I call you Don here or what? Do I kiss your ring? What do I do?"

Peter laughed and looked up to the side at Bruno who laughed, but only when he saw his Don wasn't angry. It was not in Bruno to take the lead in anything when Peter was near. "No," Peter said. "You don't have to do anything. I'm just a man . . . Like you."

"Don Salvano," Tony started but Peter interrupted him.

"Please, that Don stuff is for the old guys. You and me, we're the new generation. Please call me Mr. Salvano . . . For the time being anyway. Someday if things go right, you can call me Peter."

The sigh coming from Andy was audible. He was ready to kill for Tony, but he was unsure if he was ready to die for him. If it came to that, he probably would, but he wouldn't be happy about it, he laughed to himself. He relaxed and slumped down in the chair.

"Sure," Tony said. "Anything you say."

Peter stood and walked around in front of the desk. He put his hand on Tony's shoulder. He was as tall as Tony, and older by twenty years or more. He felt young muscle under Tony's suit jacket that Peter wished he had. He tried to keep himself in shape, but his work days were long and tiring and weren't getting any easier as the years went by. Peter said, "I'll bet you thought you were going to be killed."

"I guess I'm just not used to the formalities," Tony said.

Peter pulled a tall, dark wood chair with an upholstered seat close to the desk and said, "Please sit down. I want to talk with you."

Tony sat and tried to get comfortable, but he was still unsure of why he was there. Peter returned to his chair at the side of the desk and lit a cigarette. He blew the smoke to the ceiling. He looked at Tony and apologized, "I'm sorry about the smoke. I heard you don't like it, but this is about the only place I can enjoy a cigarette."

Tony said, "Knowing who you are, I guess I won't complain."

Peter laughed and then said, "Tell me about Al Falzone."

Tony ignored the cigarette smoke. If it were anyone else, he would tell them not to smoke around him. "What do you want to know?" Tony asked. "I mean, Al's my boss. He's OK, I suppose. Why?"

Peter took another deep drag on the cigarette, blew the smoke again to the ceiling, and asked, "Al killed Roger Tifton, didn't he?"

"What? The cops say he didn't. Tifton was robbed and killed. We got the guys who did it. Didn't Bruno tell you that?"

"I understand, Tony. I know what you did and

why you did it. I know it all. Now, if you lie to me, Tony, you're finished. You're not dead . . . But you're finished. You can go back to The Aces. You can go back to Passaic and whatever is waiting there for you. But you'll never work for me again."

Tony thought about that. The deal he had made with Al was to lie about Roger Tifton in exchange for being Made and for Teresa. But Don Salvano must have found out. Did Al tell him the truth? That would be unlikely because if he had, Al would be dead. Maybe Mr. Salvano was guessing, fishing for the truth? More than likely, the police who had changed the police reports had told someone, who told someone, who eventually told Peter Salvano. That was the only way he could have found out, Tony thought.

Tony had a lot at stake and he had to weigh his options, which he knew were few. Maybe it was time to tell the truth and try to talk his way out of it. If Peter knew the truth, and Tony continued with the lie, well, he had been back to Passaic and he had seen what happened to The Aces. He would not be able to handle that.

Peter broke into Tony's thoughts. "What kind of deal did you make with Al?"

Tony shifted in his chair and in the corner of his eye he saw Andy's hand move slowly toward the big gun in his shoulder holster. He turned slightly and raised a hand. Andy relaxed his arm. That, too, was noticed by Peter and Bruno.

"OK," Tony began. "Maybe it's time. I protected Al in exchange for him sponsoring me. I want to be Made, and I want to be Capo of the Newark territory. Al agreed."

"What else?" Peter asked.

"I don't know what you mean, Mr. Salvano."

"What else was in the deal? What else did you get?"

Tony shrugged his shoulders, not really understanding what Peter wanted. What else was he told? What lie, perhaps, could have been told? And who could he be listening to? Tony decided that the truth was the best way. He said, "I got to date Al's daughter, out in the open."

Peter smiled and said, "And I understand she's a very pretty girl," He crushed out his cigarette and lit another one. "Why do you want to protect Al . . . I mean other than the fact that he's your girl's father? Why shouldn't he suffer for killing my friend?"

Tony swallowed hard, sat forward and said, "Mr. Salvano, think about it." He had nothing to lose by that time. Either his plan would work or he would never leave this Brooklyn house alive.

He said, "I mean no disrespect but your Family is in trouble. There's a hole in the leadership. Al's stuck in Trenton with his Mexican chick. I've been there, and the place is messed up. They're hiding in a rat hole. The State Police and the FBI are hounding them. Their income is down. You're losing a lot of money. And in Newark there's no leadership at all. Now, I've been expanding, little by little. I'm turning that nickel dime poker game into a high stakes game. I'm getting people with money who like to gamble to play. I'm taking over the numbers operation there. I've got nice, clean places where people bet on horses, football, anything. I have an idea to start a high stakes gambling room, you know, a small casino type place. But I'm doing this on my own. There's no leadership there.

"So if you take Al out," Tony continued, his eyes locked on Peter's. "Even if he's not doing a good job in Trenton, that leaves two operations without a leader.

How long will it take before someone sees the weakness there and moves in? You could lose both Newark and Trenton. New York must be licking their lips at the thought of expanding out.

"I know the people who work for you out there. You've got three guys in Newark, not including me and Andy. Not one of those three could lead an old lady across the street. And in Trenton? There isn't one man who can step into leadership. You know that. Two of them came from Newark with Al. They're good at what they do, collecting and getting rough when they have to. But name one who can be a Capo."

"So what happens to Trenton if I leave Al there?" Peter asked.

"He'll continue to think of his dick before he thinks of business. He needs closer management."

"And who would you suggest as that closer management?"

"Me, Mr. Salvano. I know what to do."

"And what would you do?"

"First I'd recruit new soldiers. There are plenty of people who hang around and just wait for a chance to move up. I know a few really good guys. You need at least three new soldiers in Trenton. Chi Chi's guys there have to go. Two of them are gone already. They're angry, and it may take them a long time to figure out that you took Chi Chi out, but they eventually will. And when they do, they'll cause trouble. Second, with your backing, I'd teach Al how to be a Capo . . . A leader."

Peter interrupted again and asked, "What makes you think I killed Chi Chi?"

"Again, Mr. Salvano, with all due respect. I got the order from Al . . ."

Again Peter interrupted, "*You* got the order from Al? You took Chi Chi out?"

"Yes, sir," Tony answered, wondering if he had said the right thing.

"Al told me he had done it himself," Peter said.

Tony turned in his chair and looked at Andy. He nodded and Andy said, "I put two bullets in Chi Chi's head, sir."

Peter and Bruno shared a knowing glance. Al had lied. Peter asked Tony, "So what would you do to bring in more cash in Trenton?"

Tony leaned forward again and thought for a moment, then said, "Gambling should be expanded. In Newark there's two poker games a week. Good money, but a waste of time in the long run. I'm going start several more big dollar games there; bring in doctors, lawyers, guys with pockets full of cash. I'd do the same down in Trenton. There's got to be cash there with all the politicians and lawyers.

"And I'd open a place with other games, like I said. You know, roulette, craps, games like that. Within twenty-five miles of Newark there must be millions of dollars that we're not going after. There's probably more than that around Trenton. I figure the cops won't care so long as we don't break legs and we only let big money in. Keep the small money out, you know? Keep the games fair and honest, no crooked stuff. Plus, we'll invite the cops in, and they all have to be winners when they play. Nothing big . . . A few hundred will satisfy them."

Peter nodded and asked, "Anything else?"

"Loan sharking is a good business, but it's not a big money maker, and there's violence there that the cops don't like. And extortion is something my old gang of kids did. I'd take the money and instead of loaning it out at high interest, I'd buy into businesses when someone needs cash, become investors instead of demanding money from them. I'd make sure the businesses were good, and I'd let the owner alone to run the business if he was running it well. I'd use the businesses that were being screwed up by the owners to expand cash flow by buying things through the business, screw paying for it, and resell it and let the business fail, and then I'd sell off whatever assets the business has. And I'd leave all the damn hijacking to others who aren't smart enough to do anything else. You once told me The Aces were small potatoes. That's what all the leg breaking and hijacking can be if we expand out . . . As I know we can."

"Have you been to college, Tony?" Peter asked.

"No sir. I never went to High School. I was too busy."

"Trenton seems like a different place than Newark. I think you know that. What would you do there that's different than what you'd do in Newark?"

"I'd recruit, as I said. Then I'd move out of the slum they're in now. Then I'd meet with the State Police . . ."

"You'd meet with the cops?" Bruno asked.

"Sure," Tony said. "Think about it. Trenton is the State Capital. If we don't have politicians on the books, we should. Those guys are always looking for someone to finance their next campaign. I'd have those politicians pave the way for me. The State Police will listen, if the politicians tell them to. They don't want their budgets cut. I'd also stop all the leg breaking down there. The cops hate the violence and killing. Again, gambling and investments. Both of which don't bring violence with them. And then I'd redirect the State Police to the drug dealers. I'd have nothing to do with drugs, but I'd make sure that the drug dealers were set up for arrest. In fact, I'd work with the State Police to bust up the drug gangs. I'd put some of the new soldiers out on the street looking for drug dealers. I mean, they're just blacks and spics after all."

"Anything else?" Peter asked, as he lit yet another cigarette.

"As I said. I'd keep Al down there, but I'd have him move his wife and family there. That might keep his dick in his pants, at least cut back on the time he spends with his girlfriends. Maria Falzone is a hard woman, but she's also a good woman. She wants her husband to be powerful. She wants the money he could bring in if he was powerful. She would be the best onsite manager to keep Al in line."

Peter blew smoke towards Tony this time, but Tony didn't complain. He didn't like cigarette smoke and never let people who were near him smoke, except for Peter Salvano of course. Peter asked, "Why is it so important to keep Al? Is it because he's your girl's father? You never answered me when I asked that."

"That's part of it," Tony said, grinning shyly. "Someday he's going to be my father-in-law. Killing him would ruin what Teresa and I have. She would never forgive me, of course. I couldn't take that. It would break me, I guess. But more than that. I think he can do a good job for you . . . If he has the right guidance. And who can replace him right now? Not a couple of years from now, but right now? The guys down there might question his position and leadership, but they still have some semblance of loyalty, and I can increase that."

Peter nodded. He understood. And he knew Tony was right in everything he had said. Since before his father's death, when Peter knew he would one day take over the leadership of the Family, Peter had dreams of moving away from the Old World of violent crimes and murders. He wanted the cash to come in from operations that were quiet and as legal as possible. The gambling, he believed, was something the police might turn a blind eye to if there were no violence attached to it. And redirecting the police to drug dealers was a genius idea that he had never even thought of himself.

"One final thing, Tony," Peter said, as he put the cigarette to his lips. "Mike Colombo was killed. Why?"

Tony swallowed hard and looked down, thinking once again. He had told the truth so far; he felt he had to continue with the truth. He said, "Al told Mike to kill Roger Tifton. Apparently, Mike went to Tifton and told him he would let him live for money. Tifton gave him one thousand dollars. Mike took it and told Al that I had told him not to kill Tifton."

"Did you tell him that?"

"Hell no! . . . Excuse me, Mr. Salvano. I mean, no, I didn't. I never even heard of Tifton until Al came to L'oro Luna and cut Mike's throat."

"Al did that? Al cut the throat of his own man?"

"He's like that, Mr. Salvano. But I think he can be controlled. At least I'd like to try."

Peter crushed out the cigarette and nodded at Bruno, who immediately pushed a small red button on top of the desk. The door behind Tony opened and the old man who had greeted Tony and Andy at the front door stood there. "Come with me," he said.

Tony stood. This was it. Maybe he had gone too far. Maybe he had insulted the Don. Maybe he had given the Don his ideas and now he wasn't needed anymore. Teresa filled his mind. If he died, she would live, but he wouldn't have her. There was nothing he could do.

Andy stood and started for his gun. Peter said, "Calm down, Andy. Sit down, and stay here. Nothing bad is going to happen."

Tony nodded and Andy sat. Tony walked to Andy and bent to whisper in his ear, "If I don't come back . . . Kill them all." Then he followed the old man out of the den. They reached an open door that led down to the cellar. Tony followed the man down. The cellar was dimly lit. At the bottom of the stairs, Tony stopped and looked around. Three men, all big and old but mean looking, stood behind a rectangular table that was covered in a white linen cloth. A single candle was burning in a gold candlestick. A knife, the blade shined to mirror brilliance, the handle gold and encrusted with rubies, lay on the table, the point of the blade away from the three men, pointed at Tony.

The old man said, "Stand over there," pointing at the table. Tony walked there. The table separated Tony from the three men. The man in the middle spoke, "For generations the Salvano Family ruled Napoli. Men swore allegiance to the Family. An oath was taken that could never be broken. To violate that oath meant death. Nothing is more important than the oath to the Family. Any sacrifice must be made when called upon to do so. Once the oath is taken, a man may never leave the Family. Anthony Moretti, are you ready to take this oath of loyalty and allegiance to the Salvano Family? If you aren't, you may leave freely. No one will ever hold anger against you if you walk away."

"I'm ready," Tony said. He was surprised, of course. He had never imagined that he would be initiated into The Family that day. He had feared just the opposite. But who sponsored him? Surely not Al. Peter would never accept that knowing that Al had killed his friend. Who else? Maybe Peter had become impressed enough with Tony to sponsor him himself? But it didn't make any real difference. Becoming a Made Man was the next step in Tony's plan.

The man said, "Will you swear on your eternal soul that your life is now owned by the Salvano Family?"

"Yes, I swear it," Tony said.

"In the old days, a man's hand was cut. The blood being the symbol of what the man would be willing to give to his Family. Today we merely prick the man's finger for a drop of blood."

Tony held out his right hand, palm up. "The old way," he said. "I respect the tradition."

The three men all smiled and nodded to each other. The man picked up the blade and laid the edge on Tony's palm. With a quick movement he sliced open Tony's palm and the blood ran across the blade and down onto the white linen. Tony didn't flinch or show any pain. He kept his hand outstretched. The man took a small card from his inside jacket pocket. "This is the Holy Card of San Gennaro, the patron Saint of Napoli and of the Salvano Family." He held the card to the candle's flame and it started to burn. He placed the burning card onto Tony's bleeding hand and the three men looked deeply into Tony's eyes. There was no sign of pain there. The card turned to ash.

"Anthony Moretti, you are now a member of the Salvano Family. You may go now and always obey your Don."

****

While Tony was in the basement, Peter spoke to

Andy. "You and Tony are friends?" he asked.

"Friends, sure. But he's my boss, too."

"Why?" Peter asked.

Andy had to think about that. He knew he wasn't as quick as Tony, but he knew how he felt, and that is what he wanted to express. He wanted to express it well so that Mr. Salvano would understand. He said, "Tony took me away from The Aces . . . Away from Passaic. I seen what's left of them. Their lives are screwed up. I don't know what I would'a done if Tony hadn't taken me away from there.   I'd probably be dead or in jail, ya' know? I don't wanna' be there, ya' know? I thank Tony for doing that for me, ya' know?"

"Would you kill if Tony told you to kill?"

"Sure . . . I guess I'd do whatever he says t'do."

"Would you die for Tony?"

Andy lowered his head and tried to think that out. But he went with his feelings once again. He looked up and said, "I don't wanna' die, ya' know? But if it meant that Tony would go on livin', I guess I would. Sure. I owe him that much. 'Course, I wouldn't go outta' my way lookin' to get killed either."

"Do you feel good when you kill someone, Andy?" Peter asked.

"Feel good? I don't know," Andy said. "I kind'a like being better and stronger than other people. I know I ain't smarter than a lot of guys. Sometimes I dream about stickin' knives in people. That's funny, ain't it? I mean is that strange?"

"No, Andy," Peter said. "I think that's just you. Now listen. I want you to protect Tony. People are going to try to kill him. Can you do that?"

"No offense, Mr. Salvano. But I'd do that anyway. You don't have to tell me that."

"That's good, Andy. That's loyalty. One more thing. You still live at home . . . With your mother. Right?"

"Yes, sir." Andy answered simply.

"Your father is dead?"

"I don't know. He just left one day and never came back. I suppose he could be dead."

"Your mother is Sicilian?" Peter asked.

"Yeah, I think so."

"Your father is Italian?"

"I really don't know," Andy said. "I was real young when he left."

"Andy, you need to move out of your mother's home. You are a man now. You need to be on your own. You should always love and respect your mother; you should always financially support her. You should visit her often. You should take her shopping and to church. But you shouldn't live with her. That is what a child does. Find a place of your own soon."

"Yes, sir," Andy said, a little embarrassed but understanding what he had to do.

Peter smiled. He stood and walked to Andy. He held out his hand, and Andy stood, taking Peter's hand.

****

Tony lowered his hand, letting the blood drip onto the concrete floor as he walked away from the table. He walked up the stairs slowly and returned to the den where Peter and Bruno and Andy waited. A trail of blood was left behind as he left the basement and walked to the den. He clinched his fist when he walked into the den so as not to drip blood onto the carpet there. Bruno smiled when he saw the clinched fist. Peter stood and said, "You did it the old world way. That's good. The old guys will like that. They'll think a lot of you."

"I thought the guys down there would be impressed," Tony laughed.

Bruno poured four glasses of grappa. They drank the strong liquor down quickly. Peter then said, "I want to talk to Tony alone."

Bruno and Andy walked out of the room, closing the door. In the den Peter told Tony to sit, and Peter took the big chair behind the desk.

"Does it hurt?" he asked.

Tony laughed and said, "Like hell!"

Peter smiled. He pulled a rolled gauze bandage from the drawer in the desk and handed it to Tony. "Wrap it in that," he said. He lit yet another cigarette, blew the smoke upwards, and he began, "OK, I want you to take over Newark. I'll have Bruno phone the men there . . ."

Tony broke in and said, "Please don't do that. I want them to work for me because they know that's the right thing to do. If you tell them, they will always know I'm not their real leader. They'll question everything I say, wondering if it's your order or mine."

"But I do give the orders," Peter said.

"You do . . . But the men have to follow me without question. I don't want them always wondering if they have to check with you on everything I say. Let me handle that problem, please. I know how to do it."

"OK," Peter agreed. "I'll give you a chance, but

not forever."   He paused and rubbed his chin in thought, then said, "But what about Al?"

"Can I assume you want me to take over Trenton, also?"

"For the time being, yes.   Until it's straightened out down there. And then we'll see what's best. But I want you to understand that Al Falzone is not a permanent part of the operation. His life is temporary, understand?"

"Then that's going to take some intervention from you, Mr. Salvano. Until tonight I worked for him. He's going to object."

"I'll take care of that," Peter said. "I'll talk to him personally.   But I want you to understand that Al Falzone is not a permanent part of the operation.   His life is temporary, understand?   Now, you have six months to make the changes in Newark you spoke about. Can you do that?"

"Of course, Mr. Salvano."

"Then I want Trenton straightened out after that. You see, Tony, I want the money to continue coming in.   I have some investments I want to make. Eventually, I want to be able to retire to a legitimate life. I think your ideas are what I've been looking for. I want to move away from the old ways.   I want to move away from the guns and the violence.   I think you can work with me on that."

"Mr. Salvano," Tony said. "To be honest, I want the money, too. I think I can make that money without the cops breathing down my neck. I believe that there are businesses out there that will make a lot of money without having to kill anyone to get it."

"What about your friend, Andy Pecora?"

"He will always be useful.   That new business life isn't going to happen overnight."

Peter liked what he heard. He liked this young man, and he believed Tony might be the future he was looking for. He wouldn't tell this to anyone, but Peter wanted to keep the illegal money coming in. There was too much of it to let go of, and he wanted money to invest. He needed front people, like Tony Moretti, to bring that money in. He had politics in mind for himself, maybe even mayor of New York or something more. He needed the money, and he needed to be distanced from the source of that money. In time he knew he could do this.

"I have one question about Trenton. If Al's family moves to Trenton, won't that put some miles between you and Teresa if you're up in Newark?"

"No, I thought about that. Teresa is going to start college in the fall. I'll wait until then to move Al's family south. That will give me time to improve Newark."

"You really love that girl, don't you?" Peter asked.

"Mr. Salvano, I'm going to spend the rest of my life with her."

"Tony, my wife and I are having a little party next Saturday. I'd like you and Teresa to come to that party. I want to show you off, and I want to meet this Teresa myself. She must be something."

"She is, Mr. Salvano. She is."

"Just one thing, Tony. While you're there, there will be no talk of business, understand?"

"Of course, Mr. Salvano."

****

Montclair, New Jersey

Tony and Andy drove back from Brooklyn, both of them excited about what the future would hold for them. Andy was singing along with Elvis' "Are you lonesome tonight", out of tune of course. Tony was laughing, trying to ignore the pain in his hand.

"Tell you what," Tony said. "Let's go see what Maria is cooking for lunch."

"Yeah, right," Andy laughed. "You just wanna' see your girl. You ain't never been that interested in food."

"OK, so that's the truth," Tony said. "Let's go there anyway."

As they got near the Hudson River, the rain started - a cold, icy, wintery rain. The wind blowing across the bridge made Andy head for the Lincoln Tunnel. But they got to Montclair, and Andy parked the Cadillac in the driveway.

"You sure I should go in with you, boss?" he asked.

"Hell yes," Tony said. "You're going to be my best man. Might as well get used to being part of the family." That made Andy feel good. He patted Tony on the shoulder and opened the door.

They ran for the front door through the rain and knocked and rang the bell, standing in the lashing rain. Al opened the door. As they stood there, in the rain, he scowled and said, "What the hell you two want?"

Tony pushed his way past Al and said "Come on Al. Be nice. Get used to it." As Andy walked past Al he stopped and whispered, "You know what can happen if you ain't nice, Al."

Teresa heard them and ran downstairs. As she

always did, she jumped into Tony's arms and kissed him.   Then she saw his bandaged hand.   "What happened? Is it serious?"

"No," Tony said. "Just a scratch."

But the gauze wrap was red with fresh blood. Teresa held his hand, looking at all the blood, and said, "Maybe you should see a doctor? Andy, take him to the emergency room."

"He's gonna be OK, babe," Andy said.   "It's a good thing."

"How is a cut hand a good thing?"

Maria walked from the kitchen wearing her usual dress with a full skirt, pearls and hi-heeled shoes. She saw Tony's bandaged hand and, knowing what it was, she smiled and returned to the kitchen.

Al knew also. He walked away to an open bottle of whiskey and poured a drink. 'That damn kid,' he thought.

Teresa insisted that she put a fresh bandage on Tony's hand.   In the downstairs' bathroom she carefully washed the cut and took a bottle of iodine from the medicine cabinet. She opened it and dabbed some on with a cotton ball. Tony pulled his hand away quickly and said, "Ouch! Shit! Damn it! That hurts!"

"Oh Tony, don't be such a baby," Teresa said, wiping more iodine on the cut. She wrapped a fresh cotton bandage around his hand, and holding his hand in hers, she said, "Oh, Tony, it looks so bad. What happened?"

"Nothing for you to worry about," he said. "Hey look, we came for lunch. Are you going to let us starve?"

****

Teresa was scared. At first she didn't want to go to Peter Salvano's party. But Tony was insistent. "But I don't have anything to wear," she complained. He took her into New York, to Saks on Fifth Avenue. The sales ladies there explained what she needed, and she and Tony walked out two hours later with arms full of boxes and bags.

Teresa was resplendent at the party. She wore a black cocktail dress with simple but elegant gold jewelry. Tony wore a dark suit that he had paid a few hundred dollars extra to have sized and finished in less than an hour. The doorman at Peter's building was expecting them; he wasn't expecting them to arrive in a white Cadillac with Andy Pecora driving. Andy handed the keys to the doorman and said roughly, "Park it, and keep it clean." Andy was wearing his best suit, a grey pin striped double breasted. It did little to hide the bulge under his left arm. He pushed his way through the crowded sidewalk, leading Tony and Teresa into the building.

The elevator ride took what seemed like forever to reach the penthouse apartment. A woman dressed in a black and white maid's uniform opened the door to Peter's apartment and then stepped back cautiously as Andy stepped inside, stopped and looked around. Peter walked to them, smiling graciously, a glass of champagne in his hand. "Oh, welcome!" he said. "Andy, I'm so glad you could come. Please, there's liquor at the bar; anything you want." Tony nodded, and Andy went to the bar.

Peter held his hand out to Tony who took it. His hand was still bandaged, and he winched as Peter shook hands with him. "Oh, I'm sorry, Tony. I forgot. Is it healing alright?"

"It's fine," Tony answered.

Teresa said, "No it isn't. I wish he'd see a

doctor."

"I'm sure you'll be OK, Tony."

Tony said, "I'm sorry about the entrance, Mr. Salvano. It's just that Andy likes to take care of me."

Peter interrupted, "Nonsense. I understand. And I'm glad you have someone like Andy to protect you. Let's just not talk about it here. Most of these people are friends and business associates. They know nothing of our business." He turned to Teresa and smiled at the young beauty. "So this is Teresa. My, but you are more beautiful than I had been told."

"Thank you, Mr. Salvano," she blushed.

"Would you like some Champaign?" Peter asked. "Maybe something softer?"

Tony looked at Teresa, and she said, "Thank you, no. Maybe later."

Peter started to lead them into his home, when Tony stopped him. He had been bothered for days about the invitation. Peter wanted to keep his two business worlds separated, yet he had invited Tony to the party. No other man or woman from that other world was there. He asked, "Why am I here, Mr. Salvano?"

"Well, Tony. I guess I just wanted you to see how I live and what you can expect in the future . . . If you're as smart as I think you are."

Teresa smiled. That's what her mother had said she wanted for her daughter. Teresa wondered if that was what she wanted, however. She loved Tony and nothing would change that. But did she want to be part of the world her mother and father had lived in? Her mother dreamed of riches and wealth and power. Teresa would be happy in a small house somewhere with Tony and children. But she would accept whatever came, as long as she could be with the man she loved so deeply.

"Please come inside," Peter said, waving them into the grand apartment. It was furnished like nothing Tony and Teresa had ever seen or dreamed of before. To them it was a palace. The furniture had all been picked out by Carol, Peter's wife, working with the best interior designers money could buy. Massive gold and crystal chandeliers hung from the ceiling. Several large chairs with red Chinese silk upholstery stood like sentries, guarding the priceless paintings on the walls, original pieces by some of the most sought after modern artists in the world. The floors were made of marble and fine woods, with rare Persian carpets laid perfectly on them. A staff of waiters and waitresses mingled with the guests, serving champagne and waiting to fetch anything anyone wanted.

One long wall held shelves from end to end, and on those shelves were vases, sculptures, framed artwork, and clocks of gold and silver. Next to that wall was a glass wall that looked out over the lights of the City. It was almost too much for Tony and Teresa to take in.

"There are people here you'd like to meet," Peter said. He waved to one man, a tough looking man of about fifty years. His rugged face bore a scar across his chin. Tony thought, 'This guy's either a Capo or a cop.'

Peter introduced him, "Tony, I'd like you to meet Detective Captain Robert Wolf." The Detective held out his hand and shook hands with Tony. Tony grinned. Detective Wolf did not know Tony, but Tony made a mental note to invite him to the opening of the gambling room he was having built in Newark.

Peter led them through the elegant room and introduced them to the guests, one by one, couple after couple. They were all wealthy businessmen and their expensive wives. Gold and diamonds decorated gowns, wrists, and necklines everywhere. Peter waved at a tall, beautiful blond. She was wearing a white dress with a splash of rhinestones across her bodice. Her thick, silky hair hung long, across her shoulders. She excused herself from the people she was with and started towards Peter. She held a glass of Champaign expertly as she moved like a Princess across the floor. The hand holding the champagne flute had a big diamond ring on it, perfectly positioned so that everyone could see it as she held the glass. Peter whispered to Tony and Teresa, "I'm going to introduce you to my wife. She knows nothing of our business." Tony nodded.

"Carol," he said brightly. "I'd like you to meet two young people I met the other day. This is Anthony Moretti and Teresa Falzone. This is Carol, my wife . . . Mrs. Salvano."

"I'm so glad to meet you," she said. "And Teresa, you are beautiful; I hope you know that."

"Thank you, Mrs. Salvano. And you are beautiful enough to be in the movies."

They laughed and Peter asked, "Carol, would you please take Teresa and introduce her around? I think a glass of soda would be appropriate. Maybe some champagne, if she would like to try some. I need to talk business with Tony."

He took Tony by his arm and led him away, leaving the two ladies behind. They walked across the room to a door that stood open a few inches. Peter opened the door, and they entered Peter's office. It was as grand as the rest of the home, the walls lined with dark polished wood, shelves of books, and Asian artifacts. A desk of elaborately carved walnut sat directly in front of the two men. Two dark leather chairs sat in front of the desk, and a tall brown leather chair sat on the other side.

Peter walked around the desk and sat in the tall chair. He waived Tony towards one of the chairs, where he sat, wondering why the hell he was there. He had been told it was a party. But was it? There were no other doors in the room, so it was unlikely anyone was waiting to put a bullet in his head. And Andy was out there, at the bar and wherever there was food. He wished Andy could be with him. Tony shifted uncomfortably, leaned forward and asked, "OK, why am I here?"

"As I said, I wanted you to see how I live, Tony. I'm very proud of how I live. I have a gorgeous wife; I have four children in a very expensive private school; I have a chauffeur who handles my Mercedes very well. I own buildings all over New York, Chicago, Los Angeles and a few other places, I own a construction company, and I have money in the bank. I take my wife to Europe once a year. I have a yacht tied up in Bermuda."

Tony smirked and asked, "So what? Am I here to listen to you brag?"

Peter leaned back and laughed loudly. He stopped long enough to light a cigarette. "My wife won't let me smoke in the house. But I don't let her in here. Would you like a cigarette? A cigar perhaps?"

"No, I don't smoke."

Peter blew smoke towards the ceiling, relaxed back in his big chair, stared deeply into Tony's eyes, and then began, "I want you to see what can be . . . For you, I mean. You're young . . . Someday you won't be. The people you and I work with are from a different world. I like the way you think, Tony. You have ideas like my own. I see bright things in your future."

"Excuse me, Mr. Salvano. But I think we've

talked about all this before."

"You're right, of course. I keep forgetting I don't have to talk down to you like I do with the others. Anyway, there's been a change of plans."

"You're taking Newark away from me?"

"No, not at all. You're off to a good start there. I'm speaking of Al Falzone. I spoke with him . . . Several times. He's very angry. He hates you, and he's a very violent man. You may be in jeopardy."

"I have Andy," Tony said simply.

"And you're very lucky to have such a loyal bodyguard."

"So what? What are you getting at?"

"I don't want Al around anymore."

"Are you asking me to kill Al Falzone?"

Peter smiled, took a long drag on the cigarette and blew the smoke up above Tony's head. But he did not answer.

"Look, Mr. Salvano. You know I'm going to do whatever you ask me to do. If you want Al dead, well, he's dead. But that's not a good idea right now."

"Why?"

"I thought I explained all this to you already. Because he still has men in Newark and Trenton who are loyal to him. Give me time to break that loyalty."

"I thought I told you to get rid of Al's men in Newark?"

"You did, and I will, but give me time. I've only been at this a short time. If the killing starts it will only delay what we both want. Look, I'll get rid of Al when I don't need him anymore . . . But I'll make it look like an accident. It won't look like a murder. No one will know. Just let me do it my way."

Tony sat back in the chair, and Peter smoked the cigarette down to the filter. He crushed it out slowly and deliberately. He was thinking, and Tony was thinking of his options. There wouldn't be any killing at the party. But if Peter thought he was being disloyal, if Peter did not get what he expected, then Tony could be facing trouble in the following few days. He was relieved when Peter said, "OK, Tony. I guess I have to trust you. I want the future you can see. If you think Al should stay alive, then so be it. But I want him controlled. I don't want any trouble from him. He killed a good business friend of mine and cost me a lot of money. He's not talking to me or Bruno in the tone he should. He's not respectful any longer. I don't trust people who are disloyal. Sooner or later he *will* die . . . And not of old age."

"You hate Al that much?" Tony asked. Peter didn't answer, but Tony knew the answer anyway. Peter Salvano was greedy. He had a taste for buckets of money, and he liked the power he had assumed when his father died. The murder of Roger Tifton took a lot of money away from Peter. That, he had come to believe, was unacceptable. Al Falzone had to die for the indiscretion of taking money away from Peter Salvano.

Tony stood and held out his hand. Peter hesitated, to make a good show of being in charge, and finally stood to shake Tony's hand, this time very gently in deference to the bandaged cut. They both returned to the party.

TWENTY-NINE

Newark, New Jersey
September 1961

As Don Peter Salvano had instructed, Tony had turned the Newark operation around in six months. Tony was surprised that first day, six months ago, when he and Andy Pecora walked into L'oro Luna. Andy stood behind Tony, grinning maliciously and ready for trouble when his boss told Ted Bianci and Louie Lombardi that he was taking over from Al Falzone. The surprise was that neither man objected. Tony had anticipated an argument, maybe a fight. Both were, in fact, happy at the change of leadership.

Louie Lombardi said, "The word is out that you were Made. That's great, and congratulations. I think you being the boss here is the right thing to do."

Andy relaxed, maybe a little disappointed that there wasn't going to be a fight. Tony asked Louie, "Why?" He had to know if these two men were telling the truth or lying to please Tony, and more particularly to please Andy Pecora. If they were lying, nothing he had planned would work. And in spite of what he had told Peter Salvano, these two men, former crew of Al Falzone, would be the foundation of Tony's new crew. He was not going to get rid of what was left of Al's

305

Newark crew, at least not yet. He would bring them to him; he would earn their loyalty.

He needed experienced people, people whom he could trust, because he knew he couldn't be everywhere at the same time. He would, eventually, be splitting his time between Newark and Trenton. Ted and Louie would have to be there to lead the new crew.

Louie looked at Ted, and Ted had some anger in his voice when he admitted, "When Al killed Mike, I was ready to kill him. If he weren't a damn Capo . . . I would have. Me and Louie don't respect him no more. He just ain't the kind of leader we need or want. I mean, when would he kill one of us? Since you've been here, we've been making more money than ever before. For me . . . You're my Capo, Tony."

Louie stood and wanted to give Tony the mandatory Italian hug and kiss on the cheek as a greeting and welcome. Tony held up a hand, laughed and stopped him. He said, "That's one of the changes were going to make around here. No more of that kissing crap. Lots of things are going to change. We're going to run this as a business and not as some gang of thugs. My name is Tony and that's what you'll call me when you're talking to me. No more Capo and no more public talk of Mafia and organized crime. This is a new world. No more old world crap. What we do here stays in this room. And what we're going to do is different than what you've been used to. No more hijackings, that's out completely. We're going to cut back on putting money on the streets, gambling will be our major income from now on."

In six months Tony had recruited two new soldiers, good men in their twenties who knew how to take orders and keep quiet about it. They came from the streets, from a local gang, the normal place to recruit from. They weren't teens anymore, and they were ready to move up.

He had established a gambling room, as he called it, a small casino, above a dry cleaner's near L'oro Luna, the first of many. It was a high stakes, one large room casino with a popular roulette wheel, two craps tables, and two blackjack tables that surrounded a poker table, where the buy-in was three thousand dollars. A bar was located at the far end of the room, where drinks were free and urged on players to make them gamble more with less chance of making smart bets.

The room, once a warehouse storage room that took up the entire second floor of the building, was large and elegant in decoration. Thick red and gold carpet covered the floor. The walls had been done by the finest finish carpenters using the best woods. Crystal chandeliers hung from the ceiling. Cocktail waitresses in short skirts and black stockings kept the drinks fresh at each table and received big tips for each drink they brought to a player.

Clients were, as Tony had planned for years, doctors, lawyers, and business owners, anybody with money to gamble away. Many tens of thousands of dollars were bet every night. And wealthy people came from across the State to hand their money over to Tony with a smile on their faces.

Money that was to be put on the street for loan sharking and broken legs was instead used to invest in a string of private auto finance companies. Tony had Ted Bianci and Louie Lombardi put pressure on auto dealerships to use their new, legal, finance companies.

Small businesses on the edge of financial failure had Tony as a new investor, and they welcomed him, because instead of paying extortionist level vig, their businesses were saved and made profitable by the cash Tony invested with them. He started buying up dry cleaning operations and cocktail lounges, cash operations from which money could be easily skimmed. He bought a large commercial laundry that served restaurants. Again, Ted Bianci and Louie Lombardi expanded that business by 'selling' that service to as many restaurants as they could find.

To keep the businesses going and profitable, he made changes to the operations and made sure competition stayed far away by using Ted Bianci and Louie Lombardi again. And Tony went into the money laundering business, running illegal cash from other Families and Capos through these businesses for a fee.

The cash was flowing in as regular as an ocean's high tide and just as strong. Bruno was happy at the cash paid up; Michael Funno, Manny Esposito, and of course Al were less happy. Their businesses had not changed, and their incomes were flat at best. The police kept after them and were leaving Tony alone. They were being shown up by a kid. They could not match the income Tony had. And they didn't know how to do business any different than what they were already doing.

Al, at Tony's order, was home in Montclair every Thursday evening and stayed until Monday morning when he returned to Trenton. He wasn't happy about this, and his family saw the change in him. No longer did he make Sunday morning pancakes. He no longer coached the Little League team. He was angry most of the time. He drank a lot at home and yelled at everything and everybody. He wasn't the father they remembered.

To top off Al's anger, at the end of Teresa's senior school year, before leaving for College, she had packed a bag and left to move in with Tony for the summer. Al threw a fit; he screamed, he yelled, he put his fist through a wall. Maria ignored his rampage and helped Teresa to quickly pack. She promised to bring the rest of her clothes over soon.

Maria was happy for her daughter. She had started planning the wedding, going from store to store looking at wedding dresses, talking to bakers about huge cakes. "It's never too early," she would tell Teresa. "Yours will be the biggest wedding ever."

Tony had told Al that after Teresa went off to college, he was to move his wife and son down to Trenton. Al argued about this. He wanted to keep his girlfriend. It was easier for Al with her than with his wife who never stopped complaining about his position in the Salvano family. His girlfriend couldn't care less, as long as the money was there.

But he also knew he had to do what Tony told him to do. It had gone beyond the secret they kept about Roger Tifton; Al was now displaced as a leader and was now working under Tony's leadership. Until Al moved his family to Trenton, Tony had Andy make sure Al was home in Montclair every Friday, Saturday, and Sunday.

Teresa had been gone for three months, living at Tony's apartment in Newark, a place both she and Tony called 'home'. She would start college in two weeks. They came back to Montclair every Sunday for lunch and dinner with Maria, Little Al, and of course, a drunken Al.

Each work day, Tony wanted to stay 'at home' with Teresa, but Andy arrived every morning to remind him of work that needed to be done. Teresa was happy playing the role of 'housewife'. While Tony was gone, she cleaned the apartment, drove the Ford station wagon Tony had bought for her to the grocery store, and phoned her mother to get recipes and cooking advice for dinners. And each day, while she was alone, she knelt and said a prayer of thanks to God for allowing her to be with Tony. "Please God," she would pray. "Let this go on forever. I love Tony so much. Please God."

****

Montclair, New Jersey

Al's anger didn't subside with time. He was drinking more every day and venting loudly every day, too. That day in September was the worst. He had been drunk when he arrived at the house Thursday evening. He had driven alone from Trenton, drinking from the fifth of vodka. He parked his car half in the driveway and half on the front lawn. He stumbled across the lawn to the front door and pounded on it because he couldn't get his key into the lock. He stayed drunk through Sunday. He didn't eat anything, and he slept on the couch or floor in the living room, rather than in his own bed. He couldn't stand being with Maria, when he knew there was a blow job waiting for him in Trenton.

Sunday that weekend found Teresa and Tony at the Falzone home for the afternoon and for dinner. Al was loud and obnoxious; they did their best to ignore him. They sat outside, on the back patio, where Tony and Andy tried their best to bar-b-cue hamburgers. Teresa and Maria sat and watched, having a good laugh at the two of them, because neither really knew what they were doing.

After Teresa and Tony had left to go home that evening, Al stumbled to the bar in the living room and opened a fresh bottle of Four Roses Whiskey. He threw the top away and drank from the bottle.

"That won't help, Al," Maria said. "She's off to school in a couple of weeks. Let it be."

"Shut up!"

"Don't tell me to shut up! If you were any kind of man you'd be moving up like Tony is! I want Teresa to have what I never had!" There, she had said it, she thought. It was about time it was out in the open. She had come to hate Al. He wasn't the man she had married, and she didn't see a future with him. Divorce was on her mind; it was just the Church keeping her from finding a lawyer. But soon, she was sure, soon she would say 'to hell with it' and leave him.

Al drank from the bottle twice more, holding it by its neck, spilling liquor down his chin, onto his shirt. He was glaring at Maria. Why did he have to be there with her when he could be with Margarita and the blow jobs she did so well? It was that damn kid, Tony, that was it. That damn kid had taken everything from him. First his job and crew and then his daughter. He had waited long enough for the kid to make a mistake. The damn kid might never make a damn mistake. He had to do something to make his daughter break up with the damn kid.

"Oh, Al," Maria said. "Come on. Put the bottle down. I'll make some coffee. You have to sober up so you can go back to Trenton tomorrow."

He threw the whiskey bottle across the room, frightening Maria. She screamed as it flew past her. It broke on the wall just inches from her head. Shards of glass hit her cheek and drops of blood appeared. He ran, stumbling, across the room and grabbed Maria by her hair and hit her with a closed fist hard across her cheek. She screamed again as she fell to the floor. The pearl necklace she was wearing broke and pearls ran across the carpet. Al kicked her in the stomach, kicked her again, and kicked her again. He pulled her to her feet, ripping her blouse. She was bleeding badly and too hurt to scream again.

He slapped her and then back handed her. A punch to her mouth opened her bottom lip. He hit her again and again. Al was in a psychotic state were all he could see in front of him was hot red hate. He wasn't thinking; he was just lashing out, letting hatred take over.

Blood was flowing from Maria's face, eyes, and ears. Her eyes were swelling fast and closing. Her mouth was full of blood. He threw her against the wall, and she slumped to the floor, unconscious. But Al kept kicking her, in her stomach and at her head. He reached down and hit her, over and over again until her face was nothing but blood. He couldn't stop himself; he wanted to kill her, to be finally done with her after too many years of her complaining and berating him over what she saw as his failure.

Little Al was watching from the stairs. He was terrified. He bit his thumb until it bled and he wet his pants. He was crying, his mouth open in a scream, but no sound came from him. He was pulling at his hair. He was stamping his feet on the stairs. He turned and ran to his bedroom. He hid under his bed for the rest of that evening, until it was dark.

Little Al was shivering, shaking uncontrollably for hour after hour, waiting for someone, anyone, to come save him from his terror. He couldn't stop from wetting himself, and his bowel opened; watery feces pooled under him. He waited for someone to come to save him, but no one did. When he finally did crawl out from under his bed, the house was dark, and he was alone. He walked slowly, carefully, down the stairs, cautiously looking for his father. If his father was still there, he would run from him, he decided; he would run and hide.

He went to the living room where his mother lay, covered in blood. She was very pale and barely breathing. He bent to her and shook her, covering his hands with her blood. "Mama . . . Mama . . . Mama," he kept repeating as he shook her. But she wouldn't move. He screamed and screamed again. He slumped onto the floor and started crying.

Neighbors had heard what was going on, the beatings and screaming and yelling and cursing, but they were afraid to intercede. In the middle of the night, when Little Al was screaming, a couple of the neighborhood men found the courage to go to the Falzone home. They found Maria and phoned for an ambulance. No thought was given to phoning the police.

Little Al had run to his room and under his bed when he heard the neighbors at the door.

****

Newark, New Jersey

Tony and Teresa were in their apartment laughing and having fun, trying to cook some breakfast together. They were trying to cook a frittata, making a mess of it. There was more egg and tomato on them and the floor than in the fry pan. The phone rang, interrupting their fun. It was Louie Lombardi.

"Tony," he said. "It's your girl's mother. She's in Saint Agnes Hospital."

"What happened?"

"You better get here, Tony. It's bad."

Andy had driven to his own place for the night. They had Teresa's Ford, but Tony thought that maybe she shouldn't be driving it, if what Louie said was true. So Tony phoned for a cab. He took Teresa to a chair and made her sit while he waited for the taxi. "It's your mother," he said. "Something happened. She's in the hospital."

"Oh my God! It's my Dad, isn't it? He hurt her, didn't he?" She seemed to know somehow. It wasn't a premonition; she had worried that something like this would happen someday. It was only a matter of time, she had seemed certain of that. Al had been so angry for so long; he was always drunk. He wasn't the same father she remembered. She had been seeing him as a dark monster, keeping that vision to herself. If she had told Tony of her thoughts, he would have found the meaning to his nightmare. He would have done something to stop Al, but Teresa never shared her feelings on her father with him, and Tony hadn't yet told her of his nightmare.

"I don't know," Tony said. He held her hand and tried to comfort her, to ease her worry. "Maybe she just tripped or something. We'll get there as soon as we can. In the meantime, let's not make something out of what's probably nothing."

The taxi came, and Tony gave the driver a hundred dollar bill. "Get us to St. Agnes Hospital in Montclair fast!" he ordered. "Screw the speed limits and traffic lights. Don't worry about the cops. I'll fix everything."

The driver did as he was paid to do. There were no police. They avoided getting into a couple of accidents as they sped through red lights. They skidded to a stop in front of the emergency room entrance. Teresa ran inside with Tony at her heels. The room was a mass of people, crying, bleeding, in pain. A man sat in a plastic chair, his shirt covered in blood. He had been stabbed; he was holding a hand to his stomach but the blood seeped through his fingers. His eyes were vacant as he stared off into nothingness, dying as he waited for a doctor to help him. It was near mayhem. They weren't going to wait with the rest of these poor people. Tony went to the front desk, slammed his fist on the counter and demanded, "Maria Falzone! Where is she!"

The nurse, a black woman who had stepped back away from Tony, pointed with a shaking finger down a hallway. Tony took Teresa by her hand, and they ran down the hall. Halfway down, there was a uniformed cop standing in the hallway, leaning against the wall, his thumbs tucked into his work belt. He saw Tony coming and stood upright.

Tony said, "Maria Falzone."

The cop reached for the door handle behind him and opened the door. They stood in the open doorway and couldn't believe it was Maria they were looking at. Maria was in a bed, covered with a white sheet that was stained with her blood. Her head was visible, but she didn't look like Maria, because of the stitched cuts and bandages all over her face and head. Both her eyes were swollen shut and bright red. A doctor and a nurse were standing at opposite sides of the bed. Machinery buzzed, and a drip of blood was flowing into Maria's arm. The doctor turned and said, "No visitors."

"I'm her daughter," Teresa said. She went to her mother and took her hand. Maria was still unconscious. Her face was colorless, save for the cuts and swelling that were everywhere. There were fresh stitches along her lower lip. Her eyes were so badly swollen, that even if she were awake she would not be able to see. Teresa started crying. Tony took the doctor's arm and pulled him aside.

"How is she?" he asked.

"Who are you?"

"I'm Tony Moretti," he said. "You've heard of

me?"

"Of course," the doctor answered. He was
surprised to see how young this man was who was
reputed to be the head of all criminal organizations in
Northeast New Jersey. To the Doctor, Tony couldn't
be more than 20, maybe a little older. He had no idea
Tony was only 17 years old. "I know who you are," he
said nervously.

"Then tell me how she is."

"She's been hurt badly. There's a concussion
and internal injuries. She's lost a lot of blood. We're
going to have to remove her spleen. One of her
kidneys isn't functioning. I don't know if we can save
that yet. It's the head injuries I'm most worried about.
Now please, you and the girl must leave so we can
work here."

Tony looked hard into the doctor's eyes and
said, "She's going to live, Doctor. She's going to live.
Understand?"

He took Teresa back to the hallway and to a
bench across the hall from her mother's emergency
treatment room. She sat, still crying and wiping her
eyes with the remnants of a tissue. Tony walked to
the police officer at Maria's door and asked quietly,
"Do you guys know who did this?"

"Not so far," he answered.

"Where is her husband?"

"Last I heard they haven't been able to talk to
him or find him."

"You mean he's gone?" Tony asked.

"I guess so," the cop said. He shifted nervously
from foot to foot and then added, "Look, I've been
standing here for over an hour. I don't know what
they're doing or if they found Mr. Falzone. You better

call the station."

Tony returned to Teresa and sat close to her. He put his arm around her shoulders and hugged her to him. "Teresa," he said. "I'm going to leave you here, OK? I'm going to go make a few phone calls to try to find out who did this. I'll be back soon. You wait here. I won't be long."

"My Dad did it," she sobbed. "He did it."

"I'll find out who did it and take care of it."

She looked up at him and said, "Don't hurt him, Tony. Just find him. Don't hurt him, please."

Tony kissed her quickly. Her lips tasted of salty tears. He squeezed her hand in his and walked away. Near the end of the hall was a nurse's station. Tony went to it and demanded a telephone. The young nurse behind the counter picked up a phone, laid it on the counter and then backed away.

Tony dialed L'oro Luna. Ted Bianci answered. Tony said, "I want the whole crew and all our friends out on the streets. I want everybody out now. I want Al Falzone found. Don't hurt him, just hold him for me. One hundred dollars to the man who finds him."

He quickly dialed Andy's apartment number. Andy answered on the third ring.

"This is Tony. I want you to drive down to Trenton right now. Get to that piss hole pool hall the guys hang out in. Get everybody there out on the streets. Have somebody go to Al's friggin' apartment. Have them wait there. I want Al Falzone brought back to Newark if he shows up there. Don't hurt him, just bring him to me."

"You got it, boss," Andy said without asking 'why'. His boss had told him what to do, and he would do it. He raced outside to the Cadillac.

Tony next phoned Bruno in Brooklyn. He explained what had happened. Bruno said, "That's bad. Look, Al's a Capo. You better speak to your Don." He gave Tony the direct phone number to reach Peter Salvano. "Don't speak in detail, Tony. The cops may be listening in."

"Yeah, I don't really care."

Tony dialed the number, and Peter answered. Tony said, speaking plainly, "This is Tony," when Peter answered. He told Peter what had happened. "I want him," he said. "Do I have your permission?"

"I'm sorry. I don't know who you are or what you're talking about. Are you sure you have the right number?"

"I don't have time for this," Tony said. "I want Al . . . If you know what I mean."

"I don't know what you're talking about. I would advise you . . . Whoever you are . . . Not to hurt anyone. That would be a crime no one would appreciate."

"But . . ."

Peter decided to just speak plainly. If anyone was listening, and he gave Tony permission to kill Al Falzone, he would be arrested and charged. So he said in plain language, "I know how you feel, Tony. But not right now. It was you, as I recall, who had a plan for Al. Now, things haven't changed. You can find him and see if he did this, but nothing else."

"Can I turn him over to the cops?"

"I don't care about that," Peter said. "The cops are nothing."

Tony returned to Teresa. She was sitting where he had left her. She had stopped crying, but she stared straight ahead as if she was in a trance, looking at something far, far away. He took her hand and said, "Teresa, baby. You OK?"

"Yes," she said in a near whisper. "This happened because of me."

"What! What did you do?"

"Daddy never wanted me to be with you. If I had done what he wanted . . . If I hadn't moved out . . . This wouldn't have happened. It's all my fault."

Tony knew she was right in saying Al didn't want them to be together, of course. Al hated Tony for taking his daughter away from him. How often had he told Tony that he wanted her to marry a good man, outside of the business? Al let that anger build inside of him, and that, added to the alcohol that had warped his brain, caused him to go crazy. He had lashed out at the closest thing to him, and that, unfortunately, was Teresa's mother.

'If I had told Peter Salvano the truth, Al would probably be dead, and none of this would have happened,' he told himself. But if Teresa ever found out that he had told Peter and Al was murdered as a result, she would have hated him forever for having her father killed. Now this; and what would happen to them? What was she thinking? Would she continue to love him? Could she continue to love him?

He brushed the hair from her eyes and said, "It's not your fault. It's my fault."

Teresa turned to look at him. "How?" she asked.

"I've taken the Newark territory from him. He hates me, even though he has Trenton. He doesn't realize that he hasn't lost anything . . . But you. He believes I've taken you from him. It was building up inside of him for months. His anger was boiling inside of him, and it just burst out. My God, Teresa. If you had been there instead of with me, it might be you in there where you mother is. It's all on me, Teresa. Not you."

She stared up into his eyes. There was questioning there, wondering if what he said was the truth. She asked, "Do you love me, or are you out to hurt my father? To take everything from him?"

"I love you, Teresa. Your father and I have business together. It's a tough business, you know that. I've got plans, and your father is scared of those plans. My plans are different than everything your father has become used to. You are the biggest part of those plans. Our future . . . Our lives together . . . That's what all my plans are about. He thinks he's going to be pushed aside, but he's wrong. I've tried to tell him he's wrong. I've tried to tell him that being with his family was important. I tried to talk to him about being a grandfather to our kids. I'm not sure he understood or believed me. He and I are different kinds of people. We have different visions of the future. That's all."

"Is he going to be pushed aside, Tony? Is he going to be hurt?"

"I just talked with Mr. Salvano. I told him what happened and that it looks like your father may have done this. Mr. Salvano gave me orders not to hurt your father. That means he isn't going to be hurt. I had no intention of hurting him, and I wanted to be sure Peter wouldn't hurt him. If he wanted to hurt your father, I would have protected him. I've told everyone to find him and not to hurt him." Tony paused for a moment and then said, "I would never do anything to hurt you, Teresa. You're my whole life and my future. If having you means losing everything else, I would lose everything else. I would walk away today, if you would come with me. If you would come with me, we'd just drive away and start a new life somewhere. You have to believe that."

They sat for over an hour, speaking very little to each other, waiting for some report from the doctors. Nurses and doctors and technicians with machines went into and went away from Maria's room. Heavy footsteps coming down the linoleum covered floor caught their attention. It was two Police Detectives in cheap shoes that made too much noise on the linoleum floor. Their sports jackets and ill-matching pants were as cheap. Tony recognized one as being on his payroll. He said nothing because the other might not be his employee.

They stopped in front of Tony and Teresa. Tony stood and waited. "I'm Detective Morrison," the one not on his payroll said. "Miss Falzone, I'm very sorry about what happened to your mother."

"Thank you," she said. "Have you found my father?"

"No. Do you have reason to believe your father did this to your mother?"

Tony was holding Teresa's hand. He squeezed her hand just enough to tell her she shouldn't be talking to the police. Tony spoke up and said, "As soon as he's found, I'll let you know. I don't know if he did this. He may be unaware of what's happened. Nothing will happen to him before you guys get to talk to him," and with that, he sat down.

Morrison looked down at the seated Tony Moretti. He knew who this young man was and the power he was accumulating. 'One day.' He thought, 'I'm gonna' have to deal with this kid.' But not that day.

He said, "Alright. Remember that I talked to you, and remember that what happened is an assault. There are laws against that sort of thing . . . No matter who does the assaulting. Understand?"

"Oh, sure thing, Detective," Tony said. "I got it.

Are you leaving now? Shouldn't you be out looking for whoever did this? Or do you think whoever did this is hiding in the hospital?"

The two Detectives walked away, leaving Tony and Teresa alone again. They remained seated for hours, waiting. A nurse brought them two paper cups of coffee and two ham and cheese sandwiches. "That was nice of her," Teresa said in a weak voice as she laid the unwrapped sandwich on the bench next to her. "But I couldn't eat anything." She sipped at the bitter coffee but couldn't taste it.

At half past three in the afternoon, the Doctor who had been in Maria's room when they arrived walked out of the room. Tony and Teresa jumped to their feet and ran to him.

They waited, standing in front of him, waiting for the Doctor to say something, afraid to ask. The Doctor looked exhausted. He had been with Maria for twelve straight hours. He said, "She's in serious but stable condition. She'll live. She's still unconscious. We're going to leave her unconscious for the time being. In the morning we're going to operate to try to repair some of the internal damage."

"Can I see her?" Teresa asked.

"Just for a minute," he answered. "Just you, though."

Tony ignored the Doctor, and he walked past him into Maria's room with Teresa. The woman didn't look like Maria Falzone. Her face was twisted out of shape and was swollen due to her broken jaw. Her eyes were surrounded by ugly red swelling. There was a mask across her mouth and twisted nose to bring oxygen into her. The sheet covering her had been changed, this one clean and white.

She had been beaten so badly that Teresa could hardly recognize her. Although the Doctor had said she was stabilized, she didn't look any better than she had hours before. But they had stopped giving her blood. Teresa remarked on that and said, "That's a good sign, don't you think?"

They had cleaned her face of blood but that only exposed all the damage Al had inflicted. There were cuts and bruises everywhere. Teresa at first wanted to pull the sheet away but she was afraid of what she would find under it. She bent down and kissed her mother lightly and quickly on her forehead. Tony took her by the arm and said, "We better leave. We'll come back in the morning." Teresa nodded, and they left. Louie Lombardi was waiting at the entrance to the emergency room. He tossed his cigarette into the gutter and opened a car door for them. "Thought you'd need a ride, Tony."

"Yeah, thanks, Louie. Back to my place, OK?"

Teresa stood at the open car door and said in a frail and tired voice, "No, I want to go home, Tony." She quickly looked up at him and then said, "I want to go to my mother's home, please."

He nodded, and Louie drove them to Teresa's home in Montclair. Teresa walked very slowly up the flagstone path to her front door. Tony told Louie to have someone pick him up there in the morning. "I want to be kept up to date on Al," he said. "When he's found I want to know."

Louie handed Tony a pistol and said, "Just in case, Tony." He took it and tucked it under his belt at the small of his back. He followed Teresa to the front door. Neighbors were at their windows watching. No one dared step outside.

At the door, Teresa used her key to unlock and open the door. She turned to Tony, standing in the open doorway, and said, "I think we shouldn't be together tonight."

"I'm not going to leave you alone here," he said. "If your father shows up, there's no telling what he'll do. If I have to, I'll sleep here on your front porch."

She nodded and stepped inside and let Tony in behind her. The house was dark and cold and quiet. The late evening light racing in through the front window fell on the stain of dried blood where Maria had lain. Teresa looked at the ugly stain and quickly looked away. "I don't want to sleep with you tonight, Tony," she said and walked away to the kitchen. She searched for something to clean up the blood stains. Tony sat in a chair and laid the pistol on his lap.

He tried to understand what Teresa was feeling, but he couldn't. Yes, she loved her parents, both her mother and father, in spite of the change in her father. They had been good parents to Teresa, spoiling her with clothes and everything she ever wanted. Yes, she knew the business her father was in. And yes, Tony thought, she may have accepted the fact that her father had almost killed her mother, although he doubted she would ever forgive him. But would that affect her love of him? He couldn't understand why it wouldn't. But he also couldn't understand what she was thinking.

Tony thought back on the beatings he and his mother had taken from his drunken father. It was bad; those nights were terrifying, but never this bad. In the end, he hated his father and had little feelings left for his mother, who refused to protect her child. Teresa had obviously never been beaten by Al, at least he didn't think she ever had been. Maybe, he thought, she was just a girl wanting her family to be perfect and now finding out that her family was as far from perfect as a family could get? Maybe she was feeling grief at the loss of her perfect family?

Sitting in the chair, alone in the living room, the memory of the nightmare came back to him. Was Al the dark monster that would come between Teresa and him? Could he have seen it coming? Should he have done something to keep it from happening? Should he have been warned? Was it a mistake to try to keep Teresa's family together? Was the nightmare a message that he had ignored? Maybe he made a mistake insisting Al come back to Montclair and not stay in Trenton?

Upstairs, Little Al slammed open the door to his room. Teresa, in the kitchen, jumped at the sound. Tony reached for his gun. If Al was in the house, he would be dangerous. But it was only Little Al. He ran down the hallway and down the stairs. He was screaming like a demented banshee, jumping up and down, and waving his arms about madly. "SISTER! . . . SISTER! . . . WHERE HAVE YOU BEEN! WHERE'S MOMMY! WHAT'S GOING ON!"

Teresa bent and hugged the boy with her one free arm, holding a wet towel she was going to use to clean what she could of the blood in the other. He was hysterical, stamping his bare feet on the floor like a baby. He was covered with feces and urine. Teresa stepped back away from him because of the filth. He was flailing around and screaming like a crazy person. "Mommy's alright," she said trying to calm the boy. "She's in the hospital, but she'll be home soon. I'll be here with you."

"I SAW WHAT DADDY DID! I SAW HIM HIT MOMMY! WHY DID HE DO THAT?" he shrieked. His eyes were flared; his arms were thrashing at the air above his head. He was jumping around and stamping in puddles of his urine and feces. Foamy spittle ran from his mouth and green mucus ran from his nostrils.

"I don't know, baby. He's coming home soon, and we can ask him." Teresa wanted to go to her brother, to take him in her arms, but he was filthy. She reared back, away from him.

"NO! NO! I DON'T WANT HIM HERE! I'M SCARED! HE'LL HIT ME LIKE HE HIT MOMMY."

"You saw him hit Mommy?" Teresa asked.

"YES! YES! YES! I'M SCARED, SISTER! I'M SCARED!"

"There's nothing to be scared of, Alley. I'm here with you now. Let's go upstairs and get you cleaned up. A nice hot bath, OK?" She took the boy's hand, and that at least stopped him from screaming and flailing.

Tony watched from the chair, not knowing what to say or do. Little Al was ten years old, and he was screaming like some child maniac. He had dirtied himself. The kid was insane, Tony thought. It was more than what the boy had seen the night before. It had to be the end result of what had been his life.

Tony was aware of all the boy had suffered in his ten years - being ignored, the constant scolding and lecturing, being left alone in the house so often. He had tried to be the boy's friend, but that did no good. "Oh shit!" he said out loud. Tony had promised to take the boy to New York and to museums there. He had forgotten. Business had gotten in the way. Maybe, he thought, if he had spent more time with Little Al, maybe he wouldn't be crazy. 'He's going to be trouble when he grows up,' Tony thought.

He wanted to stay awake in case Al came back to the house. But sleep overcame him. He dreamed of Teresa . . . This time without the dark monster . . . But she was crying in his dream. He held her, but she would not stop crying, and it hurt him to not be able to stop her sadness. Hours later Teresa went downstairs to find Tony asleep in the chair. She stood at the bottom of the stairs looking at him. She shivered and tried to understand why she would feel so far from him because of what had happened. Tony had taken no part in it. He had been nothing but good to her. They had been together for so long; they had loved each other for so long.

Now she looked at Tony and tried to remember all the things that had made her happy, but everything had changed; the happiness had suddenly escaped her. A veil had been lowered between them. A tear fell from the corner of her eye as she watched him, slumped back in the chair, breathing deeply and slowly, the gun in his lap that he would use to protect her. She turned and went back upstairs to see if Little Al was still asleep.

The phone woke Tony. The sun was lighting the room. He smelled coffee. He shook his head to try to clear it from sleep and picked up the phone. It was Andy. "I got him, boss. Found him in Trenton trying to get to his whore. He's really fucked up. Been drinkin' a lot."

"Bring him to the L'oro Luna. I'll be there."

Teresa was standing in the entry to the kitchen. She held a mug of coffee in her hands. She was pale, her hair was a rumpled mess, and her eyes were streaked with eye makeup that had run down her face with her tears. She hadn't slept; it took more than an hour to calm Little Al and get him cleaned up and into bed. Then she had to stay with him for another hour to get him to sleep. He was terrified, and all she could do was speak softly and try to comfort and reassure him.

His room was fetid with the smell of human waste. She had put him in her bed, and when he finally fell asleep she tried to clean up his room as best she could. Under his bed, lying in the puddles of urine and feces were Little Al's hand drawn pictures of naked women. They shocked her; she had not known he was doing this. They were beyond obscene; they were pictures of torture and death. All she could do was call them 'sick'. It was just another reason for her to cry. She ripped the pages into shreds, took them into the bathroom and burnt them in the tub, washing the ashes down the drain.

She stood in the kitchen doorway, looking at Tony and asked, "You have him?"

He pushed himself out of the chair; his back and neck were stiff, but he pushed the pain aside. The pistol fell to the floor, unnoticed. "He was in Trenton. He's OK. He's pretty drunk. Andy's bringing him home."

"You're going to bring him here?" she asked.

"To the L'oro Luna."

"OK, that's good. I don't think Alley should see him right now." Teresa said. "When he's sober I want to talk to him." She turned away from him and started up the stairs to her room. She didn't say goodbye, she didn't thank him, and there was no thought of a kiss. She just turned her back on him and walked upstairs, carrying her mug of hot coffee.

Tony did not answer her. He had to see Al, to talk to him before he would let him get close to Teresa.

"How's Little Al?" he called out.

"I don't know," she said stopping half way up the stairs without turning to look at him. "He went to bed after I got him cleaned up." She would not tell him of the pictures under the boy's bed. They made her feel ashamed.

He said, "He saw what happened, Teresa. My God, that could scar him forever."

"I know," she said. She was not looking at him. She sipped at the coffee without offering him any. "I'll take care of him."

"What can I do, honey?" Tony asked. He started for the stairs but she went up and out of his sight, away from him, without looking at him. He was startled that she would just walk away from him so abruptly. She was angry, she was hurt, and she was scared. But Tony couldn't figure out why she was angry with him. What had he done? He didn't know. All he had wanted to do was help her.

Then it came to him once again. It was the nightmare! He knew it now. The nightmare was a premonition that he hadn't understood, that he had forced himself to ignore, a message of what was to happen. If he had believed it, maybe he could have done something different; maybe he could have changed things? But he had pushed it aside, not taken notice of it, and now she was leaving him.

'My God!' he realized. 'She's leaving me!' The room was suddenly caught in a tornado, twisting and turning around him; it was about to throw him off his feet. His eyes were aflame blinding him to everything but the reality of Teresa. He fell to his knees, and a flood of tears burst from his eyes. He wanted to scream, but he couldn't.

The gun! It was the easy way out. She was gone from him, and life had no meaning. He crawled across the room and tried to focus through the whirlwind in his brain. Sight was useless through the tears that wouldn't stop. Then his gun was there, in his hand. All he had to do was pull the hammer back, put the gun to his temple, and the pain would come to an end.

But Teresa was still out there. That single thought brought sense back to Tony. He forced himself to his feet, and he threw the gun across the room, onto the couch. He had to live . . . For Teresa.

He had to be alive for her, for that someday when she would be back in his arms. His head was aching, throbbing; his stomach was twisted in knots. He ran for the front door, and outside, at a bush next to the steps, he vomited.

THIRTY

Newark, New Jersey
September 1961

Ted Bianci had gone to the Falzone home to get Tony. He had parked at the curb in front of the house and waited two hours for him. Ted saw Tony rush from the house and throw up. He ran to him. "You OK, Tony? What's a'matter? You OK?"

Tony wiped his mouth with a handkerchief and grabbed onto Ted's arm.

"Help me to the car," Tony said. He was unsteady on his feet; the world was spinning around in front of him, away from him. He couldn't see through the spinning fog.

On the way down the flagstone path to the car, Ted, trying to say something because he didn't know what to do, explained, "Andy wanted to come but Al's really messed up. It's best that Andy stay with him."

Tony sat in the front seat of Ted's brand new Buick, but he took no notice of it. The ride seemed to take forever. He didn't recognize where they were going. He leaned his head back and closed his eyes. She was gone from him, he knew that. He needed to figure out what to do. He had to get her back . . .

Soon . . . Somehow.

When they got to L'oro Luna all of Tony's newly recruited young soldiers were standing on the sidewalk in front. No one would get inside past them; police, no one. They stopped talking; those who were smoking crushed out their cigarettes because they knew Tony didn't like the smoke.

None of them had ever seen Tony in the state he was in. Instead of his expensive suit, he wore wrinkled tan cotton slacks and a white shirt that was spotted with vomit. His face was pale, and he stumbled as he walked to the door.

They backed up a few steps leaving a respectful distance for Tony to walk into the bar. No one said anything. Ted wanted to help him, to hold onto him, but Tony shrugged him away. The door was opened for Tony, and he stopped in the doorway when he saw what the men had done.

Inside, Al was sitting on a hard backed wooden chair in the middle of the tavern. All the tables and chairs had been moved to the walls. Andy stood behind Al, his arms crossed. He didn't look happy.

Al was tied to the chair, his arms behind him; thick rope wound around his chest. He was a mess; his suit was torn and mud covered, his hair knotted and hanging over his forehead.

"What the hell is this?" Tony asked. "I thought I said he wasn't to be hurt."

Andy said angrily, "The som'bitch puked all over your car."

'He's not the only one sick because of this,' Tony thought. He had to fight the urge to take Andy's gun and blow Al's brains out.

"So why tie him up?"

"He was hittin' an' kickin' everybody, boss. I had to tie him up so he wouldn't get hurt by somebody. The guys were pretty mad, ya' know?"

Tony went to Al. His head was slumped forward, his eyes closed. Tony grabbed a shock of hair and pulled Al's head up. Al's eyes opened. "You fuckin' bastard kid," he slurred when he looked at Tony through bloodshot eyes.

A couple of the new soldiers had entered the bar behind Tony, agreeing they would protect him, but really wanting to see what was going on. He turned to them and said, "Get a bucket of cold water. Put some coffee on. I want him sober."

One of the men ran and got a mop bucket from a back room. He filled it with cold water and carried it to Al. He paused and then threw it at his face. Al screamed, choked, and woke up. He swore, but he was awake. Tony untied Al's hands and unwrapped the rope that bound his chest. Al jumped to his feet. Andy grabbed him from behind and pushed him down onto the chair.

"Al," Tony said. "Be smart for once in your damn life. You're in trouble. You caused me a lot of trouble. You don't know the trouble you've caused me. You caused Andy here a lot of trouble. Your son and daughter are wrecks because of you. Your wife is in the hospital."

"Fuck you, kid." He looked up at Tony standing in front of him and spit. Tony moved away quickly, and the yellow phlegm flew past him.

"Al, you're testing my resolve to keep you alive. I promised your daughter that you wouldn't be hurt. Let me keep that promise. Look, you need to sober up. The guys are making coffee. You're going to drink as much as it takes."

Tony waited at the bar, sitting on a stool, while

Al, still sitting in the chair in the middle of the barroom in soaked clothes, drank two cups of hot coffee and then a third. Andy was standing in front of him. It was threat enough to make Al finish the coffee. When he thought the time was right, Tony stepped forward and stood in front of Al.

"Why, Al?" he asked. "Why the hell did you do it? My God, man! She's your wife! You almost killed her!"

"Fuck you, kid."

"Your wife is in the hospital. She almost died. Your daughter is nearly crazy over all this. Your son is crying like a crazy man, and he shit himself and wet his damn pants. Why, Al?"

"Because of you," he said, spitting the words out. "I hate you, you son of a bitch. I hate you. You're everything that I hate and everything that's gonna' destroy me."

Tony thought about that. Al was right at least on one point. Tony was going to end the rule of people like Al Falzone. Al was the old world. Al was the violence and stupidity. Al's time was just about up. All the men of that world were almost out of time.

"OK," he said. "I can accept that. But can you accept it? I've taken over Newark. I've changed things here. Next I'm going to change things down in Trenton."

"You're taking over my territory?"

"Oh, you're going to be there. You're going to go back to Trenton, and you're going to stay there. For your daughter, you're going to stay alive. But you're going to take your orders from me, Al. Mr. Salvano gave you to me, do you understand that? I own you now. You work for me now. You'll do what I tell you to do. But you'll be down there permanently now. You're not going to see Newark or Montclair again. You're never going to see your wife again. You're not going to see your children again."

"You son of a bitch," Al said, spitting out the words.

"Al, I'm the only one keeping you alive. The cops want you. I can give you to them. Peter said that was OK. But I won't . . . I won't because of Teresa." Tony paused and put a hand to his forehead. The room began spinning in front of him again. He had to control it; he had to stay in control. He forced his head to clear but a throbbing headache shot pain through him.

He said, "Peter wanted you dead months ago. He knows all about Roger Tifton. He knows you killed him and why. I talked him out of it . . . For Teresa's sake, you son of a bitch. And I'm going to keep you alive . . . For Teresa's sake. Now, are you sober enough to talk to Teresa? She wants to talk to you, but you're not going to the house. You'll talk to her by phone, and then you'll never talk to her again."

"You fuckin' kid!" Al slurred the words, spittle shooting from his lips. "You come in here and try to take my territory and now my fuckin' daughter! You fuckin' kid! I should put a bullet in your fuckin' head!"

Tony told his two soldiers to take Al by his arms and walk him to the back of the bar. There was a pay phone there. Tony dropped some change in the slot and dialed the Falzone home. Teresa answered.

"This is Tony," he said. "Your father is here with me. Do you want to speak with him?"

"Bring him here, Tony. I'll keep Alley in his room."

"I can't do that, Teresa. He's really messed up. He's acting crazy. I don't know what he'd do. If he tried to hurt you . . . Well, I couldn't keep my promise to you. Just talk to him now."

Al grabbed the phone from Tony's hand. He said, trying to sound like a sweet, loving father but still slurring his words because of all the alcohol, "Hi, baby. How are you?"

"How am I? Shouldn't you ask how Mama is?"

"I'm sorry about that, baby. I just had too much to drink. Is she OK?"

"Am I the reason, Daddy?"

"No, baby, you're not the reason. I couldn't hate you baby. I love you baby. It's that damn Tony you've been with. He's no good, baby. He's a liar and a cheat. He's been using you, baby. He's been touching you and using you to get me. You need to stay away from him, baby. He's no good, baby."

She said nothing, and for a moment there was silence. Then she hung up. Al held the phone close to his ear and said, "Hello, baby? You still there, baby?" Tony took the phone and hung it up.

He told Andy, "Take him back to Trenton. Take two of your guys with you. Don't hurt him. Take him to his apartment. Kick his whore out and tell her not to come back. Clean out everything she owns. Give her five hundred bucks and tell her to leave town. Tell her if she ever comes back." He paused, and then he said, "Just tell her."

He turned to Al and stood only inches from him. He said in a low and threatening voice, "You stay there, Al. I promised Teresa I wouldn't hurt you. Don't make me break that promise. I'm going to be down there in a day or two. Until I get there, I want you to stay inside your apartment. Don't even walk out your front door to get a breath of fresh air. Food will be brought to you. Booze will be brought to you.

I'm going to have your telephones ripped out of the walls. I'm going to have two guys there watching you. Don't challenge me, Al. Mr. Salvano told me what to do, and I'm going to do it. If you disobey me, you'll be disobeying him. Got it?"

Al didn't answer; he just sneered and silently mouthed a few insults. Tony turned away from the man, waved his arm in disgust and said, "Get him the hell out of here."

Andy grabbed Al's arm and roughly dragged him, kicking and screaming, from L'oro Luna. There were eight men, including Ted Bianci and Louie Lombardi, inside L'oro Luna with Tony after Andy had left. None of them spoke a word. They all watched Tony pace around the room, thinking. He stopped suddenly, took a deep breath and said, "Somebody give me a car."

Ted Bianci quickly tossed the keys to his Buick to Tony, who caught them and walked fast out of L'oro Luna. Tony hadn't done much driving up to then, but he managed. He drove fast, but not too fast. He drove to Teresa.

He pulled the car into the Falzone's driveway in Montclair. Al's car was still there, where he had left it, half on the driveway and half on the front lawn. For the first time that he could remember in his whole life, Tony was scared. He loved Teresa so much that he hurt inside for fear of what could happen. He had heard what Al had told her. Could she believe him? Could she hate him now?

The truth; that was the thing. But could he tell her the truth? Could he tell her about Roger Tifton and the Mexican whore? Could he tell her about Mike Colombo and how her father had slashed his throat? He pounded his fist on the steering wheel and got out of the car. He stumbled once walking across the flagstones to Teresa's front door. The door opened before he could knock.

She had washed her face and her hair had been combed back off her forehead. But her eyes were still filled with tears. She held a twisted wad of tissue in her hands. She had changed clothes and was wearing loose fitting blue jeans and a white shirt, the sleeves rolled up. The knees of the jeans were wet. "Come in, Tony," she said. Inside she had been straightening up the house. She had been on her knees scrubbing blood from the wall and floor. She had put furniture upright where it all should be. All the broken things had been cleaned up and disposed of.

She stood in the open doorway. Tony put his hands on her shoulders but she shrugged away from him. "I've been thinking, Tony," she began. "I think we need some time away from each other . . . Some time to think."

"What? Time to think about what?"

She folded her arms in front of her and looked him in his eyes. "You're my father . . . My father is you. I think I was attracted to you because you're like my father. You and he are in the same business. I always thought my father was brave . . . dangerous in an exciting kind of way. I always thought of him like a romantic pirate, sort of. I never thought about all the bad things he must do. I used to think of you the same way."

"I'm not anything like your father, Teresa. I'm different. I have different ideas. I think differently. I could never do what your father does."

"What if one day you do to me what he did to my mother, Tony? What if the business does to you what it did to him? The business made my father what he is today. I'm afraid it will do the same to you. What if someone comes up and tries to take your business away someday? I'm frightened, Tony. I don't know what to do."

He took a step closer to her, but she shrugged from him once again. "Don't touch me, Tony. Please don't touch me."

"I would never hit you. That will never happen, Teresa. I love you so much . . . I could never hurt you. Please don't do this."

She was quiet for a moment and then said, "I'm going to stay here and take care of Mama when she comes home."

"What about college?" Tony asked. "You start there in a couple of weeks."

"I'm not going . . . Not right now, anyway. I need to take care of my mother. I'll think about college later."

"We'll get a nurse in," Tony pled. "Full time . . . The best there is."

"No, Tony. I need some time. I need to take care of Mama. She's been so good to me . . . She loved me so much. I need to be good to her now. I need to show her I love her, too."

"What about us?"

"I need some time away from you, Tony . . . To think. I need to figure it all out. I'm really scared, Tony. I need some time. I don't know what to do, and I need to figure it out."

The last time Tony cried was when he was eight years old. He had stood by and watched his own father beat his mother, but nothing as bad as Al must have done to Teresa's mother. Time after time his father had hit her, and Tony could do nothing. He huddled down in a corner as his father raped his mother and she screamed and pled for him to stop.

He cried that night, alone in his bedroom, and

promised himself that he would never cry again. He promised himself that one day . . . Someday . . . He would stop his father. He did, that day when The Aces challenged him to hit back, to stop him. When Teresa stood in front of him and said what she had said, tears filled his eyes for the second time since that day so long ago. He fought to keep them from bursting loose. The loss, he felt, was unbearable. How could he go on without her? He turned and ran down the flagstones, leaving her standing in the doorway.

The nightmare he had suffered through so many times had come to reality. The dark monster, Al Falzone, had finally put himself between him and Teresa. That's what Al wanted all along. Everything Tony had done could maybe be acceptable to Al . . . Except his being with Teresa. That was what had driven Al to insanity. Tony thought that maybe Al had known what he was doing when he beat Maria so badly. Maybe he had known what the result would be.

Al, the dark monster of Tony's nightmare, was successful in breaking up the love affair. And Teresa had run away.

THIRTY-ONE

Newark, New Jersey
December 1961

Each month since September, on the first of every month, Teresa found an envelope in her mailbox. The envelope was blank, not addressed, and there was no return address and no stamp. Inside each were twenty crisp and brand new one hundred dollar bills. Teresa assumed they were from her father; perhaps his way of some small penance. But with no other income, the money kept her going.

There was more brain damage to Maria Falzone than the doctors at the hospital had imagined. She could not speak or walk. She was in a near catatonic state. She remained bedridden, and her left eye, so badly damaged, eventually had to be removed lest infection spread. Her jaw had been broken badly, wired back together, and never healed properly. The doctors recommended surgery to repair the jaw. Teresa wanted to wait for her mother to show some improvement before sending her back to the hospital.

Teresa spoon fed Maria soft foods, she changed her diapers and bed sheets as often as needed, and she lovingly sponged her daily. She read books to her and talked to her not knowing if her mother could hear her or even understand what she was saying.

She cleaned the house, washed clothes for her mother and brother daily, and ordered food to be delivered from the A&P. She left the house only to get the mail each day from the box at the front door. She was exhausted by the end of the first month, but she was inwardly proud and happy to be a good daughter, even though Maria couldn't tell her that. Maria had loved Teresa all those years, bought her things and cared for her. It was, to Teresa, her chance to say thank you.

And then there was Little Al, Teresa's brother. He had never fully recovered from the trauma of seeing his father almost murder his mother. Little Al had never had a close relationship with his father. While Al was coaching Little League and being a good neighbor, Little Al was ignored, except when his father berated him and yelled at him for even the most minor indiscretion or accident. A spilled glass of milk at the dinner table brought pounding of fists on the table and yelling at the least, and often a slap across the face. The only thing Al could seem to do was criticize his son, tell him he was stupid for not doing well in school, and accuse him of things Little Al didn't do.

Maria had doted on Teresa, buying her clothes and taking her out to lunches and dinners. She had spent all those years grooming Teresa and teaching her how to attract boys, the right kind of boys who could one day bring her wealth. Little Al wanted attention from his mother but seldom got it. She was never mean or cruel to the boy; she just didn't have time for him. Her days were taken up raising beautiful Teresa.

In the months after Maria returned home from the hospital, Little Al wanted to help his sister. He would come to her when she was cleaning or taking care of Maria and ask what he could do. Teresa thought she was being kind to the boy when she said, "Not now Alley," her pet name for her brother. "When you're older." So he retreated to his bedroom and to his fantasies.

He discovered masturbation while he hid under his bed drawing childishly obscene pictures of naked girls and women, many of them depicted being tortured, cut, and beheaded. He had completely lost control of his bladder, wetting his pants a half dozen times every day and every night in bed, and then crying, hitting himself, and banging his head against a wall, until Teresa came to him and brought him clean clothes. She tried to comfort him when this happened, but then she would hear her mother's moaning, and she would leave Alley and run to her mother.

Little Al refused to leave the house, even to step out onto the back patio. He told Teresa he was scared his father was waiting out there for him, behind a tree or in a shadow. He refused to go to school; the school authorities and police knew well who his father was and did nothing to force him back to school.

Neighbor's visited and brought casseroles, cakes and other things. Teresa took the food gratefully, as she had never learned to cook very well, but she politely refused their help. "I really want to take care of Mama myself," she would tell them and thank them for their kindness.

Christmas was forgotten that year. The calendar was a meaningless piece of paper stuck on the kitchen wall. Little Al asked if Santa Claus was coming. Teresa hugged him and said he wasn't. That the best present they could ask for was for their mother's good health. A neighbor brought a large wreath and hung it on the front door one night.

The neighbors could see how the stress and work was affecting the young girl. She had lost weight, her hair hung long and needed washing, and her clothes appeared to have been worn for days at a time. She was obviously sleeping in her clothes, when she slept, which wasn't often.

The house was always spotless, however, because she worked like a slave to keep it that way. The boys in the neighborhood took good care of the yard to try to lessen her work load. But her eyes clearly showed the exhaustion she was feeling. It didn't take long for this to be passed from person to person and finally to L'oro Luna and from there to Tony.

Tony ordered that he be kept current on what Teresa was doing. He wanted to do something to help her, but he was scared, frightened; he didn't know what to do to get her love back. He didn't want to do anything that might anger her. He made sure the $2000 was delivered to her mailbox in the middle of the night on the first of every month. That's all he could think of doing.

****

Trenton, New Jersey
December 1961

Tony had been in Trenton since mid-November. The Newark operation was working well. The gambling room was making tens of thousands of dollars, and the police left it alone, since everyone from the Chief of Police to the local patrolmen were allowed in, and they always walked away a winner. Tony went back to Newark twice while he was in the process of opening a second gambling room there, but being that close to Teresa tempted him to go to her. So he stayed far away in Trenton and let others do the work. Tony sent Andy back and forth between Trenton and Newark, carrying orders and money.

He had opened an Italian restaurant near the Government buildings of the State Capital. He named it Il Sole Italiano, The Italian Sun. Sort of a contrast to L'oro Luna, The Gold Moon, he explained. The back room of Il Sole Italiano was where the crew met and did business. He abandoned the dirty pool hall and decided not to burn it down.

He found a third floor place in Trenton big enough to open a gambling room, and it turned out to be more successful than the one in Newark. There were politicians and government people with money in Trenton, and they were all allowed in. He had hired the same people who decorated and finished the place in Newark to make it a twin. It was shortly making a half million a year profit.

In both Newark and Trenton, he opened and expanded his betting parlors where anyone, rich or poor, could place bets on sporting events. He hired people who knew how to make the odds always profitable for the house without cheating anyone.

As he had planned, and as he had explained to Peter Salvano, he had used his new politician friends to arrange a meeting with the Director of the State Police. Without asking for anything in return, Tony told him he was going to help him clean up the drug business in Trenton, because he hated drugs, Tony explained. Nothing had to be asked for in return, because the Director knew the good publicity that would be his for cleaning up the city's illegal drug trafficking.

Tony's new soldiers were out on the streets, looking for drug dealers in the slums and black areas of every part of the State. Tony started making anonymous phone calls to the State Police, reporting drug dealers, and when and where drugs were moving around the State. The Director, of course, knew who was making the anonymous phone calls, but all he was interested in were the results. The State Police became so fascinated with the accurate details they were getting, they kept adding more and more men to the drug taskforce, pulling them away from the fruitless investigation of Tony Moretti's growing gambling empire.

Al Falzone spent those months alone in his small apartment. Two of the new Trenton crew sat in a car in front of Al's building doing twelve hour shifts. They didn't complain because they knew they were doing what Tony Moretti wanted them to do, and someday they would have more important work to do and more money.

Al was kept in all the whiskey he could drink. Secretly, unspoken to anyone, Tony hoped the whiskey would finally kill him. Once a week, on Tuesday afternoons, Al was taken from his apartment and brought to the new restaurant, through the back door, where, in the back room, Tony met with the Trenton crew.

Al didn't know why he was there, and he didn't ask. He stayed drunk most of the time and was often loud and obnoxious in the back room while the meeting was going on. No one wanted him there because he was drunk all the time, but no one said anything. Tony wanted everyone to be sick of seeing Al and not miss him when he was dead, so he kept bringing Al there. Whatever loyalty might remain had to be broken and done away with.

It didn't take long for word of Teresa's distress at home to reach Tony. When it became obvious she was killing herself taking care of Maria and Little Al, a team of nurses showed up at Teresa's door. They would work in eight hour shifts, twenty-four hours a day, seven days a week, they told her. At first Teresa objected, saying she didn't need the help, and she certainly couldn't afford it. But they did as they were instructed and told her that her father was paying the bill and wanted her to have the help. Teresa relented. She thought that her father was at least trying to say he was sorry.

Everything was moving smoothly, too smoothly for Andy who started to complain about wanting some action. Driving back and forth between Newark and Trenton, carrying cash, delivering orders from Tony, wasn't enough to satisfy his craving for excitement. But his loyalty to Tony was more important to him than anything else.

He drove Tony's Cadillac, he had more money than he could spend, he was Tony's fulltime bodyguard, and he remembered Don Peter Salvano's admonition that someone, someday, would try to kill Tony. That was the life he had chosen, to protect Tony Moretti and to kill for him. It was, he knew, a better life than he would have had if he had stayed in Passaic. He could not imagine what he would be doing were it not for Tony. He would be either dead or in jail, as he had told Tony and Peter, he was sure of that.

He did get a job that was out of the routine that Tuesday, when the two men who were to bring Al Falzone to the crew's meeting got tired of waiting for him outside his apartment. He was a half hour late, not stumbling down the stairs as he usually did. They walked up the three dank flights of stairs and knocked on the apartment's door. There was no answer and no sound from inside. They shared their fear that Al had slipped out somehow, without them seeing him. There would be a price to pay for that. The door was locked;

they debated for a minute or two whether they should phone Tony or break the door down. They decided to break in. No sense alerting him if Al was merely passed out on the floor from too much booze.

It took only two kicks for the thin door to collapse. Inside was eerily dark, with yellow light filtered through old blinds that were drawn down tightly. And in the center of the room, Al Falzone was hanging by his neck. A hole had been cut in the ceiling and the rope tied around a joist. There was a wooden chair lying on its side beneath Al. His eyes were open, his skin grey with death, and he was completely naked. His clothes had been thrown in a far corner, on the floor, in a pile.

The two men struggled to cut the rope and get Al down. They laid him on his rumpled, unmade bed. "What the hell do we do now?" one said to the other. They talked about their options and finally decided running to Tony was the only thing to do. They both ran from the room and down the stairs. At the car, some sense found its way into their fear. One of them went back up the stairs and into Al's apartment. At first he walked inside, and then, rather than be near the body, he waited in the hall, closing the broken door behind him. The other drove as fast as possible to find Tony.

It was a week before Christmas. "Shit, what a present this is gonna be!" the young soldier said as he spun the car around a corner.

****

Montclair, New Jersey
December 1961

The morning Al Falzone was laid to rest was cold, but the sky was clear and as blue as any day in spring. The many trees in the cemetery in Montclair were barren of leaves; the remnants of snow from two days ago lined the branches. The snow had been cleared around the grave site and green blankets, imitating a summer lawn, had been placed encircling the hole Al would be lowered into. Folding metal chairs, five rows deep, were lined up on four sides of the open grave. They were all taken by men of criminal organizations from around the Northeast, and their women. In the back rows of chairs were neighbors of the Falzone's and friends from the Little League Al had coached so long ago.

Tony stood at the rear of the crowd, facing the foot of Al's bronze casket, Andy at his side as he always was. Teresa sat near her father as the Priest read prayers in Latin that no one understood.

The ceremony lasted an hour. A few people stood and went to the casket to lay single roses on the closed top. Everyone watched as the casket was slowly lowered into the ground. One by one, most people walked up to Teresa and expressed their sorrow and sympathy. Some people just walked away. Eventually Teresa was left alone, still seated, still crying.

The short December afternoon was signaled by an early afternoon setting sun. A slight evening breeze made the cold air feel even colder. Teresa shivered, pulled her brown wool coat up tight around her and stood. She turned to start on her way home and found Tony standing behind the rows of chairs. Andy stood away from them, at what he thought was a polite distance, watching.

"What are you doing here?" she snapped.

"He was my boss. I'm just showing my respect."

Teresa walked around the chairs to Tony. Suddenly she reached out and slapped him across his face. He didn't move.

"You killed my father," she said and slapped him again. Again he made no movement.

"I didn't . . ." Tony started but she slapped him a third time.

"Don't lie to me, Tony. You killed my father."

"Teresa," he began. "I kept your father alive. People wanted him dead. I kept him alive for you."

"Don't lie to me, Tony. You killed him . . . Just be a man and admit it."

Tony said nothing. Teresa turned and walked away.

Andy walked slowly to Tony, stood at his side, and asked, "You OK, boss?"

"Yeah, I'm OK."

He put his hand on Tony's shoulder as a friend would and said, "You gotta' keep hopin', boss. Somethin' is bound to happen. I think she still loves you, ya'know? I think she's just angry and confused. She's under a lot of pressure, ya'know? She don't know the truth. Just keep hopin' and don't give up on her, OK?"

"I want you to find out who killed Al."

"You don't think he done it himself?"

"No . . . It's too convenient, Andy. I think he would have tried to kill me before he killed himself. He hated me, and he wouldn't have taken that hate with him to hell. No, I think somebody killed him and made it look like suicide. Get the police reports . . . Get the Medical Examiner's report. I think we have a murder here, and I want to know who."

"Who do you think did it?"

"I don't know. Maybe one of the guys. None of them liked him. Newark was angry about Mike Colombo's murder. The Trenton people just are disgusted with him. Maybe somebody he pissed off that we don't know about yet. But I'm sure he didn't kill himself."

THIRTY-TWO

Trenton, New Jersey
April 1962

Andy had phoned Tony at his Trenton apartment from a public phone two blocks from L'oro Luna. It was a phone call with a lot of danger behind it, and he didn't want to use the phone in L'oro Luna, where others could hear. He had been up in Newark for over a week, asking questions and getting answers. It's where the months of his investigation of Al's death had led him. He sounded desperate and anxious. "You ain't gonna' like this, boss," he said.

"I'm not going to like what, Andy?"

"Not on the phone . . . It's too much to talk about like this. Some other people shouldn't hear, ya' know? You gotta' come on up to Newark, boss."

"OK, I'll get one of the guys to drive me . . ."

"No, boss! Don't do that. It ain't safe. Don't trust nobody, boss. Stay where you are and lock your door. You still got that .38 I gave you?"

"It's that bad, Andy?"

"It's that bad, boss. I'll come get you. I'll leave right now. Lock your damn door, and don't let nobody but me in."

He slammed the phone down and ran for the car. Tony had bought a new Cadillac, this one black in color and as nondescript as a big Cadillac could be. The white Caddy had been great for the kid Tony used to be, but he had grown up very quickly in the last few months. The *man* Tony needed something more refined, more adult, more of the car a man of respect would be seen in. Andy jumped in the brand new Cadillac and gunned the engine. He broke every speed law there was getting to Trenton.

Tony had moved to an expensive apartment on the eleventh floor of a High Rise apartment building populated by politicians and government officials and a few very wealthy people. The apartment had been furnished by a local interior decorator. Everything was new and expensive and perfect, and reflected Tony's wealth.

That day he had been planning on leaving to check on the building of a new gambling room, but he stayed at home as Andy had suggested. The .38 revolver was in a nightstand next to his bed. He went to it, checked to see that it was loaded, and, as an afterthought, locked the door to the apartment. He sat and waited, trying to stay calm, but it was hard.

'It's about time,' he thought. Sooner or later he had known that someone would try to kill him. There were a thousand reasons why people would want him dead, but the one he had never been able to let go of was the fact that he was just a very young man running a big criminal organization. Only the new soldiers were his age. Not one man who had worked for Al in either Newark or Trenton was younger than he was. He had just turned eighteen in January.

But every one of them knew he had the backing of Peter Salvano. Maybe that bullet proof vest of protection had worn thin? Maybe he wasn't as important to Peter as he had been? He had always had the thought in the back of his mind that when he had changed the business from leg breaking to high stakes gambling, would Peter have any more use for him? Tony's income had grown very fast, also. He was making cash in the six figures annually. Did Peter's greed want that money now?

The hours had dragged by slowly; the sun had set and the apartment was dark but Tony left the lights turned off. The dark was a better place to hide in than the light. He had closed the drapes and pulled an armchair against a wall directly across from the door.

He held the pistol and wondered if he could actually kill anyone. He had found it easy enough to order Andy Pecora to kill someone, people who needed to be killed to further his plans, people who had been standing in his way. But could he himself pull the trigger?

The knock on the door startled him. He jumped from the chair and backed against the wall.

"Boss . . . It's me, boss . . . Andy . . . You there, boss?"

Tony dropped the pistol on the chair he had been in and went to the door. He quickly unlocked it and opened it. Andy pushed his way in and closed and locked the door behind him. He looked around the blackened room and felt on the wall for a light switch. The light hurt Tony's eyes for a second or two. He rubbed them and then asked, "What the hell happened?"

"You better sit down, boss. This is somethin' ain't gonna be easy t'fix."

Andy led Tony into the kitchen and sat him at the table there. Andy quickly put on a pot of coffee to brew and then sat across from his boss. He said, "I found out who killed Al."

"That's great, Andy. Now I can tell Teresa . . ."

"Boss, it ain't that easy. Let me explain."

It took nearly an entire pot of coffee, shared between the two of them, for Andy to tell what he had learned and for Tony to ask enough questions to believe the unbelievable story.

Andy explained that Peter Salvano was responsible for Al Falzone's death. Peter had never gotten past the fact that Al had killed Roger Tifton. His anger had grown over the years. Peter and Roger were partners in a real estate scheme that involved a complicated fraud that Andy didn't understand.

"That's OK, Andy. We can get the details later," Tony said, urging him on.

Because Al had killed Roger Tifton over something as stupid as the Mexican whore, the scheme fell apart and Peter had lost millions of dollars. Peter had wanted all that money, he had made plans for it, and those plans crashed at Tifton's death. Peter wanted revenge; he wanted Al murdered for the growing hatred he had for Al. But he didn't want any possible connection to the murder.

The FBI, Andy explained, had never given up trying to link Peter to his father's Mafia family. Peter needed buffers between him and the crime organization he had inherited. Bruno Massetti was that buffer. When Peter's mother was alive, it could not be thought criminal for Peter to visit his aged mother. Since his mother's death, Peter had only been to the Brooklyn house once, when Tony was brought into the Family. Peter had taken precautions that day, and Andy's police contacts confirmed that the FBI did not have a record of that day.

At first he wanted Tony to kill Al openly and

quickly, but Tony gave Peter what sounded like good reasons to keep him alive, not the least of which was Teresa, of course. Peter's anger at the loss of the millions of dollars he could have had working with Roger Tifton had grown out of control. Day by day the anger had grown and festered into a burning sore inside of him. It was tearing at him; he had a hard time thinking of his other businesses, and they were suffering. Eventually Peter couldn't wait any longer; Al Falzone had to die so that Peter could sleep again. He had Bruno go to the New York Gambino Family and paid for an assassination of Al Falzone.

"I kind of figured he would do something like that someday," Tony said.

"Yeah, but that ain't all of it."

Peter wanted to place the guilt for the murder on Tony. Tony had come too far too fast in Peter's opinion, as Tony had figured. Rumor had it that Peter was in fear of Tony becoming so powerful that he would be able to push Peter aside and take over the Family. He wanted to stop Tony, but he couldn't step out in the open and do it. Tony had to take the fall for Al Falzone's murder without any connection to Peter. Peter would take care of two problems with one stroke.

There was some manufactured evidence that Andy couldn't get the details on. Soon it would be placed in the hands of the New Jersey State Attorney General that would lead the police and the FBI to Tony. That evidence would directly connect Tony to Al's murder. But Peter reasoned that if Tony were arrested and charged, he might talk of Family business and Peter Salvano's position as Don of the Family.

So Peter had put a contract out on Tony. It wasn't a contract with the Gambino Family. Peter needed one person to take the contract so that that one person could be eliminated, too. It was a secret, limited contract, not publicly known. Ted Bianci, one of the original soldiers when Al formed his Newark crew years before, had the contract. Ten thousand dollars was the contract fee, a huge amount of money for Ted in those days. He would be rich, he thought. What he didn't know was that after he killed Tony, Bruno Massetti would make sure he wouldn't live long enough to spend a penny of it.

"I ain't seen Ted for about a week, boss," Andy said. "I think he knows what I'd do if I see him. None of the guys up in Newark have seen him. But that means he's after you. He's good, too, boss. He might be good enough to get you."

"OK, Andy. Good work. I have to think about this. Look, I'm a little hungry and I know you're always hungry. Go get us a pizza and some beer, OK?"

"You gonna be OK here alone, boss?"

"Yeah, I've got your gun, and I'll keep the doors locked. I'll be OK. I just have to think about this."

Andy left, and while he was gone, Tony paced around the apartment. He left the pistol on the kitchen table, but he made sure the front door was securely locked, and he pulled a chair against it. He came to the conclusion that he had only two options. If Andy was right, and he trusted that Andy was right, Peter would never relent . . . Unless he had to. The problem was getting him to that point where he realized he had no choice but the one Tony would offer him. It would be that or death at the hands of Andy Pecora.

Ted Bianci was another story. That one was easy. Ted had made a wrong choice, and he had only days to live. All Tony had to do was find him. Tony had too many men in Newark and Trenton. Ted had taken a very private contract so everyone else would still be loyal to Tony. All he had to do was tell them to find Ted. That was easy.

So Tony settled down in his favorite chair, an upholstered easy chair he had found in a second hand furniture store so long ago. It reminded him of a chair at his parent's home in Passaic and one he had in the small apartment in Newark. It was upholstered in a rose pattern, unusual for a guy to like, but it was just like the chair he had grown up with and the one he had when he had Teresa with him. It didn't fit in with the expensive and modern furniture the interior decorator had chosen for him, but he liked it. It reminded him of the love he had lost.

His mind was eased now that he knew what he had to do. He relaxed and thought of his home back in Passaic; it had been a very long time since he had thought of that. He wondered how things were back there. Was his father working or drinking between jobs? Were his mother's hands still wrapped inside her rosary beads? Had anything changed? He recalled that day four years earlier when he finally hit his father and then hit him again. He had hurt the old man badly, but had he changed the man? He thought when all this business with Peter was straightened out he might drop by there and see if anything had changed.

The soft knock on the door startled Tony out of his thoughts. He jumped from the chair and ran to the kitchen for the gun. 'That's stupid,' he thought. Would Ted knock on the door before killing him? He went to the door and without opening it he said, "Yes, who is it?"

"It's Mrs. Ogilvy . . . From down the hall."

"What is it, Mrs. Ogilvy?"

"Have you seen kittims?" Mrs. Ogilvy was an elderly lady, a widow, who had lived in the apartment tower since it was new. She was one of the first tenants. She was a nice old lady who baked banana bread and gave too many of them to Tony. She was a pest, but she was also a nice old lady. Kittims was her old grey cat.

"No, Mrs. Ogilvy. I haven't seen your kittims."

"Oh, please Tony. I'm so upset. Please help me."

Tony pushed the chair away and opened the door to let Mrs. Ogilvy in. She was crying into a small lace hanky, as she stepped into the apartment. Tony glanced to the left and right in the hallway. There was no one there. He closed the door and went to his neighbor.

"I'm sure kittims will come back, Mrs. Ogilvy. She knows where her food is. I'm sure she won't be gone for long."

"Oh, Tony, will you help me find her, please? I'm so upset."

"I'm expecting someone here soon . . . Business. As soon as that's done, if kittims isn't home, I will help you find her. Now, I think you should go home and wait for her. Have a good cup of tea. She'll be home soon. She knows where her food and water are. As soon as she gets hungry, she'll be there."

"Do you think so, Tony?"

"I'm sure."

They walked to the door, and Tony opened it for her. Ted Bianci was standing at the door. He smiled.

Tony said, "Now see, Mrs. Ogilvy. Here's my business appointment. Now you go home and wait there, OK?"

The old lady nodded and wiped her nose. She walked away, her head bent and shoulders slumped. Ted pushed his way into the apartment. He closed the door behind him and stood with his back to the door.

He drew a pistol from his jacket pocket.

"What about Mrs. Ogilvy?" Tony asked.

"She's an old lady . . . She didn't look at me . . . She was crying . . . She won't be able to ID me."

"Good, thank you Ted. How much do you want to walk away?"

"I been paid Tony. If I walk away I'm dead. It's me or you."

"Suppose I give you a way to walk away?"

Ted didn't answer right away. He knew Tony was smart; he'd made everybody rich and kept the cops off their backs. There had to be a reason for the Don to want him dead. And he had to leave a few feet of cheap rope the Don had given him hidden somewhere in the apartment. He didn't know it was the evidence the police would find. It was just something Peter had told him to do. His immediate instinct was to accept Peter Salvano as being more dangerous than Tony Moretti.

"Where's Andy?" he asked.

"On his way up to Newark. He's carrying a bag of money."

"You want your girl to know anything? I can get a message to her if you want."

"Nah," Tony said. "My mouth is real dry. Can I get some water?"

"Shit Tony, I can see the damn pistol on the table from here."

Ted slowly raised the pistol and pointed it at Tony's head. He pulled the hammer back and was thrown to the floor when the door crashed open against him. Andy jumped on Ted's back with both feet, knocking the air out of him. Tony took two steps and kicked Ted at the side of his head. He and Andy pulled the man to his feet. His gun was lying on the floor a few feet away. Andy spun him around and hit him hard across his jaw. Ted fell backwards, unconscious.

"Where should I take him?" Andy asked.

The length of rope, cut from the rope that had been used to hang Al Falzone, had fallen from Ted's pocket. "Tie him up with that," Tony said. "I want a message sent. We'll take him up to New York. I want to dump him in front of Peter Salvano's condo building."

"You gonna let him live?"

"Nah," Tony said, walking away. "Cut his damn throat before we dump him."

****

Manhattan, New York
April 1962

They waited across the street and at the corner, diagonal from Peter's condominium. It was nearing 4 AM; it was very dark. The streets of Manhattan were deserted at that hour. There was a doorman who was standing inside the big glass doors to stay out of the early morning cold air. Andy started to get anxious to dump Ted who was in the trunk of the car, tied and gagged. They had wrapped him in an old sheet that Tony had found in the basement of the apartment building, in a pile of trash.

Tony was calm and told Andy the doorman would walk away soon. Andy couldn't figure out how Tony could know this, but he trusted his boss. He waited. All he wanted was a cigarette, but with Tony sitting next to him, that was not possible.

And as Tony had predicted, the doorman did walk away. He went for coffee to stay awake and the bathroom after the coffee. It would be five, maybe ten minutes before he returned to the door. That would be enough time.

Tony nodded, and Andy started the engine of the Cadillac. He pulled to the curb, left the engine running, went to the rear, opened the trunk and grinned broadly as he slit Ted's throat. Blood was gushing all over the sheet as he pulled Ted from the trunk. He dropped him hard on the first step at the front door of the building. Ted bounced but stayed on the marble step. Andy raced back to the car, and they drove away slowly. No sense attracting attention.

THIRTY-THREE

Manhattan, New York
May 1962

It was ten minutes to five in the afternoon. Peter Salvano sat at his desk in his thirtieth floor office. He had been shaken by the body of Ted Bianci being dumped at his doorstep. He knew who did it, of course, but he didn't know what to do about it. The police interviewed everyone, including Peter, but no one knew or had seen anything. The police, of course, had their suspicions about Peter. After all, his name was Salvano and his father had been Don Pietro Salvano. But they had no evidence as usual.

Peter knew it was only a matter of time before something would happen. He had spoken with Bruno Massetti in Brooklyn three times, and all Bruno could tell him was that he knew nothing. Bruno had put the word out on the street. Who killed Ted Bianci? There was a reward for good information. But either no one knew anything, or everyone was too frightened to talk.

Peter knew, of course, that it was Tony Moretti. The thought of Tony coming after him was a nightmare. It was badly interfering with his work. He couldn't concentrate on anything. The slightest noise made him jump.

The intercom on his desk buzzed. It was his secretary. Peter pushed a button and asked, "Yes, what is it?"

"There's a Mr. John Brown here to see you. He says it's very important."

"What does he want?"

"It's about the Fox Hunt development, Mr. Salvano."

There wasn't any Fox Hunt development. It could only be one person. But what could Peter do? There was no place to run. There was no place to hide.

"Alright, send him in," he said. He had no choice. Face up to Tony, flatter him, buy him off. Offer him anything.

The eight foot tall solid oak double doors to Peter's office opened and Tony walked in. He was wearing an expensive navy blue double breasted suit. He carried a brown leather attaché case and wore thick rimmed glasses. It was Tony, no doubt about that, but he didn't look like the Tony Peter knew.

The doors were shut, and Tony walked across the big office to Peter's desk. He laid the attaché on the floor and sat in one of the leather chairs in front of Peter's desk without being invited to do so. Peter was scared, frightened so much that his mouth hung open in silence.

"Well, Pete," Tony said. He had never before called the Don anything but Mr. Salvano. "Things change so damn quickly, don't they? Ain't it just amazing?"

Tony took the false eyeglasses off and put them in the breast pocket of his suit. He crossed his legs casually and took in the richly furnished office. "You've got a really nice place here," he said. "I'm very anxious to take this away from you, Pete."

"What do you want?" Peter stammered.

"What the hell do you think I want? I want to know why you tried to frame me for murder and then have Ted kill me."

"I don't know what you're talking about. Someone's been lying to you." Peter was sweating in the cool office. His hands were shaking. "What do you want? Money? I can move you up. Do you want Bruno's place? I can do that."

Tony leaned back in the chair and smiled. Peter was getting very pale. Tony thought he might faint any minute now. He laughed. Each of them sat in silence until Peter's secretary buzzed again.

"I'm sorry to interrupt, Mr. Salvano. You're wife is on the phone."

Peter's hand was shaking as he picked up the phone. "Yes? What do you want? I'm very busy."

"I am sorry, dear. But there's a messenger here, a very nice young man named Andy something or other. He has some very important papers about a Fox Hunt development. Should he wait here, or should I send him to your office? I didn't know if you were going to come home soon or not."

Peter almost vomited. He managed to swallow the bile that rose in his throat.

"Dear? Peter, what shall I tell him?"

"No, send him here. I'll be awhile."

"Alright. Please don't be too late. The children would like to have dinner with you."

Peter hung up the phone. All signs of life had drained from his face; the room was spinning around him, out of control. His family! His family!

Nightmarish visions flashed before his eyes.

Tony leaned forward and asked, "So Pete, are you OK or what? You look like shit."

"Why?" was all Peter could ask.

"Why? Because you tried to kill me you son of a bitch. You really screwed up."

"But my family . . ."

"That's just a warning, Pete. They're OK. Nothing is going to happen to them. I just wanted you to know how easy it would be to kill you and every-friggin-body you love. Now I'm going to explain what changes are going to be made. The bottom line here, Pete, is . . . You're now out of it. You're done. You're not a Don anymore."

"You can't do that . . ."

"It's done, Pete. You're going to live, and your family will go on living so long as you keep your damn mouth shut and you stay out of the business. It's all mine now, you see, Pete. I own everything."

"But the other families . . . New York."

"I've contacted them. They're going to start getting money from me. I'm paying up to them. They couldn't give a shit what happens to you. You're nothing, Pete. You're not worth the scab on a pig's ass."

"The Capos . . . What about the Capos?" Peter was spitting out the words, saliva was running from his lips.

"I'm going to talk to them. They'll understand. Look, Pete, they owe you nothing. They've seen your face maybe three times in four years. They don't know you anymore. And I have plans. They'll like the plans I have."

"So you're taking over?" Peter asked.

"No, not really. I'm not *taking* over, Pete . . . I've already taken over."

"But you're just a fucking kid."

"Face the facts, Pete. I'm old enough to kill you and your whole family if you screw with me. Now just calm down and accept what will be. I mean, you're rich and all that. You don't need the money. Just live with it because you don't have a choice."

Tony stood, picked up his attaché, put on the phony glasses and walked out.

That evening as Andy drove Tony back to Trenton, Andy broke the silence in the Cadillac. He said, "You did it, boss."

"Did what, Andy?"

"You took over. I always knew you could, of course. But you really did it."

"We have to deal with Bruno Massetti and Michael Funno and Manny Esposito first. They might complain a little."

"How you gonna' handle them, boss?"

"I don't know yet, Andy. I'll have to think about that. Damn, I've got a headache."

"You want I should stop and get some aspirin, boss?"

"Nah, let's just get home."

Tony leaned back in the front passenger seat against the black leather and closed his eyes. The pressure of the business and his ongoing plans were heavy on him. He tried to think of other things. And there was only one other thing he could ever think about.

"How's Teresa doing?" he asked.

"She's doin' OK, boss. Her mom ain't so good, though."

"Does she ever wonder where the money is coming from since her father died?"

"Nah, But I think she knows, boss. She ain't stupid."

Tony thought about her, picturing her in his mind. He longed for the day when he could be with her again, when he could feel her lips against his, when he could hold her and make love to her.

Tony had never been religious. He had spent his days working rather than going to Church. But, he often felt, if there was a Heaven it couldn't be any better than having Teresa lie next to him all night, every night. He had to get her back someday soon. That day had to come, he thought. He was too young to spend the rest of his life without her.

"Is she getting out of the house?"

"Yeah . . . You know."

Tony sat upright again and asked suspiciously, "No I don't know. Tell me. Is she seeing anyone?"

"Hey, boss. Sure she goes out now and then. The nurses are doing most of the stuff for Maria. It gives her more time, ya' know? She's young. What can you expect?"

Tony rested his head back again. He had to wash the visions of Teresa with someone else out of his mind.

"Up what she gets to three grand a month," he said.

"Sure, boss."

They drove for another half hour. Andy thought Tony might have fallen asleep. He was surprised when Tony asked, "You still see your mother, Andy?"

"Sure I do. Most Sundays I take her to Church, and we stop at the bakery to get rolls and shit. I pay her rent and give her cash. There's no way she could live on that damn Social Security check she gets."

"You go to Church, Andy?"

"Yeah, my Ma wouldn't have it no other way."

"How about Confession and all that stuff?" Tony asked.

"Nah, that ain't for me. The damn Priest would have a heart attack if he was to hear all I done." They both laughed at that, and Tony leaned back again.

"I've been thinking about my folks. Do you know how they're doing?"

"Sure, I ask about them all the time."

"How are they doing? I haven't seen them in a couple of years."

"They're OK . . . You know . . . 'Bout the same . . . Nothin' real bad and nothin' real good . . . You know."

"Is he working?" Tony asked.

"Last time I heard he wasn't. Your Mom is working in a diner somewhere."

"Start sending them some money, Andy. I think I'll stop in and see them soon."

Another five miles went by, and Andy asked, "You ever worry about all this Mafia shit? I mean, ain't you supposed to get permission to kill a Made Man? I mean Chi Chi and Ted Bianci were both Made a long time ago."

"I don't think all that stuff is important anymore. Most of the old Don's are dead or too old to worry about. That Omerta thing is being chipped away at. A lot of guys up in New York are talking rather than spending the rest of their lives in prison. Money is the important thing, Andy. It seems like if money can be made, then all the old rules can be tossed out. The old rules don't matter much anymore. And if they do . . . We're making enough money to break the rules."

Tony opened his right hand and looked at the scar across his palm. The act the old men put on was funny, laughable, but he had to do it. He had to move up to make his plan complete. He ran a finger across the scar.

THIRTY-FOUR

Brooklyn, New York
June 1962

Bruno Massetti sat in the old Don's den in the Brooklyn house, in the old Don's chair, behind the old Don's desk. On the other side of the big desk the two Capos, Michael Funno and Manny Esposito, sat in comfortable chairs. They were all that was left of the old days when Don Pietro ruled like a medieval king. In secret, in words they would never speak, they longed for the old days. The power, the fear, the ability to do anything they wanted was what was missing. They waited without talking, chain smoking and looking from one another. They were nervous, uncomfortable, and unsure of what was going to happen.

Tony had called the meeting. He had told Bruno, when Bruno wanted to clear the meeting with Peter, "Don't do that, Bruno. I'm calling this meeting. There are changes we need to talk about. Do what I tell you to do." Before that phone call from Tony, Bruno had tried to phone Peter. He found that the private number he had always called Peter on had been disconnected.

Tony's reputation, earned at the age of 18, was

respected by everyone in the family. He was feared as they would fear a man twice his age, and there was no one who would challenge him, at least not alone. He had a small army of new soldiers he had personally recruited, young men from the streets and gangs who were loyal to him and no one else. And he had Andy Pecora. So the three men sat and waited.

The meeting was to start at 7 PM. At twenty past seven Tony walked into the den, followed by Andy Pecora and five of Tony's newly recruited soldiers. The five were young, tough, strong, well dressed in good suits, white shirts and ties, and willing to do anything to advance in the crime family. And they were all armed. Bruno, Michael and Manny had never seen any of them before.

They circled the room and stood at the walls. Andy stood behind and slightly to the left of Tony who walked to the center of the room.

"What the fuck's this?" Manny Esposito demanded.

"Be patient, Manny," Tony said. "Good things are going to happen. Be patient."

"Then why all the guns?"

"Just in case, Manny. Just in case."

Andy pulled a chair away from the wall and placed it in the middle of the room, where Tony could sit. Michael Funno and Manny Esposito turned in their chairs to look at him. He sat and crossed his legs. "Things are changing," Tony began. "Peter Salvano is out . . ."

"What the hell you mean 'out'?" Michael Funno demanded.

"He's decided to retire . . . Sort of. Anyway, Pete wants to devote his time to his legal businesses and his loving family. He's taken this strange idea into his head that the pressure of the business might be bringing on an early death. He's out."

"Pete?" Bruno growled. "Is that the kind of respect you show to your Don?"

"Pete isn't the Don anymore. The Salvano Family doesn't exist anymore."

Bruno asked, "And that's your decision is it, Tony?"

Tony smiled, looked from man to man, and said, "I've made a deal with New York. From now on you each pay up to me and I pay up to New York. If you want to argue about Pete being out . . . Go to New York and argue with them."

Michael snarled his question, "So you're making yourself the new Don, is that right?"

"The days of the Dons are over, Mike. I'm Tony to you guys, Mr. Moretti to your men."

"That's bullshit!" Manny said.

Tony ignored Manny. He said to everyone, "Don't be stupid. Things have moved beyond you. The old days are in the past, and a new way of doing business is here. Learn to live with it, and your incomes will increase."

Manny and Michael looked at each other. Bruno's face was red with restrained rage. Tony spoke to Bruno, "How much have you guys been paying up to Pete?"

Bruno hesitated and then relented, "Fifty percent . . . You know that."

"From now on you pay up to me . . . Twenty-five percent."

Manny snarled, "You think you can buy loyalty by cutting back on what we pay up?"

"I don't want your loyalty, Manny. I want your money. Be patient. Things are changing."

Tony locked his eyes on Bruno's and said, "From now on Andy Pecora will come here on the first of every month. He will examine the books, and you will give him the money. Don't give him any trouble, and don't hold out on me. You can stay here and live out your life in comfort. Fuck with me, and that life will be cut very short."

Mike Funno stood up and said, "I'm a Made Man. I've been in the Salvano Family for over twenty years. You're a fuckin' kid, and you come in here and try to take over just like that?"

"Sit down, Mike. I'm a Made Man, too. Don't forget that." Tony slowly raised his right hand, palm up, so that the three men could see the scar running across his palm.

"But there are more changes. You and Manny keep everything you have and run your businesses as you see fit. You don't need my permission to do anything. Expand anywhere you like. You're independent . . . So long as you pay up to me and New York, no one will interfere with whatever you do. And I'll keep the cops off your back so long as you don't do anything stupid. But I'm going to open gambling operations and sports books and numbers in your territories. I don't want any trouble from you on this. They will be mine, and you won't have any part of them. You'll stay out of them, and you won't talk to anybody about them. Understand?"

"We're on our own?" Manny asked.

"So long as you don't do anything stupid. Deal drugs or kill someone and you won't get any help from me. Expand wherever you want. Do whatever you want. I don't care. And by the way, I'm giving Bennie Rizo, Frankie De Luca and Louie Lombardi to you.

They're from the old days . . . Pete and Al's old crew. I don't want them, and I don't need them. They're yours."

"I need to talk to Don Peter about this," Bruno said. His voice revealed how unsure he was, how dangerous the words were.

"Go ahead, Bruno. You've got his home and business numbers. Phone him."

Bruno's hand hovered over the phone. He stared at Tony, waiting for him to say something. When he didn't Bruno decided to risk it. He picked up the phone and dialed Peter's home number, since the private line had been disconnected.

Peter answered on the seventh ring. "Hello," he said.

"This is Bruno . . . You there?"

"I don't want to talk to you, Bruno. Don't call here anymore."

"But . . ."

"I'm having all my phone numbers changed in the morning. Leave me alone." The line went dead. Bruno slowly placed the phone in its cradle and looked at Tony.

"OK," he said. "So you did it. You fuckin' did it. Is all the crap you said true?"

"It's all true, Bruno. You guys are on your own to do whatever you want. I get twenty-five percent. You stay away from drugs and don't start any wars, and I'll keep the cops away. We got a deal or not?"

Manny and Mike stood and turned to Tony. Tony laughed and said, "None of that kissing stuff. Let's just shake hands like businessmen and walk away."

****

The drive back to Trenton was long and slow. The car with Ton's new, young soldier followed. Tony rubbed his eyes and leaned back in the rear seat of the Cadillac. He had visions of Teresa running through his mind, but that wasn't unusual. She was seldom far away from his thoughts. During the day, and especially at night when he was in bed alone trying to sleep, she would be there in his mind, and when sleep finally did fold itself around him, she would fill his dreams.

Andy looked into the rearview mirror at his boss and said, "We made it, huh, boss? We really made it."

"Yeah, I guess so. There's a lot of work to do."

"Ain't you happy, boss?"

"Yeah . . . Sort of."

"Somethin's missing, right?" Andy knew, of course. He had become so close to his boss that he felt he could almost read his mind, anticipate what he was going to say, know what he was feeling.

"Yeah . . . Sort of."

"Why don't you just go see her, boss? Just go knock on her door and marry her."

"I wish I could, Andy. I wish I could."

Tony closed his eyes and moaned faintly.

"You got a headache again, boss?" Andy asked.

"No, I'm just tired," he lied. His head was throbbing again.

"Get some sleep. We got a couple hours to drive."

"I was thinking, Andy. Let's make a stop in

Passaic. I think I want to see my folks."

"You sure, boss?"

"Yeah, I'm sure."

****

Passaic, New Jersey
June 1962

The street of old red brick attached homes hadn't changed for the better in the years since Tony had been there. There was more garbage in the street; the buildings seemed older somehow, and more drab. Tony stood on the sidewalk and looked up and down the street. It was near 9:30 PM; two of the three street lights on the block were not lit. Three boys, young and black, stood at the corner and suspiciously watched the man in the expensive suit and the big Cadillac he had arrived in. No one else was outside that warm summer evening.

Tony turned and walked up the four concrete steps to the door of the home he had been raised in. Inside he walked up the two flights of stairs to the apartment where he had once lived. The door was locked; he tried the doorbell, and when no one answered, he assumed it was still not working after all those years. He knocked and knocked again a little harder. The door opened, and his mother stood there, one hand on the door.

"Yes?" she said. "What do you want?"

"It's me, Mom."

Graziella stared, frowning, trying to understand. "Anthony? Is that you Anthony?" She looked him up

and down, trying to see her boy under the expensive
clothes. She looked older than he remembered her.
Her hair was gray and tangled; she wore an old
housecoat dress, buttoned down the front. Her
breasts hung flat against her chest. Her eyes were
sad and sickly from a life of pain. She held a rag of a
dish towel in her hand and would not move aside to let
Tony in.

"Yeah, Mom," he said smiling, holding his arms
out for her but she stepped backward, away from him.

"What do you want? Why are you here?" she
stammered.

"Whatta'ya mean, Mom? I came to see you . . .
And Dad."

"You've been gone for years . . . Without a word
to let me know you're alive or dead . . . And now you
show up here in a million dollar suit you got by
stealing, and you want me to say I'm glad to see you?"

"It's not a million dollar suit, Mom. Look, I'm
sorry but I just want to see you and Dad again. I've
been helping you out . . . Sending you money."

"Yes," she said. Her face reflected her dislike of
everything her only son had come to. "You send me
money you got through stealing. I don't want that kind
of money. And I haven't been keeping it."

"You haven't been keeping it?"

"No, I've given every dirty penny of it to the
Church . . . And I light candles for you, and I say
prayers for your soul. You've damned yourself to hell,
Anthony. You're not my son anymore. Now go away .
. . And come back when you've repented to God and
stopped being a criminal."

She slammed the door and Tony heard the bolts
being thrown, locking him out.

Tony walked down the steps and outside to the sidewalk. He stopped at the Cadillac, his hand on the door handle. The three boys had approached. One of them asked, "Who you, whitey?"

"I'm nobody," Tony answered. He opened the car door and slid in the front seat.

"Let's go home, Andy."

As Andy drove away he said, "I'm sorry, boss. Don't worry. It'll all work out."

THIRTY-FIVE

Montclair, New Jersey
February 1964

Tony had joined one of the new 'Health Clubs' in Trenton, and he and Andy were regulars there. Andy continued to over eat, but his weight had been stabilized by the workouts he was doing alongside his boss. Tony had begun heavy and hard workouts, building up his upper body, broadening his shoulders and thickening his arms. He found the hard work and sweat helped whenever thoughts of Teresa filled his mind. And those thoughts had not lessened over the years. His love for her, his yearning to hold her in his arms, to feel her lips on his, grew stronger every day.

Tony had nine of his one room casinos – gambling rooms as he called them – twelve sports booking rooms, and in every inner city spread across Northeastern New Jersey, he had a string of numbers operations. He opened his latest gambling room three blocks off the beach in Atlantic City. Everyone he worked with, his trusted soldiers, his accountants and lawyers, even Andy had advised against moving into Atlantic City.

"That's a place for families, for their summer vacations. It's not a place for gambling," they would say.

But Tony knew different. Once, many years before, Atlantic City was a place for smuggling liquor into the Country. During prohibition, in the birth years of the American Mafia, Lucky Luciano and others would spend time there. And there used to be gambling back then. "One day," Tony predicted, "Atlantic City will be wide open for gambling for anybody and everybody. There's going to be legal gambling and big casinos." Were it not Tony Moretti saying this, they would have laughed at him.

Each gambling room was elegantly and expensively decorated; each was open only to a select few wealthy men and women, and of course politicians and police. Only those people who could afford to make big bets and of course to lose big bets, were allowed in. Breaking legs to collect debts was a thing of the past.

The police and politicians would always walk away winners. They wouldn't win more than a hundred dollars, maybe a little more, but they were happy and let the illegal gambling continue. Gambling might not be legal, but no one was getting hurt, no one was being intimidated, there was no extortion, no drugs, and no murders. So the police let the rooms remain open, and they enjoyed the extra income they provided.

Losers at the tables and at the sports booking windows – and most guests were losers – had enjoyed a good time, free liquor, good music and entertainment. One evening Frank Sinatra, a New Jersey native, dropped in at the new gambling room in Atlantic City. He lost a few thousand dollars but walked away happy enough to return a few nights later with Dean Martin and Sammy Davis, Jr. Tony was there that night. Sinatra shook his hand and congratulated him on his success.

Things were going well for Tony. He was happy with the business; it was what he had planned those many years ago when he first told The Aces he had ideas. All he needed was to be in on the inside, and he knew he could change things, turn 'organized crime' into an organized business.

But he was never able to forget Teresa. All the years since the last time he had seen her had not erased her vision from his mind and dreams. The death of Teresa's mother, Maria, gave him a chance to see her once again.

Friends and neighbors gathered at the gravesite that cold, grey morning. Maria would rest next to her husband. She had suffered a long, slow death, with many months of great pain she could not understand, as her damaged brain could not fathom it.

The death of her mother was a blessing and relief to Teresa. She hated to see her mother suffer and wondered why God did not take her sooner, why did He allow her to go on suffering for so long? The priest who came regularly to visit Maria could not answer the question. "God has his plan for all of us, Teresa," he would say. She thought that maybe God had little to do with it.

Tony stood with Andy at the curb, a distance from the grave site. He watched as the priest said the necessary prayers. The ceremony didn't last as long as at Al's burial. The small gathered crowd all expressed their sorrows to Teresa, and as they began to drift away, Tony walked to her.

She was dressed in black, with a black lace veil over her head and tucked under the collar of a very plane black wool coat. She had a rosary wrapped in her fingers. She was dabbing at her eyes with a white hanky held in her black-gloved hands.

There were five people standing with her when

he walked to her. He called her name softly. She turned and her face reddened when she saw him. She pushed the veil back, off her head, revealing the lustrous hair that Tony longed to touch once again.

"What are you doing here?" she asked.

"I came to show my respect. I'm very sorry about your mother."

Teresa looked up at Tony. He was not close, although he wanted to be. She made no effort to get closer to him. There was a distance between them. Was that foretelling something, Tony asked himself?

She stared at him not knowing what to say. What could she say? Among the small group of people standing with Teresa was a man wearing an Army uniform. Everyone but this man slowly drifted away. The man put his arm around Teresa's shoulders. Tony looked surprised and shocked, angry. He walked to them.

"I'm sorry, Tony," Teresa said nervously. "This is my husband, Edgar Henderson."

Edgar wore Captain's bars on his shoulders, and on his collars were the brass Caduceus badges, telling Tony Edgar was a doctor.

Teresa turned to her husband and said, uncomfortably, "This is Tony Moretti, Edgar."

"Oh yes, the famous Tony I've heard so much about," Edgar said. He held out his hand, and Tony shook hands with him. The touch sent a shivery chill up Tony's spine.

"Yeah, well I haven't heard anything about you."

Teresa glanced sideways and saw Andy standing fifty yards away. She looked up at Tony and said, "No trouble, Tony. OK?"

Edgar spoke up, "Look, you two have a lot to talk

about. I'm going to go to the car and have a cigarette. Take your time. It was nice meeting you Tony."

He walked away, past Andy, who gave him a look that would frighten most people. At the funeral car, he leaned against the front fender and lit a cigarette, watching his new wife and Tony Moretti.

"How long have you been married, Teresa?" Tony asked.

"Two months. Edgar was one of Mama's doctors. He was seeing her for months. We got to know one another very well."

"I see. I am sorry about your mother."

"Thank you," Teresa said. "But it's actually a big relief. She was suffering for so long. I'm sure she's at peace with God now."

Tony was quiet for a moment and then said, "He's in the Army."

"Yes. I guess they needed him more than I do. He's going to Vietnam in two weeks."

"That's too bad," Tony said.

"Doctor's don't have guns. They just help people who were hurt in the war. It's what he does," she said pointedly. "He helps people. He'll be OK."

"I hope so . . . For your sake."

"He was drafted, Tony. Isn't that terrible? They drafted a doctor. That means they expect this to be a terrible war, don't you think? They're drafting so many young men now. I've read that they are building up the army there. I'll bet they'll never draft you though, will they."

"That would be tough," he said grinning. "I don't exist."

"What does that mean?"

"I don't have a birth certificate. I was born in Italy. I don't have a Social Security Number. I don't have a driver's license. I've never filed an Income Tax Return. I've never been arrested. No one has ever taken my finger prints. There's not even a parking ticket with my name on it. I never even went to High School. Even the electric bill where I live is in Andy's name. There's a record somewhere of a baby entering this Country with his father and mother. Other than that . . . I don't exist."

"You're lucky . . . I guess," she said and looked away from him. It was hard for Teresa to look at Tony. After all that time, there was still something inside of her that stirred feelings that hadn't been there for years. She was fighting off what she felt. She wanted to hate Tony, but all she felt was fear.

"No, your husband is lucky, Teresa."

"He's a good man, Tony. He's a good doctor. He's kind, he cares about people, he's very smart, and he was very good to my mother."

"Do you love him, Teresa?"

"I guess I do," she said, lowering her eyes again. "I'm not sure what love is anymore, Tony." She paused for a moment, wondering if she should run or stay.

She said, "After my father . . . After you. I guess I do love him. I mean I loved my father in spite of all he was. I think I love Edgar. He's so different than my father. I know he's kind and gentle with me, and I know he'll never hurt me like my father hurt my mother."

The words were like white hot knives being stabbed into Tony's chest, into his heart. He felt his stomach twist. He wanted to scream. She was gone; he knew that now, but his love for her, his desire for her, that would never be gone.

"I guess you think he's different than me, too?" he asked her, a little anger and spite in his voice.

"I don't know, Tony. You frighten me. Will you turn out like my father? Will you . . . Would you ever hurt me like he hurt my mother? I don't think Edgar would ever do that."

It was all over, he felt. She would never return to him now. The wall that had been built between them was too tall, too strong. What was he going to do? He wondered if life had any reason now. Would he be able to keep her vision in his mind and dreams or would she fade away over time? That damn nightmare had come true. She was gone.

"Is there anything I can do for you?" he asked.

She looked up at him, smiled a little, and said, "No, I'm OK. Thanks for the money and the nurses by the way. But I don't need it anymore."

"You figured out it was from me?"

"At first I thought my father was sending it. But when it all just kept coming after his death, I kind of figured it all had to be from you. Thank you for it all. It really helped."

They stood facing each other, four feet apart, without speaking for what seemed like hours to Tony. The world was spinning away in front of him.

They looked into each other's eyes. He wanted to take her into his arms and tell her how much he loved her and wanted her. But he knew it was too late. She was someone else's woman now.

He was about to say goodbye, when he heard someone call, "Sister! Sister! I want to go home now!"

It was Little Al, Teresa's brother. He was walking towards her, his pants stained with urine. His hair was a greasy, uncombed mess. He was picking his nose. He wore what once had to be a white dress shirt that was now wrinkled and hung loose outside his pants. His shoe laces were untied. Spittle was running out of his mouth and down his chin.

"Is that Little Al?" Tony asked in a shocked voice.

"Yes. He's really in bad shape. Edgar says he should be in a home somewhere, where he can be taken care of. He needs psychiatric help, the poor kid. But he won't leave me. I feel so sorry for him . . . But I don't know what to do. I try to take care of him but nothing I do seems to help."

"Is it because of your mother?" Tony asked.

"He watched my father . . . You know that . . . He watched as he beat Mama. It must have been terrible. He was there all night, all alone, with Mama there bleeding on the floor. We were . . . You and I . . . I just can't imagine what he went through."

Tony remembered that terrible night all too well. If he hadn't insisted that Al go home for Christmas, all this would not have happened. If he hadn't insisted that Al go home every weekend, Al would have stayed in Trenton with his whore, and Maria would be alive, and Teresa would be with him. It was all his fault, he knew. He had wanted to do something good, but he told himself that he didn't know what good was. He should have thought it out. But he was thinking only of Teresa. He had wanted her to have a father; he wanted her to be with her whole family. And this was the result.

"Is there anything I can do?"

"What can you do, Tony? I don't want to be mean to you, but it was my father who did this to him. You and my father are so much alike . . . What can you do?"

Tony shifted nervously and pleaded, "Teresa, I'm nothing like your father. I thought you knew me better than that. If you only knew what I've done . . . All that I've changed . . . How different things are now. It's not like the old days."

"I don't want to argue, Tony. Look, I have to go. Please take care of yourself." She put her gloved hand out and Tony took it, gently, and he felt a shiver inside of him. "Regardless of everything," she said. "I don't want anything bad to happen to you."

She turned and started to walk away. Tony said, "Call me if you need anything."

She stopped for a second, she didn't turn, and then she walked away. Tony watched her walk away from him and to her husband. He never thought he could feel such pain. Her words were like a punch in the stomach. Andy walked up to him. He put his hand on Tony's shoulder. Tony said, "Let's go get drunk."

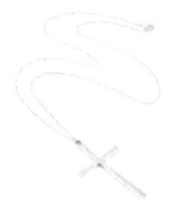

THIRTY-SIX

Montclair, New Jersey
October 1964

Little Al had been on a stew of six different medications for five months. In one respect they were doing some good. He had stopped wetting himself at least, but his nighttime bed wetting continued. A month after starting on the drugs, Little Al took a step out the back door of the house, onto the patio, all by himself. Since witnessing his mother's beating and subsequent death, he had not left the house except to go to his mother's funeral. Teresa's husband, Edgar, had talked him into doing that.

"I'm going, Alley," Teresa called as she was leaving for the cemetery. "Edgar and I are going. You'll be home all alone," she had said.

"NO! NO!" he screamed and fell to the floor, kicking his feet and pounding his fists on the carpet. And once again he wet himself. Teresa had to clean him up and help him into fresh clothes.

Edgar sat him down and talked calmly to him. He had come close to building a bond with the boy. But Edgar knew Little Al needed more than he could give him. Finally, Little Al relented and rather than be alone in the house, he went with Teresa and her husband to the Church and to the Cemetery.

This day Teresa was at the sink, washing the breakfast dishes. Her day would be the same as the day before and the day before that. She would prepare three meals and hope that her brother would eat some of each. She would wash the dishes after each meal. She would vacuum and dust, she would do one or two loads of laundry. She would comfort Little Al when he started screaming over something so innocuous that often Teresa did not know why he was screaming.

That day in autumn, as she stood at the sink, wash cloth in hand, she watched Little Al open the sliding glass door and take a tentative step outside, onto the patio. Teresa dropped the cloth into the soapy water and dried her hands on a kitchen towel. She stood for a moment, unsure of what she should do.

But there he was that cold autumn day, standing outside, all alone, with no effort from Teresa. There was hope, she thought. The mélange of drugs he was taking had calmed him. They hadn't stopped his bedwetting, but they had stopped his wetting himself during the day. He was not screaming at nothing anymore. All that was good, Teresa thought. The bad part was that Little Al had entered a world of foggy visions and near trancelike periods, where he would sit and stare out at some unseen thing for hours. He started talking, almost normally, but often that talk was of things Teresa could not understand and could not follow the logic of.

Little by little the boy made strides in leaving the house on his own. There were long periods of time when he seemed capable of taking care of himself, in spite of sudden onsets of periods of total inertia when he would sit on the floor or on a chair for hours and just stare at nothing. If he could hear Teresa when she spoke to him during these periods, he would not or could not answer. But Teresa thought it would be good for Little Al to be outside, on his own, for as long as he could.

He started to take walks around the neighborhood; the children playing on the street would stop their play and stand aside when he walked, like some smiling machine, past them without a word, without looking at them. Their parents had warned them not to bother Little Al, not to try to talk to him, not to laugh at him, and certainly not to get too close to him.

One day Teresa asked her brother if he wanted to go to the Mall. To her surprise he said 'Yes' and seemed excited to go. They walked together to the bus stop. Teresa dropped the coins into the slot while Little Al watched intently, learning.

Days later, Little Al told his sister he wanted to go to the Mall again.

"I have to clean the bathrooms today, Alley," Teresa said. "How about we go on Saturday? We can go then, OK?"

"No, Sister," he said in an almost normal voice. "I'd like to go today. I can go by myself, Sister. I know how to do it." He was smiling, something she had not seen him do in years.

"Are you sure, Alley?" she asked. "Do you remember where the bus stops? And where you get on the bus to come home?"

"Of course I do," he said, pouting like a child. "I'm not stupid, Sister."

So Teresa stood at the front door and watched Little Al walk down the street to the bus stop at the end of the cul-d-sac where their house was. He waited there, looking down the street for the bus to arrive. When it did, he got on, drop his coins into the slot, sat next to a window, and the bus drove away.

The doorbell rang two hours later. Teresa ran to the door. 'Oh my God!' she thought. 'Something's happened to Alley.' She opened the door and found Little Al standing there. He had a small white paper bag in his hand.

"For you, sister." He said holding the bag out to her. She took the bag and opened it. Inside was a Hersey's chocolate bar. She didn't know what to say. He had brought her a present!

In the days that followed, Little Al went out by himself every day. Trips to the Mall extended into other trips, longer stays away from home. Teresa made sure he always had some money with him; she had taught him to look for a taxi when he wanted to come home and no buses where nearby.

Then the day came when Teresa was sitting in her living room, waiting for Little Al to come home. 7 PM rushed by, then 9 PM. She began to panic. At 11 PM she phoned the police.

The Police Officer on the line said, "I'm sorry, lady. He has to be missing for 24 hours before we can take a missing person's report."

"He is Al Falzone, Jr." Teresa said. "Do you know that name?"

The police officer on the other end of the line said nothing for a few seconds. Then he said, "Yeah, lady. Ain't he dead or something?" He hung up.

The name 'Falzone' had lost its power. Little Al came home the next morning. Teresa ran to him and hugged him. "Oh God! You're, OK! You're OK!"

Little Al pulled away from her and said, "Of course I'm OK. I can take care of myself."

"Where were you? I was so scared."

"I was with my friends," Little Al said as he took his coat off. He tossed it onto the floor and started up the stairs to his room.

Teresa picked up the coat and hung it in the closet. She hesitated at first, but she had to know. Alley had found friends? That was wonderful on one hand, and scary on the other. Who were these friends? She had to know; she had to protect him from the world. It was her responsibility.

She walked up the stairs and stopped outside Little Al's room. The door was closed; she tried the knob but the door was locked from the inside. She knocked again and said, "Alley, Open the door, will you? I want to talk to you."

"Go away, sister," he said.

"Alley, please. I want to talk to you. Please open the door."

A few seconds passed, and she heard the lock being turned. He opened the door and stood in the open doorway, blocking it so Teresa couldn't go into his room.

"What?" he said caustically.

"Who were you with, today?" she asked, smiling as best she could.

"My friends," he answered.

"Who are they? Do I know them?"

"They're *my* friends, Sister. Not yours."

Teresa stood at the bedroom door and looked at her brother's face. For the first time in as long as she could remember, there was anger there. She had seen fear in him before; she had seen expressions of loss and depression, but never before had she seen

Little Al angry. He wasn't a boy anymore. He was as tall as Teresa, and she realized that she couldn't treat him like a boy anymore. She felt frightened; he was big enough to demand and big enough to hurt her if he wanted to. Would the drugs stop that? She didn't know. So she walked away and went downstairs.

The next morning Teresa had made pancakes for Little Al, his favorite breakfast. He ate four and asked for more. Until that day Teresa and her mother before her, had always said that four were enough. That day Teresa gave him four more. He was happy. She took the opportunity to sit with him and drink her coffee while he ate.

"You had a good time while you were out, didn't you?" she asked, smiling.

"Yeah," he said through a mouthful of pancakes.

"Did you go to the Mall?"

"No."

She drank some coffee. 'Take it slow' she thought. Don't press.

"Where did you go?"

"Saw my friends," he said.

"That's good, Alley. I'm glad you have friends. Do you have fun with them?"

"Yes."

"Oh, that's great. What kind of things do you do?"

Little Al shoved the last big forkful of pancakes into his mouth and said through it, "We sing a lot."

"Sing! Oh that's wonderful! I didn't know you could sing!"

Little Al stood from the table and said, "I gotta go."

"Where are you going, Alley?" Teresa asked. She was worried. Would he be gone for days again?

Little Al went to the hallway closet and pulled his jacket out. He put it on and went to the front door. Teresa followed him and grabbed his arm. He spun around and grabbed her by her shoulders. His eyes were fiery and a terrifying look of rage colored his face. "I'm going to see my friends!" he said, his voice a low animalistic growl Teresa had never heard from him before.

He pushed her away roughly and left the house, slamming the door behind him. Teresa ran for the garage and got in her Ford station wagon, the one Tony had bought for her when they were in Newark together. She would follow him, she decided. She had to be sure her brother was OK. If he had finally found friends, that was good, but she had to be sure.

She waited at the curb in front of her house. She could see down the street to the bus stop where Little Al waited. The bus arrived, and he got on. Teresa drove away slowly and followed the bus. Fifteen minutes later the bus stopped, and Little Al got off. She stopped and waited a block away, hoping he would not see her. Another bus arrived, and Little Al got on. She followed once again. They went towards New York and into the Lincoln Tunnel. Out of the tunnel the bus drove into the big Port Authority building, the City's transit station for buses and subways. Teresa panicked. She pulled into the public parking area, found a place to park and ran to the stairs to get to the bus terminal. By the time she found the bus Little Al had been in, he was gone.

THIRTY-SEVEN

Trenton, New Jersey
May 1965

Tony sat alone in his apartment. It was Tuesday, and Tuesday's were always slow since he stopped having the weekly meetings in the back room of the Il Sole Italiano restaurant. Since Al's death there really was no need for the meetings. His people knew what to do.

He was considering going to the gym and getting a heavy work out, but he felt lazy that day. He had one of the new color televisions, but there wasn't much to watch in color. He had a baseball game on; the Yankees were playing Minnesota. The Yankees weren't doing well so far that year, but it was still early in the season. He was only half paying attention to the game. Teresa was filling his mind once again.

Business had settled down to a routine. Everyone knew what they were supposed to do, and they did it. Tony had hired the best people he could and paid them well. His new soldiers had been turned into tuxedo wearing guards in the gambling rooms and suit wearing guards in the booking rooms. They were polite rather than fearful. They opened doors for customers. They smiled and carried on polite small talk. But everyone of them had a slight bulge under their left arms, where they carried a gun in a shoulder holster.

The dealers at every table in the luxurious gambling rooms where young ladies. They were all attractive, all smiling, and all knew how to get the players to make just one more bet. If the players stayed at the tables long enough, they would lose. That was how the odds worked and everyone working for Tony knew that.

He had hired six young black men to run the numbers operations in the inner cities, where twenty-five cents bet on a three digit number might bring wealth to the bettor. The other people who worked for him objected to this. Blacks were OK in the kitchens, cleaning homes, doing heavy work outdoors, but not in Tony Moretti's Family.

Tony ignored these complaints. He never answered these complaints; rather he just turned and walked away. These men brought in a lot of cash, and they were willing to work in neighborhoods where Tony's white employees wouldn't dare go. There was money in those neighborhoods, and Tony wanted that money. Andy complained once, and Tony told him, "The only color I care about is green, Andy. There's money there."

He had an open bottle of Pabst beer sitting on the table next to his favorite chair, the upholstered chair with the red roses on it, but he was ignoring it. Unlike so many of the people he worked with, he had never had a thirst for hard liquor. He never smoked, and he never had tried any drugs. He had a vision for his future, and that made him keep his mind clear. That vision still had Teresa as its center. After all the years, he had not forgotten her or stopped loving her. And all too often he would cry himself to sleep at night, in his bed, all alone.

Andy would be there soon with the bag of cash he had picked up from Bruno Massetti in Brooklyn. Bruno, Andy had told him, was old and ill. Andy thought he might have some kind of cancer. He was thin, drawn, and weak. His sister had passed away, and one of his nieces had moved out. The two nieces remaining with him weren't taking good care of Bruno, Andy told him. The house wasn't being cleaned and maintained as it used to be. The sisters were fat and lazy, Andy reported.

Without speaking it, Tony couldn't care less. Bruno had questioned him when he pushed Peter Salvano out. He was never truly loyal to Tony; he never would be truly loyal to Tony. Were it not for the New York threat, he and the two Capos would not have turned over any cash to him.

Tony would have to come up with some other plan to receive the money from Manny Esposito and Michael Funno. It was such a small amount of money compared to the millions he was bringing in from his gambling operations, he could easily do without it. But he wanted to keep the Capos under his thumb, afraid of him. He didn't want them complaining about his operations in their territories. They lived on their loan sharking, extortion and hijacking businesses. He didn't want any part of that, and he didn't want them lusting after his business.

But he would think about that later. His mind was on Teresa once again as the ballgame went on, unnoticed by Tony. Where was she? What was she doing? Was she happy? Did she have a family? Children? When these thoughts filled his head, tears threatened to burst from his eyes. His love for Teresa had never diminished, in fact over the years he felt more of a yearning for her, more love of her. She was as fresh and beautiful in his mind as that first day, so many years ago, in Pop's Candy Store.

He wiped the tears away with the back of his hand and was reaching for the beer when the phone rang. He got up and turned the volume down on the T.V., and walked to the phone. "Hello," he said on the third ring.

There was a faint buzzing but no one said anything. "Hello," he repeated. "Is anybody there?"

"Tony," Teresa said. Her voice was weak and faint, almost too soft to hear. "It's me, Teresa."

"Are you OK?" 'Oh my God!' he thought. What was wrong? Why was she calling him? She must be desperate.

"I'm fine . . . But I need your help, Tony. You said to call you if I ever needed help."

"What's wrong? Are you sick?"

"I don't want to talk over the phone, Tony. Can we meet somewhere?"

"Yes . . . Certainly . . . But how did you get this number?"

She answered, "I phoned the Lora Luna. It some explaining but they gave me your home number."

Tony's heart was jumping, his head was spinning, and he had trouble breathing. The very sound of her voice stirred the feelings for her that he had never lost. Now he had the chance to do something for her, to help her, to show her he still loved her and wanted her. He would do anything. No amount of money was enough. He would kill for her. But he knew he had to stay calm. She was married and beyond him. He would not tell her how he felt; it would be an intrusion into her life.

"Where are you?"

"I'm at home."

"I'll be there as fast as I can. It'll take a couple of hours. Wait there for me. Will you be OK until I can get to you? Should I send some men to protect you?"

"No, Tony . . . Don't do that."

"Will you be OK?"

"Yes, Tony . . . Thank you . . . I don't deserve your kindness."

He paced the apartment while waiting for Andy. When Andy did arrive, he had a canvass bag filled with thousands of dollars in small bills in his hand. He said, "It's light again, boss."

"Forget that," Tony said as he grabbed a light jacket from the back of a chair. "We have to get to Teresa's. She's in some kind of trouble."

Andy didn't wait for an explanation. It was important. He knew how his boss had been suffering for such a long time. Tony had never expressed what pain he was feeling, but Andy knew. He could see it, he could sense it. He tossed the bag into a far corner and bills spilled out. No matter, neither of them noticed.

They ran down the stairs, not willing to wait for the elevator. Tony's new Cadillac, light blue this time, sat at the curb. They jumped in, and Andy sped away. Twice Tony told Andy to speed up. It seemed like they would never get to Teresa.

After an hour and a half of driving too fast and too dangerously, Andy finally spun the car into the driveway of Teresa's home. The sun had set and the spring's night air was cooling off. There was a breeze moving through the trees. Black clouds foretold rain that night. Tony jumped out before Andy could bring the car to a full stop.

Teresa was standing at the open door. She was crying, a tissue was wadded in her hands. She stepped aside for Tony, and he led her into the house. Andy followed, closing the door behind him.

As Andy would, he had his big gun out, expecting some kind of trouble. Teresa saw this, put a hand to her mouth, and Tony said, "Not now, Andy. We don't need any guns right now." He put the gun back in its shoulder holster and stood against the closed door.

Teresa turned to Tony and fell into his arms. She was sobbing and shaking. Tony spoke over her shoulder, "Andy, how about some water? And maybe see if there's any tea in the kitchen." Andy walked as fast as his bulk would allow into the kitchen.

When they were alone, Tony gently pulled her away from him. She looked up at him, pleading in her eyes. "Oh, Tony . . . I know I don't deserve it but . . . I just don't know what to do. I don't know who to turn to. I'm so awfully alone, Tony."

"Tell me what's wrong, Teresa. I can fix anything."

"It's my brother Alley . . . Little Al. He's been arrested. He's in jail."

"Arrested! For what? What did he do?" Tony was confused. Little Al was a psychotic mess the last time he had seen him. At Maria's funeral he had seen a boy who looked like he should have been institutionalized.

"He was found with drugs. They say he was going to sell them."

How was it possible he could be out dealing drugs? The kid was wetting his damn pants. He was a mess.

"What kind of drugs?" he asked.

Andy returned to the room with a tall glass of

water. He handed it to Teresa and said, "Hey, the both of you need to sit down. Whatever's wrong, the boss can fix anything, Teresa. Don't worry, babe. Everything's going to be OK now."

"Thank you, Andy," she said. Tony took her by her arm and led her to the couch. She sat, drank a sip of water, and Tony sat a few feet away from her. Andy returned to the kitchen, telling them he had a kettle on and would make some tea. He said he had found some Lipton tea bags in a cupboard. And he had found a bottle of scotch. 'Maybe that would help her,' he thought.

"He thinks a lot of you, Tony, doesn't he?" she said when Andy had left the room. She tried to smile a little. Her face was colorless, she wore no makeup. Her eyes were bloodshot from hours of tears. He wanted to take her in his arms and tell her how much he loved her and needed her, but she had moved on. She had a husband and a new life.

Tony looked around the room. Little had changed; there was no new furniture; everything looked like it had that time he had walked into the house to take her to the Christmas dance so many years ago. Swedish modern had gone out of style years before, but Teresa had changed nothing. The same bright colors, the same gaudy lights and pictures on the walls. Surely a doctor's income would be enough to buy new furniture? He asked her why nothing had changed.

"I thought Alley should have some stability. I thought that if the environment changed, it might not be good for him. He was almost OK here, as long as he stayed inside."

"But . . ."

"It was hard, Tony. He was constantly wetting himself, he couldn't stop. At night he would wake up screaming. He would tell me about his nightmares. They were always about Daddy hitting Mama. I would change his sheets and dress him in clean pajamas. He was scared to be left alone anywhere. I had to sit with him every night while he went to sleep. He kept jumping at the slightest sound."

"That's bad," Tony said. "I wish you would have let me know. I could have gotten the nurses back again. They could have taken care of him. You look exhausted."

"I am exhausted, Tony. You don't know how many times I almost picked up that phone. But I just couldn't."

He had to wonder why she was taking care of her brother all alone like that. What the hell kind of husband did she have? Was he too damn busy taking care of other people and ignoring his own wife? Tony felt his temper rising at the thought. Maybe he had better have a talk with the guy. Better yet, maybe Andy should have a talk with him.

"Where's your husband?" he asked. "Is he with Little Al?"

Teresa gripped the glass tightly and looked into it. Tears appeared in her eyes again. She said without looking up, "He's dead, Tony. He died in Viet Nam."

"Oh, Jesus Christ! I'm so sorry, Teresa." He touched her hand but she pulled away from him. He wouldn't push. It wasn't the right time. 'Patience,' he thought.

"He was only there for two and a half weeks. They say he was sent to something called a forward aid station. I don't know what that is. They say some Marines were badly wounded. He went there to help them. He was operating, they say. He was saving lives. There was a mortar attack. He was killed along with a lot of other poor guys. They gave me a Bronze Star for him. Hardly a fair trade, was it?"

"I'm so sorry," Tony said. And to his own amazement, he really was sorry. The girl he had loved for so long had been hurt, and that hurt him. He hated to see her mourning so, even if it was for a man who had taken her from him. That was why she was all alone, taking care of her brother all by herself. It must have been terrible, he thought.

"It's OK," she said. "It's been awhile. It hurt at first. But . . . But I just couldn't bring myself to feel more than sorry for him. I mean, he was such a good man. He did so much good. I feel really guilty that I couldn't grieve."

Much to Tony's regret, he felt good about that. He was ashamed inside of himself that her words made him feel good. A good man had died a needless, senseless death. He should have felt bad about that, but he didn't. She didn't really love him. She married him because he was a good man and for no other reason.

"But Alley needs help. God, Tony. He wouldn't survive in prison. He'll die there."

"Did he kill anyone?" Tony asked.

"No, of course not."

"Then he won't go to prison. But how the hell did he get out of the house? He was so . . . messed up the last time I saw him."

"The Veteran's Hospital. Because I'm a . . . a war widow I guess . . . The doctor's there were seeing him. I used to take him once a week. It was really hell in there, all these guys in really bad shape, just sitting around, waiting for someone to take pity on them. I almost cried at seeing all of them the first few times I took Alley there. They didn't want to see him at first because he wasn't directly related to Edgar. But I pleaded. I told them I had nowhere else to go, and Alley really needed the help. So they agreed to see him, and they never asked for a penny from me.

"They gave him some new drugs. I'm not sure what they were, but there were six pills he had to take every day and one more he took twice a day. They really spaced him out, but he was able to be almost normal within a few weeks of starting on them. He started going outdoors even. First just into the back yard as long as I was with him. Little by little, over a month or so, he got used to it . . . As long as he stayed heavily medicated.

"He was really spaced out on the drugs. So often he would just sit and stare out at nothing. But he wasn't wetting himself anymore, and he wasn't afraid to be alone. I think his nightmares ended. Of course, he never stopped wetting the bed at night. At least he didn't wake up every night screaming in terror. I was thankful for that.

"He started going out, away from the house, by himself. At first I was grateful for the time alone. But he got into a bad group, apparently. Hippies I think. He stayed out overnight once, and I was in a panic. The police wouldn't help. When he came home, he refused to tell me where he had gone. The next day he went out again, and I tried to follow him, but I guess I'll never be one of those television private eyes. I lost him in the Port Authority building up in New York. After that I never tried to follow him again.

"I made sure he always had enough money with him to get back home. I'm guessing his new friends wanted that money because when he did come home he never had any money left. I think they might have turned him on to some bad drugs. Mixing whatever prescription drugs he was taking with what they were selling him was bad.

"He started staying out all night for longer and longer periods, and he would never tell me where he was. I had no idea where he was sleeping, if he was eating, if he was getting into trouble. I was so scared, Tony. The police say he was selling and transporting drugs for his new friends, and they were keeping him high in return. After awhile he began to refuse his medications here at home, but he was only here for a day or two before leaving again anyway. I think he was medicating on whatever they were giving him."

"How do you know they were giving him drugs? Did the police tell you that?" was the obvious question, and it came from Andy, who was standing in front of them, unnoticed, with a tray holding two big mugs of steaming tea.

"He told me, Andy," she answered and smiled kindly up at him. "He said they were giving him what he called 'funny looking pills'."

Tony and Andy looked at each other, both wondering what the hell was going on. Tony said, "He just up and told you? Just like that? And there was nothing you could do to stop him from going up to New York?"

"I didn't know what to do. He's big now . . . I was scared. He could hurt me, you know." she confessed.

"You should have called me a long time ago," Tony said, and he immediately felt sorry for saying that.

Andy laid the tray on a coffee table and said, "Hey, boss. That ain't important now. We're here, and we gotta' do somethin', right? Let the past be the past."

It was not often that Andy told Tony what to do. "You're right, of course," Tony said. He asked Teresa, "Does he have a lawyer?"

"Yes. I've got his card somewhere. I'll give it to you."

"What jail is he in? Who made the arrest?"

"He's in New York. In Brooklyn."

"Brooklyn?" Tony said. "What the hell was he doing in Brooklyn?"

"They say he had nearly two pounds of heroin. He was supposed to bring it to someone who would buy it. The police found him wandering around aimlessly at two in the morning. He was lost, I guess. He's never been to Brooklyn before."

She paused and drank some of the hot tea. She smiled up at Andy again, telling him it was good and thanking him. She looked down at the floor and said, "I know I have no right to ask you . . . But I just don't know what to do. I don't know who to turn to. His lawyer says he should plead guilty and maybe get only five to ten years. Tony, he'll die in prison. He'll never survive."

"Does he have a trial date yet?"

"Next week . . . Monday morning."

"OK," Tony said. "Get the lawyer's card for me, and I'll take care of everything."

"Can you?" she asked. "After all I've done to you? After how I've hurt you?"

"Don't worry about it, Teresa. I'll take care of it."

While Teresa was getting the lawyer's card, Tony told Andy, "Get ahold of Bruno. Brooklyn is his territory. I want to get the name of the cops involved and the judge, and tell Bruno I want it today . . . Not tomorrow . . . Today."

Andy went to a telephone hanging on the wall in the kitchen and phoned Bruno Massetti. He told him

what Tony had said. Bruno said, "Yeah, I'll get on that
. . . But I ain't feelin' too good today. I'll have one of
the boys do it in the mornin'."

"The boss said today, Bruno."

"I said I'd get it done. Ain't that good enough for
the kid?"

****

Brooklyn, New York

Bruno's answer to the order Andy had given had
upset both Andy and Tony. That's not the way things
were supposed to operate, they both knew. They went
to the kitchen, leaving Teresa alone for a few minutes
while they talked.

Andy said in a low voice, "Boss, I don't think
Bruno is gonna' do what you want. Not today and not
tomorrow."

"I agree," Tony said. "There's something wrong
out there. I think it's time you and I made a call on
Bruno.

They stayed the rest of the day with Teresa until
she had calmed down and Tony felt he could leave her
alone. It was past 9 PM by the time they drove out to
Brooklyn, where Bruno still lived. The sun had set on
the way over, and Tony thought that the setting sun
might just be a foretelling of what was happening with
the remnants of Peter Salvano's Family.

Don Pietro's old house in Brooklyn had not aged
any better than Bruno Massetti had. Although Andy
went to see Bruno on a regular basis, to pick up the
money and examine the books, Tony hadn't been there

in years. The yard that night was full of weeds and yellow dandelions. The roof had pealing shingles; the house needed a fresh coat of paint. The neighborhood, too, was changed. So many of the old homes had fallen into disrepair, and a couple of them had been abandoned and were standing empty. The streets were lined with trash. It was what Tony had seen in so many of the old neighborhoods; the old people were dying off, and the young were moving to the suburbs.

He was shocked when he saw Bruno at the front door. The once big, strong man was shrunken, bent and grey. Most of his hair was gone and what was left was colorless. His face was unshaven; his clothes, an old plaid flannel shirt and corduroy pants, were rumpled and dirty. He coughed into a dirty handkerchief rather than say 'Hello'.

He walked slowly and unsteady, leading them through the musty house to the den, where all business was done going back to the days of Don Pietro Salvano in the 1920s. He lowered himself into the big chair behind the desk. He coughed again and then asked, "So what's wrong?"

"I should ask you the same question, Bruno. How sick are you?" Tony asked, concerned although he wasn't sure why.

"Sick enough," he answered. "Does that bother you?"

"I'm sorry, Bruno. I was just asking. You don't have to like me . . . You just have to do what I tell you to do."

"Yeah, for a little while longer, then I'll be free of you," Bruno said in a raspy, phlegm filled voice that was full of hate for the young Tony Moretti.

There was no sense arguing with the old man. Tony saw he was dying; it was just a matter of time.

But that was what Tony had seen in his visions of the future, when he joined with The Aces all those many years ago. The old ways of organized crime, of Mafia, were quickly dying, and his vision of organized crime, business without the violence that society would not accept, was the future. The old 'gun slingers' were quickly dying off. The violent crimes were being left to others, to the blacks and the Latinos. Threats, extortion, murders, leg breaking to collect illegal debts, would eventually die off with Bruno and his generation. Political power and business power was the future. Bruno would never understand that, even if he lived for another fifty years.

"OK, Bruno," Tony said as he pulled a chair closer to the dust covered desk. The chair seat, upholstered in the heavy brocade of a generation past, was worn thin and had an unrepaired tear along the edge. "For now, I need to know what cops and judges in Brooklyn are on the payroll."

Bruno said nothing. His bloodshot eyes seemed locked on Tony's, the loathing he felt for Tony and all he represented was evident. He coughed into his handkerchief but said nothing.

"Bruno, did you hear me? Tell me who you have on the payroll."

"There ain't nobody," he said, his voice a gravely grind, yellow spittle dripping from the corner of his lips.

"You don't have anybody you're paying off? Not one cop? Not one low level politician? I don't believe it. What the hell happened?"

"People out here don't give a shit about you, Tony. You're a nothing out here. Your thing is across the river, over in Jersey. What the hell do they care about what goes on over there? You think your reputation has spread all the way to New York? Most of these cops out here don't even know who the hell you are. They don't care about you. Sure, you got money but you're a nobody here."

Tony stood, throwing the chair back against the wall. He glared down at the old, sick man. Bruno was done. As it turned out, Bruno had let every operation the Salvano Family had once run in Brooklyn go to other Families. There was nothing left there . . . And Tony was happy about that. He didn't want to be associated with the old world.

Tony had waited too long to find another bank for payments from the Capos. He had to move the bank out of New York, make it somewhere closer to home.

"Give me the books, Bruno."

The man stared at Tony, hatred glaring from the old man's dead eyes. But he didn't move. In his mind he was thinking, 'Go ahead, kid. Kill me now. It's a better way to go than what I got.'

Tony turned to Andy and said, "Get the books." Andy went around to the back of the desk. He reached down and opened the bottom drawer of the desk and pulled two old, worn ledger books from it. Andy stood next to Bruno, looking down at the old man. He demanded, "You hand these books to your boss." He held the books out for a moment. Bruno finally took them from Andy and dropped them on the desk, the effort causing him to suffer a wracking cough that seemed not to end.

Tony took the books, and he and Andy walked out of the house to the car. As they drove away, Tony asked, "Who takes care of him?"

"Bruno? Nobody I guess. I heard there's only one of his nieces left and she's moved into some kind of nursing home. I think he might be there alone."

"He never got married, did he?"

"No, he had a girlfriend a long time ago. I heard they had a couple of kids but they never really got married, ya'know? The kids are out in Oregon. I don't think they care a whole lot about him. They never had much to do with him when they was growing up."

"Who owns the house?

Andy shrugged his big shoulders and answered, "I guess Peter Salvano still has the deed. I mean I guess he inherited it from his old man. I really don't know. I'd be kinda' surprised if Bruno owned it."

Tony thought for a minute, looking out the window at the old houses as they drove past them. He said, "When Bruno dies . . . Burn the damn house down."

"You got it, boss."

"We're going to need someplace for the Capos to send the money. Have you got any ideas?"

"Yeah, I been thinkin' about that. But you ain't gonna like what I been thinkin' about."

"OK, so tell me."

"Look," Andy started, as he weaved the car through the streets of old homes. "I can see what you're doin'. I like what you're doing. You got high roller gamblin' goin' on. And I can see what that's bringin' in, more cash than I ever thought I'd see. That's good because it keeps the cops off our ass. Smart, ya'know? So I was thinkin', why do we need them old fuckers? They still doin' loan shark business and sellin' protection. That's what we was doin' when we was kids with The Aces. Breakin' legs and throwin' bricks through windows is old stuff. The cops don't like it, and the people I think are sick of all that kinda' crap." Andy paused for a minute, took a deep breath, and then went on. "Why not let them go? Let the cops keep goin' after them like we do with them drug pushers down in Trenton. Let them take the heat while we keep rakin' in the dough. We don't need 'em, do we?"

Tony thought about that. He liked what he had heard and wished he had thought of doing that himself. "You know Andy, you're right again. I hate those old guys anyway. They still owe loyalty to the Salvano Family, and that family doesn't even exist anymore. They never will be loyal to us like they should be. To them it's like they were taking orders from their kids. They still have dreams of the old days, of shooting guys in the streets and running backroom speakeasies. No, you're right."

He looked out the car's window and the dark night sky above. It perhaps was time to move on. It was perhaps time to make the next move in his plans. Yes, it was time. He said, "Go ahead and pass the word down that they're on their own. They don't need to pay up anymore. And when the cops and New York come after them . . . well, let them take care of themselves. They shouldn't come to me for help. And besides, they're either holding out on us, or their income is shrinking. Anyway you look at it . . . It's time to move on and away from them."

****

Tony had been paying up to the New York Gambino organization for a long time, ever since pushing Peter Salvano aside. Close to a million a year had been given to them, and the amount was increasing as Tony's gambling operations expanded. Tony considered the payments to be nothing more than protection and extortion. As long as he paid up, they left him alone. It was time to get something back for that payment.

He made two phone calls to New York, both to Capos of the Gambino Family. The Capos operated in Brooklyn, and they had a book of corrupt police and politicians that Tony needed access to. Within an hour after making the calls, he found out who Little Al's arresting officer was and what judge would sit at Little Al's trial. Ten thousand dollars was filtered up the appropriate chain through the Gambino Family to politicians and police, and five days later Little Al walked into Teresa's house, a free man . . . Or at least a free boy.

Tony and Andy had waited outside the Brooklyn jail where Little Al was being held. He was a mental mess when the guards walked him to the front gate, one guard holding each of Little Al's arms. Little Al was drooling and talking to himself. He seemed unaware of what was happening, where he was or where he was going. The guards roughly shoved him into the backseat of the Cadillac, one of them sneering, "Good luck with that," to Andy.

They drove him home as quickly as they could. He slumped down in the back seat and said nothing to them, not even to answer when Tony asked if he was OK. He seemed to be in some other world all by himself. He did wet his pants in the back seat of Tony's car. He had been off his medication for over two weeks.

Teresa was happy but worried about her brother when Tony and Andy all but carried the young man into the house. She was in shock when she saw him, holding her hands up to her mouth to stop herself from screaming. Tears once again filled her eyes.

Tony and Andy got Little Al upstairs and helped Teresa take his filthy clothes off. They walked him into the bathroom and lifted him into the tub as Teresa filled it with hot water. That seemed to relax Little Al. He leaned back in the tub and his muscles loosened up a bit. He was filthy because the guards were unable to get him into the jail's shower. His hair was matted and crawling with bugs from the dirty mattress and pillow he had slept on, on the floor of an isolation cell.

Between the three of them they managed to clean him up and dry him off. Andy picked him up in his arms and carried him into Little Al's bedroom. He laid him on the bed, and Teresa pulled a blanket up over him. Little Al fell asleep almost immediately.

Teresa knew she had to get her brother back on his medication, and she remembered how hard it was to get him started on it. She anticipated he would fight and argue about going back on the cocktail of drugs that allowed him to be almost normal.

Little Al slept for only three hours and then was awake, walking down the stairs completely naked, asking for pancakes. As she thought, he did fight taking the pills. But Teresa had asked Tony and Andy to stay after bringing him home. When he pushed Teresa away and threw one of the bottles of pills against the wall, Andy grabbed him by his shoulders, lifted him off the ground and said, "Take your fuckin' pills you little shit. Your sister wants to help you. Be thankful you ain't somebody's bitch in jail right now."

Little Al was truly frightened. He started crying like a baby but he took the pills and ran off to his room. He didn't refuse his pills after that. In a matter of days he was as normal as he would ever be.

Teresa made a pot of coffee and asked Tony and Andy to sit with her in the kitchen. Andy quickly finished a cup and said, "You guys have somethin' to talk about. I'll go wait in the car."

He left Tony and Teresa sitting together. They

drank their coffee, in uncomfortable silence. Teresa was staring out the window. A bird was jumping around from branch to branch as she watched. Tony wished he could read her mind, to know what she was thinking. He wanted Teresa so badly, he loved her so much, he wanted to touch her, to hold her in his arms and feel her close to him, but he also knew there was a curtain between them. He finally asked, "What do we do now?"

"I don't know, Tony. I can never thank you enough for doing what you did for Alley."

She stopped there, and Tony added, "There's a 'but' in there somewhere, Teresa."

"Yes, there is. There's so much come between us, Tony. I keep thinking that if it weren't for us . . . Being together when we were kids . . . My parents might both still be alive today. I don't blame you . . . I blame myself."

"Can that be repaired?" he asked.

She looked from the window to Tony and asked, "Why do you love me, Tony? Why haven't you moved on?"

"Why do I love you? There's an empty place inside me that can't be filled without you. I love everything about you, and I dream of you every night. I love your touch, I love the way you feel, I love the way you smile and laugh. I love the way your hair is always so soft and flowing like a gentle ocean. I love your eyes when you look at me. I feel like I'm in hell when you cry and I can't stop you from crying. I want to make you happy, and nothing else matters except that.

"Christ, I'd give everything up for you Teresa," he went on. "I look at you today, and I feel the same longing for you as that first time I saw you in Pop's Candy Store. You are the most beautiful woman I've ever seen. No one, anywhere, can come close to you. No one has ever made me feel the way you make me feel when I'm close to you. I'm not sure I believe in heaven, but I guess the simple touch of your hand on mine has to be better than anything heaven can offer. It's stupid to say I'd give my life for you, but I guess I'd take a bullet for you anyway. I'd do anything for you. Inside me, there's something that wants you near me forever. I've done a lot in my life; I've come a long way since those days back in Passaic, but there's still that empty place . . . Where you're supposed to be.

"I guess I'll never get over you, Teresa. I love you . . . I always will . . . And it's as simple as that."

Teresa smiled a sad smile. She sipped at her coffee and then said, "If you weren't who you are . . . If it weren't for my father . . . If it weren't for so many things."

Tony twirled the coffee in his cup and then stood. He walked out and he and Andy drove away.

****

The doorbell rang interrupting Teresa's lunch. She had made a small sandwich. There was a package of some kind of plastic wrapped deli meat in the refrigerator; she didn't bother to look to see what it was. Money was short for her, so the bread was some pasty white stuff she had bought in a discount store, where she had bought the meat. It didn't matter.

Little Al had locked himself in his bedroom the night before and had not come out yet. Teresa was used to that by that time and had accepted the fact that he would never improve. Little Al, she felt, would never be anything more than what he was. The best she could hope for was some stability.

She went to the door. A woman, middle aged and dressed well in a good quality business suit, pale blue, which set off the small string of white pearls around her neck, stood at the door, smiling. She carried a large brown leather bag hung from her shoulder. She smiled in a manner that said she could be trusted.

"Hello, Mrs. Henderson?" the woman asked.

"Yes," Teresa answered. "What can I do for you?"

"I'm Dr. Patricia Simpson, Mrs. Henderson. May I come in and speak with you?"

Teresa hesitated. Letting a stranger into the house was a bad thing, something that had been drummed into her since childhood. Strangers could be dangerous. Strangers could have guns and orders to kill. But that was because of her father's business she thought. Her father was dead, and his business was dead with him. Teresa had nothing to do with her father's business when he was alive and certainly since his death. There was no reason to fear someone from her father's past. This woman didn't look dangerous, and she said she was a doctor. So Teresa stepped aside and held the door open for Dr. Simpson.

They sat in the living room. Dr. Simpson took the room in quickly. She was a psychiatrist, and she was trained in observation. The room was well furnished, she saw, but everything was old, out of fashion, well used, and most pieces had some kind of noticeable wear or damage, and needed to be replaced.

The room was very clean, which told her Teresa cared for her environment. Teresa's clothes were also well used; the colors were faded, and wear from age was obvious on everything. Dr. Simpson wondered why. She thought that maybe the young woman didn't get out of the house often enough to buy new things. Her brother, Dr. Simpson assumed, was the problem, as had been explained to her.

Teresa saw her looking around the room. She said, "I apologize for the house."

"Why? It looks nice to me."

"Who are you, Dr. Simpson? Why are you here?"

"I am a psychiatrist, Mrs. Henderson. I manage a Care Home in Buffalo . . . Upstate New York. Your brother was referred to me as a possible long term resident."

"Who referred him to you?" Teresa asked. She knew the answer, of course. It was Tony. No one else would have done that.

"I'm afraid I'm not at liberty to reveal that at this time. But let me tell you about Browne's Residence Hall."

Dr. Simpson slipped the large soft leather bag off her shoulder. She reached inside and pulled out a color brochure, handing it to Teresa. She opened it and flipped through the dozen pages, each of which was in full color and very professional. It depicted a castle-like building of grey stone, inside of which were elegantly furnished rooms, sitting rooms, dining rooms with white table cloth covered tables, libraries, T.V. rooms, recreation rooms with pool tables and card tables and game tables and ping-pong tables. It showed a big music room with a concert size grand piano. A huge swimming pool inside a glass dome at the side of the building appeared on another page.

The brochure contained photos of six different bedrooms, all appointed well enough for European royalty to feel comfortable sleeping in them. There were pictures of gardens filled with roses, manicured shrubbery, fountains and ponds, and trees with tables and chairs sitting in the shade under them. Another page displayed a picnic area near a lake, and a summer house sitting out at the end of a wooden boardwalk that stretched over the lake. White swans were swimming in the lake. But what Teresa noticed was that nowhere in any of the pictures did she see fences or guards or locked cells.

"This is all very nice, Dr. Simpson. But why show it to me?"

"Mrs. Henderson, I've read your brother's medical file."

"How did you get that?" Teresa interrupted.

"It was given to me," was all she would say. "In any case, I think your brother could benefit greatly by long term care as a resident at Browne's. Would you consider registering him there?"

"It's as simple as that?" Teresa asked. "I just hand my brother over to you and I go on with life? Are you kidding me?"

"No. No. I invite you to come to Browne's . . . With your brother of course. Spend a few days with us. See if you like it. Meet the staff. See how well our residents are doing. Let your brother use the facilities. If you agree, register your brother and he will be well taken care of, and I guarantee his health will improve. If you don't like what you see, take your brother home."

"I assume Browne's is a place to care for people with mental illnesses," she said. "But I don't see any fences or guards. Can your patients just leave any time they want?"

"First of all, the residents at Browne's are not called patients, Mrs. Henderson. We have a staff to resident ratio of three to one. That is three staff to every resident. We keep a close eye on our residents, but we never force them to do anything. In time your brother, as is the case with every resident, will come to see Browne's as home and have no desire to leave. Our care and treatment will at least stabilize your brother, and possibly lend to some progressive cure."

Teresa was trying not to be too interested, but she couldn't help wondering if this offer was something she should consider. She asked, "So, I assume you keep everyone well drugged up?"

"Not at all," the Doctor said. "Oh, we have pharmaceuticals available when necessary, but we rely more on care, continued psychiatric care, and well planned activities that we have found often return our residents to the ability to live as others live, I guess what everyone calls normal, although we don't use that term. Look," Dr. Simpson said. "I know what caused your brother's problems. I've read all the reports . . . Police reports, medical reports, and others. I think your brother can be helped. The drugs he is taking now will only delay any improvement. Oh, they calm him down, but you've seen what can happen if he is allowed out . . . On his own. I know all about that, too. Mrs. Henderson, I can help your brother. Please let me."

"This looks very expensive," Teresa said. "I can't afford much. I'm on a Veteran's Widow's Pension."

"The cost has been taken care of. There will be no cost to you."

Teresa smiled in thought. So Tony had once again come to her rescue. 'Why does he continue to care about her? Why doesn't he just walk away?' She wondered, but she knew the answer.

"I'm not sure Alley will come with me . . . If I choose to go there."

"That's a situation I'm often faced with. Many of our residents were in very bad shape when they first came to us. Many refused to visit Browne's." She reached into her bag again and took out a cardboard packet. She handed it to Teresa. One of these pills every four hours will calm your brother. If you are not demanding, he will go with you . . . . For a pleasant drive."

"But won't he be suspicious when I pack his suitcase?"

"Don't bring any of his clothes with you. We have a clothing store at Browne's, and everything will be provided for him. It's sort of an all inclusive retreat." She smiled, laughed a little and said, "The clothes are all the latest styles and fashions, but I daresay they are too modern for me. Our residents all seem to like them, however. It seems the brighter the color and more extravagant the design, the better."

Teresa took the pills and said she needed time to think. Dr. Simpson gave her a business card with her name on it and a phone number at Browne's Residence Hall. "Please phone me, Mrs. Henderson. Your brother needs our help."

Three days later Teresa gave Alley one of the pills, telling him it was a new one from his doctor. He argued at first but Teresa told him he would not have to take the other pills if he took this one. An hour later he walked with her to her car. He didn't argue or fight once again. He was, on the drive up to Buffalo, rather friendly and happy.

Teresa and Little Al stayed at Browne's for three days. She was very satisfied with everything she saw, and Little Al seemed to like it, also. Teresa did register Little Al at Browne's Residence Hall, where he was to spend the rest of his life.

THIRTY-EIGHT

Trenton, New Jersey
October, 1967

Tony had done what he had always wanted to do. From that first day in DeSonoto's Pizza when he had approached The Aces, he had an idea, a plan. It had taken nine years of hard work and great risks, but his plan had been accomplished. He was completely independent, disconnected from all the old Mafia life. He had invested his profits from the gambling businesses in legal businesses.

He owned seven Italian restaurants throughout the State, a string of dry cleaners in Newark and Trenton, apartment buildings, and two office towers near the State Capital Building that were always fully occupied. He had a large commercial laundry. And his latest acquisition was a trucking company that had been run out of business by Latino gangs who were hijacking every truck they could find. Tony bought the company cheaply and set five of his new soldiers, with Andy to lead them, after the Latino gangs. Three months later the hijacking had stopped, and the trucking company became successful.

He had opened an office in one of his high rise buildings in Trenton, near his apartment and a block from the Governor's office. Tony's office was in a corner of the 9000 square foot office space, and it was glass walled on two sides. Outside were eight employees who kept the books, answered phones, paid the bills, and presented an absolutely legitimate front to whoever walked into the office.

The business of the gambling rooms, betting rooms, and numbers operations were all handled out of the back room of L'oro Luna in Newark and kept separate from Tony's legal businesses. Tony had learned about off-shore bank accounts, using Caribbean banks to hold all the money from gambling.

Andy had an office next to Tony's. It perhaps wasn't as big, but it was big enough for a pool table, a big T.V., and a comfortable couch for Andy to take his naps on.

Tony was 23 years old and a popular guest at the parties thrown by influential politicians and businessmen. They knew him as a smart young investor and business man. The years had clouded his background of leading a crime family. He was just an exciting young, very wealthy man to be near and to brag about knowing. Rumor had it that he had attended college in Europe and was a genius at business. Tony did nothing to begin or dispel that rumor.

Tony had not given up his days at the gym. He was very fit, very muscular, and very strong. The young women and many of the older women tried to attract him. He was always polite and gracious and mannerly, but he had acquired the art of turning down their advances while leaving them feeling wonderfully in love with him.

Tony was sitting at his desk that afternoon, trying to understand financial reports that his accountants had prepared. 'What the hell does all this shit mean?' he said to himself. No one knew he had never attended even one day of High School, more or less the colleges and grad school so many people assumed he must have attended.

He flipped through the pages to find the end of the report and the one entry he understood, the profit. His secretary's voice came through the intercom, "There's a Mr. Pelto here to see you, Mr. Moretti."

"Who? Who did you say?" Tony couldn't believe he had heard right. Could it be Richie Pelto . . . From The Aces?

"Mr. Richard Pelto, sir. Shall I send him in?"

"Yes, please, right away. And tell Mr. Pecora to come in here, too."

His office door opened and Richie Pelto walked in. But this was a man and not the skinny little book worm kid Tony remembered. He was broad shouldered, and he stood tall with a confidence he hadn't had as a teenager. Richie was dressed in a good quality brown tweed sports jacket and grey slacks. His hair was short and neatly combed. He looked very different than he did in his days with The Aces.

Tony jumped to his feet and almost ran to him. They hugged each other and laughed and slapped each other on their backs. Andy walked in and stopped. "What the hell! Is that who I think it is?"

Richie held out his hand, and Andy slapped it away. "A damn handshake ain't enough, Richie. Come here so I can hug you!"

Andy picked Richie up off the floor and spun him around. All three were laughing and throwing friendly punches and slapping shoulders. It took a few minutes, but they finally calmed down. They retreated to a couch and chairs, and Tony, ignoring the intercom, just shouted, calling loudly for coffee to be brought in.

"So what the hell brings you here, Richie?" Tony asked as one of the ladies from the office poured coffee for the three of them.

"You ain't lookin' for no job are you?" Andy laughed.

"No, I've got a good job. That's what I came to see you about." Richie waited for the woman to leave the office, closing the door behind her. He reached into his inside jacket pocket and pulled out a small black case. He opened it to reveal a gold FBI badge and an ID card with his picture on it. "I'm with the FBI."

Tony and Andy looked at each other. The smiles had fallen from their faces. Tony turned back to Richie and asked, trying to sound like it was a joke but it wasn't, "So, you've come to arrest me?"

"No, I wouldn't do that. You did too much for me, Tony. I owe you too much." Richie was serious; it wasn't a joke to him. Inside, Richie knew that Tony, the smart kid who had taken over The Aces so many years ago, had saved his life. He had let Richie go.

"What did I ever do for you, Richie?" Tony sat back and asked.

"You let me out . . . You let me leave The Aces. You didn't have to. You could have said no when I said I wanted to go to California and start college. That one thing changed my life and saved me, Tony. I was never like the rest of The Aces, you know that. I had to be a part of it or be a target back in Passaic. I was tired of getting beat up and having my lunch money stolen. But I always wanted to go to college and get an education. It had been burning inside of me since grade school. I wanted something more . . . Something better. You did that for me and I'll owe you for that for the rest of my life."

"So you came here to say thanks?"

"Yes," Richie said. He sat forward on the edge of the couch. He spoke softly, in a conspiratorial tone, "Something's going to happen, Tony. You need to know. And I could lose my job over this. I'm supposed to be taking a sick day. So no one can know I was here and told you."

"They're coming after me?" Tony asked.

"No . . . Not you . . . Peter Salvano is going to be arrested and indicted for Interstate Fraud. He's stolen millions from people in his real estate racket, and we have the evidence. He'll do twenty years or more."

"Good. I hope he gets more."

"Think about it, Tony," Richie explained. "Salvano is a punk. He's scared of everything. We have a five year file on him, and we know him better than he knows himself. He'll do anything to keep out of jail. Washington is prepared to offer him witness protection for life if he rats on all the Mafia stuff he knows about. Hoover is obsessed with breaking up the Mafia Families. He wants Salvano to rat out everybody he's ever done business with."

"That means you, boss," Andy said.

Tony nodded. He realized the danger he was in. Although Peter Salvano and he had not seen each other in years, Peter knew too much about Tony's early years. The murder of Chi Chi Torrel, the murder of Ted Bianci, all the crimes, all the money. It could be the end for Tony.

"You know I've been out of that life for awhile now, don't you Richie?" Tony asked.

"I know all about you, Tony. J. Edgar has a thick file on you . . . But we can't prove anything. You've got a lot of friends whether you know it or not. People like you all the way up to D.C. But if you're not careful . . . Well, Hoover will get you, too. He's a very dangerous man. A lot of people are going to fall when Salvano starts talking, Tony."

"What are you telling me, Richie?" Tony asked.

"I'm not telling you anything, except that I owe you one, and you maybe need to watch your back. That's all I'm telling you. I'm a cop, Tony. I'm a good cop. I wouldn't be part of anything illegal."

Richie stood and said, "I'm going to leave now. Forget I was here. I don't want to know what you're going to do. My advice is to pack a suitcase full of money and leave for Mexico as quick as you can. But we're even now, Tony. You saved my life, and if I saved your life, I'm happy."

****

Peter Salvano left his office at ten past six that evening. He was a little late; he and his wife were having dinner with friends but he had some business to finish at his desk. Carol would understand; she always did.

He was feeling good about himself and how he had managed to make up for all the lost money from The Salvano Family crimes. It would have been a shorter learning curve had Roger Tifton not been killed. He could have taught Peter how to cheat people. But Peter wasn't exactly stupid. He learned all on his own, and he was worth many millions, most of it acquired by the fraudulent land deals he had started.

Western land was cheap, he had found out. He would start a new corporation that would start a wholly owned corporation that would start yet another corporation and have that junior corporation borrow money from a small bank in some small western State's town. A stretch of desert somewhere would be bought cheaply and roads would be put in. The land would be subdivided and sold off piece by piece. Once sold, the junior corporation would file for bankruptcy, and the other corporations would simply close their doors and fade away into the night. All the money taken from investors would wind up hidden in overseas banks where Peter had access to it as needed, while he was sheltered from the fraud through layers of corporation filings and front people who didn't know he existed.

When he stepped from the elevator that evening, the building's doorman greeted him and opened the door to the street. "I'll need a cab, Billy. It's too damn cold to walk." Peter had taken to leaving his Jaguar sports car in the basement parking garage of his condominium and walking the few blocks between his office and home. Age was catching up with him, and he needed the exercise, he told himself.

Billy ran to the curb and waived down a yellow cab. He opened the rear door, and Peter jumped in. He gave the driver his home address. The driver lowered the flag and pulled away from the curb. He drove for two blocks and took a left turn. Peter looked out the window and said, "You're going the wrong way, driver."

"Shut you damn mouth," the driver said.

"What's going on here?"

"I said, shut up. You'll find out soon enough."

Peter had no idea what was happening. A kidnapping for ransom? Carol had access to their personal accounts, but there wasn't more than a hundred thousand there. He would have to get the money from one of the Caribbean Island banks.

But maybe it was one of the people he had stolen money from? OK, he would just buy his way out, he thought. Money can buy anything. So he sat back and waited. There was no sense trying to overtake the driver or to jump from the moving taxi. Just wait, he said. He was sure he could talk and buy his way out of anything.

They drove on, out of Manhattan and across the bridge into Brooklyn. They seemed to be driving in circles, making turn after turn and doubling back on themselves. How many times had Peter done that in those years when he had to make the trip to see his father and mother? It was past eight PM when the cab stopped in front of the burnt out shell of the Brooklyn house where Don Pietro Salvano once lived and ruled from.

Andy and two of the soldiers who worked directly for him opened the door of the cab. "Get out", Andy said. When Peter didn't move he was dragged from the cab and the driver sped away. Peter's arms were held twisted painfully behind him as he was taken into the burnt ruins. Parts of a few walls still stood; burnt wood and charred furniture filled the interior.

"What do you want, Andy? Why are you doing this? You want money? I'll give you whatever you want."

"Shut up, asshole," Andy said. As Peter was held by the soldiers Andy drew a pistol with a silencer and held it a few inches from Peter's forehead. He smiled as Peter started crying. He was sweating and shaking, tears fell in streams across his face. "Please Andy . . . Please Andy," was all he could say before Andy pulled the trigger.

Peter was found the following morning. The gun lay nearby, no fingerprints on it. The police took pictures of everything including the dead rat that had been stuffed in Peter's mouth. It was an old Mafia sign identifying someone who had talked or 'ratted out' Mafia dealings. The body was found in Peter's father's house. All the signs were there to convince the police and the FBI that the Brooklyn mob had killed Peter.

THIRTY-NINE

Trenton, New Jersey
May, 1968

Tony sat alone in his office, staring out the windows across the State Capital. It was half past twelve, but he wasn't interested in lunch. The morning had been taken up with a breakfast meeting with some people who wanted money for some charity or something. He wasn't sure what it was, but he gave them a few thousand anyway, if for no other reason than to not have to listen to them anymore. Tony had the reputation of a businessman who supported many charities, and he was always being approached by one or another to give more. They never seemed to have enough.

Andy had taken the day off. He said he was taking a new girlfriend down to Atlantic City. He had to check in with the three horse betting parlors there and see if the gambling room was doing OK. So he took his new girlfriend with him and they would spend the night there. With Andy gone, Tony found he had no one to talk to for any reason other than business. That's the way Tony's life had been for several years. Only Andy was left. Only Andy knew where they had been, what they had shared, what Tony had done.

Only Andy knew the dream Tony had ten years ago, the dream that had come true, except for Tony's loss of Teresa.

That loss, the pain of the loss, had never left Tony's heart. There wasn't a day go by or a night asleep alone in his bed that Tony didn't think of Teresa and long for her to be with him. The hurt was becoming unbearable. His love for Teresa had grown every day. But he knew there was nothing could be done about it. She was gone . . . Forever.

Andy got back early from his day away, rather than spending the night in Atlantic City as he said he would. He knocked on Tony's apartment door at half past seven.

"Hey, Andy," Tony said happily. He was glad there was someone he could talk to. "How was your day? I thought you were going to spend the night with that girl. What, did she turn you down?"

"She was fantastic, boss. She was great. Best girl in the world. But I didn't want to spend the night with her. I think she's interested in somebody else. I got done what I needed to get done, so's I came back home."

Tony asked, "So how is the Atlantic City operation going, Andy? Any problems?"

"Nah," he said. "Things is just great, ya' know? Let's watch the game, huh, boss? We can talk business later."

"I'm bored, Andy," Tony said. He went to the kitchen, pulled two bottles of beer out and opened them with the church key opener that he had hung on a string from a cabinet handle, as he had done in the small apartment in Newark. He handed one to his friend. They settled back in comfortable chairs.

"Yeah, I got that," Andy said. "You been lookin'

bored for awhile now. Tell you what. Tomorrow you take the day off, and you and me will go somewhere . . . Have some fun, ya'know?"

"You know, Andy, you're right again. That just might be what I need. I need to get away . . . If only for the day. The office is boring the hell out of me. A little vacation, right? Nobody at the office will miss me. I don't even sign checks anymore. The whole damn place runs like I'm the invisible man. Sometimes I think they don't even know I'm there."

He turned on the T.V., and they watched a night game; the Dodgers were playing. The game gave them enough time to finish five beers each. At midnight, Andy left and Tony went to bed. He dreamed of Teresa once again. The same dream; he was holding her in his arms, and they kissed. They were walking along a deserted beach somewhere. The gentle waves lapped across their bare feet as they walked, holding each other closely. The sound of the ocean rolling in was calming and peaceful. He felt good and happy. But he knew in his sleep that it was just a dream. She was gone from him.

The nightmare of the dark monster hadn't engulfed him since losing her years ago. But her memory was still with him and would always be there. He gladly welcomed the dreams and the thoughts of her. It was better than not having her at all. His love for her had not diminished over the years, and the pain he felt for not having her had not diminished either.

When he woke in the middle of the night, he first looked at the picture of Teresa in the silver frame that sat on the night stand next to his bed. She was smiling, and she was beautiful. Every time he woke, morning or night, that was the first thing he looked at.

The next morning Andy and Tony left in Tony's Cadillac. It had been so many years that they had dressed in suits that they both wore suits that day without considering anything else, even on a vacation day. "So what should we do, Andy?" he asked as they started away from the curb.

"I been thinking, boss. I been thinking about the old days. You know, back when we was kids? You know what I want?"

Tony laughed and said, "No . . . Tell me what you want, and I'll bet it has something to do with food."

"Yeah, you got it. I want one of them greasy cheeseburgers we used to get at Pop's Candy Store."

"You're kidding, right?" Tony said and turned to look at Andy behind the wheel of the brand new Cadillac, this one black like one he had had before. "Refined," Tony had said. Andy's bulk was of bragging proportions. He had an undiminished appetite that seemed to grow every year. He had to buy new suits twice a year because he outgrew them so fast.

"No, I really got this thing for one of them. Let's go up there, huh, boss? Whatt'a ya' say, huh?"

And so Andy took them back to Passaic, where it all had begun. Pop's hadn't changed much; the parking lot wasn't as crowded that afternoon as it would be after dark when the local kids would gather there. Andy parked the car inside the lot rather than at the curb in front of the red fire hydrant. They had grown away from that life where the police would look the other way when they blocked a fire hydrant. They walked inside.

They found a vacant booth at the rear and sat. A waitress came to them. She didn't know who they were, so she was a little short tempered with them after a long day taking orders. Tony recalled the Saturday afternoon that he had first met Teresa there. The waitress knew who he was, and she was scared. 'Things change,' he thought.

Andy ordered his cheeseburger, a large fries and a thick chocolate shake. Tony shook his head and ordered a coffee.

"I'm not really hungry," he explained.

Music was playing on the jukebox, but neither of them recognized the tune. "The music was better back then, boss," Andy said.

"Yes, it was."

Tony looked around the diner. There weren't many people there at that time of day, not as many as would crowd the place at night. More adults than would have been there in his time, but not many young people. Most of the tables and booths were filled with people eating lunch and enjoying egg creams. His eyes went from table to table and person to person. 'Times sure have changed,' he thought. The customers were different. The kids were dressed in what Tony thought was 'wild' clothing; bright colors and strange costumes, and their hair was long, to their shoulders, both boys and girls. 'Times have changed,' he thought again.

He looked, and then stopped, when he saw Teresa. She was sitting in the same booth, on the other side of Pop's, where he had first seen her ten years before. She was wearing a simple light blue sweater with a small gold cross on a thin chain that hung around her neck and rested on the sweater, just as she had worn that day he first saw her there. She wore tight fitting Capri pants that did justice to her curves, just as she had worn that day. And she was as beautiful as she had been that day. She was alone and smiling. She was looking at him.

Their eyes found each other, and her smile broadened. Andy said, "Go on, boss. Don't be stupid."

Tony slid out of the booth and found it hard to

walk to her. His knees felt weak, they were about to buckle under him, and his head was feeling light; his feet couldn't feel the floor under him. His heart was beating fast, and he had a hard time breathing. His mind was filled with visions of her in his arms, but he knew that wasn't going to happen, and that hurt. Maybe she wanted something . . . Maybe she needed something. He would do anything for her.

Everything around Teresa was a grey blur. Only she was in focus. His head was spinning away. He found himself standing at her booth, looking down at her, longing for her, not really remembering how he had gotten there.

"Sit down, Tony," she said. She was smiling up at him. Her hair was long and soft, the way he remembered it. Her makeup was light, the way he remembered from so long ago. Her eyes were bright, and she looked happy to see him.

He did sit, across from her. Keeping the table between them was proper, he thought. He stopped himself from reaching out to her. 'She wouldn't want that,' he thought.

"Hi, Tony," she said softly, gently, still smiling.

"Hello . . . I'm surprised to find you here."

"I wanted to talk to you. Andy arranged this."

Tony looked across the room to Andy. He was grinning like a kid on Christmas morning. He shrugged his shoulders. So this was planned. That great new girl Andy had spent the day with was Teresa, and there never was a trip to Atlantic City.

"I don't know what to say," he stammered. "What do you want?"

"I want to apologize to you, Tony."

"For what? I don't get it."

"For everything. Andy told me everything yesterday."

"Yesterday? He was supposed to be with a new girlfriend."

"Yeah, he lied, I guess. We spent the day together. He came to my house. I almost didn't let him in. I was frightened at first. But I'm glad I did. We had lunch together, and by the way, we need to put him on a diet. He eats too much," she laughed.

"He told me about Roger Tifton," she said. "That man's death was the cause of all that has happened between us, Tony. I didn't know anything about that. I wish I had. I know everything that happened now. It wasn't you, none of it was you.

"He told me about my father hating you so much because you were always seen as smarter than he was. He was frightened that you would shut him out, take away his power and money. He was afraid you were taking me away. Tony, I know my father did that to my mother to break us apart. He knew what my reaction would be. He wanted you and me to not be together. It was a terrible thing to do, but I know now why he did it.

"Andy told me how you had protected my father from Peter Salvano even after all the bad things my father did and all the terrible things he said about you. You protected him for me, I know that now. Andy told me that Peter had my father murdered because of Roger Tifton, that he hired killers from New York, that you had nothing to do with it. All you ever wanted was to protect my father and try to give me the family I wanted.

"I didn't realize that it was you who made my father come home that Christmas and the weekends afterwards. I thought he just wanted to be with me . . . With his family."

Tony said, "Yes, and I'm sorry about that. Your mother would still be alive today if I hadn't done that. I feel terribly responsible."

"Don't, you couldn't have known. I know you did that for me. You just wanted me to be happy, to have a good Christmas, to have a good family."

Tony nodded and looked down at the table, unable to look at her when he said, "But I am responsible for all the bad that has happened. I should have known . . ."

"Don't feel that way, Tony. No one can see into the future. You were just trying to be good to me . . . As you have been all these years. Anyway, Andy told me about the money you sent to me and the nurses. I thought at first my father was doing that. But I guess my father really didn't care what happened to his children. I guess I knew it was you when the money and nurses continued after his death.

"It seems my father was involved with another woman down in Trenton, and that's all he cared about. And Andy told me how you made that woman leave and never see my father again.

"He told me about how you got Alley out of jail and the debt you owe to the Gambinos. He said that debt is weighing heavily on you. Andy explained how terrible the Gambinos are and how you have to pay them money for helping you. He told me that you're paying for my brother's stay at Browne's . . . Although I figured that out for myself. No one else could have done it. I was so terribly alone . . . Except for you, of course. I know that now."

Teresa paused for a moment. She touched his finger tips, tentatively, slowly. "I was wrong about you Tony. I'm sorry."

"OK," Tony said, still wondering what was happening. "I guess I'm glad you know the truth . . .

Although I'm going to have a long talk with Andy later on." He turned and looked across the room at the broadly grinning Andy Pecora, who looked happier than Tony could ever remember him being. Andy had seen how Tony's separation from Teresa had been so terrible for Tony and how his depression over her loss was deepening. It was easy for him to see how Tony had never lost the thought of her. It was the only failure in his boss' life. He was worried about his boss. So Andy made it his job to help his boss, to right the only wrong he could see.

Tony turned back to Teresa. They sat without speaking, their eyes locked together. Tony fought the urge to put his hand out, to touch her hand. Teresa must have read his mind because she took his hand in hers. She squeezed his hand lovingly. She smiled and asked, "Do you still have the apartment in Newark?"

"Of course," he answered. "I couldn't give that up. It's too special. It was our home for a long time. I bought the building so I wouldn't lose it. I go there now and then . . . Just to get away. There's good memories there for me."

"It wasn't our home for a long enough time, Tony," she admitted. "Tony . . . How do I say I'm sorry for everything? I've hurt you so badly. I was terrible to you. I wanted to hurt you, and all you did was be good to me. All you ever did was try to help me. I was so wrong for everything I did to you."

"OK . . . I guess I accept your apology if that's what you want . . . Although you don't need to apologize. I understand everything. I couldn't be angry at you. I never was angry with you."

"So you forgive me, then?"

"Forgive? There's nothing to forgive. You were doing only what you thought you had to do. You didn't know the truth, and you acted on what you knew. You were protecting and helping your family. I understand that. I wouldn't expect anything less of you."

She squeezed his hand again. She looked down, forcing her eyes away from Tony. She asked in a quaking voice, "Do you still love me, Tony?"

Tony didn't hesitate when he said, "Teresa, I've never stopped loving you. There's never been anyone else . . ."

She interrupted him to laugh, look up at him, and say, "Yes, Andy told me you've been living like a cloistered monk."

Tony glanced across the room to Andy once again. He had a mouthful of cheeseburger but that didn't stop him from grinning again, meat juice and melted cheese ran from the corners of his mouth.

He turned back to look into her dark eyes and went on, "You've been in my heart . . . You've filled my dreams every night, Teresa. I would give up everything if I could have you. There hasn't been a day go by since that day we met right here all those years ago that I haven't loved you more than the day before. There hasn't been a day go by that I haven't thought about you. When I close my eyes, you're always there . . . Beautiful as you always have been . . . As you are now . . . Soft and wonderful and smiling and happy. Do I still love you? Every day I wake up and I wonder how to go on living without you that day. I go to bed every night wishing you were with me . . . I wake up every morning wishing you were there next to me. You are everything to me, Teresa. You are life to me. The day will never come when you aren't in my dreams, in my mind, in my heart. There is nothing that could ever make me stop loving you. Tell me what you want me to do . . . Tell me what you want me to give up. Anything."

"Well, you don't have to give up anything," she said. "I love you, too, Tony. I know that now. I've never stopped loving you. I was just so confused and scared . . . I'm yours if you still want me."

Tony didn't know what to say. He gently grasped her hand in both of his. He couldn't tear his eyes away from hers. 'This has to be a dream,' he thought. 'This can't be really happening.'

She pulled her hand free, slowly slid from the booth and stood next to him. She bent, ever so slowly, and knelt on one knee. She said, "Tony Moretti, my love . . . Will you do me the honor of becoming my husband? Will you marry me?"

Pop's was deadly silent as everyone there watched what was happening. Tony looked around the room and at Andy who said loud enough for everyone to hear, "Do I gotta' go over there and make you say yes?"

Tony stood, pulled Teresa to her feet and took her into his arms. They kissed, and he spun her around. Pops erupted in applause. Andy was yelling, on his feet, dancing around wildly, and clapping.

****

The wedding was supposed to be a small affair at St. Ignatius Church. A handful of friends were invited. More than a hundred people showed up. Some were business acquaintances, a few were from Tony's crime days, some were from Teresa's neighborhood in Montclair, some who knew of the years past were just curious to see the famous Tony Moretti marry Al Falzone's daughter, the joining together of two famous families. News people were there with their flashing cameras and too inquisitive questions. Andy asked Tony, "You want I should clear the place out?"

"No. Might as well let them stay . . . Only if they don't disrupt the wedding. Watch the news people. If they go overboard with all this, have some of the guys show them to the exit, but do it quietly."

Teresa was resplendent in her white gown and veil. Little Al, who had responded well enough to Dr. Simpson's care, was able to walk her down the aisle. Andy Pecora, Tony's best man, stood next to him at the altar, as he had stood next to him for ten years. It was a wonderful day for Tony and Teresa.

There was a small reception at Teresa's house. Andy's men stood watch at the curb, keeping uninvited people and news people outside and away. That evening Andy drove them to Newark where Tony and Teresa wanted to spend their first night as a married couple in their 'home' there.

The small apartment was exactly as Teresa had last seen it. Nothing had changed. The old chair that she had wanted to get rid of was still there. The bed they had picked out and spent so many afternoons and nights in was still there. A tear found the corner of her eye as she walked in and saw all the familiar things.

They awoke next to each other, as they had so many years ago, with the sun streaming in the lone bedroom window that still held the old air conditioner.

Tony Moretti had risen from poverty, slums, and a violent home. He had a dream as a child, a dream of being wealthy and powerful and respected. He had used what his environment had offered him. He had risen to the top of his chosen lifestyle and business. He fought through the barriers established by the people he would replace, he moved away from the violence he had seen all around him to a position of influence in business and government. Yes, he used violence as he rose in power, but that was the only tool Tony knew. It had been learned from beatings at home, gang wars on the street, and seeing the Mafia wreak pain on those around him. And what powerful man anywhere in the world has not used violence for gain?

In the end, Tony had finally gotten everything he wanted, wealth, power, respect and the one woman he had loved his entire life.

FORTY

Long Island, New York
Christmas Eve 2008

Tony was only sixty-four years old, but the years had not treated him well. The pressure of his chosen life had aged him beyond his years. His hair was grey and thin. His face was sunken and drawn, without much color. His eyes were old and dark ringed. His once muscular body had shrunk to the frail body of an old man. His once broad back and shoulders were hunched after carrying the weight of his business for so many years.

In his chosen business he had always been seen as a 'kid' who had risen too fast, no matter how many years passed by. As he expanded his income and businesses, many Families in New York became envious of his success. For years it was a struggle, one that year after year had become less wanted by Tony.

He sat in the big, soft chair he always sat in, the one with the rose patterned upholstery, near the big fireplace in his home on Long Island, where the flames would keep him warm and ease the pain of arthritis that had overtaken his shoulders and hands. His children were in the kitchen having a good time preparing the big turkey and all the trimmings for dinner that night. Donny, his son and oldest of his three children, was trying to help, but his two sisters, Lorraine and Terry, were saying he was more in their way than a help. They were laughing and having a good time.

There was an eight foot tall Christmas tree in the living room with stacks of presents underneath. Tony had one grandchild, a daughter, Donny's daughter, whom he doted on and had bought too many gifts for that year as usual. Lorraine was pregnant and Tony would have his second grandchild in March.

He had never smoked cigarettes or cigars like so many of the other men he worked with. But in retirement he had taken to smoking a pipe in the evening. Not that he particularly liked it, but he thought it made him look dignified and refined.

The house was warm, brightly lit inside and out with lights and wreaths. It would be a good Christmas, he thought. Donny came in from the kitchen. He had heard the cars in the driveway. Tony's hearing wasn't as good as it used to be; he hadn't heard the cars.

"I've got a little Christmas surprise for you, Dad," Donny said.

"Not another tie," Tony laughed. "I don't need any more ties."

"Not a tie Dad." He went to the door and opened it. Andy Pecora stamped the snow off his shoes and entered the house. His wife, Angela, and their five children and three grandchildren were with him. His arms were full of wrapped presents.

"Hey, Andy!" Tony said. He struggled to push himself out of his chair gripping the pipe still in his teeth. "And you brought the kids. That's great!" Andy was not as big . . . Fat . . . As he had been so many years ago. A good marriage had slimmed him down to just being big.

Andy's children and grandchildren all ran to Tony, all hugging him at once and all saying at the same time, "Merry Christmas, Uncle Tony, Merry Christmas!"

Andy said, "I brought something else, boss." He turned and Jay Schoemer walked in. His wife Nancy, their two children and two grandchildren behind him. Then Norman Rocque walked in, stumbling clumsily over the threshold. Richie Pelto followed holding his grandson. His wife and daughter at his side. They were all laden down with brightly wrapped Christmas gifts.

Tony didn't know what to say. The pipe slipped from his teeth and fell to the floor. "My God! Where'd you all come from?" was all he could manage.

As the gifts were being spread out around the tree, Andy threw his big arm around Donny's shoulders and explained, "This kid arranged it all. He found us all and got us all here. That's a good kid you got, boss."

Donny said, "Not all by myself, Dad. Uncle Andy did all the leg work. I just used the computer and gave him what I found."

Tony's two daughters and granddaughter came from the kitchen and joined the mob of friends. The younger children all ran in excited play around all the colorful presents under the tree. They were all talking at once about what Santa Claus would bring them that night.

The older ones introduced themselves to each other, and Donny uncorked a half dozen bottles of good Chianti. After awhile everyone had settled down to talking and helping out in the kitchen. Tony and Andy stood near the fireplace, each with a glass of the good red wine in hand. A picture of Teresa, framed in silver, stood on the mantle; the picture Tony had kept all those years on his nightstand. Andy picked it up and said, "How long has it been, boss?"

"Five years, two months and three days," Tony answered, choking up again as he did every time he thought of the death of Teresa. He had sat at her bedside everyday during those terrible months that the cancer took her. There was no cure, the doctors had said. Nothing they could do seemed to be able to save her. Their children wanted him to go home, to sleep a little, to eat, lest they lose him, too. But he would not leave her side until she was gone.

"It's a shame she had to die so young," Andy said.

"Yes, but we had thirty-five wonderful, wonderful years together. And she gave me three wonderful kids, a granddaughter and another grandkid on the way. I see her in every one of them." Tears filled his eyes once again. Years would not intervene and ease his pain at the loss. Andy saw this and put his big hand on his boss's shoulder. He wanted to ease the pain but he there was nothing he could do.

"You really loved her didn't you, boss?"

"I've loved her every day since that first day I saw her," he said, trying to smile past the tears. "I still do, Andy. She's in here," he said touching his chest. He pointed to the side of his head and tried to say, "And she's in my memories." But he couldn't get the words out. "She always will be," he managed. He wiped the tears away and took a long drink of the strong red wine.

He had to stop; there were old friends who needed him. He had a responsibility to them, a responsibility he had carried his whole life. His plan had been for his life, to better his life, to bring him out of the slums and poverty. But that same plan had placed responsibility on his shoulders that weighed him down for fifty years. His plan had been dependant on fulfilling that responsibility to others.

Norman, still alone in the crowded room and looking uncomfortable and out of place, walked hesitatingly towards them. He had a mug of coffee that he held up to proudly show Tony and Andy. "Been dry for almost a year now," he said.

"Good for you, Norm," Tony said. "I'm proud of you. Keep it up, hear?"

"Yeah," he said sadly, "It's tough though. Bein' all alone and all that."

"Still no woman in your life, Norm?"

"You know me. One ain't never been enough."

Jay saw the three standing alone and walked over to them. He hadn't lost any of his muscles with the onset of age. He was as big as he ever was, and his hair had not yet turned grey, which belied his real age. Tony looked at the three men and realized that although he was younger than all of them, he looked ten years older.

Andy patted Jay's shoulder and said, "Those are great kids you got."

"Thanks, Andy. I'm real proud of them."

Tony asked, "What are you doing now, Jay? Did you ever get that gym you used to talk about?"

"Hell, I got three of'em," he said proudly. "Doin' good, too. Young people, particularly the women, they can't get enough of workin' out. Got a thing 'bout dancing to crazy music and kickin' an' stuff. They call it exercise, believe it or not. They dance around and work up a sweat. But they pay good money to do it."

"That's great," Tony said. "I'm glad to hear it."

Andy looked across the room and said jokingly, "Hey watch out. The cops are coming."

Richie Pelto was approaching, smiling and happy to see everyone. "Nice place you've got here, Tony."

"Thanks, Richie. You still with the FBI?"

"FBI!" Andy said holding up his hands over his head and spilling drops of red wine from his glass. "Hey, I didn't do it, copper!"

"No sweat, Andy," Richie said and laughed. "I retired a couple of years ago. I figured 35 years were enough for anybody. The young guys coming up are better than I ever was. It's a new world out there. All science and computers now. We have a nice place down in Florida. You guys have to come visit some time. Bring the grandkids. They'll love the beach."

The five men stood in a circle, none saying anything. Time had taken its toll. They had all changed from those days as teenagers hanging out in DeSonoto's Pizza Parlor. They weren't The Aces anymore. They had all grown up. Tony finally said, "I wish Eddy could have been here."

Jay replied, "Yeah, that was a real tragedy, him killing himself and all."

Andy said, "I kind'a wish I hadn't treated him so mean when we was kids. I feel bad about that."

Richie added, "What about Joey Castellani? How come he isn't here?"

Andy answered, "Me and Donny tried to find him, but we couldn't. I don't know where he is. Maybe dead for all I know. He was always mad at somethin', remember? That temper of his probably got him in trouble somewhere."

They were quiet again until Richie asked, "Tony,

how's it been with you.   You look like you've done well."

"I'm retired now.   I still have the trucking company . . ."

"Yeah," Andy interrupted.   "The Aces Interstate Trucking Company he calls it.   Ain't that somethin'? Named the damn company after us!"

"What about everything else?" Richie asked, still naturally suspicious even after retirement.

"Don't worry, Richie. I'm clean.   Things got too profitable in Jersey and New York started moving in. I didn't have the manpower to stop them, and I really didn't want to anyway. I'd had enough of the struggle. I had believed that the old world of organized crime was dead, but it wasn't. I stalled it for years, but in the end the guys who use violence never really went away.   So I kept the trucking company, sold off the restaurants and dry cleaners, and let them have the rest.   All the gambling rooms, the horse betting, the numbers. I kept the real estate, good investment there. My son Donny runs the trucking company now. He's doing great, too.   Smart kid.   Takes after his mother. He's opening another distribution warehouse, down in Atlanta this time."

"Yeah, that's great," Richie said. He paused and everyone was quiet again. Someone had to say it, so Richie said, "We're all sorry to hear about Teresa."

"Thank you. All of you," Tony said, but he knew the tears would come again if he spoke of the only woman he ever loved. So he said quickly, "But how about we see how that food is coming? I know Jay and Andy here could eat a horse while we dig into that turkey."

They all filtered off, except for Andy and Tony who stayed behind and watched The Aces as they walked away. Andy took a sip of his wine and said to his boss, "We had some good times, didn't we boss?"

"Yes, Andy," Tony said. "We had some good times."

THE END

EPILOG

Some facts about this story:

The reader may think it strange that young people, mere teenagers, are the center of this story, as they grow up and live through fifty years of troubled lives. But in the world of organized crime, recruits into the various crime families don't come from college campuses, and they are not grown men when they enter the life. They come from the streets, the slums, the teenage gangs.

Charles "Lucky" Luciano, Meyer Lansky, and Frank Costello, who together brought the competing Mafia Families of the 1930's and 1940's into a single criminal organization called 'The Commission,' all came up from their pre-teen and teen years in early 20th Century New York street gangs.

In 1914 a teenage Luciano and fellow teen Lansky formed a gang that dealt in extortion. Eventually, as mere teens, they moved into bootlegging and smuggling during prohibition. By the time they were 20 years old they owned a string of 'speakeasies' in New York City.

In 1931 Luciano brought an end to the violent competition between New York Mafia families by forming the "Five Families" and organized the entire criminal world of the United States into one

"Commission" which he headed.

The characters in this story are, of course, fictitious. I was raised in Northern New Jersey and as a teen and young man I came to know many people who lived lives as depicted here. Although the story is a fiction, the reality of such lives as you will read here is not fiction. Those tragic lives still exist today in many inner cities, and the people living those lives are the fodder from which organized crime will feed.

The lives of teens in the street gangs of the fifties and sixties were sad and should never be thought of as colorful or heroic. Too many died young, senseless, and useless deaths. Too many were caught in a morass of poverty and horrible home lives that left few of them any opportunity to leave the 'life.'

While reading this story one may wonder why the lovers, Tony and Teresa, don't just run away and start lives independent of their families. You would have to grow up and live lives in the communities depicted here. Only a few of us were able to see beyond the boundaries that fenced us in and successfully leave. Only a very few of us could see a world outside the few blocks of city we knew. The lives they live and have chosen for themselves leave few options for them.

The lives of Mafia 'soldiers' – associates of crime families who are called upon to inflict pain and commit murders as ordered by their superiors – are as tragic. They often live their lives in poverty and hardship until they spend years in prison or die an early death. Few of the soldiers ever "move up" in the Crime Family they are a part of. To "move up" is to gain a promotion within the Family. A soldier, having special talents, might rise to be his Capo's underboss or Consigliore - advisor. One of hundreds might become a Capo of his own crew. One of thousands would ever become a Don or Capo di tutti Capi.

****

Early in the story mention is made of a New York Street gang called 'The Mau Maus.' This gang did actually exist in the 1940s and 1950s. It was a violent precursor to many of today's New York street gangs. They led the way for followers in dealing drugs and committing murders.

Throughout the story, reference is made to "vig". This is a shortened version of 'vigorish' or the interest charged by loan sharks. Interest could be as low as 2% or 3% a week up to as much as 10% or 15% a week. A person or business taking a loan of this sort had to pay the vig at a minimum each week. If, once or twice, the vig was not paid, it was added to the loan. Normally, three weeks missed was never allowed. Force was then used to collect what was owed.

The 'Don', or head of the crime family, was – and in fact still is today – a man of absolute power and extreme wealth within the world of organized crime. His orders are always obeyed, and the life and death of any member of his family is in his hands. In the language of organized crime, the Don is the Capo di tutti Capi.

The Caporegimes, often called Capos, who owe him loyalty, have spent a lifetime working their way up in the crime family they belong to, from street gangs and petty criminals. They are leaders of 'crews' of soldiers who steal, commit acts of violence, extort, and collect the debts owed to the Caporegime.

Mention is made of a real estate transaction involving a 'Straw Buyer'. A Straw Buyer is a person who uses his name and or credit to buy real estate for another person who, for whatever reason, cannot buy the property himself. This is an illegal transaction. As a Criminal Investigator, I have put several people in jail for 'Straw Buyer' transactions.

****

I hope you have enjoyed this story and feel the joy and pain of the two lovers as they grew into adulthood. Please understand who they are and forgive them for what they do. Choice is not part of their lives.

Arthur A. Lee

www.ingramcontent.com/pod-product-compliance
Lightning Source LLC
Chambersburg PA
CBHW030755260626
47169CB00001B/57